BRIGHT AND TENDER DARK

BRIGHT AND TENDER DARK

a novel

JOANNA PEARSON

BLOOMSBURY PUBLISHING
NEW YORK · LONDON · OXFORD · NEW DELHI · SYDNEY

BLOOMSBURY PUBLISHING
Bloomsbury Publishing Inc.
1385 Broadway, New York, NY 10018, USA

BLOOMSBURY, BLOOMSBURY PUBLISHING, and the Diana logo are trademarks
of Bloomsbury Publishing Plc

First published in the United States 2024

Copyright © Joanna Pearson, 2024

All rights reserved. No part of this publication may be reproduced or transmitted in any form or by any means, electronic or mechanical, including photocopying, recording, or any information storage or retrieval system, without prior permission in writing from the publishers.

This is a work of fiction. Names and characters are the product of the author's imagination and any resemblance to actual persons, living or dead, is entirely coincidental.

Bloomsbury Publishing Plc does not have any control over, or responsibility for, any third-party websites referred to or in this book. All internet addresses given in this book were correct at the time of going to press. The author and publisher regret any inconvenience caused if addresses have changed or sites have ceased to exist, but can accept no responsibility for any such changes.

ISBN: HB: 978-1-63973-289-0; EBOOK: 978-1-63973-290-6

LIBRARY OF CONGRESS CATALOGING-IN-PUBLICATION DATA IS AVAILABLE

2 4 6 8 10 9 7 5 3 1

Typeset by Westchester Publishing Services
Printed and bound in the U.S.A.

To find out more about our authors and books visit www.bloomsbury.com and sign up for our newsletters.

Bloomsbury books may be purchased for business or promotional use. For information on bulk purchases please contact Macmillan Corporate and Premium Sales Department at specialmarkets@macmillan.com.

*Again, for Matthew,
bright, dark, and tender.*

Contents

2019

    Grand Mal   9
    Unit 7C   29
    r/JusticeforKarlie   52
    The Veldt   70
    The Dark Forest   101
    The Weeper   122

1999

    Universal Love   153
    The More Loving One   162
    The Gathering   178
    Bonedigger   199
    The Walk-In   220
    Karlie   234
    Dark   257

2019

    When We Were Gone Astray   269

BRIGHT AND TENDER DARK

From LoveandLegacy.com:

Karlie Richards (July 13, 1980–January 8, 2000)

Margaret Karla "Karlie" Richards of Sycamore Grove, NC, darling daughter, sister, and friend, went to meet her Heavenly Father in the early hours of January 8, 2000, after a brief but extraordinary life during which she was most cherished and loved . . .

From Reddit.com/r/karlierichardshauntings:

[wandatwothree]: Karlie was mythic from the start; her death only secured that status. I was also a member of UNC's class of 2002. I didn't really know her, but we were in the same freshman art history class. Karlie was the sort of person you couldn't help but notice: xylophone laughter, hair like spun gold, a way of gliding across the lecture hall. There was a seriousness to her whole demeanor that I'd never seen before—that I definitely didn't see in any of the other students. She was regal. We were all kids compared to her. She sat close to the front, so the light from the back of the projector cast her in this orb of illuminated dust, and you could tell she was taking in every word the professor said. Her face was always very attentive when she wasn't speaking. She was someone you wondered about, who inspired curiosity while she was alive. But after she died, she morphed into legend. People kept saying they were seeing her ghost everywhere, but that's what happens when you can't stop talking about someone, then drink too many two-for-one rail drinks and spook yourself . . . That's a recipe for a ghost right there. But that's not Karlie.

[prettyprettyliars]: I started my first year in Chapel Hill the fall after she was murdered, so the tragedy was fresh on everyone's minds. There were these new security call button stations all over campus and self-defense classes at the gym, and they encouraged everybody, especially the girls, to sign up. The RAs were required to lead sessions on personal safety. Maybe they were actually trying to accomplish something, but we thought it was all a big show, a way for the members of the administration to make themselves feel better.

Everyone believed that the kid they'd charged with Karlie's murder hadn't done it. We knew the real killer was still on the loose. Three of my friends were assaulted at frat parties within the first two months of school, so, you know, some things never change. The bad guys were still out there, business as usual.

Anyway, that's when we started seeing her. Karlie. It wasn't long after the night my friend Sarah had come home crying from Sig Ep that we noticed this girl down at the basketball court at Hinton James. We spotted her from our dorm window, way below us. She'd show up at night. Never talked to anyone. We'd watch her, walking back and forth from basket to basket, her face too far away to make out clearly. We went down to try and catch her a few times, but she'd always vanish. Finally, we managed to get a good look, and I swear to God, it was Karlie. Exactly as she appeared in all the photos. Karlie herself. Just staring right back at us.

[devilmaycare432]: I arrived at UNC a couple years after Karlie was killed, and there was a rumor that if you went over to the apartment complex where she was murdered, you could summon her. The owner of the complex still had her unit blocked off. No one wanted to live there, but people did want to sneak down there late at night, with beer or a joint or whatever. They kept breaking in, and the owners kept boarding the place back up. I went with a bunch of people once during my junior year, even though it seemed like a big joke at the time. Like going to a haunted house. We were all drunk and acting stupid, and it was a while before we realized our friend Tara had wandered away. When she came back, something was off. You know when people say it looks like someone has seen a ghost? That was Tara. She wouldn't speak for the rest of the evening. Everybody felt bad about it. She never did talk about whatever it was that happened to her that night. Then the worst part was about ten years after we all graduated, Tara was murdered by a jealous ex. All of us who'd been there, those of us who were still in touch—it freaked us out. I now believe she saw Karlie there that night, and that Karlie had been trying to warn her.

[vyper9]: Lots of people saw Karlie after she died. Lots—me included. She was really haunting the place. Haunting it vigorously, appearing for all sorts of people—or so they claimed. Mainly down at those crappy student apartments where she died, but other places, too. Davis Library. McCorkle Place. By the highrise South Campus dorms. Behind the Forest Theatre. People swore they saw her darting into a convenience store close to campus for a pack of gum, or sitting on the patio at Carrburritos, idling outside various Franklin Street bars—Linda's, He's Not Here, Top of the Hill . . . Classic spots, the Chapel Hill circuit. Karlie was everywhere, like any enthusiastic undergrad might be. Only she was dead.

Yet she lingered. Can't say I blame her. I'd haunt the shit out of people, too, if I got murdered and the wrong person went to prison and my true killer went free, and everyone, everyone, everyone was talking about it but getting the story all wrong. I'd be pissed. I'd want to correct the record. Isn't that how ghosts are made?

From *The Daily Tar Heel*:

January 9, 2000

Chapel Hill, NC—Chapel Hill police are seeking any information regarding a young woman found slain inside her off-campus apartment on January 8. The body of nineteen-year-old UNC undergraduate student Margaret Karla "Karlie" Richards was discovered in the early-morning hours by a friend after she failed to respond to phone calls the previous evening.

"Right now, we're looking into all possibilities," Police Chief Hank Askins said. "While we don't have any reason to believe there's an active threat to the community, we're encouraging community members to be mindful of their surroundings and take reasonable precautions."

The exact cause of Richards's death has not been disclosed, but police are investigating the case as a homicide.

Greta Longley, a UNC senior who also lives in the off-campus Trailview Crest apartment complex at 253 Arendale Road, says this event has rattled the community.

"It's horrible," she said. "She was this vivacious, active presence on campus. Stuff like this just doesn't happen here."

Another resident of the complex, who wished for anonymity, reported hearing people coming and going at Ms. Richards's apartment late into the evening of January 7 and into the early-morning hours of January 8.

"I didn't make too much of it at first," he said. "I mean, college students keep late hours, you know? But at one point I got up to go to the bathroom and heard arguing. I saw a guy standing right outside Karlie's apartment. Big glasses. A limp when he walked. Kind of—well, he looked confused and upset."

Another nearby resident who expressed the desire for anonymity out of concern for safety also attested to the fact of at least one late-night visitor at Karlie's apartment.

"I heard someone drive up," the witness stated. "But I couldn't make out the car. It definitely pulled in right by her place, though. And then there was a man shouting. It was too dark to see his face, but he was waiting there, right outside Karlie's apartment. He gave me the creeps. Everything was quiet after that."

This witness is also fully cooperating with police.

The UNC spring semester is set to start on Wednesday, January 12. According to acting chancellor Bill Sterling, the semester will begin as scheduled, but with a "heavy pall cast over our community."

"Karlie was a wonderful spirit and a dynamic intellect, according to all who knew her," Chancellor Sterling said. "She was a beloved member of our university family who exemplified the Carolina way."

Sterling also announced a campus-wide remembrance and candlelight vigil in the Pit at 5:00 P.M. on January 13. This tragedy will also accelerate plans for additional safety measures and trainings on campus, university officials said.

At this time, Chapel Hill police are looking for an individual of interest in connection with the Richards case, a male seen by witnesses near her apartment shortly before the estimated time of her death. No suspect has been named at this time. Chapel Hill Police have posted an anonymous tip line. Anyone with information related to the case may call 919-555-0198.

2019

Grand Mal

Joy's freshman roommate had claimed that if you were being attacked, you had to throw a fit: fall to the ground, froth at the mouth, growl, fling your arms, spout gibberish. Karlie demonstrated vividly and with an ease that suggested she'd previously employed such a tactic successfully. She looked like a Holy Roller, someone in the grip of ecstatic revelation—nothing like an actual epileptic. Joy knew because her father suffered from epilepsy. But an attacker would hardly know the difference, Karlie promised. The exact details wouldn't matter. So go bananas with it. Vomit, if you're able. Let your eyes roll back in your head. The attacker would be so startled, so wary of whatever dread affliction or malevolent spirit had seized you, that he'd scamper off, harmless, into the shadows.

In another of Joy's most vivid memories of her, Karlie presided over a group of their dormmates, passing out piping-hot break-and-bake cookies straight from the toaster oven, along with hand-annotated chapter summaries printed from a book called *I Kissed Dating Goodbye*. The girls, glossy-haired and chirruping like a cluster of morning songbirds, sat cross-legged atop her lofted bed, sprawled across her lavender comforter. They perched on her desk or straddled her desk chair. Cooing abundantly, they filled the room with soft exhalations and murmurs of assent. Their sweet breath combined with the scent of fresh-baked cookies, mango body lotion, and tropical fruit hair conditioner to turn the air madly, clashingly fragrant, like that in a fine ladies' boutique. Karlie, her very name like a filigreed pink greeting card, was leading a small group derived from a large all-campus evangelical organization. She had a way of noticing the friendless and ushering them toward her, cultivating some secret specialness they each possessed until it bloomed. Already, at age eighteen, she held herself with an unflappable maternal authority. Even then, as it was happening, this was a scene at which Joy could gaze but never truly enter, stuck outside, Little Match Girl–style, her fingers icy against the metaphorical glass of a specific sort of faith, or lack thereof, that blocked true access. Joy had a chemistry exam looming. She was the sort of girl who took looming chemistry exams seriously. There was no space for her—her seriousness, her worldly anxieties—there, in her own blessèd dorm room. She would have to trudge back to the library, but not before her roommate paused and smiled. Karlie knew her type and pitied her, handing Joy a cookie for her troubles. Even in this dismissal, Joy glowed with a sanctified warmth. Everyone was a bit more radiant in Karlie's presence, and Joy was not immune.

This moment occurred, of course, before Karlie went through a phase of rebellion—a personal Rumspringa during which she discovered drinking and the fact that a *blow job* did not mean blowing gently against the nether regions of a person you love. Those were the innocent early days, when she still used terms like *front-bottom* instead of *vagina* and collected lip balms flavored like pineapple soda and endorsed books that argued godly young women should refrain from kissing anyone until their wedding day. Submission to the right sort of authority, Karlie said, was glorious. Liberating, even. It was a doublespeak so calm, so self-assured, that Joy envied her certitude.

Despite all this, Karlie possessed a brutal practicality. While her providential faith armed her with untroubled optimism in many respects—God would guide her through that Spanish quiz she hadn't studied for!—she had an array of strategies when it came to certain exigencies. She was a collector of tips gleaned from Oprah, ways to jab a pickpocket in the throat or how to escape from a trunk in the event of a carjacking. She could change a flat in the time it took AAA to show up; she could remove a stain from white linen with her own spit. God would nod approvingly. She was prepared: pink Mace, a dainty purse-size first aid kit, double-sided tape to secure a bra strap, emergency tampons, granola bars, a Swiss Army knife.

Not two years after she and Joy first met, Karlie was dead.

It happened during the latter days of Karlie's apostasy, when she'd reportedly started to waver in her rebellion, to consider returning to the fold as prodigal daughter. Her story would have made a most excellent faith journey, real road-to-Damascus stuff for the fresh converts. A few days earlier, she'd gone out drinking. It was the end of winter break, early January, most students yet to return to town. According to those who'd accompanied her, Karlie had stayed out until the wee hours, and despite her ready laughter, something seemed amiss. There was a nervousness to her that night, a distracted way she kept glancing over her shoulder. She was supposed to hang out again later, friends said, but after she stopped answering phone calls, a friend went to check her off-campus apartment the following morning. He found Karlie's body on the living room floor. There were no signs of forced entry. It appeared Karlie had invited the killer, whoever he was, into her home. The story of her murder was covered salaciously by reporters for months.

Joy wasn't in close touch with Karlie at that point, but her friends knew that Karlie had been her freshman roommate—that she'd left her little prayer notes and Easter baskets and had generally treated Joy with all the love and attention a kindergarten teacher might bestow upon a reluctant student. During Karlie's time in the wilderness, Joy had run into her once or twice, leaving at the point when Karlie seemed ready to pair off with whatever frat boy or admirer was closest at hand. Karlie's business, Joy figured. Whichever version of her Joy got, who was she—lonely and awkward, still overcoming the stutter that had plagued her throughout her childhood—to judge? The last time Joy saw Karlie was at a terrible Y2K New Year's party, a moment that now seemed ominous, imbued with foreboding in light of what happened afterward.

"She was magnetic," Joy told her friend Sari. They had been studying together in the stacks not long after Karlie's death. "She wasn't supposed to end up like this. She didn't deserve it." Even though she hadn't bought into everything Karlie had believed, Joy still thought of her as fundamentally *good*—a genuinely devout person, someone merely trying on wildness for size.

Sari made a little sucking sound through her teeth and looked hard at Joy. She knew better. Joy knew better. But goodness and badness were flawed premises anyway; the former offered no real protection, and as for the latter, well, nobody deserved to end up murdered. It wasn't right to turn Karlie into a morality tale, an innocent led astray. But it was also hard not to fall back on old habits, hard not to provide oneself reassurance, to seek out the fatal flaw and correct for it with numerous precautions. Never be a woman out alone, in the dark, after drinks. Never invite the enemy in. Punishments abounded.

Joy thought of Karlie's trick. She wondered if Karlie had even had the chance to try it: a practiced series of convulsions while she uncapped her Mace. She told Sari about Karlie's method but Sari just shook her head. They both volunteered for an intimate-partner-violence support line; they were minoring in women's studies. They were already practicing their world-weariness. They thought they knew things.

"Come on, Joy," Sari had said. "You know it doesn't work that way. I mean, I could argue that the safest thing for all of us would be to rid the planet of men. But you wouldn't want that, would you."

She wasn't really asking a question.

Face burning, Joy turned away. Sari had recently learned about Joy and the sociology professor—it was a thing that was not a thing, not really, not beyond Joy having taken one too many of his classes. And it was over now, besides. But it had been *something*, this non-thing she'd instinctively kept hidden. Joy was still consumed by it; she thought about it all the time. Him, her professor. Professor Jacob Hendrix. Sari did not approve. Now, cheeks still hot, a nauseous feeling overtaking her, Joy thought again of her former roommate. Had Joy somehow invited this trouble? Had she unleashed it upon Karlie? An unwitting snake with an apple? Joy had wanted to taste the apple, too. She'd wanted to gobble the whole thing.

Decades after graduation, she and Sari have remained in contact, trading emails now and then. Sari's an ACLU attorney who works with Title IX complaints, a dedicated person who lives by her principles. Joy is a person who has, admittedly, dined out a few times on the story of her roommate's death. Everyone's interested in murder as long as it doesn't touch them. The story makes for rapt listeners, granting Joy the weirdly exalted status of the true-crime adjacent, shameful and delicious. Joy always whispers an apology afterward, feeling the sordidness of her own soul.

They eventually arrested someone for Karlie's death and charged him: a young man who hung out regularly downtown, picking up odd jobs or service work, occasionally panhandling—someone most locals recognized on sight—who, it seemed, had developed an obsession with Karlie. He'd previously only been picked up for minor charges, shoplifting, loitering, alleged Peeping Tom antics. Joy watched him on the news footage, shuffling along in shackles, mouth agape like a fish flung ashore, bewildered eyes. He lived with his mother, had an eighth-grade education. It troubled Joy, the whole thing. But life, for the living, went on.

And then, all these years later, a letter arrives addressed to Joy. From Karlie.

THE LETTER IS a sort of time traveler—the envelope worn with the years, unopened. Originally addressed to Joy's college apartment, the text is written over and crossed out. It's Joy's son Sean who finds it, slipped into an old book of hers, the collected poetry of John Donne—a book he's borrowed for English class. The letter has made a long and improbable voyage through time after having been tucked away and forgotten, never even opened. A miracle. An artifact of an old-fashioned epistolary era. Sean hands the letter to Joy with the solemnity of someone who has grown up on Snapchat. Joy's hands tremble at the sight of the familiar handwriting. She dares not open it.

The letter hits her at a bad time. She has been taking long walks by herself at night, thinking, skittering out of the way of oncoming traffic, watching people live their lives behind windows. She's been having trouble sleeping.

Karlie was on her mind even before the letter arrives: Joy recently happened upon an article online about the guy who'd written *I Kissed*

Dating Goodbye. Now he regrets it. He is divorcing his wife and leaving his pastorship. He's lost his faith and no longer identifies as a Christian. It all seems too sad to warrant any schadenfreude.

Joy is getting a divorce herself.

She and her husband had spent the year she was approaching forty debating whether or not to try for a third child—a luxury child, Joy's work friend Martha had quipped, as if the child were an expensive tennis bracelet. Joy feigned laughter even though Martha's words made her vaguely queasy. Martha had a daughter—an only child by design—and the kind of unquestioning surety about decisions that often left Joy both uncomfortable and a little envious. Joy herself always saw things from too many angles, paralyzed by possibilities and potential outcomes. This theoretical third child would be wonderful, but wearying, her husband conceded. He and Joy were already too exhausted to have sex, which seemed a prerequisite to obtaining said luxury child. Plonking themselves down in front of the television, they sometimes touched hands. It was the best they could do. They ultimately decided to forgo the metaphorical tennis bracelet in the name of their marriage. By then, though, Joy's husband seemed to think there was no longer a marriage worth saving. He'd moved on, peremptorily, it turned out. Without her knowledge and against her will.

You're constitutionally unhappy, he said. *It oppresses me.*

I'm not depressed.

I didn't say you were. Constitutionally unhappy. It makes me unhappy, too. Your unhappiness makes it hard for me to breathe.

He made the unhappiness sound like the core feature of her personality. A suffocating force. The way that Joy looked at the world, pinched and vigilant, bracing for fire ants, falling branches, and tax deadlines, rather than celebrations. But her unhappiness allowed her to get things done!

The divorce has turned bitter. There is money involved—her husband's, originally—and Joy has come to the slightly paranoid conclusion that he will stop at nothing to keep it. But this isn't even the part that is getting to her. It's the fact that her husband is now having a third baby without her—with a younger woman he met through work, fresh-cheeked and fresh-egged. It is insulting in such a classic and retrograde way that Joy feels she can't mention it to anyone, that she must feign a carefree attitude about the whole situation. Let some other poor woman's pelvic floor get busted out like an old screen from its frame. Joy has better things to do.

I'm sorry, goose. XOXOXO

Karlie had written this on the envelope's exterior, rounded letters along the edge, smudged but legible.

The words ripple through Joy, giving shape to an inchoate thought that had been dormant inside her for all these years, a virus awakening, tingling through her nerves again.

She must find her old professor. Professor Hendrix.

IT'S A DAMP gray day when both her sons are at their father's. The house is too quiet without them, suffused with a ghostly absence. In the bathroom mirror, the face that stares back at her belongs to a haggard old woman.

She and Professor Hendrix have not communicated in years. He took a position at a small liberal arts college in Georgia after her junior year. A few years ago, he'd returned to the university town where Joy still lives, the place where he began his career, to retire. She'd heard this through a loose network of his former students—the admiring ones, those filled with unrequited intellectual adoration. Joy both scorns and relates to these former students. Her professor seemed old when she'd been his student, but now he will be a senior citizen inarguably. Joy works as a grant writer for a women's health nonprofit, and she wonders if he'll find conversation with current her engaging. She assumes he is still interested in the things he studied over the course of his career: nondenominational Protestantism, cults, the prosperity gospel, televangelism. Younger women.

She could go to him. She knows all his old haunts. The youthful her inside herself, the hopeful girl, alert to every tender shoot, thirsting for beauty, for love, gives a little flutter like a wintering bird catching a ray of light. He is elderly, Joy reminds herself, and she is very sad. This is nothing—she will find him and have a drink, catch up. He is simply an old mentor of sorts. But her skin flushes and prickles at the thought.

"KNEEL DOWN HERE," her roommate had said.

It was cool outside, the leaves brushed with the first reddish tinge of fall. Karlie was wearing a long woolen scarf around her neck that, when combined with her green peacoat, made her look like a girl from a college catalog—bright, perky, ready to learn. Wearing only a thin long-sleeved shirt without a jacket, Joy shivered beside her. They'd gathered in an outdoor amphitheater that belonged to the university, a wooded place surrounded by trees. Karlie's friend Jamie—a born-again kid from Mount Airy, hopelessly blond and handsome, a smiling, musical-loving boy who, it seemed, had translated all his repressed desires into a kind of ebullient evangelism—was with them. The homoeroticism of the Jesus that Jamie described was so painfully obvious to Joy that her cheeks reddened whenever he spoke of Him.

"There," Jamie said, touching the nape of Joy's neck gently, guiding her head forward. Joy let him, like it was all new to her—and in a way, it was. It was different here, with Jamie and Karlie. She had not yet confessed the truth about her father, or about her status as a wayward preacher's kid. Through the trees they could still hear the sounds from one of the upper quads: students shouting, music playing from a boom box.

Karlie and Jamie had brought Joy directly there from a small on-campus meeting room in which a group of students gathered to listen to Clay, one of the professional leaders of the all-campus evangelical group, the Gathering, share his personal faith journey. Clay was older, handsome in the way of an outdoor educator, and his voice had trembled at key moments when he spoke. Clay and his cousin Kent had grown up hard. There'd been darkness, Clay said, a moment when they'd come to a kind of crossroads. He and his cousin might have ended up somewhere else entirely, a chilled and lonely place, but for the power and glory of Almighty

God, their ever-loving Father, and His grace. Here Clay was, leading a campus youth organization, and here was his cousin, in graduate school.

"Ask Him to enter you," Jamie said softly, kneeling beside her. Joy could feel the afterglow of Clay's testimony still, all that promise. The Holy Ghost was coiled somewhere nearby, ready to unfurl into an all-seeing, all-knowing mist. "Ask Jesus to enter your heart."

Karlie knelt beside her, their knees touching—a meaningful heat transmitted. Or maybe Joy was just cold. She glanced at Karlie.

"Go ahead," she said. "Ask Him."

The sun was already dropping, somewhere out behind the trees, the road, the hill, and Joy could hear the whoosh of traffic. Jamie's eyes were closed. He seemed to radiate peace, beneficence. Karlie, too—tipping her head back, lips parted slightly, as if she were awaiting some divine dispensation. Joy wanted this also. She wanted to be free of her loneliness. Already she'd gone to frat parties with two other girls from her dorm, pleasantly ordinary college students who wished only for the trappings of a pleasantly ordinary experience: beer pong, formals, all-nighters, pizza. She'd stood stiffly in a corner, until a boy with a pockmarked face sauntered over and asked if Joy was in his anthro lecture. When she was unable to formulate any answer, he'd left her standing there, alone.

At the amphitheater, Joy spoke to God silently, forming the words neatly in her mind like a prayer. Jamie gave her hand a squeeze, and Joy watched Karlie's lips moving, offering some intercession on her behalf.

She waited. Nothing happened.

Finally, as if they'd all agreed to it, they stood. Jamie and Karlie were beaming.

"You did it, Joy," Karlie said, and there was a new lightness Joy felt in her head, a strange, ebullient, hollow feeling—but maybe that was the cold, too, the rush of blood from her head to her feet.

"Joy!" Jamie said, giving her name its full meaning and weight, her name, which had always clung to her like a cruel parody. How had her parents not known better than to give her, their sallow, serious, frowning daughter, a name of elation?

"Thank you," she said, although she didn't know what she was thanking them for.

The next day when she went to her professor's office hours, Joy felt emboldened. No one had ever taught her to flirt, so her only coyness, her one move, was to play contrarian: She told him what happened. Her recent salvation. He chuckled slightly.

"Another soul saved, another notch in their belts," he said, turning to the shelf of books behind him, moving several volumes to pull out the bottle of bourbon he kept there. From his desk drawer, he withdrew two glasses and poured each of them a drink.

"No, it wasn't like that. They're my friends," Joy said, but the flush of the cold amphitheater returned to her then, her cheeks growing hot once more. She wasn't simply another heathen converted, a tally mark on their scorecard.

He shrugged and took a sip from his glass, gesturing for Joy to drink also. She drank, unable to tell if the burning in her throat was the threat of tears or the alcohol.

"I'm sure they are."

Joy had been meeting him here, regularly, for months now, since the day he'd noticed a particular question she asked in class about the First Great Awakening. There must have been a clue in her voice, in the way she gazed at him, that conveyed friendlessness and hunger. *Preacher's kid*, he'd said, pointing at her with one long, pale finger after the rest of the class had left. *You're lost. I know your type.* Joy had nodded, although technically she was unsure if she still counted as a preacher's kid. Her father's seizures had grown worse. What for so long he'd managed to frame as a divine gift, as the hand of God—descending only rarely and electrifyingly—bestowing ethereal visions during his postictal states, had now turned into something vicious and frequent. A curse. It had soured her father's mind, leaving him gray-faced and distant, hardly able to get out of bed. A turning of the spiritual milk, he called it. Her mother helped him negotiate a medical leave. On recent visits, the only times she saw him was shuffling to the kitchen to microwave a mug of soup. He hadn't set foot in the church for over a year. Her father, it seemed to Joy, was now more lost than she was.

Joy's professor had told her he'd found himself similarly overwhelmed by the vastness of this large university when he'd first arrived as a student. Questioning, just like her. Newly distanced from his family back home—not in quite the same way as Joy, but enough so that he understood. He simpered knowingly, although she'd told him very little about herself. He wasn't wrong. It felt like a magic trick, the way he'd read her so easily.

"Anyway, I felt it," Joy had said to him that day, which, with a little distance from the experience, almost didn't seem like a lie. "It felt different from before. From back home. In my old church. This felt real." Already the sip of bourbon was making her brave—or maybe it was the illicit atmosphere of these meetings, which had become more and more regular, in her professor's office, sharing drinks. Something pulled taut between them, invisible, daring one of them to be the first to pluck it.

"Oh, yeah?"

He raised an eyebrow, his eyes twinkling in amusement. Behind him, there was a photo of him with his wife in front of the Parthenon. She looked like a nice woman, ordinary—which made Joy hate her all the more.

"Yeah," she said, and as they talked about her experience, Joy could feel a kind of effortless revision happening, the cold air becoming a kind of clarity, the rushing sensation in her head when she'd stood up like being reborn, a God-ghost burrowing into her chest parasitically, causing a blossoming of her hard little unripe heart.

"Do tell."

"I felt faint. Like something was coming over me. A mystery. It was weird."

In her mind, Joy was articulate, sensitive to the vagaries of experience—but with her professor, she still used the crude monosyllables of late adolescence. It was like the blaze of her professor's intelligence rendered her stupid. He drank the rest of his bourbon in a gulp, but Joy could see through the blur of his glass that he was smiling, trying not to laugh.

"That feeling of mystery," he said, "is probably something we could summon right here. In this dusty little office. It wouldn't take much."

"That's not what Karlie says," Joy told him. She shared with him what Karlie had told her of signs she's received: a message intuited from a bit of green ribbon blowing directly into her path, a butterfly alighting on her nose and filling her with an extraordinary sense of comfort, the time she'd been half asleep and swore she witnessed a seraphic messenger, felt the distinct pressure of heavenly hands on her shoulders while she prayed.

Professor Hendrix nodded. Joy could still see amusement in his eyes. He poured himself another bourbon.

"I'd like to meet this Karlie," he said. "She sounds like a real wonder."

Joy shrugged. Perhaps he was joking, but people did say this about Karlie, who was very convincing, and also beautiful in a soft, womanly way. She had large eyes and a pretty mouth and face, the full arms of an old-fashioned milk maiden. Everyone loved her—Clay, the other leaders of the evangelical group, her peers, the rest of the girls in the dorm. She looked like someone from a Vermeer; Joy had seen those paintings in their art history class and thought of Karlie immediately. The whiteness of her cheeks, that untouchable gaze of hers.

Professor Hendrix seemed to intuit her thoughts, because he pulled himself closer, scraping the chair across the floor. He let the scoop of his hand fall on her knee, where it rested warmly. His face was across from hers, their breath mingling. This was the closest they'd ever sat.

"I mean as an interview subject," he said softly. He was writing a paper on young evangelicals. "If she's willing to participate."

She nodded. Other powers seemed to be working on her then—the bourbon, the cramped space of the office, her professor's hand on her knee.

"I'll show you that feeling of mystery," he said, his voice very soft, very close to her ear. "We can surely conjure it."

———

JOY FINDS HER professor at the bar. It is the one near campus that he frequented back in his teaching days. She had seen him there many times, flanked by eager graduate students and seniors from his honors seminar, hands awhirl as he spoke, basking in the glow of all that attention. She never went. She'd never been invited, but she walked past many times, crunching through the leaves and stealing jealous glances through the window.

She is no one, she reminds herself—even with those long, bourbon-soaked talks during his office hours, the way he'd touched the back of her neck just so, a feeling like the Paraclete summoned. Joy was no one to him. It was all subtext without text.

Now, her professor sits in a booth alone.

He sees her standing outside and waves. It feels like he's been waiting for her to appear, like the whole thing had been prearranged, predetermined. Joy pushes open the door and walks up to him, watching his inscrutable smile. There is always part of him, she feels, that is gently amused and laughing at her. She finds she already wants to leave.

"I know you," he says. "You're . . ."

"Joy," she supplies.

"Joy!" He repeats her name like he means it.

He looks so old, so changed from what she remembers that she almost can't bear it. She still feels the same inside, like an earnest college girl, but she wonders if he thinks the same seeing her. She is middle-aged; he is an old man.

"What are the odds? Sit, Joy, sit!"

His smile hurts her. He seems to be recalling an oft-told joke, grateful, like she reminds him of a time he loved and has almost forgotten.

"It's good to see you," he says. He's already beckoning to the waitress and ordering her a drink—bourbon, like old times. She doesn't have the heart to tell him that it is something she only pretended to like, for his sake.

She sits down in the booth across from him and looks directly into his face. Words do not come to her. The unopened letter from her past, from Karlie, rests in her bag.

"You could say 'It's good to see you, too,'" her professor says, and his voice is jovial, but Joy can see the mildest irritation in his gestures, in the way he picks up his glass quickly and drinks.

"I read something and thought of you," she says, telling him about the article she saw, about the *I Kissed Dating Goodbye* guy, the tawdry sadness of it, how it prompted her to think of Karlie and her Bible studies, of him and his academic work. She mentions her own divorce, making light of it, easy-breezy, like a fun-time girl. He laughs in his familiar way again, as if Joy is unbearably precocious, but then his laughter sputters to a cough.

She never quite liked his laughter, Joy realizes—the smugness of it. Her anger toward him is finally coalescing after all the years of uncertainty, and she can feel it burbling up now, like the need to retch.

"Karlie," she says quietly. "Why? Why did it have to be her?"

A look passes over his face quickly, darkening it, but he remains impassive. Carefully, he folds up his napkin into triangles, then takes another sip of his drink. There is music playing, an old B-52's song from another era that might as well have been an age of buggies and oil lamps—they are insulated by the music, the clatter of silverware, the voices of other customers. Joy feels alone with him, in a strange bubble of privacy. *Roam if you want to . . .* Finally, he speaks.

"People are complicated, Joy," he says slowly. With one knobby finger, he traces the circumference of his glass, then holds it up to the dying light from the window, as if inspecting for impurities. "Karlie was very complicated. I think you may never have fully appreciated that."

"She was my friend."

"No doubt of that. I like to think she was mine as well." He sighs very deeply. The B-52's are playing and playing—*without wings, without wheels*—with a Möbius strip–like endlessness, and the dusky bar seems to be the maw of some sick carnival ride. "It was a tragedy," her professor says softly, in the special, fatherly voice he used when she was riled. She's always hated this voice, which indeed reminds her of her own father—sunken-eyed and silent, his uncut hair fanned out against his pillow pitifully, like the halo of a failed saint.

"You killed her," Joy says quietly. "Karlie. My roommate. It was your fault. She was so good before she met you. You ruined her."

At this, he laughs, but his eyes have turned hard, bleak.

"Joy," her professor says slowly, dabbing at his lips with the folded napkin. His hands are liver-spotted now, with none of the power she recalls. "I know you're under a great deal of stress. With your divorce. I'm going to ignore what you just said. You're beside yourself."

But she cannot stop herself. All those old days are rushing back to her.

After Joy had introduced them, toward the very end of their freshmen year, Karlie had agreed to participate in Professor Hendrix's studies. They began to meet regularly.

He's interviewing me for his research, Karlie had told Joy. *We talk about the historicity of the Gospel, modern evangelical movements, that kind of thing, you know . . . He's so smart,* and her eyes shot heavenward, but Joy could see the way a blush rose up her neck, the extra care she put into her appearance before they met. And Joy saw the tiny bruise on Karlie's neck, a devil's kiss. She began dallying in the hallways outside Professor Hendrix's office, trying to catch glimpses of them together, trying to comprehend exactly what was going on—but she knew. Of course Joy knew. She idled near the departmental building, waiting to see them exit together, watching as a casual familiarity grew ever so subtly over time between them, his arm on Karlie's shoulder, Karlie wearing his sweater as it got colder.

When Joy stopped showing up to her professor's office hours and he said nothing, that was the end of it for her. She continued to attend class the rest of the semester but turned taciturn, reluctant, careful to do only the bare minimum. Professor Hendrix never sought her out or asked why. It was like whatever they'd once shared was simply a figment of Joy's imagination.

"It was your fault," Joy repeats, although she's hardly sure why she's saying it. Karlie made her own choices. There is another man in jail, evidence tying him to the scene. Open and shut. This man across from her, her former professor, had an alibi. What's more, he's pitiable now, impotent, a king dethroned. Maybe there's a way she still longs for him to see her, an approving gaze she still might earn. Maybe she is simply cruel.

Yet she places the letter from Karlie on the table for him to see, like it's proof.

He shakes his head and puts his hands into the sparse hair at his temples, pressing as if to stop an ache in his head.

"You were jealous," he whispers. "You wanted me to cross that line with you."

"No."

"You hated her."

Joy thinks of all those days she waited outside his office, listening to voices inside—his, Karlie's. She'd laugh softly, he'd murmur something, she'd laugh again, but soon there were other sounds. Joy stood by the door listening, a terrible heat spreading over her.

The truth is that Joy's professor never so much as kissed her, although his every gesture seemed to promise it: fingers on her shoulders, her back, sending shivers down her neck. His breath behind her ears, at the nape of her neck. The barometric pressure between them thick, ominous. Promises, signals, implications, leaving her like an arrow pulled back on a bow but never released into flight.

"I never hated her," Joy says, which is true. She'd loved Karlie. But she'd also envied her, for the way she lived in the world with a sense of ownership, for the way she took things.

He shakes his head again, like it's all very sad to him. He takes another drink. She sees he is still in possession of his most notable attributes, superciliousness and composure.

"Poor lost preacher's kid with her poor sick-in-the-head daddy."

She stands to leave, her bag knocking over her bourbon and spilling it onto Karlie's letter. Giving a little gasp, she tries to rescue the letter, but it's already wet. She plucks it from the puddle of liquor.

"I'm praying for you," he says mockingly.

She scoffs. There's bourbon dripping from Karlie's letter onto the toes of her boots.

"God, I hate you."

She means it in every possible way.

He doesn't answer her. He says nothing when she leaves.

OUTSIDE THE BAR, Joy stands on the corner, catching her breath. Her teeth chatter. It's grown colder now, but not nearly as cold as she feels, and it is already dark although barely past five P.M. In late November, the weather in North Carolina is alternately balmy, then unexpectedly cool. Some students pass by still wearing shorts, whereas others have broken out their jackets. A little shudder passes through her that has nothing to do with the temperature. She presses a cocktail napkin she's grabbed against the damp part of the letter.

She and Karlie were close only during that first semester of freshman year. By sophomore year, they lived apart, and Joy rarely saw her. She'd stopped speaking to Professor Hendrix entirely by then, although for reasons that were inexplicable to her, Joy took two more of his classes.

With Karlie, she remained pleasantly aloof. They bumped into each other now and then before Karlie died, but they never again spoke of Professor Hendrix. He left for his new job the semester after Karlie's death, and Joy moved to an off-campus apartment with Sari and some of the others she'd met in her women's studies seminar. It was a relief not to be seeking some grander plane of being. She felt at ease with her new friends, slump-shouldered former high school nerds made good, vigorous people who invested themselves in things like the college radio station or environmental action campaigns or slam poetry. Once, not long after graduation, Joy had looked up Professor Hendrix at his new college and emailed him. He'd never responded.

Joy tries to shake off the thought of him—a mean old man. Pathetic. She walks away from the bar, ignoring the clusters of laughing students who block the sidewalk. Professor Hendrix does not rush out to try to stop her or apologize. Joy doesn't turn around to look, but she knows he is seated peacefully in his booth, finishing his drink in neat sips, untroubled by their encounter.

Her husband's lawyer has sent another threatening email to Joy, trying to get her to sign a bunch of papers, accede to his demands. She hasn't yet. He's riled the defiant part of her. She won't go down without a fight.

Instead of walking back to where she parked, Joy heads in the opposite direction, entering a part of town close to campus where there are million-dollar houses and streets shaded by stately trees. Her hands are still shaking, so she stuffs them into her pockets. The boots she's wearing are a half size too small and pinch her toes. She walks anyway.

She is walking to her husband's house—the new house he shares with the woman who will be his new wife, her replacement. When Joy gets there, she stands at the foot of the drive so she can see into the glowing windows of their kitchen.

There are silhouettes moving: her husband, her sons, the new woman with the baby inside her. Joy can see them as shapes, like figures in a shadow play. Maybe if she looks long enough, she will really see. She watches them readying dinner and wipes her cheek in the dark.

Karlie's letter is in her pocket, half ruined. There's not enough light to read, but Joy pulls the letter out anyway. She opens the envelope and turns on her phone's flashlight:

December 1999

Dear Joy,

Thank you for introducing me to Prof. H., and I'm sorry—I know in becoming close to him I took something from you. But whatever it was you thought he offered—approval and safety, maybe, or wisdom—it's a false promise. He's nothing special—really, he's worse than nothing special. He's petty, flawed, vain. I'm not just saying that to make you feel better. It's over between us, anyway, whatever was going on between us in the first place. I'm sorry.

I know you've been following me. I've seen you on campus. I saw you duck into the stairwell when we were leaving Howell Hall. And I saw you that day outside his office, pretending to look at the bulletin board. Another time at the coffee shop, I pretended not to notice you. I didn't want to embarrass you. I don't blame you. I know it hurt you, seeing us together. But a part of me likes to think I protected you from something. Maybe I'm justifying myself, but . . . you're better off. Trust me. Now, someone's started driving over to my apartment. At first, I thought it was Prof. H. But then I remembered you, following me on campus. And I finally saw the car. Is that you who keeps showing up at my apartment? Driving the "BMW"? I hear it pull up, watch its cyclops eye crawling slowly up my wall . . . I won't hold it against you, but could you please stop? Maybe it's not you in the BMW. But it's someone.

I wish I could learn to pray again. There I was, <u>lying on the living room floor</u> of my apartment, thinking that, trying to find the words that used to come so easily to me, and I saw one of my <u>signs</u>! (You know! Remember when you *said everything's a <u>Magic Eye image</u> to me?) It'd been there all along, and I'd noticed it before, but I saw it differently this time. I'd been thinking of you, how even though we still talk on occasion, <u>vent</u> to one another, nothing's ever been quite the same since back when we were roommates . . .*

I love you, goose. Merry Christmas!
Karlie

Joy blinks, and blinks again, then folds the letter back into its envelope. A precious, perishable thing, filled with Karlie's characteristic arbitrary overuse of emphasis, all her exclamation marks and underlining. She'd understood how Joy had felt the whole time. And yet Karlie was wrong. Joy had never been following her, had never come to her apartment. She'd been following only him. Her professor, on campus. She hadn't had a car during college, much less a BMW. A sick, strange sadness uncurls in Joy's stomach.

A door of the house opens, and out comes someone into the dark. Joy hears the clunk of a trash can being pushed toward the curb. She clicks off the light on her phone quickly and holds her breath, motionless.

The wheels of the trash can rumble closer and closer, then stop. There, in the dimness, Joy sees her, swimming into focus, a shadowy woman-shape with the unmistakable swell of pregnancy. Her eyes seem feline, reflecting ambient light from the other houses.

"You," the woman says, her voice like a knife. "You again. You're trespassing. I could call the cops."

She moves closer to Joy, her belly a taunt.

"You've got to stop doing this," she says. "You've got to leave us alone."

Joy hears the door of the house open again, and someone steps out.

"Maggie?"

That's the woman's name. It is her husband's voice saying it. Joy can see his outline, backlit on the porch, peering into the darkness.

"You all right?"

Joy grips Karlie's letter tight in her fist, but she lets the rest of herself slump to the cool cement. She lies on her back, looking up into the starless sky. Then she lets all that feeling course through her. Unlike Karlie, she knows how to do it right. She saw her father so many times. She watched it happen, an ungovernable force, a wordless thing, like being possessed by something—God, perhaps, or a lesser demon.

"Jesus, John. There's something wrong with her. She's . . . Are you okay?"

"Joy?"

She hears the stricken sound of her husband's voice, his feet pounding down the path—her husband, running to her aid.

Her arms seize and jerk like she's been shot through with electricity. She lets her head fall back, her mouth foam. Her arms stiffen and jerk from their sockets. Her tongue has gone rigid in her mouth. Joy lets them scream at it, at her display—this new woman and her husband, the two of them hovering over her like abiding angels—but this time, it truly feels real. Like getting struck by lightning. Or holiness. Submitting once and for all.

Unit 7C

It's a crap job no one wants, which is why KC takes it: a couple dollars more than minimum wage, plus a steep discount on his one-bedroom, an upgrade from the studio he chose initially. For what he saves in rent, the job's worth it—makes his place almost free. He just covers utilities. In exchange, he's hassled all night long by drunk nineteen-year-olds. They are forever locking themselves out of their apartments, letting toilets overflow, setting off smoke alarms. Thursday nights he spots them, bolting across the parking lot like startled antelope, or laughing, hyena-ish, on their balconies. While he sits reading on his tiny balcony in the evening, they dart past him, strangely beguiling in their foolishness, their innocence. Flushed and shouting, they embark on youthful missions. High-gloss hijinks with fake IDs. Casual, testosterone-driven destruction. Preening displays of breasts and upper thighs at Pantana Bob's. Beer drinking and mating rituals at fraternity court. Oh, what younglings, these little animals. He is not yet twenty-one himself, but regarding his neighbors—his peers, technically—is, to KC, like regarding a different species entirely.

KC is the night manager. He gave himself this title for the purposes of a résumé recently concocted to apply for a summer research position. In truth, he's never actually been offered anything so formal as a title. He wasn't even sure how much the property management higher-ups knew about the arrangement until he received, after his first four months and a turn of the calendar year, an actual W-9.

He was recruited one day in the laundry room by Gus, the guy who does regular maintenance and oversees the office during the day. Gus has a glass eye, a hip injury, and a VFW decal on his car—also, a ghoulish way of leaning out of the office window with a cigarette dangling from his lips when young women walk past. KC had avoided him at all costs.

"Anderson, right? 11B?"

KC nodded, the clean laundry warm as fresh-baked bread in his arms.

"I've got a job for you if you need it."

KC froze, uncertain how to respond. This seemed like the sort of abrupt overture that led to one becoming a drug mule or something equally unsavory.

"Work from home. You're here all the time anyway, right?"

KC felt himself flush at the obviousness of his isolation. So obvious that a one-eyed man beaten up by life saw it and, probably, pitied him, rather than vice versa. He was young and ought to be having *the time of his life*. The implicit pressure to do so was everywhere. It was stifling. It was enough to make a person want to retreat to his white-walled one-bedroom with a mattress in the corner and good high-speed internet.

"I guess," KC said, because in truth he *did* need money. There'd been discord with his old suitemates, and KC had needed to move out quickly. The cost of leaving the dorms abruptly—well, he'd taken a financial hit. Unlike these lords and ladies of the manor in their pastel collared shirts and Daddy's Mercedes, he was putting himself through school. He had a partial scholarship and a work-study arrangement at the library. But it was always tight, not having the advantage of family support.

Gus turned out to be all right. He got KC set up with a key to the office, showed him how to transfer the after-hours phone line to KC's cell, gave him suggestions on how to handle the most common issues. For maintenance requests, KC's job was to try and stave off acute disaster. Only in the direst situations was he authorized to call an emergency plumber. Generally, the goal was to placate the resident until morning, when Gus would handle the situation. Mostly, Gus explained, KC's job would consist of letting drunk kids back into their places when they lost their keys. You were supposed to check an ID and cross-reference that with the leasing list in the computer system, but half the time the kids didn't have their IDs on them, either. Just make sure they seemed legit, Gus said.

When KC asked what that meant, Gus swept his arm over the sea of shiny vehicles, gleaming tokens of affection from parents invested in the comfort and long-term success of their offspring, parked in the complex lot and shrugged.

"You'll know."

Gus shoved him gently in the shoulder then, the kind of slo-mo gesture KC saw among the frat boys who loitered outside the bars downtown—possibly ironic in this instance, since Gus himself had also spent years observing the antics of the young.

"It's why I noticed you, kid. Wondered how you snuck in."

And then Gus doubled over in a fit of uproarious laughter, although it was more a paroxysm of coughing, really. Emphysema, KC thought. It was how his dad had sounded the last time he'd seen him. This, however, was a cough-laugh of genuine fondness.

They are of similar tribes, KC now understands. Gus had seen it from the start. Outsiders. Despite his textbooks, his respectable GPA, the paper he'd recently written on subverted gender roles in Shakespeare's comedies, KC is an interloper here, at the university, in this apartment complex full of joyful, blundering young people. He can afford neither blunders nor joy.

On Fridays, he walks the premises with a little bag, picking up trash. The girls, sparkling and bare-shouldered, call to one another, silver bracelets loose on their careless wrists reflecting light. Beloved girls, polished and clean. They do not notice him anymore. It would be humiliating if they did, but there is something inherently overlookable in KC now, an invisibility that makes him feel, among his peers, like a ghost. He is lucky in this regard, but it is easy to forget sometimes that he exists on the same timeline as everyone else.

The girl sitting by the swimming pool is also like a ghost, startling him with her suddenness. She sits on a backpack beyond the radius of light spilling from a nearby window. In the low light, she is spectral, her face hollowed and bluish with shadow. The pool is closed, its large brown cover heavy with fallen leaves. It is a terrible pool, even in summertime when it is open—dirty and too small, never not overcrowded. Someone is always vomiting into it or losing a twenty-four-karat gold necklace that KC will be called upon to fish out of the drain. The gate is locked now.

The girl steps forward and points to the little hedge and a bit of brick wall near a spot where the fence dips lower.

"I climbed over," she says without offering a greeting. "It's nice and quiet in there."

He nods, noting the gleam of an empty soda can, a plastic grocery bag, a receipt for Chinese takeout lying on the ground. He'll pick those up later. It's almost eight P.M., too early for anyone to have ventured out, but he can hear the sounds of friends arriving, knocking on doors, greeting one another, ready to pregame. It's late in the semester, the last days of classes before the exam period starts. No one else is here in the center of the complex besides this girl and him.

"You work here," she says.

He's seen her, he realizes, around town, smoking outside the diner off Main.

"Yeah. You live here?"

"No, down the road."

"Oh, the Rosemont?"

She laughs and shakes her head.

"I'm between places. Bad breakup. I'm staying with friends right now."

He gauges that her heartbreak over this breakup was not too severe—or else that heartbreak becomes her. She has long, white-blonde hair and a chocolate-colored mole on her left cheek. There's something unkempt about her, scraggly and unwashed, yet she is beautiful enough that it looks intentional, a look someone has cultivated for a grunge photo shoot. Yes, he remembers her—can recall having seen her standing by herself near the bus stop downtown, or under the café awning. The students all travel in packs, but not this girl. He feels the pang one gets around another like-minded person.

"KC," he says, offering a little semi-ironic salute that he immediately regrets. He was not always so awkward, was he? But if she's noticed his social clumsiness, her face does not betray her.

"Lydia," she says, throwing her backpack over first, then grasping the fence so it rattles and pulling herself over. She jumps lightly to the low brick wall and then to the ground beside him.

"So, you must've already heard about the show," she says, peering up at KC. Her pupils are large and dark, and he wonders if she's on something. Then again, the light is very dim.

He shakes his head.

"*Murder Real Estate: The World's Most Haunted Places?*"

He shakes his head again.

Lydia pulls her long hair into a skein and twists it round and round, wrapping it into a bun at the nape of her neck. Her skin is pale, luminous under the nearby streetlamp. She has, KC thinks, the sharp collar bones and long, ethereal hands of an angel. She shifts and the light changes, creating the illusion of bruises down one side of her face. When she is not speaking, her lips do not quite close all the way, revealing a toothy wedge. Her posture is poor. And yet even in her imperfection, there is a rightness to her, an ease in the way she inhabits her body. A unity of form and being. His throat aches just watching.

"It's a true-crime docuseries," she explains. "They want to film here. On the girl who was killed."

There are stories about a college girl who was killed years ago, the details of which have morphed over time into the stuff of urban legend. He's never even been sure exactly where it happened. There are nearly identical apartment buildings all over this stretch between the interstate and the university campus.

"Oh," he says. "Sure. Gus'll be back tomorrow. He's in touch with the owners."

Lydia shakes her head, touching his arm.

"No," she says. "Another ex of mine is part of the crew. Owners already denied the request."

"That's too bad." She is, KC thinks, a girl of many ex-boyfriends, something that marks her, maybe, with a certain level of danger. He ought to be on guard.

Lydia studies him.

"You've got access, right?"

There is a whooping sound behind them: three guys in untucked button-down shirts, who waft thick clouds of cologne as they climb into a Jeep.

"I mean, if they said no already . . ."

"Listen," she says. "They'll pay you."

He can't even look at her. The pull is too strong—money he could use, Lydia, standing so close he could bite her. He looks at a spot of darkness beyond her shoulder—a tree, the lower wing of the apartment complex.

"The episode won't air for ages. Please."

He meets her eyes and nods.

Her smile is iridescent, a luna moth, there and gone.

LYDIA'S EX SHOWS up in a van after midnight the night of filming. KC suggested Tuesday, a slow night for lockouts and alcohol poisoning. The ex is named Brian. He's thin, with a goatee and an earnest manner. As he hefts video equipment from the van—he's strong for a wiry guy—his ragged T-shirt reveals patches of slender torso. His crew consists of only one other guy: Mike, prematurely graying, schlubby, in his thirties, KC guesses, with an impressive Tom Selleck–style mustache.

Lydia comes, too, their broker. Also, as she's explained to KC, she's interested. She's a true-crime completist, a Murderino, has listened to all the podcasts, watched all the old episodes of *Dateline* and *Unsolved Mysteries*, all the feature-length documentaries on the Night Stalker, the Manson family, the Golden State Killer.

"I know the details," she says, drawing a figure eight on the ground with the toe of her shoe. "Everything. Please don't think I'm a freak."

"Far from it," KC says with a little too much sincerity. He looks down, cheeks warm.

"A lot of people consider the case unsolved. The guy they charged had no history of violence and the IQ of an eight-year-old," Lydia explains. "Toby. He's the one who found her first. Called the cops from a pay phone anonymously—but he was crying and confused. He was talking about a dead girl, but he didn't give an address or anything, so the call was uninterpretable at first. Police only realized the call's relevance later, after another friend showed up to check on Karlie and found her and called again. A witness spotted Toby downtown early that morning, looking agitated and acting strange, so that didn't help his cause. Karlie's door was left unlocked, so he'd entered and he left fingerprints, trace evidence, all over the scene. It was completely contaminated. He was obviously present after she was dead, but I don't think he did it. He'd been picked up once in the past for voyeurism, so that didn't look good. But they were friendly with one another. She was always sweet to him, and everyone said he adored her."

They're following Brian and Mike down the sloping parking lot, past wing B of the apartment complex, down to where wing C sits, unoccupied, still under renovation. Below it, there is a narrow brown creek and a sad little public park with rusted swings and a cracked basketball court. A stand of trees blocks the view of another neighborhood sitting farther back, above the crest.

"I'm trying to find people who knew her," Brian says. "Friends, classmates, members of the campus religious group she belonged to."

"There's a professor she was close to," Mike adds. "This guy, Hendrix. He's the one we really want to convince to talk. Apparently very popular with his students—maybe a little too popular, you know? He's always turned down interview requests. We're hoping we can find someone who knew both him and Karlie. Maybe they'd shed light on the relationship. Or even convince him to talk to us."

KC has a ring of master keys, a thudding in his chest. He can't afford to lose this night manager job now that he has it, but what Brian has offered him—well, it *is* good money. He needs good money. Not only for school, not only to support himself, but also for the rest of his life. For it to fully take shape. There will be costs involved. So far, he's fudged his way along as much as he can, using tips and tricks gleaned from message boards and private Facebook groups.

"It's definitely that one, ground floor, in the corner," Brian says, pointing to the far end of the shuttered wing, unit 7C. He's holding up his phone, comparing the building to an image from an old news story. KC understands now why the original name of the complex was changed, the numbering of the units altered, why the current owners have planned for this corner unit to be converted to storage space. There's still old signage in the backroom that reads TRAILVIEW CREST in weathered green all-caps letters, but no one uses that name for the complex anymore. It occurs to him that he was completely incurious not to have wondered about this before.

The four of them move closer, huddling around KC as he fits the key into the lock. The door has swollen in its frame, and it takes a full-body shove to open. Inside, the apartment is dank, stale-smelling, still untouched by the contractors. The carpet has been pulled up, and KC notices that there's a small, dark blotch on the bare floor. The kitchen, with its cheap cabinets and particleboard, sits farther back, an old white refrigerator glowering. The whole place, KC feels, is suffused with a deathly stillness. A cold prickling moves up his spine. He could believe, in this moment, that places absorb their most awful occurrences.

"Let's get some room tone," Brian says to Mike. "I'll shoot some B-roll of the exterior and work my way in."

KC moves closer to Lydia. It's inadvertent, a reflexive action. Her warmth is comforting in the cold room. Someone hits a light, and the splotch on the floor comes more clearly into view—a brown Rorschach blot.

"That's where they found her," Lydia whispers. "There were other prints in the living room, but the crime scene techs apparently messed up the superglue fuming—you know, that's how they preserve the prints? So the prosecutors just ignored that."

"Prints could have been anyone. A friend, a classmate," Mike calls over his shoulder. "I stand by my theory they cleared the professor too soon. Now, y'all shut up."

They oblige, moving silently through unit 7C: the tiny bathroom, the empty bedroom with bare, pocked walls. The shades are pulled shut. By a baseboard, KC sees a number two pencil. He picks it up, feeling the indentations where someone gnawed it—a nervous habit he himself shares—the texture strangely intimate in his hand, and slips the pencil into his pocket. Karlie's, he thinks—although sure, it could have been dropped by someone else, Gus, a cleaner, anyone over the last twenty years. Slight though the pencil is in his pocket, it feels significant.

KC and Lydia keep clear of Brian's camera while he gets a shot of the living room, the stain on the floor stark and accusatory. Brian works quietly while they watch.

"See?" Lydia whispers to KC. "Scratch marks."

She points toward a faint series of scratches along the wall, which KC believes could just as easily be ordinary wear and tear, the marks left by a heavy shelf being repositioned against the wall. But he's transfixed by her, the conviction on her face.

"There was a bloodstain found on the scene, but the crime scene investigators were unable to extract DNA for analysis or typing so the prosecutors weren't able to use it. I suspect Karlie drew blood from her assailant. We know she was asphyxiated. Strangled. No ligature, but by someone's hands according to the medical examiner's report, which indicates larger physical stature and passion—male rage. It's such an up-close-and-personal way to kill someone. If he held her down here, and she was lying like this"—Lydia throws her arms above her head so her shirt rides up, and he can see the intimate lunar scoop of her belly, the band of her lavender panties peeking out, hip bones like handles he could grip—"then she might have been reaching over here. We know the medical examiner didn't obtain semen from her vaginal cavity during the autopsy, but there was trace semen in her cervix, which might actually suggest an earlier sexual encounter, not from the night she died . . . Anyway, that sample was also deteriorated enough that they couldn't extract DNA. But if she'd been lying here—"

Brian is grabbing Lydia then, roughly, yanking her to her feet. She stifles a little yelp. KC sees how Brian's fingers dig into the soft flesh of her arm.

"I'm trying to work," he says through gritted teeth. The suddenness of his irritation is startling. "You know I need quiet."

He pulls her toward the kitchen, out of earshot, speaking quietly to her, a rush of hot words that KC can't make out.

When Lydia returns, she says nothing and will not return KC's gaze. Chastened or seething, he cannot tell. Brian resumes his filming, and KC watches the pink splotches on Lydia's arm slowly begin to fade.

It's almost two thirty A.M. when they begin to hear loud voices from the upper parking lot, shouts, laughter—the sounds of apartment residents returning home slicked with sweat and spilled drinks, sticky with hormones and makeup melting from around their eyes like dead pageant girls. There's a terrible club the undergrads frequent, and KC remembers going during his freshman year, the girls all scantily clad and smelling of self-tanner, everyone crowded on the campus shuttle bus from the high-rise freshman dorms. It was a claustrophobic space, the club, darkened to hide the cheapness of its interior, the music assaultively loud, people jammed everywhere. Wherever he tried to move, someone groped at KC—hot breath down his neck, a stranger's hands on his buttocks. The girls around him all laughed at this, like it was a game, like they were fruit being plucked and squeezed for ripeness. KC would back his way into a corner, bracing his shoulders against the wall, watching. His suitemates had all returned to the dorm exhilarated, damp, letting their shimmering garments fall to the floor of the suite like snakes molting their skin. KC had hated it. He'd refused to ever go back.

"Y'all smoke?" Mike asks. They've stepped back outside under the moon, white and austere above them beyond the trees, and he is rummaging in the passenger side of the van for something. It's cold. Lydia shivers, and KC finds himself wishing he were wearing a sweater so he could offer it to her.

"Sure," Lydia says.

KC watches Lydia, the flame from the lighter passing briefly over her face as Mike hunches before her. She inhales, coughs gently, then touches KC's hand, passing the joint to him. They sit together, staring down the moon, sharing. An acrid warmth has blossomed in KC's chest, in his head, his heart. It has been a long time since he's allowed himself to loosen the reins of his control, and this—sitting here, beside Lydia and the film crew—feels reckless. The ghost of Karlie Richards looms somewhere nearby—a cloud passing, a bird calling, invisible fingers tickling the base of KC's skull.

"I'm fucking starving," Brian announces. "Me and Mike'll go pick up burgers."

Lydia has let her head loll back. She sits semi-reclined on the sidewalk.

"We'll wait here," she says, her voice rich and sleepy. She reminds KC of his old cat, the way it curled luxuriously in the sun—even though they are here in the chilly dark. Lydia herself is somehow both light and warmth.

"Guard our shit," Mike says, lifting himself deftly for someone so large into the passenger side of the van.

It's quiet for a while after they leave—a feeling of relief. It is good for Brian and Mike to be gone so they can speak freely, KC thinks, good for it to be only the two of them. There's also a sense of anticipation—palpable, looming over KC and Lydia like the threat of thunder. He watches it pass over her, a shivering in her shoulders.

"Come on," KC says, taking her hand, which is soft but surprisingly cool. "It's too cold out here. Let's go back inside."

The apartment, when they reenter, seems more ordinary this time. An empty room in need of new carpet, a paint job, fresh appliances. An anonymous space that might be claimed by any nineteen-year-old. They sit on the floor, knees up beside each other, facing the blank wall. The long-armed shadows of trees waver before them.

"Karlie was, like, this Christian debutante princess," Lydia offers eventually. The empty space, the silence, demands to be filled by something. "Beautiful. Smart. She could have become anything she wanted in the world."

"I hate this story already." KC cannot help that he sounds weary. The story of Karlie Richards—well-off, beautiful, white, like all celebrated murder victims—is still sad. But all the forgotten murdered girls—poor girls, troublemakers, brown and Black girls, the ones from the wrong neighborhood, the strung-out ones, the undocumented, the wrong-bodied or unpretty, the girls who never stood a chance—their stories are sad, too. All those girls, all those women, young and old, famous or nameless, hovering everywhere. A whole host of dead girls, their names a silent litany. It is unspeakably sad. KC's head feels unmoored from the rest of his body, a loose dreamy feeling. He thinks of his own mother and father, who are not speaking to him, and feels the vaguest nostalgia, like he's thinking of old acquaintances.

"Everyone looked up to her," Lydia continues. "She was perfect. And then she rebelled."

"A tale as old as time," he says. "Go on."

"She got involved with one of her professors. That guy Mike mentioned earlier, Hendrix. He was among the primary suspects at first, but his wife provided an alibi for the entirety of that evening, for whatever that's worth. He also claimed his health condition would have made him unable to assault Karlie in such a manner, got a doctor's note and everything that said he would have been too weak or something, which sounds like bullshit if you ask me. Plus, there was more and more circumstantial evidence that made the guy with the mind of an eight-year-old the most convenient culprit. I remain suspicious of the professor, but I think there are other possibilities, too. She knew a lot of people. Beautiful, provocative, daring—you know, she was that type—you either wanted to *be* her or be *with* her."

"Oh, God. Of course she got murdered."

"Don't be an asshole."

KC doesn't answer.

"You don't know what it's like," Lydia says.

They sit there, with just the faint whoosh of passing cars marring the silence. Lydia holds herself stiffly. Then, seeming to soften toward him, she swipes her finger over her phone, holding the lit rectangle up: a photo of Karlie—a candid shot in which her head is thrown back, her eyes squinting shut with wide-mouthed laughter, abundant blonde hair filling the rest of the frame. They gaze at the photo for a long moment. Karlie's eyes betray a deep pain even mid-laugh—although maybe he only sees that now, in retrospect.

"Look at these."

Lydia has found a list of "Karlie hauntings" on Reddit, many written by past tenants back before the apartment complex was renamed and remodeled. She reads them aloud, letting her free hand fall on KC's forearm, tracing abstract shapes there ever so lightly. His whole brain tingles with her touch while he tries to listen.

[kev4kev85]: One day I came home from class and someone (something?) had put a Bible on the floor. Opened. It wasn't from my shelf. I didn't even own a Bible, but you know they say Karlie was ultra-religious. I have no idea where this Bible came from, but it had something red smudged on the page, like bloody fingerprints or something . . . I didn't touch it for days, just left it there. I was too afraid. I told my friend about it and asked him to come by to get rid of it one weekend when I was away, but when he showed up to get it, it was gone. Totally disappeared.

[ADclp7690]: My girlfriend lived there, in the actual apartment, only five or six years after it happened. She also knew that guy Clay who led the Christian group Karlie had been a part of—they were from the same hometown—and she swore he wasn't right afterward. He wasn't the same, like he was guilt-stricken or something, at least according to her. Anyway, my girlfriend was totally creeped out living there, and she'd asked to switch, but they wouldn't at first. She swore that if you lay down on the living room floor at the exact right spot at night, you'd be flooded with this terrible feeling . . . You couldn't breathe, and it was like there was someone squeezing your neck. Like you could feel the life seeping out of you the longer you lay there. One night we got drunk and tried it. I can't even explain what the feeling was like, but I wouldn't wish it on my worst enemy. I felt so angry, so filled with hatred and rage that I might have hurt anyone who came near me, and that freaked me out. I didn't tell my girlfriend about that—that it was a terrible feeling, but not the one she'd described. We left and went to my apartment afterward and drank a lot. Neither of us wanted to talk about it. Not long after that, she broke her lease because she had to get out of there. But I don't know, it was like we were cursed after that. Something dark had a hold of us. I still believe that's why we broke up.

[dirt430lawya]: I had some buddies who lived in the apartment next to the one that was Karlie's. They said that in the middle of the night they heard sounds of someone screaming. It was always the same time of night, when the moon was full. The screaming always sounded like it was coming through the walls, from the unit next door. But when they went over, there were these two guys who lived there, and they were sound asleep. But it happened all the time, on a regular basis, those screams.

[aleximan530]: I've heard they've still got that piece of carpet from Karlie's apartment, the one with the blood stain, stored somewhere in evidence. I have an uncle who works in a lab and he says they ought to try retesting it now. He says the technology's improved, and even though it's old they should see if they can get anything else out of it.

[boymomstace2]: People always told me I looked sort of like her, which unnerved me, and I happened to live in the same complex where she was killed. One night this group of drunk frat guys started calling out for me, but they were shouting her name at me—Karlie, Karlie, Karlie. It freaked me out, even though they were smiling like they were just having fun. I knew I needed to run. They started chasing me. They chased me all the way through that little patch of woods and down the hill that leads into that next neighborhood, and I swear, I was not in shape to run, but I felt this energy surge through me. It was like Karlie was helping me or something because she didn't want it to happen to another girl . . . I ran so fast I lost them. Later, I heard that a group of guys, the same ones who'd chased me, I think, drove up through campus, like, super drunk, hollering and throwing beer cans out their windows. They accidentally hit this old woman who was out late walking her dog and it was tragic . . . but a part of me kept thinking, wow, that could have been me.

"Are these supposed to be ghost stories?" KC says.

Lydia shrugs, clicking her phone back off. She lifts something that's fallen to the floor, a brown square. KC recognizes it as his wallet.

"Hey, that's mine," he says, reaching for it, but she moves away from him, crab-like, holding the wallet out of his reach.

He leans over her, trying to grab it, until she's on her back on the ground and he's floating over her, their bodies suddenly in tantalizing proximity. His chest hovers above hers. She's giggling. In the dim room, her face glows beneath his, her mouth just below his mouth.

"Oh, look," she says, pointing above him to the ceiling. "A swan!"

He turns obediently to look, but his eyes graze over nothing but an expanse of discolored and flaking white paint.

"See?" she says, sounding pleased, a young girl who has found a rabbit in the clouds, the face of the man on the moon. "See the wings there, and the long neck?"

"Sure, a swan," KC says, but already he's turned back toward her, holding her eyes with his own gaze. The heat and flush of her cheeks seems to rise up beneath him, warming him.

"I dare you," she whispers.

"Dare me to do what?"

They are inches apart now, breathing each other's exhalations. He's propping himself above her with one arm. The wallet is still tight in her fist. She is smiling. He can feel her heart thudding under his. He could kiss her, KC thinks. He could—

She twists away from him, laughing, and opens his wallet, plucking out several cards. She holds them up for inspection.

"Kristina Claire Anderson," she says, holding up his student ID, then turning to study him. There is something awful in how her face changes. She is not cruel. She is thoughtful. Curiosity, then a soft look. It's worse, her pity, the way she assesses him differently now.

"I see why you went with KC," she says, tucking the ID in its fold and handing him back his wallet.

The previous moment, filled with possibility, has transformed to ordinary disappointment. Humiliation, even. He thinks of his former suitemates in the dorm and the argument they had, the way all his suitemates looked at him, like he had a sickness. *It's not about that*, one of them said. *It's you. You've changed. Your personality. You don't mesh with the rest of our suite now. Like, on an emotional level.* Which was fine because he'd have wanted to leave the suite eventually anyway, once he was ready, but they sprung it on him before he'd had the chance to work out any of the details, before he'd had a chance to do much of anything. Campus housing told him he was entitled to finish out his lease, but by that point, he'd wanted none of it. He needed to get out. And then there were his parents. He recalls that awful weekend spring semester of freshman year, the last time he'd visited them—scared, but eager. His father fell into a fit of coughing that left him speechless. His mother stood there, staring at KC blankly, almost without recognition. And then she touched his hair— newly cut, the strange feeling of it shorn above his ears. She touched him so hesitantly it was almost tender. *But you were such a pretty girl*, she said eventually, and that was all she would say.

Lydia reaches over to pat his shoulder, and he can tell it's meant to be conciliatory, an apology of sorts, but it's the wrong move. He flinches, humiliated by such a sisterly gesture. Anger is welling up in him, and he feels it: how he could slap her, the heat buzzing through his hand, the red mark of his handprint across her cheek. Could he ever be angry enough to do that? Or to hurt someone far worse?

These perfect girls. Everyone obsessed with them. Acid rises in his throat. That photo of Karlie Richards. Golden. Frozen in time. Her smile infuriating with its secrets.

KC says nothing. He walks back outside, letting the cool of the night air calm him. Lydia follows. They stand there, silent.

And then the van pulls in. Brian and Mike are back, stepping out of the truck with paper bags greasy and redolent of burgers. Brian passes the food around, and they all eat quickly, quietly. The hunger KC wasn't previously aware of is there now, a gaping hole in his belly. When he finishes, Brian stands over them, a shadowy figure leaning against the van. He's lit a cigarette, and KC watches its cherry float up and down.

"We should finish up," he says. "Ready, Lydia? KC, you want to help out?"

UNIT 7C

Lydia extends her hand to KC to help him up. He accepts grudgingly.

"They don't do full reenactments," Lydia explains. "Only partial scenes. I'm playing Karlie."

"We need a bad guy. Here," Brian says, handing KC a black hoodie. "You play the professor. Don't worry, I won't get your face."

KC takes the jacket, ignoring the funny fluttering in his chest. It's after three A.M. He has class in the morning. There's no good reason for him to be here.

But Lydia is looking excited now, eager to play the role of victim. Brian positions himself at the edge of the walkway with the camera at his shoulder. Mike arranges the audio equipment, although there are no speaking parts—only the whisper of night sounds, the occasional car passing at a distance.

KC creeps over to the bushes, trying to channel a certain menace, then kneels behind some overgrown brush. Brian gestures with his hand, and KC stands up, taking a few cautious steps to where Lydia pantomimes peering out the door into the dark.

"KC, listen, buddy. Your walk, man. It's off. Try it more like this."

Brian mimics what he wants, an exaggerated masculine swagger.

KC nods, feeling the heat travel up his cheeks, thankful now for the low light, the hood pulled forward over his face.

And then his phone rings. He looks down and sees it's the apartment after-hours line, delivering a message to his voicemail.

"Sorry, I gotta go."

"But we're almost done," Lydia says, and though she is pale and lovely as a lit candle in a darkened church, KC sees now she's just an ordinary girl with an ordinary whine. The truth is this phone call, whatever it is, is a relief.

"Duty calls."

"You'll come back?" Lydia asks.

He nods, knowing that he won't. Soon enough, the most dedicated early joggers will be out, their headlamps bobbing up the sidewalks. It is a degradation to be called upon at such an hour, but he welcomes it at this point, whatever straightforward humiliation awaits him: shit overflowing onto a bathroom floor; some sophomore's Tiffany ring that needs to be fished out from the gunk in her garbage disposal; a freshman who keeps losing his key; two swaying ogres from the water polo team fumbling, trying over and over to open the wrong apartment door. It is an act of self-flagellation, his submission to these callers, his eager subservience. In the mind of the resident calling, the matter will always be an emergency, no matter how small, a thing that absolutely could not have waited. It does not occur to any of them, the residents who call the after-hours line, that KC might be sorely inconvenienced, that he might be trying to sleep. The residents of this apartment complex have all grown up accustomed to Siri and Amazon Prime and meal delivery apps, and though polite, they forget that he is not a robot engineered to address their needs.

After listening to the voicemail—a plumbing emergency, sure enough—he makes his way up the hill to wing A, the second floor. All is quiet at this hour, still not yet four A.M., the lights off in almost every apartment. Wing A is thickly shadowed, cloaked in an unnatural dark, only a blinking, red Emergency Exit sign visible at the distant stairwell. He'll mention to Gus tomorrow that the exterior lights have gone out and need replacing.

"Hey," an invisible voice says from the far shadows. "We got locked out. Are you the manager?"

It's a girl's voice, slurred and low. There's a gnawing sensation in his chest. A primitive instinct urges him to flee, but he walks toward her instead. Or rather, toward them. Two girls, one in tights and a corduroy miniskirt, the other in jeggings and a midriff-baring top. First-year students—no older, he thinks. Whereas something has accelerated in his own mind, a premature aging of sorts, that leaves him feeling wearied and ancient, his peers, other college students, all look bright-faced and absurdly young. Babies. Babies still delighted by the world, its bounty of offerings, their whole futures stretching before them like an endless buffet of pleasure. So it is for these girls who look like apple-cheeked children to him, young enough to be in high school. The girl in the miniskirt totters a little, still graceful, foal-like, in her lanky youth, and KC imagines the nips of cheap vodka they've nabbed, the warm, conspiratorial giggling. To have friends like that. There's a twinge of pain in his chest.

"Gotta toilet to unclog," he says, an indirect answer. One of the girls has moved closer—a little flirtatiously, although maybe that's just the vodka coursing through her. Weariness passes over him again.

Maybe it's the hour, the awkward clothes, the strength he now appreciates in the second girl. She has swimmer's shoulders, her exposed abdomen as tautly muscled as a Junior Olympian's, and as she moves closer, he realizes she hovers above him, taller by at least four inches, maybe more. Physically imposing, despite her girlish wiles. This is clearly some sort of setup. He is alone, outnumbered. Vulnerable, always, on all fronts. He's always been unnerved, undone, by pairs or packs of girls—their knowingness and sardonic laughter.

"We're locked out of this one," the first girl says. She gestures to the door behind her. "Can you let us in?"

Reluctantly, KC nods, extracting his phone for its light, which casts an eerie glow on the girl's face. He doubts himself again. From this vantage, she is innocent, innocuous. A small-town country girl from eastern North Carolina indulging in the first excesses of college life, exhausted now, ready for her own bed, which probably has pink throw pillows, the walls of her room still bearing a photo from her high school prom. He notes the spread of freckles across her slightly upturned nose. Maybe he even recognizes her.

"Hey," the girl says. "I know you . . ."

There's a stuttering recognition happening in KC's mind, a flipping of mental files, and then he knows: She's the one who always slips into class at the last minute, with hoop earrings, a high ponytail, and an aggressively unfashionable rolling backpack. He admired her, actually, for the audacity of her response one day when the professor asked a question about Marxist economies, admired it all the more because she'd always seemed so young, so uncertain. To see the professor elicit such a response from this unassuming pea shoot of a girl with baby-fine wisps of hair escaping her scrunchie was a satisfying surprise.

"History Seventy-Four. With Phillips? You sit in the back left."

She smiles now, pleased at this bit of loose kinship.

"I got special permission to take the course," she offers, a bit of unnecessary information, but there's obvious pride in her voice. The pleased way she looks at him, as if ready to accept his approval, makes her seem, momentarily, even younger.

The other girl, with her swimmer's shoulders and long dark hair, has crossed her arms across her chest, her one hip cocked to the side—a stance of obvious irritation and boredom.

KC pulls out his key and opens the door for them. The apartment inside is cool and tomb-like, nothing but oblong shadows and the buzzing of a refrigerator. A humming blankness. Every apartment in the complex has the same layout, though, so he can trace the contours in his mind without seeing.

The girl claps her hands, almost too gleeful, and KC feels one more hint of misgiving. He is exhausted, though. There is a quiz in his class the next morning. Normally he manages to get a decent chunk of sleep during his shifts, but tonight he'll be lucky if he can get a twenty-minute nap.

The girls enter the apartment in an exploratory fashion, fumbling for the light switch. The first girl, his classmate, pauses to look back at him. She smiles a smile that holds suppressed giggling. He wonders for a second if she's flirting with him. But that would be ridiculous. The girls are just tipsy.

"Thanks. You're the best," the first girl says.

"Jesus, I've got to pee so bad," the taller girl adds to no one in particular, and her voice is pleasantly low, older than her appearance.

KC stands for a moment, hesitant, watching as the tall girl clumsily opens the door to what is actually a coat closet, not the bathroom. Not his business, he thinks. Maybe she's hanging up her jacket. There's a toilet three doors down that still needs unclogging. He walks away.

THE SURPRISING YET unsurprising news that there's been a theft does not reach KC until late the following afternoon. It's like finding out he's failed a test he didn't study for and knew he was probably going to fail—inevitable, but still a blow. The girls in unit 23A report that, after having stayed at a friend's the previous night, they returned to find their apartment door open, all their most hockable belongings gone, muddy footprints on the floor.

"Dumb kids," Gus says of unit 23A. "Forgot to lock up."

KC is underslept, his head pounding. He offers nothing.

"Still. Owners want me to do a once-over of the whole place. Come on, you."

KC follows Gus numbly, handing him fresh light bulbs, watching as he tests doors and picks up protein bar wrappers from the bottoms of stairwells. The late-autumn sun sits low in the sky, casting a cold, searing light directly into KC's eyeballs. He follows Gus down the slope toward wing C, where the contractors have set a large demolition bin filled with broken plywood and strips of ratty carpet. The voices of children rise from the park below. They run, brightly colored in their jackets, over the brown grass and among the rusty playground equipment.

"You know a girl got killed down here?" Gus says mildly. "We get junkies breaking in sometimes."

He is pulling out his keys to open the door to Karlie's apartment, but KC knows the door is still unlocked. He never locked it back. KC took the key to 7C off the ring and put it in his pocket last night with his wallet, but he hasn't seen it, he realizes, since his wallet fell out. He scans the walkway quickly for its silver glint. There's a catch in his throat like a stuck chicken bone. He recalls Lydia last night, her expression as she'd looked at him, not unkindly, but with sudden understanding. Sympathy. It makes him feel sick all over again.

Gus frowns, also noting the missing key, then gently tests the door handle, which seems almost animate at that point, easy, waiting, ready for his touch. And when the door swings open to unit 7C, there is Lydia, like an apparition reappearing. She's sleeping on the floor, using her backpack as a pillow. The spill of her pale hair, her parted lips, make her seem even more vulnerable. The squeezing sensation in KC's heart—he's not sure if it's longing or hatred. What he does know is that Brian's money has already been transferred to his account, and he cannot afford to lose his job.

"Oh, hey," Lydia says, eyelashes fluttering, a stricken look crossing her face. KC watches as she registers his presence: friend rather than foe, sudden relief.

"Well, well," Gus says, "our intruder."

"No, I didn't—" Lydia says, her eyes darting to KC's. In the daylight, he is better able to see how she is visibly unbathed, her hair limp with grease, an actual streak of dirt going up one cheek like a street urchin.

"Hand over the backpack," Gus says.

"Oh, no. I didn't take anything."

She clutches the backpack to her chest, eyes searching KC, waiting for him to explain, to rescue her. He will not meet her eyes. Instead, he studies the dark splotch on the floor: someone's blood, from years ago. A distant tragedy.

"What are you doing here, then?"

"She told me I could crash here for the night," Lydia says, pointing at KC, her index finger trembling.

KC doesn't think before he responds. Something sweeps through him there in unit 7C, filling him with a defiance he hasn't been able to gather during his past two decades of life, twenty years of having been walked over. The word flies out of his mouth before he can think.

"Liar."

"I'll stay here with her," Gus says to him. "You go call the cops."

Lydia recoils as if slapped. KC walks away.

IN THE WEEKS that follow, guilt eats at him, whether it should or not. He looks for Lydia everywhere but finds no sign of her—no flash of her pale ponytail, no fluttery sylph loitering by the leaf-covered swimming pool. The thought of how he sold her out gnaws at him, even if she sort of deserved it. He can't keep the tainted money.

KC asks around about a film crew at the nearest coffee shops and bars, leaving a note with his contact info for Brian, who eventually calls him back. Through Brian, he manages to track Lydia to where she's currently staying at another friend's apartment. He withdraws the entire sum he was paid in cash and leaves it in an envelope with Lydia's name on it at the front desk. Perhaps he is noble. Or perhaps he lacks the ruthlessness necessary to survive.

Months later, when KC is still on campus after most of the students have finished up final exams for the spring semester, he'll find himself alone in his underfurnished apartment, searching for something mindless to stream on his laptop. And there he sees it listed in a pop-up ad: *Murder Real Estate: The World's Most Haunted Places: The Karlie Richards Story.* Apparently the episode is airing much sooner than Lydia had claimed, and yet the memory of that night of filming already seems distant to him. He finds a link to the episode on YouTube and clicks play.

As he watches, KC feels the weird shiver of his recent past moving through him. He recognizes Brian speaking in the voice-over, although it's hard to focus on the words—something about new claims of a missing rape kit, evidence implicating a cult in the western part of the state in some sort of illegal activity—because what KC is struck by is Karlie. It's that photo of her, the most familiar one, made famous by all the news articles, of Karlie, blonde and glowing, head tipped back in laughter. Even frozen there as an image on the dusty screen of his laptop, she emanates a kind of magic. Brian is saying something else, something KC doesn't quite follow, speculating as to why Karlie might have been targeted. Despite the air of documentarian authority, KC thinks, the show still has a sensationalistic vibe, the theories and supposedly crucial leads as flimsy as any of the internet rumors KC has read—especially as the footage shifts to a grainy reenactment of the night of Karlie's death.

And there it is, flashing across the screen: Lydia cowering in the doorway as Karlie, peering out into the unknowable night, already sensing betrayal. She is so young, Lydia, so terribly young and uncertain. He shivers again. It turns out there is no shot of him crouching in the nearby bushes, playing the bad guy. Still, there's real tension to the scene. Something terrible awaits that poor girl frozen there—a bad boyfriend, a stalker, an angry, nameless figure in the dark. Hunter and prey. You can see it in her eyes.

But KC is nowhere, nowhere at all.

r/JusticeforKarlie

The bulk goods stand in tall, stacked towers: clear bins of couscous, red lentils, navy beans, carob chips, wild rice, pistachios, spelt flour, big chunks of candied ginger, dried pineapple. Pumpkin seeds, basmati, cassava flour, almond meal, tricolor quinoa. Provisions for hungry suburban homesteaders—strategic people, survivors with sacks ready to fill. Joy drifts past these items with wraithlike uncertainty. She is haggard, under-caffeinated, overwhelmed by options. Her house is empty, her cupboard bare. In the produce section, Joy moves past stacks of bananas, piles of sweet potatoes, the heirloom apples heaped in all their blushing abundance, jostling a display of kabocha squash with her big, blunt hip bones. A mother carrying her baby in an Ergo maneuvers to eye a pallet of baby basil plants, and she and Joy almost collide.

"Excuse me," Joy says. The croak of her underused voice is almost unrecognizable. The woman presses her lips against the baby's downy head accusatorily, backing away as if Joy's the bad fairy at the christening. There's a crate of turnips at Joy's feet, the whole store a bountiful obstacle course, a maze of nourishment. Joy is in the way, somehow always in the way—the unwieldiness of her physical presence not entirely explained by size.

A convex mirror above the purple onions reflects a distorted image of Joy. All her angles have grown oversharp of late, and there's a starveling look to her already hawklike face. She carries the reusable shopping bags on her arm, dutiful in that way. She votes in local elections, supports her neighborhood food co-op. Joy is here to get ingredients to make cupcakes for her son. She is a person who ought to get some credit for something—a little leniency, given how she tries.

Ethan has requested cupcakes for the school's Holiday Festival. It is the sort of school where cupcakes must be organic, allergen-free. No unnecessary chemicals or dyes. Another parent, Amelia, has told her of a suitable mix the co-op stocks. Amelia has also endorsed simply buying overpriced cupcakes premade from the in-house bakery, a tactic Joy herself has employed in previous years.

But this year will be different. Joy is determined to make the cupcakes for Ethan herself, and they will be green, his favorite color. A Christmas color also, although the school's festival is scrupulously inclusive of all the winter holidays, and Ethan insists on reminding her of this. These will *not* be Christmas cupcakes. She's found a recipe online that suggests using spinach to color the cake batter. The co-op does not make green cupcakes—only an airy, white vanilla or a moist, dense chocolate, both delicious. But not green! Joy can imagine the surprise and pleasure that will appear on Ethan's face when he sees what she's done. Cupcakes that are his favorite color! Made specially with him in mind! It's the sort of thoughtful act Joy's own mother might have undertaken for her when she was little, the kind of extra step Joy herself always seems unable to make, even though she loves her boys—desperately, urgently, she does.

Right around the dairy case full of old-fashioned glass bottles of local milk, she almost runs into Maggie. Joy's heart clenches in her chest. She cannot breathe.

Joy lets out a little gasp, and the curly-haired woman apologizes, despite the fact it's Joy—oafish Joy, arms full of spinach—why didn't she think to grab a cart!?—who is at fault.

The woman facing her is not Maggie at all but another woman with curls pulled into a messy topknot and a similarly broad, open face. Joy's both relieved and disappointed. It's a problem, what she does—her sudden crushes, the way her capacious loneliness shoots out its fast-growing tendrils like an invasive species, covering and smothering people in waxy leaves. She becomes enamored before she even fully knows someone, noticing this fact only after the objects of her affection have been completely subsumed by her infatuation, shaped into whatever vessels will best carry her hopes for them. She used to think it was the same thing as falling in love. And maybe it's not so different? By one way of accounting, Joy's fallen in love scores of times. By another, hardly ever. You could take a different definitional approach and say it's not love at all that she's been seeking but rather something else—deep care, a gnostic spark. She's always searching for someone who might finally see the flame of her secret self and shelter it with a benevolent palm. Maybe that's not love at all. Maybe she simply wants someone to see her and understand. She's perhaps too suggestible? Or too prone to projection?

It's the sort of thing she and Karlie might have discussed during that fall of freshman year, Joy supine on her loft bed, letting her hands fall over the sides, a languishing sort of pose—like Millais's *Ophelia*, a poster reproduction that you would tack onto the dorm room wall to convey you were a darkly romantic, literarily minded sort of girl. Karlie would sit in the beanbag chair below, reaching up at times to brush her hand against Joy's—a peculiar sort of touch, one Karlie never explained, but one that meant something to Joy. Reassurance of sorts. A suggestion of something else. Something larger, more profound.

Maybe all Joy's ever wanted is simple approval, plain old affection, draped in fine language to make the intensity of her longing less pathetic.

She's humiliated, here, now, the morning after what happened at John's new house. There's a pain at the back of her head, an insistent throbbing that makes her wonder if she went down harder than she thought. Had her head struck the sidewalk? It had seemed at first like a gentle process, one she would have sworn was outside of her control, her body floating downward. Ophelia again, swept along with the current. Poor old passive Ophelia. Poor old passive-*aggressive* Ophelia. Had she fallen asleep? Joy—not Ophelia—with no gentle brook to carry her, no flower crown. Had she willed herself into a kind of fit? Her muscles are sore, like her body had truly seized.

Joy gathers the cupcake mix, egg replacer, cane sugar, baking powder, a container of special all-natural frosting, and makes her way through the checkout, bargaining that she'll have the rest of the dry ingredients tucked away somewhere at home.

There are already poinsettias out by the checkout line, a little display of holiday stollen made fresh in the bakery, even though it's seventy-five degrees outside. Absently, Joy rubs a finger over a poinsettia petal, velvety to the touch.

"Looks like an interesting dinner tonight at your place," the clerk says at checkout.

Joy realizes she hasn't purchased any regular groceries, her assemblage of items odd and incongruent. One of her hands flies up to her face, a bewildered gesture, a reflex. Her mouth twitches uncertainly; she covers it, hiding the nervous itch of a grin, her face trying to split open into a hysterical grimace. There's an urge to explain herself to the clerk—the cupcake recipe, her son's school, the spinach as a natural dye source—but the clerk has pink hair and a pierced nose and is only making small talk, after all. Joy already feels hulking and strange, aware that she's been prone to a terrible overearnestness since childhood. She simply smiles and nods.

"I love spinach."

The clerk grins and shrugs.

"It's a great vegetable," she says, handing Joy her bag.

BACK HOME, JOY arranges her cupcake ingredients on the counter like a lineup of suspects and puts a pod into her espresso machine. John left it for her, acting like it was a concession on his part, when the machine had originally been an anniversary present. A gift, from him to her. *Her* machine, from John, who doesn't even drink espresso! There—let the record show—is John's version of generosity.

But it's a nice espresso maker. As it purrs and clicks, the smell of espresso rises, almost too bitter for Joy, like she has a hangover, except the hangover is shame.

Maggie had sounded angry at first, filled with reproach, but then she'd seemed on the verge of tears. She'd wanted to call 9-1-1. She'd held Joy's hand—gently, so gently, it made Joy's eyes burn, a salty ache at the back of her throat—hovering ghostlike over her. Thank God the boys hadn't seen. (Or had they?)

"She's got to go to the ER and get checked out at least," Maggie insisted, pleading, urgent but calm. Joy understood then why John preferred her. A better woman, this Maggie. A good soul. Joy tried to muster a bracing hatred, but it fled from her. Too exhausted to resist, she'd relented, squeezing Maggie's hand tighter and feeling relief despite herself, while the beginning of something else bloomed inside her chest.

"I was faking it," Joy wanted to announce, but suddenly she wasn't so sure. She felt woozy, like if she stood up too fast, she'd faint. She pictured her mother—much younger, hair still a glossy brown—cracking eggs over a mixing bowl, the sunlight piercing the kitchen window at an unavoidable angle, forming a sharp triangle of light. A memory long unretrieved rising unbidden. Her mother singing her favorite hymn, *Joyful, joyful, we adore thee, God of glory, Lord of love.* Joy saw her own skull as one of those eggs, the pain running through the crack. Blinking hard into that sharp light, the hurt blinding, she wished for her mother's cool hands against her brow, her mother's voice. Only, her mother spoke now with Maggie's voice, wore Maggie's smooth, unvarnished brow.

"Maggie," Joy whispered at the touch as of fingers brushing back her hair—which seemed as bald a declaration as any, the obvious squish and squelch of her caramel-soft heart revealed in two syllables. She'd been grateful for the cover of darkness, the bleating of downtown traffic a few blocks up through the trees, the nervous way John kept clearing his throat.

John had driven her to the ER entrance, pausing in the drop-off circle. The parking garage was eight dollars an hour, a football field away.

"I'll stay," he said. "I can let you out here and park and come back."

She'd tried to interpret his face in the dark, weighing the authenticity of his offer. The last time they'd been at this ER it was two years before, during Joy's protracted miscarriage. The clinic wouldn't see her for fear she was hemorrhaging. Sean and Ethan had been old enough to mind themselves at home. She'd wondered if John was thinking of this, too—of the last time they'd been here, blood running down her legs and puddling in her shoes, saturating the towels they'd brought. Joy, stunned into impassivity; John, weeping outright.

He wouldn't meet her eyes, sitting there at the ER entrance while he waited for her response. There'd been a quiet falseness between them these past two years, as if someone had replaced the tableau of their life together with a trompe l'oeil painting of it—the doors and windows would no longer open, but neither dared acknowledge it.

Earlier in their marriage, he'd looked at her square in the face, and often. They'd laughed more. They'd opened the kitchen windows to welcome the scent of early-budding flowers and grass clippings, and the windows had obliged. Earlier in their marriage, the notion of another child occurred to them both as a grace that might befall them. An incidental thing, something they'd be content living with or without. Like rain or sunshine. Weather happened, but you did not will the weather. You did not set out to make snow fall or wind blow. You simply accepted weather as it came and dressed accordingly. Whatever storms or sun, they'd face together.

A pregnancy. They took it as good fortune.

But what followed had been a misery: first the spotting, then the uncertain ultrasounds, the scanty heartbeat, a genetic test that was unpromising. *Inevitable loss* was the phrase her doctor used, although the baby, for some reason, kept going in its halfhearted way, inching ever closer, at an agonizing pace, to eventual demise. The doctor had pressed his hand against Joy's while she gulped down her sobs—because that was the thing, wasn't it? You only knew how badly you wanted something once it was taken away from you in slow degrees. Only then did you realize.

Further complications developed. By the time she got to the ER, there was a question of keeping the uterus, which, through some strange, distancing defense mechanism, Joy had come to imagine as a little travel carry-on bag, an object apart from herself—one she might not have much use for any longer, but from which she could not fathom parting. Her vision faltered. There was a steady, hot rush between her legs. Jellied clots. They feared she might be bleeding out.

She fell in love with the doctor who guided her through the whole ordeal. Briefly, at least. There was no other word for it. He was a goofy-looking man in his late fifties or early sixties with a monk's tonsure, a doughy face. Decidedly unhandsome, unprepossessing, and yet her eyes welled up whenever she so much as spoke his name. She pulled up his image on the hospital website to study it, reading his message to her in the patient portal over and over, as if she might find some new comfort there. She thought of him—his ordinary, capable eyes, the comfort in his voice—in the way one might think of a crush. Obsessively, longingly, tearfully. She almost made one more appointment with him just to hear him speak to her, simply to be in his presence.

She knew better and so did not.

"Your grief is compounded. You're still mourning your father," John observed afterward, but Joy resisted being psychoanalyzed. Her father had died not so many months prior to her miscarriage, but that had merely been the final act in a slow-motion fade that had been happening ever since her seventeenth birthday. She'd been losing him forever, her father. Losing, losing, lost. Like her youth. Like the lost child, nothing but a clump of tissue, a tantalizing notion offered by the gods then snatched away.

It all passed—the anguish, Joy's desperate feeling toward the doctor—as it often did, and that's how she learned her flippancy. *Luxury child*, she quipped afterward, borrowing her colleague Martha's term for it, mimicking her bravado, because the notion was there now, a question mark between herself and John. Luxury, like a tennis bracelet. Unnecessary, possibly ill-advised, yet also tempting. A lovely novelty to solve all the creeping sadness in their marriage that had so recently been made plain. There was no reason to be sad. She was already—as they'd have said in her father's congregation—mightily blessed. It would be—had been—an act of audacity to want more. To open herself up to that want was unbearable, an invitation, perhaps, for the universe to steal what good fortune she already had and took for granted. Un*bear*able. She was punning! Always cleverer than people realized, her stolid nature concealing her wit.

"Seriously. I don't mind staying," John was saying to her, Joy's thoughts returning to last night. One of the security guards was trying either to wave them off or to figure out if they needed assistance. John turned to look at Joy, and the reddish lights from the Emergency signage turned his face sickly.

"I'll be fine," she said, relieving him of his performance of politeness.

She wanted him to leave because she knew she would not go back into that ER—no way. On pain of death she would not reenter that place. Well, maybe if a limb was semidetached from her body, maybe then. She heard John's jaw click, felt him wanting to protest, ready at least to offer an *Are you sure?* And holding back. He'd want to get home to Maggie, his new life. The sad part, Joy thinks, is that, who wouldn't? The thought of Maggie—her wide, lightly freckled face, her seed-pearl teeth and small but elastic mouth, the light brown curls—somehow warmed her, sitting there, in the passenger seat of John's car. It was ludicrous to entertain the thought they'd ever be friends.

Joy, at nearly forty years on earth, ought to know better. She pities her former self, mucus-soft like a deshelled snail, weeping under the harsh ER lights while they crossmatched her blood. Never again.

Soon there'd be a new baby, not her own. A sibling for her sons—and this thought still festers.

She sips her espresso, scrubs at her eyes in their sockets with her fists. A failure, a sloven who cannot fulfill the basic feminine task of keeping house, driving away others with her excessive need. Joy's too weary to heat up milk for the espresso. There probably isn't milk: yet another thing she should have picked up at the co-op. She slumps into the kitchen chair, wincing, pressing her fingers to the spot where her left temple throbs. Maggie's face keeps floating up, an apparition emerging from a migrainous dark. Joy slugs the rest of the espresso like it's a shot of tequila. Her throat burns. She chews the grounds, then spits.

She could vomit. Maybe she's having sympathy symptoms in response to Maggie. A pseudo pregnancy. Maybe she *is* too suggestible. Or maybe she's had too much espresso on an empty stomach.

There: Maggie's face again, aura-like, wearing such a tender expression.

There'd been an article she'd read once offering two competing TED Talk–derived visions on how to sustain long-term relationships. On the one hand there was Esther Perel's take, and on the other . . . somebody else's. But what Joy remembered was that word they used when talking about the phase of early infatuation: *limerence*. An ephemeral state, all-consuming and transient, too volatile to persist. The word itself shimmered, resplendent with the brief flame of its own meaning, mirroring itself in sound, a perfect convergence of denotation and connotation.

And yet even that understanding seemed to miss some other underlying complexity to it. A flattening. Mere shorthand.

But Karlie had gotten it—or so it seemed. *I want to gobble him up*, she'd said once of a winsome, lonely boy who seemed always to be drifting over the steps of Wilson Library with a textbook on information systems analysis and design in his hands. A grad student, they'd imagined—rightly, it turned out later. Computer science? Or information and library science? A noble genius orphan who'd grown up on a ramshackle farm and eked by on pure grit and intellect. Whole histories they'd concocted for him, their brief heartthrob, while they waited for his eyes to light on theirs, to recognize something familiar burning within them, too. Later, Joy met the boy from the library steps at a party. She'd put it together only later—that he was the same person they'd spotted there. His name was Kent. School of Information and Library Science, a brainy boy from rural eastern North Carolina. He'd been kind to her, lent her a shirt, which she never returned. But back then, when she and Karlie had first seen him from afar like that, he'd been nothing but a promise, a stripling shape onto which they could project whatever they liked. *I could just gobble him*, Karlie said, her eyes big, and, although it was a thing commonly said of babies, her intended meaning seemed almost literal, and Joy knew she understood. The pull of the gnostic spark, the platonic soulmate. To know and be known.

Had Joy ever felt any of that, the smallest drop of it, for John?

She pulls the cupcake recipe up on her phone and rises, approaching the stainless-steel refrigerator John selected for them when the last one went kaput. (She had. Yes, she'd felt it for him once. John, her blue-eyed guy, so funny and charming. But oh, how that had turned.) There's half a carton of orange juice, the hardened heel of a loaf of bread, a withered bounty of late-fall produce purchased from the farmers market back when she still had the oomph, the zeal, to be the sort of person who purchased locally grown seasonal produce, whose life was arranged by such thought and healthful vigor. The beets have grown the wizened chins of old men, the leeks and turnip greens have shriveled accusatorily. There's a box of the oat crunch cereal Ethan likes on the shelf above the stove, but only a splash of any sort of milk. Butter—there is no butter. No cooking oil in the cupboard. There will be no cupcakes without oil or butter.

Her mistake hits her almost as suddenly as her hunger—a gnawing hunger, the likes of which she hasn't felt during all these weeks that she's subsisted on nothing but air and Diet Coke and loose granola bars stashed in the console of the car, forgotten Ziplocs of her son's trail mix.

There's a rim of peanut butter at the bottom of the jar at least. Resigned, Joy grabs the leftover bread, curled and dry. Famine food. End-time vittles. She'll toast it into edibility. She'll make it work.

That's what she learned from her father before he got sick. Scrappiness. How to make do.

And yet what does she have to show for it? She and Karlie used to talk about wanting to move to New York to be writers. Joy, an essayist like Joan Didion, and Karlie, a poet. A foolish girlhood fantasy—and yet one some people managed to realize. But no, not Joy, who'd remained like a lotus-eater in this college town forever. And of course, not poor Karlie.

The toast is settling Joy's stomach. The cupcakes will have to wait. She unlocks her phone and opens Instagram, scrolling aimlessly. So many images. Elegantly plated tuna tartare with delicate sprouts and a drizzle of vibrant yellow, a stand of huge redwoods, a lone saguaro before a setting desert sun, a laughing woman in red sunglasses licking a perfect cone of ice cream. Her sons showed her how to set up her account, but she has posted only once: a perfect strawberry, arugula, and feta salad she'd made last spring. She'd planned to use Instagram accordingly—as a tool of appreciation, a way of capturing moments to frame and savor lest she not notice them at all. That's what she needed—a way of noticing her life, seeing its small beauties. That first post had made her feel virtuous, like someone living vibrantly. But only three people had liked it. She'd quickly lost interest in finding new salads to post. Her house was boring; she microwaved most of her food. Her life was decidedly monochromatic. Now, Instagram has turned into a window of passive yearning, a lookbook of lack.

A rush of hot shame floods her as she's reminded of Karlie's letter. She pulls the envelope from the kitchen junk drawer where she's hidden it beneath old billing statements and rubber bands and warranty forms. The envelope is bulky. In addition to the letter itself, Karlie had included a touching selection of useless 1999 flotsam: a stick of Joy's favorite gum, gone hard with the years, and a desiccated cherry-cola flavored Bonne Bell Lip Smacker. Joy puts these items aside and retrieves the letter, smoothing its folds as she rereads it, the words returning to her, sing-songy in her mind, like a taunt.

I know you've been following me.

But Joy had never, would never! Yes, there was a certain amount of dawdling by Professor Hendrix's office. She's always been a curious person, someone apt to slow herself as she gathers her belongings if it means overhearing a particularly intriguing conversation in a café. But she'd never gone to Karlie's off-campus apartment! And the car, the BMW. She'd borrowed her friend Tatiana's beater of a Cadillac a few times, yes, to go to Harris Teeter and once to meet a friend in Durham, but that was it.

Professor Hendrix was known for enthralling his students. And enthralled she had become. She'd been but one of many to succumb. But to see him with Karlie—that was something different. Joy had sensed it almost instantly, and it was a double betrayal. She couldn't help but notice Professor Hendrix on campus, especially if he was with Karlie, couldn't resist lingering when the opportunity presented itself. She could feel them whenever they were nearby, even before they were visible, like a heat in the back of her head, a terrible awareness of their proximity that she couldn't shake. And Karlie had apparently seen Joy, had known but said nothing, the entire time. At least, not until the letter.

It's a humiliation to learn this, even now with Karlie long gone.

Someone else had been following Karlie, tracking her like prey. Joy considers the young man who went to prison, how baby-faced and disoriented he appeared in all the mug shots and media images. Was he capable of such a thing? No, that wasn't the right question. Wasn't anyone capable of anything under the right set of circumstances? The question was whether he was likely to have done it, and the answer to that seemed like it must be no. She'd seen clips of him—teddy-bear-ish build, startled face, halting speech.

She thinks again of her recent encounter with Professor Hendrix, the way he'd looked at her—fond at first, curious, prepared to be mildly amused by her foolish antics. The antics of a child. But then when she'd accused him, there was the way his mouth had twisted, his voice turning bitter, cruel. He was a man, it occurred to Joy, capable of nursing a fixation. An obsession. He was a man, she thought, who might be angered by not getting his way. She wondered what sort of car he drove back in the late nineties—a BMW? She can't recall, but even with his professor's salary, there was a moneyed quality to him, his clothing, his taste in whiskey. She'd always had the sense he was a man who liked luxuries. A BMW. It seems not only plausible but likely. She feels the bracing rush of revelation, the sense of a puzzle piece clicking into place.

The letter is evidence. Maybe the man in prison is innocent. A scapegoat. She should give the letter to someone, turn it in, explain about the professor—but at what cost? She might look like someone with a residual sad schoolgirl crush, crazed with jealousy. Or, worse, the letter might cast suspicion on her. Karlie had believed it was Joy herself lurking outside her door, watching from the dark.

A coldness runs down Joy's neck, like the slow drip of ice. Maybe she is crazed with jealousy, spinning fictions out of feeling, letting the sediment of the past get stirred up into such a haze she can't see the plain truth in front of her face. The case was solved! She needs sleep, needs to pull herself together.

Joy puts the sticky plate on the counter, resting it atop a pile of similarly sticky plates and brown-ringed mugs. She's stopped cleaning up lately. Sean and Ethan haven't said anything, but she's watched them noticing her, her behaviors, her unwashed hair.

In the bedroom, Joy kneels beneath the bed, fishing past dust bunnies and scuffed boots and worn-out running shoes until she finds it. An old shoebox.

She lifts it carefully, a relic she hasn't opened in years.

Toward the bottom, she finds the photos and keepsakes from freshman year at UNC: she and Karlie, perched on the loft bed, smiling in front of a Belle and Sebastian poster. Karlie, posing as if she's taking an exaggerated bite of pizza. A photo of the two of them at Kenan Stadium for a football game. She and Karlie in front of the Old Well, their arms draped over each other, smiling in their matching oversize light blue CTOPS T-shirts. There's another photo of Joy, Karlie, the leader of the campus Christian group, and a few other friends. Clay was the leader, only a few years older than they were, so sincere and Jesus-bearded that it was often hard to tell when he was joking. He'd lived with two other guys, one named Ian, who worked in a restaurant and was a friend of Karlie's, and a cousin, Kent, the boy from the library steps, who looked older, it turned out, when you got up close, and who was indeed in graduate school at the School of Information and Library Science. Joy had spoken to them both at that party, a New Year's Eve celebration not long before Karlie died. Her encounter with Ian had been weird, a little embarrassing. She'd wished never to run into him again, and later, when she'd learned that he'd died by suicide soon thereafter, she'd felt a strange wave of guilt, as if her wish had caused his demise. Kent was nice, unassuming, with an accent that, like Clay's, betrayed his small-town North Carolina origins. Neither Kent nor Ian had been fervently religious, which was refreshing, although they both had seemed close to Clay. Flipping through a few more photos she sees them again. Ian, Kent, Clay, their arms slung around one another.

There are also a few creased sheets of paper: an old public policy paper, a sheaf of Karlie's poems. They'd both loved poetry—but it was Joy who loved poetry more at first, regarding it with the reverence of a girl who'd grown up appreciating the rhythms of the King James Bible and May Hill Arbuthnot's *Time for Poetry*. Joy shared poems she thought Karlie might like, and Karlie had taken to them, as she took to so many things. She had a knack for writing poems, too, it turned out. And so poetry became yet more territory that Joy ceded—although it didn't feel that way early in their friendship. In those days, every transaction between them still felt like a gift.

Joy opens one of Karlie's old poems and reads it. The poem is about rivers. Rereading it, she searches for some new insight, but the words only run through her fingers again, like water, like prayer.

Joy takes a photo of the photo of herself and Karlie by the Old Well, then another photo of Karlie's poem, then creates a post on her dormant Instagram account. She selects a sepia filter, which adds a requisite moodiness, then starts to type hashtags, which quickly autopopulate for her: *#karlierichards #karlierichardsmurder #karlierichardspoetry #xokarliegonetoosoon*

She writes a caption:

Here I am with my freshman roommate, Karlie Richards. She was important to me . . . Sharing one of her poems. Miss you, Karlie. xo

The caption is mundane but honest. Joy feels a stab of the preemptive embarrassment she always gets with any public message or group response, but she posts anyway, casting her quiet voice out into the raucous public space.

It's only ten A.M. and the boys won't be back from their father's until tomorrow. She could run by the Harris Teeter later for butter. She could rest her eyes now, clear her head, maybe do a short ten-minute meditation—the kind of self-edifying habit she always swears she'll start doing regularly. A total reset is in order—after she makes the cupcakes, she'll clean the kitchen, clear out the fridge, buy fresh fruits and vegetables along with a few treats for her sons. Decide what she as a responsible citizen ought to do about Karlie's letter. Maybe take a walk, do yoga, clean the microwave, bake fresh bread—the sorts of things she imagines Maggie doing all the time.

Joy closes her eyes.

When she wakes, the light is different—shallow and gray-tinged, the soft murk of afternoon shadows swimming across Joy's bedroom. The peanut butter toast is long digested, leaving only a tight knot in her empty stomach. Her bladder is overfull in her pelvis, a dull ache.

Her phone buzzes. It buzzes again. She picks it up and sees her home screen is full of Instagram notifications. Instead of going to the bathroom, she opens the app.

The photo of Karlie's poem has over 300 likes, already over 150 comments, with more trickling in. Her follower count has risen from a total of 115 to nearly 400. And there are direct messages:

murdersleuth12
Whoa, so you knew her? Please come to our discussion board on truecrimesleuth.net. We would love to have you. #justiceforkarlie

tcmemorabilia
Wow, never seen this photo of Karlie! If authenticated, we are interested in buying photo and poem. Estimate between $150 to $350 if in good condition. Please notify if you have more and can verify provenance.

murderinette19
So, are you for real? Let's talk. If you are legit and knew KR, we would like to set up an AMA with you on our subreddit.

murderrealestate
Hello, @jloveshydrangeas. This is Brian with the production team for a documentary series entitled Murder Real Estate: The World's Most Haunted Places. You may have heard about our first season? We have a loyal viewership now. Anyway, your post happened to catch our eye, and we noticed your bio has your location as Chapel Hill. We're looking for people who were friends of Karlie's and who might be able to speak more to her relationships at the time, including that with one of her professors. As it happens, we're planning a story on Karlie Richards. Would love to get in touch. Please feel free to text or call my cell: 310-555-0112

More likes and comments come in even as she reads.

It's remarkable, what she's feeling: a hit of something so pure she's almost afraid of it. Joy's never fully understood when people spoke of the reinforcement of social media because her participation was always so minimal. She gets it now. It's validating. There's a little electric tingle with each new red dot. She can hardly turn away. Maybe it's the aftereffects of the espresso combined with her hunger, but her hands shake.

Remembering her aching bladder, she runs to the bathroom. Once she finishes, she goes to her laptop, pulls up some of the websites mentioned in the comments under her post, and there it is, a world opening before her: all the true-crime obsessives, dedicated to Karlie arcana, ready to microanalyze seemingly overlooked details of the case. Jacob Hendrix is mentioned in many of the comments, a popular suspect even though he was cleared. Joy's own name appears in one of the threads, and she perks up, reading on: *Karlie's roommate and devoted sidekick*, someone has written of her. That's all. The warm buoyancy that has been rising up in her is flattened. There's nothing more written about her, nothing of her complicated friendship with Karlie, nothing of the fact that she's the one who introduced Karlie to Jacob Hendrix in the first place. Joy *knew* Karlie—actually *knew* her, possibly even understood things about her—unlike all these armchair detectives whose only experience of Karlie was as a tragic beauty in a photo. *Devoted sidekick*. She wants to scream but there's no sound at all inside her.

She thinks of one of the long-standing arguments she and John had over the years, especially shortly after the miscarriage.

"You're drifting. Aimless," he'd insisted. "Grant writing's fine, but you're not fulfilled."

He was referring, she knew, to ambitions she'd harbored before having children and locking into her steady grant writing job, ambitions that went back to those days with Karlie. And before her sons were born, she'd done a bit: pitches to local magazines to write a couple of features, a few movie and book reviews for the alternative weekly, an article once in *Woman's Day*, another in *Southern Living*. She'd dreamed of writing a Modern Love essay, but it seemed her life lacked sufficient tragedy or hilarity, that she could not quite conjure the right jaunty voice. She'd often imagined undertaking some longer project—a book—but the subject never seemed quite right, or the research too exhausting, her own authorial voice too wheedling and uncertain.

"You sit back and wait for things to happen," John said. "That's the problem. You have to *act*, not just be acted upon."

His words had stung her. She'd been washing a wineglass after they hosted friends for dinner, and she remembers the hot suds on her hand, how she let the glass slip into the basin of the sink, where it splintered. She'd reached instinctively into the sudsy water and pulled out only the broken stem, blood beading on her hand.

But maybe John was—is—exactly right, Joy thinks now, scrolling these forums filled with people who know nothing of Karlie, who'd never met her, never shared a twelve-by-nineteen dorm room with her, and yet speculate about her habits, her little quirks. Speculate confidently! Like they knew her! Like they'd had long, late-night conversations with Karlie about God, about belief and doubt and loneliness, about the nature of truth and beauty!

Joy takes a breath and closes her laptop. She takes Karlie's letter and folds it neatly, then tucks it into the shoebox. Before closing the shoebox and placing it back under her bed, she selects a photo from it.

Her phone buzzes again.

Even as nothing more than an icon on a screen, a username, Joy has found a way to hold people's attention. They are there, waiting, all of them, for her next words.

This is how Karlie must have felt, Joy thinks.

She types Brian the producer's phone number into her text box.

> Hi, Brian, this is @jloveshydrangeas. My real name is Joy, and I was roommates with Karlie Richards. Although our friendship was brief and somewhat complicated, we were very close at one time . . . I knew Jacob Hendrix as well and was his student. Long story, but all that to say: I'd love to talk. By day, I'm a grant writer at a nationally recognized women's health nonprofit. As it happens, I'm also working on a book about Karlie—currently seeking an agent to shop my proposal. Like many others, I have doubts about how the case was handled. Glad to talk more.

Rereading her words, Joy does not recognize them as her own. A new person seems to have emerged, some other Joy filled with confidence and purpose. Once she presses send, the whole thing feels real, like something she might actually do.

She opens Instagram and edits her bio:

> Joy Brunner: *women's health advocate* *writer* *boy-mom* *rower* *espresso-lover* *writing book about the life and tragic murder of Karlie Richards*

The photo she's chosen is of herself and Karlie, from Halloween their first year together. Karlie is dressed as a box of cereal; Joy holds a knife. Too much? No, just enough. She snaps a photo of the photo with her phone.

She selects the Clarendon filter, adds hashtags, then posts the image to her account, and lets things begin.

The Veldt

There's always that risk: too much of a good thing. Take, for example, Red Bull. Or those especially delicious gummy edibles his friend Sam brought back from Colorado. TikTok. The internet in general. Video games. The terrifying intensity of a new crush. Love, or what looks like it. Sean is fifteen, young for his grade. But he knows. He's seen it in his friends—how they go surly, zombie-eyed, dull and mooing with excess. Or how they turn pale, envenomed by a poison they crave all the more the sicker it makes them. He's seen it in himself. His little brother, Ethan, is only twelve, nothing more than a child, but Sean knows—Ethan, too, will be vulnerable soon enough.

You're a thoughtful guy, his father says to him. *Wise for your age.* But what his father means is that Sean is wary. Considerate in his approach. No, not afraid. Unlike his mother, who prefers to stay shuttered inside, reluctantly venturing out into her garden at only odd hours when the neighbors won't walk past and try to engage in conversation, taking her long nightly walks under the cover of darkness. Sean knows his father worries about him someday turning out like his mother, although his father used to love her. He was devoted to her—at least until Maggie came along. Even now, his father holds his mother in such high esteem it's almost like he fears her. Or maybe he's intimidated by her, which amounts to the same thing. She's brilliant, Sean's father reminds him and Ethan, but also sensitive, which makes her difficult. *People hurt her along the way*, his father says, but explains no further. Sean could respond with the fact that now his father, too, is among those who have hurt Joy—but he refrains. Sean, in his slow-moving bravery, worries about his mother. His mother has come, over the past several weeks, to love the internet, its vast secrets and dead ends, trick doors and trip wires, all its puzzles, ready to be solved. A vast world-within-a-world.

"Mother!"

Sean calls to her again. She does not answer. She's always up before he or Ethan are, moving like a specter through the house until she reaches the crow's-nest office, in which she sits enthroned behind two big monitors, surrounded by her baubles. Her *home office*, she calls it, for work she needs to catch up on after hours, for making grant deadlines, but Sean thinks of it as more of a lair. He suspects she spends most of her time these days scrolling Twitter and Instagram, or chatting with her weird new batch of cold-case internet friends, trying to write a book about a murder from several decades ago—her recent obsession. Her face is always lit by the eerie glow of the monitors, eyes obscured by the light reflected in her glasses.

He pushes open the door to her office and at first she doesn't even move. He can see the screens, a wash of color, and it reminds him of a story he read once, in eighth or ninth grade, of a magical high-tech house where the nursery could transform into all sorts of places, most notably an African plain. The Happylife Home. Of course, things go badly. There are lions. Sean sometimes feels he could be one of the parents in this story, his mother one of the children.

"Mother . . . MOM!"

She turns to look up at him, wearing the noise-canceling wireless headphones she dons sometimes. He sees a photograph from a crime scene displayed on her screen. A dead girl. Her blonde hair fanned angelically, her eyes blankly open. There is bruising on her neck, from a set of large hands, Sean thinks—it has to be. He winces; it's horrible to behold. A further indignity to the dead girl. His mother appears unfazed.

"You have to pick me up from practice today. Dad can't. Ethan's getting a ride over to Kevin's house, so he's all set." Normally, the soccer season would have ended by now, but a game was postponed, rescheduled to early December, and now the coach has insisted on one last week of practice.

Something flickers across her face: disappointment. Dread. If he could drive already, none of this would be a problem. His mother is rarely the one who retrieves him. She dislikes driving, bridges, rain, tunnels, other parents. The list goes on. It wasn't always so bad; previously, it had been a thing she'd been able to push through, with the encouragement of Sean's father. She's an accomplished woman, educated, an integral part of a respected nonprofit. Joy Brunner is the sort of mother Sean ought to be proud of. But ever since his parents separated, Sean has watched his mother's terrors amplify with an impressive speed and intensity, especially in these last few weeks. She picks him up only at times like this, when his dad is tied up in a late meeting and Sean is unable to arrange another ride. He'll find her sitting stiffly in the car, motor running, hands clenching the wheel. She won't unbrace her shoulders until they make it back home.

"Garrett can't give you a ride?"

He sighs deeply, rolling his eyes even though this always wounds her. Deep splotches, maroon, almost purple, are blossoming all over her neck.

"I'm stuck," she says, knifing her hand toward the horrific image on-screen. She pinches her finger and forefinger together. "I need a missing piece, and it's there. I can feel it, Sean. I'm *this* close to it. But I'm stuck."

He sighs again. His mother has always been *this close* to something—something bigger than her job, her life with this family—because none of that is enough for her. The itch of dissatisfaction is always there with her, an itch she can never seem to scratch, no matter what idea, what project, what extracurricular passion to which she commits herself fully for an interval and then, eventually, forgets. This time it is a case involving a falsely imprisoned man and an innocent murdered girl—his mother's freshman roommate, he's learned. A creepy factoid. It's a well-known case, and the connection to his mother is admittedly a little unnerving. *My book,* his mother says, *I'm researching for my book.* Although often when she says this, what he actually sees her doing is scrolling through her social media accounts.

"I'm sure Garrett won't mind," his mother adds.

Sean rolls his eyes again. Garrett is, in Sean's opinion, an asshole of the worst sort: innocuous-seeming, a clown. He's clever with parents, drawing them out into laughter. Although Garrett is not handsome—in fact, there is something Ichabod Crane–ish about him—he has a certain lanky charisma, and this, combined with his oddball charm and humor, wins people over. And he is seventeen. A neighbor, with a car and license, who lives only two streets away and is also on Sean's soccer team, thus a frequent and obvious source of rides. When Sean's parents talk to Garrett, he always nods and gives that ingratiating (infuriating!) smile of his. *Sure*, he says, *it's no trouble*. Garrett is never rude to Sean, never incorrect, not technically. But everything he says is calculated, and it's what goes unsaid that puts Sean on edge—a sly mockery of facial expression, implication, and tone.

"Fine, I'll ask Garrett," Sean says, relenting. "None of this would be a problem if you'd let me get my learner's permit. I need to learn to *drive*, Mom. Everything would be so much easier."

Her head seems to jerk toward him, newly alert, a flash of something bright as lightning moving over her face. She turns back to her computer screen.

"You can't drive," she murmurs. Her words are so quiet he questions himself, what he's heard.

"What?"

"You *can't* drive."

His mother repeats herself like it's a marvel, a wonderment, rather than a simple obvious fact bound up in circumstance. Sean, who hasn't turned sixteen yet due to his pesky late birthday, is still behind on his driver's ed. And his mother is certainly no help when it comes to him getting his requisite practice hours driving under a permit. She turns back to Sean and smiles, and it's a radiance, the full force of sun breaking through the clouds, and she's moving toward him, grabbing his two cheeks in her hands as if he is a peach, a nectarine, the sweetest fruit she's ever known, and she's kissing his forehead, once, twice, a third time, the way she used to do when he was a little boy. Her mouth is stale, a kind of seeping bitterness he tries to ignore, and her lips chapped, but he closes his eyes and lets her. A grateful, hungry pecking. His mother, so often a shadowed absence. He almost hugs her back but he fears the sharp angles of her shoulder blades, the prominent blocks of her spine.

She pulls back, resting her hands at his ears, studying him, as if he's a person she's only just now seeing.

"What is it?"

"That's it. The car Karlie mentioned. The one she kept seeing. It had to have been someone else. He's legally blind, Toby Braithwaite, the man in prison. He didn't drive. He couldn't."

"Okay . . ."

"Prosecution argued Toby took the crosstown bus. That's how he got there. Simple as that. And he probably did, later. We know that he showed up at the scene. Witnesses saw him on the bus. Sure, he's the one who placed the first anonymous pay phone call to nine-one-one—you know, before her other friends showed up? We know he was there. But he's not the killer. I spoke to a guy making a documentary and he reminded me of something. There were witnesses at the apartment who heard a car drive up, then heard someone yelling. Right around the time it must have happened. Investigators concluded this must have just been another resident of the complex. But she was scared of someone. I know from my letter: Whoever it was was showing up often, watching her from his BMW."

"And the guy in prison couldn't drive."

"Exactly," Sean's mother says. "Not a BMW, not any car. I need to get back to this. Tell Garrett thank you for me." And like that, she's no longer paying attention to him.

Garrett is part of the cadre of senior guys on the team who, while not the best athletes, hold authority over the other boys. Garrett is their jester. He and the other seniors on the team tend to stay after practice, always ready with a stash of the best pot, insider knowledge of the next house party. Socially, if not athletically, they are the core of the team. Garrett is a shit player—at times, Sean would guess, he plays almost intentionally badly, both for the laughs, and to conceal the extent of his actual incurable badness. Sean has real talent; but in the current team hierarchy, this does not matter. Their team is always trounced by the opposition anyway.

Sean leaves his mother there, eyes fixed on her computer screen. He'll need to hurry now if he wants to catch the bus. He feels protective of his mother but also embarrassed. Although his parents drive a Prius with a Human Rights Campaign sticker on it, Sean knows his mother spends increasing amounts of time in the more unwholesome corners of the internet.

He's called her out on it, but she's refused to listen. *Research*, she calls it. *Toxic*, he volleys back. *You know the people who believe this stuff are crazy, right? It's bad for you, reading that garbage.*

But his mother has pooh-poohed his concerns. She has buried him, in fact, in a barrage of pooh-poohing. A verbal pooh-pooh mountain. She doesn't *believe* all that stuff, she tells him; she's merely exploring. She's curious about the nature of belief itself, how people come to believe all manner of things. She's asking questions—is that so wrong? To be curious? To dig in dark places? To take on a project and fully *commit* to its completion?

Sean tries to indulge his mother's online obsessions as one would a hobby, like tennis. He fears, however, that spending all this time online with tinfoil-hat-wearing obsessives is the surest route to becoming one.

Sean wets his hair with water from the bathroom sink. His face is too pretty—neat and symmetrical, his eyes long-lashed and large, like a fawn's. He looks like someone who ought to be in a boy band. He does well in school. On the soccer field, he is what his coach calls a natural.

It does not make sense for him to have a mother who is so strange.

During the bus ride to school, Sean is quiet, studying his phone. The other kids are mostly younger and treat him with requisite respect. He can read his book. Text his girlfriend, Lexi.

Lexi is one year older. A hottie—that's what all his teammates say. Smart-sexy, too. First in her class. She's into this writer called Anaïs Nin, likes French thrillers and little macarons from the nearby bakery and got really into bookbinding and printmaking at a special summer camp. She is, as a person, very well curated, beautiful enough to pull off notes of intentional ugliness: pleated pants, an orangey grandpa sweater, or an old lady's clumsy rolling bag. On her, these choices seem like strokes of stylish originality against her otherwise high-end brand-name clothing. Lately, he's noticed, Lexi's taken to adding a number of bold new embellishments it seems only she could pull off—a lapis lazuli necklace featuring a gold-limned scarab beetle, an antique jeweled broach shaped like a hummingbird, oversize diamond studs. Her dad has gotten really into taking her to estate sales on Saturdays, she's told him. And she is that sort of girl—the sort a father loves to spoil, the sort whose father can afford to do so. She's also a little rebellious in the way that girls who have grown up like her can afford to be. Intellectually fierce to the point of cruelty in classroom discussion. The kind of girl who has gotten special permission from their school to take a couple of university courses; one benefit of living in a college town. She intimidates Sean, if he's honest. Things come easily to him, yes, but he's a generalist. As a collection of interests, he is ordinary. Obvious. Boring, even. Smart Guy 1.0. He enjoys movie franchises based on comic books. When asked his favorite writer, he says Shakespeare.

"Relax," she'd said the other day, the second time he'd come over to her place knowing full well her parents weren't home. Her parents are both attorneys, intense doers with ACLU and CrossFit memberships who dote on Lexi, their adored only child. They've given everything to her—Mandarin classes and Suzuki method violin lessons, good bone structure, unwavering support even when, it seems to Sean, Lexi is merely proving a point. She has recently tried out for the men's wrestling team despite never having wrestled in her life. But there is not, as she correctly points out, a women's/nonbinary wrestling team at their school.

Sean and Lexi were on her bed, a tasteful beige affair, surrounded by Lexi's assortment of books and vintage black-and-white cabaret photos. They were naked.

"Relax," Lexi said again. "Don't try so hard."

He flushed then, his hands braced on her shoulders. She reached down with one hand to help guide him toward her, and it was thrilling. She had perfect hands of such unimaginable silky softness that the whole experience felt like a dream, and, dreamlike, it all began to slip away too quickly—he was wracked with a terrible trembling, a roiling shudder over which he had no control. The dream vanished, over before it truly began. This was the second time this had happened.

Lexi went to her en suite bathroom to get a washcloth and, dabbing gently, she kissed him sweetly on the forehead, like he was still a child.

"It's okay," she said, and then added, gently, "practice makes perfect."

He wished momentarily that instead she would have chastised him, humiliated him. But Lexi is sweet, if a little on the attention-seeking side, and she seemed willing to overlook this lapse, this one thing that did not come easily to him. (Or came too easily, harharhar. He allows himself bitter laughter at his own expense.) Sweet Lexi is also spicy, and she's begun sending him naughty photos from her phone. A couple videos, too. In these, she is funny and alluring, skillfully walking the line of irony as she does what she does. Perhaps even a little too practiced at it, Sean thinks. The first one was a joking striptease. The second was Lexi and her best friend, Megan, doing a silly yet sultry dance in some friend's bedroom, modeling jewelry and garments while making kissy faces at the camera. The third—well, Sean believes she is either a very good actor, or this one she authentically enjoyed.

The school is a large brick building shaded by trees. It is a Quaker school, with excellent academics. There is no football team, but there is a quidditch team. He's tried to explain it before to his cousins who live in the western part of the state. On the first day of class, everyone introduces themselves and gives their pronouns. Spots on the debate squad and science Olympiad are highly sought after. By contrast, the public high school his cousins described sounds ruggedly American, almost parodic, like something out of a teen movie.

He exits the bus as if in a dream, walking up the shaded path, his backpack slung over one shoulder. There is a recitation in Mr. Olander's English class today. A calculus quiz. A group presentation in AP U.S. History. He enjoys school, enjoys the satisfying rhythm of it. Challenge, mastery, challenge. It feels good to think. It feels good to run across the soccer field. There is a simplicity in him, he realizes, particularly when he talks to some of his more brooding classmates. He likes stuff. He enjoys things. He is relatively untroubled.

"Hey, man, wait up."

It's his buddy Trevor, jogging up the path behind him, tapping him on the arm.

Trevor is breathless.

"So I guess you heard?"

Sean looks at Trevor, his face betraying his ignorance.

"Dude, your mom got into it online last night with Megan Nathans."

"What?"

"Umm, I think it started with Megan posting about organizing a Students for Bernie event and went downhill from there . . ."

"Well, my mom really likes Elizabeth Warren."

At least, she used to, Sean amends to himself. He assumes she still must, despite the recent cavorting she's done with the wormy underbelly of the web. The cold case community seems to have heavy overlap with the out-and-out conspiracy theorists.

"Yeah, I know. The whole school knows. Your mom ended up calling Megan a Bernie Bro, and then Megan called your mom a sad, deluded Boomer, and then, well . . ."

Sean resists the urge to fact-check Megan in absentia. His mother isn't a Boomer; she's either Gen X's last gasp or the first breath of millennial. But Megan's point is that Sean's mother is obsolete. She is an older person worthy of scorn.

"Then what?"

"Your mom called Megan an ungrateful little silver-spoon-fed brat." Trevor pauses, sucking in his cheeks with a look close to admiration. "She kept going, too. It's been deleted now, but there are plenty of screenshots. The parents didn't like it, man. They're going berserk, talking about how your mom verbally assaulted a child."

There is an insistent drumming now filling Sean's chest. Megan is a state champion swimmer, Yale bound, her father head of cardiology at Duke, her mother a urologist at UNC. A powerful family locally respected. He can't manage to get a full breath. The school has an online community and parent forum ordinarily meant for the posting of small jobs and opportunities, school bake sales and volunteer events—mundane local happenings.

". . . and Megan's, like, lapping it up. She loves the attention. She tweeted the whole thing to the Bernie Sanders campaign, but they haven't responded. It's all blown out of proportion at this point."

Sean doubles over as if in physical pain. Megan is Lexi's best friend—although there's a competitive edge to the friendship, both girls bright and high-climbing. He's borne witness both to Lexi's fierce allegiance to Megan and to her private complaints, their little internecine conflicts. But they're still, as Sean's mother would say, joined at the hip.

"My mom's not been sleeping well lately," he says to Trevor.

Trevor throws up both hands.

"Hey, man. I just thought you'd want to know."

"She's been doing nothing but reading up on this murder. *Investigating.* It's like some weird fascination for her."

Trevor forces a laugh.

"No one's gonna hold it against you. Megan's a lot. You've seen how she gets."

"Maybe I can say Mom's account got hacked?"

"Dude, it was some real specific ad hominem shit."

Sean sighs deeply, hanging his head.

"Hey. I was a little impressed," Trevor says. "I didn't know your mom had it in her."

"Great. Thanks."

Trevor throws an arm over his shoulder, guiding him into the humanities building. The first bell has already rung, and the halls are beginning to clear.

"It's cool, man," he says. "People know you're a good dude."

Sean has moved now from horrified to seething. His mother is a fool. An idiot. Someone blithely allowing herself to be drawn into online spats with a teenager, making reckless accusations online. Taking deep dives into conspiracy theories with a hair too much credulity, spending all her time online with the fringiest people on the internet. Cold-case obsessives, yes, but her sleuthing has also taken her to other dark corners filled with God knows what kind of extremists. White supremacists. Anti-vaxxers. Flat-earthers. The farthest edges of the alt-right. It's all there. She's absorbed in it. She even missed a grant deadline for her work recently.

He's called her out on it, but she's refused to listen. Time and time again he's told her.

And here is Trevor, his best friend, one of the few Black kids at his school, trying to make him feel better. It's shameful. He feels like an asshole by proxy: rich, white, with a mom whose privilege allows her to indulge in the internet's worst excesses, to lash out at a kid. To act crazy. No wonder his dad left. He bites the inside of his cheek and tastes blood.

"Sean, man, in your shoes, I'd want someone to tell me."

Trevor has paused outside Sean's first period classroom.

"Yeah, no. Thanks, dude. I appreciate it."

"I'll see you at practice."

Sean nods, watching Trevor glide down the hall and away from him. His phone vibrates in his pocket. He pauses in the doorway to his classroom; he dares not check. He checks. A text from Lexi.

I heard about your mom and Megan . . . Meet after practice?

He knows exactly what this means. His mom's a liability, a loose cannon. It's over with Lexi. Her sights are set on Brown. Modern Culture and Media plus Poli Sci: a double concentration. She's on a trajectory. She will not affiliate with someone who does not support this trajectory—who, in fact, might jeopardize it. He clicks the phone off and rushes into class, head down.

The school day goes by in a sort of daze. No one says anything to him, but Sean imagines all eyes on him. The student body is overwhelmingly wealthy, the offspring of educated parents, professors and professionals, who wish to do well but also do right by the world. The school is an enlightened dream, a Research Triangle haven, a tiny Scandinavian country fueled by a university economy set among the red-blooded methane cornfields of America. There are student-led mediations to address conflicts, during which a talking stick is passed; everyone is an ally to everyone, passionate in their passions, exuberant with their goodwill and openness. Mothers do not curse at students in online brawls. It will not do.

Sean moves through the day like a robot, skillfully ignoring classmates, avoiding conversation. Ordinarily in class, he is an avid participant. Today, he keeps his eyes down, slumping in his desk, eyes darting toward the door when the teacher tries to capture his gaze. It will all blow over, he tells himself.

By the time he heads to soccer practice, the day seems to have taken notice of his distress: It has turned overcast, cool, low gray clouds

THE VELDT

threatening rain. Fitting pathetic fallacy. The barometric pressure has shifted. There is a brooding feeling in the air now, the whole sky pinched tight like a headache. He rubs his brow. The soccer field spreads before him so smooth and green it almost looks fake.

Trevor greets him, staying by his side as the coach runs them through wind sprints, then drills. They divvy up for scrimmage, and maybe he's being oversensitive, but it seems people aren't passing to him like they normally do.

"Buck up, golden boy," Garrett says to him by the water bottles at one point. "Why so down?"

It's a seemingly innocuous comment, but Sean can't help but over-read it. There's a way that Garrett has been laughing throughout practice that puts Sean on edge. He's aware that one of the other seniors, Blake, has been semicasually dating Megan Nathans.

Toward the end of practice, Sean sees Lexi and Megan approaching with their field hockey sticks. They are tawny-limbed, coltish, emitting a kind of radiance against the gray gloom of the day. Megan is tall, with the lean, square shoulders of a swimming scholarship hopeful. Beside her, Lexi appears slighter, less substantial, but together, the two girls create a lustrous effect, glowing with the flush of well-nurtured youth. The weather's mild still. Both girls are in short sleeves. Sean watches Lexi push back a bit of hair from her forehead, tightening her haphazard ponytail—everything about her so effortless, so messily beautiful. But there's uncertainty on her face, a reluctance. He looks to her, and she will not meet his gaze.

He watches as Blake lopes over toward the girls, greeting Megan with a side hug. Is it his imagination, or are they exchanging glances in his direction? Megan seems to be saying something emphatic, her eyebrows arches of surprise. Lexi turns away, her eyes downcast.

"See ya, man," Trevor says, adjusting his bag on his shoulder. Sean follows his gaze and sees Trevor's mom in her Subaru, waiting in the parking lot. "You got a ride?"

Sean hesitates. He'd like to ask Trevor for a ride, but his family lives twenty minutes in the opposite direction. It would be too much, on top of everything else, an indulgence he can hardly afford.

"Garrett," Sean says, nodding toward where the senior guys are standing.

Across the field, Garrett is engaged in some sort of pantomime that involves putting a Gatorade bottle on his head and doing a lurching kind of walk. Kevin Matthews and Jake Miller laugh appreciatively.

"Good luck," Trevor says, and turns away.

Sean can feel it before it happens, the way that animals can sense a storm or a predator stalking them. His ears tingle. There's an electric crackle in the air. A cluster of dark birds rises like a plume of ash from the tree that stands adjacent to the field.

Megan calls to him.

"Sean, hey! Come here."

Grudgingly, he obeys, submitting to the inevitable. Head hanging, he scuffs his cleats through the grass. At his back, he can feel the stillness of Garrett, Kevin, and Jake, the three of them gone silent, watchful.

He stops before them, hardly daring to look up. Megan is flanked by Lexi and Blake, her attendants.

"You never texted her back," Megan says, jerking her thumb toward Lexi.

He looks at Megan, her lovely, symmetrical face, her teeth the product of excellent orthodontia. His look is an appeal. Lexi, beautiful Lexi, is inspecting some tiny process occurring on the ground—an ant hefting a leftover chunk of granola bar. Her cheeks are flushed, and she's digging at a bit of sod with the toe of her shoe. In any other scenario, she would reach out to him, press the flat of her hand against his back to comfort him.

"Sorry," he says, although what he means is that he already knows and would like to cut short this torturous exchange. There's the boom of an approaching storm, somewhere far off still, the sky a dark, blue-plum color beyond the distant hills. The storm is rolling toward them.

Blake whispers something to Megan, and she giggles. This line of humiliation is pointed yet indirect. Lexi flushes a deeper crimson.

"Listen, Lexi," Sean says. "I know we're done but—"

Megan laughs loudly, cutting him off. She pinches Lexi slightly on the arm, a playful pinch, but Lexi does not return the laughter. Sean can

THE VELDT

see the upturned corners of Blake's mouth, feel the gaze of the guys behind him. He is standing outside the joke; he is the joke.

"For you to be done," Megan says, "you'd have to have actually started something. You and Lexi hung out some. So what. I'd hardly call it *dating*."

Sean feels the hot rush of blood into his face. He doesn't answer.

"Besides, you're what I'd call a solo artist," Megan continues. "You know—the rocket exploded before it left the launchpad? It's okay. That's common with young boys."

She laughs, showing all her sharp teeth like a predator.

So Lexi has told her everything. And now here she is, peering at him furtively from behind a lock of her hair, too cowardly to say a thing. Letting Megan do her dirty work.

"You're perfectly normal. It happens. There are online support groups," Megan says, her mouth twisting into a wicked smile. "Ask your mom. She seems to spend plenty of time on the internet. Maybe she can help." She laughs again, sourly.

"My mom's going through a rough patch," Sean mutters.

Lexi looks at him sorrowfully then, her big blue eyes rounded in astonished sadness. He catches a glimpse of what lies behind her expression: curiosity, satisfaction, relief. She is not nearly so stricken as she's been pretending, and in fact, he can see it; she's relieved.

Lexi glances at him again coolly, not a trace of pity. This is exactly how she wished for this scene to play out. A clean break. Beyond them, the clap of thunder sounds closer. Slow, fat drops of rain begin to fall to the ground. The girls turn arm in arm to leave, and Blake follows. Sean can hear the whispers and stifled laughter from the rest of the team standing behind him. He says nothing. He drops his bag to the ground, then sinks upon it. He lets his head fall into his knees, the rain hot and slow on the back of his neck.

Minutes pass. Voices moving nearby, people taking leave as the rain picks up. Finally, Sean senses an abrupt shadow: someone standing over him.

"Come on, pal," Garrett says. "Let's go."

Sean doesn't look up, but slowly he lets himself rise, hefting the damp bag to his shoulder. Although it's not cold out, he finds he's shivering, his clothes clammy with sweat and rain. He can imagine how pitiful he must look, a baby opossum swept away in a drainage ditch, a drowned rat.

Strangely, Garrett is not cracking jokes. He moves through the rain, which is coming down now in steady, pelting rhythm, with the hunched solemnity of a monk. At his car, he pops the lock in silence, then hands Sean an old towel from his back seat once they're inside.

"Thanks," Sean says, and he means it. He turns quickly to look out the window, back toward the soccer field, because he does not want Garrett to see his face. This small, unexpected kindness has made him well up. He swipes the back of his hand against his eyes.

Garrett starts the car, turning on the lights and the wipers. The radio is set to something low—vague new wave from the college station nearby. Sean wonders if perhaps in having been cut down to size he's made himself inoffensive to him, so thoroughly humiliated as to no longer be an enemy.

He steals a glance at Garrett from the corner of his eye, holding his gaze straight ahead. Garrett squints into the windshield, his big, clumsy-looking hands on the wheel. There are cystic pimples all along his neck and jawline. His nose is beaky and his chin recessed, giving him the look of an odd, flightless bird. Already, at age seventeen, he has the prematurely receding hairline of a middle-aged man. All the jokes, all the bluster, Sean can finally see it for what it is—a protective facade, something to ward off trouble, like the puffer mechanism of a puffer fish.

He and Garrett are in the same math class, which either means Sean is two math levels ahead, or Garrett is two behind, depending on how you look at it—and, given the academic standards of their school, everyone would hold the latter perspective. Merely being at grade level is considered remedial. Sean wonders what it must be like to be so ungainly, so awkward at a school filled with students of such privilege, such easy intelligence, such grace. He considers his own effortlessness and how to others—to someone like Garrett—it might seem like an affront.

It occurs to Sean that all this time he's been cowed by Garrett, perhaps Garrett might have been cowed by him. Yet now, they are allies.

". . . and seriously, kid, these girls suck. I mean, they're the worst at our school. Think they know everything. Right?"

THE VELDT

Garrett turns to him, and Sean realizes he's been talking. Sean has zoned out to the lull of the road, the shush of the wet tires.

"You're telling me," Sean says, in wounded solidarity.

"And Lexi and Megan, man, I could have told you not to mess with them," Garrett says. His hands tighten on the wheel, and Sean notes the hard knots of his knuckles. There's a change to his voice, too. The light ahead of them turns yellow, but they are going quickly, and then it's red. Garrett slams on the brakes, and they skid before stopping.

"They're conceited. Only in it for themselves," Garrett continues. "I could have told you that from the start. Trust me, dude. You're better off."

Sean feels a small pang of disloyalty even now. Was Lexi truly so bad? He thinks again to her standing there with Megan, tucking her chin in pained silence. A clever act. He recalls the way Megan laughed, the hideous stretch of her cackling mouth, laughing for herself and for Lexi. Oh, how they'd worked so well in tandem, cutting him down to nothing. Lexi, the reluctant judge, Megan, the executioner. Maybe Garrett was right.

"Sounds personal," Sean offers mildly—but he is interested. Very interested.

"Megan and I have some history."

Garrett reveals nothing further. The light changes again, and he shrugs, but Sean can see the hostility in how his shoulders are set. The hatred.

"And Lexi's just in it for The Lexi Show, man. That's all she cares about. Herself."

He doesn't explain any more than that. They've pulled up to Sean's house now, the wipers swishing back and forth, the low hum of the radio almost inaudible. There's a strange feeling in the car that Sean recognizes as embarrassment, although he can't tell who he feels it for: Garrett, the baldness of his emotion, the confessional quality of this entire exchange, or himself, the recently dumped.

"It wasn't totally nothing," Sean says, but his voice is small, and he hears how unconvincing he sounds. "Lexi and I were together."

Although it's not yet evening, the storm has turned the sky dark. A light clicks on by Sean's front door. He watches as his mother opens it and peers out, offering a tentative little wave to them.

"Your mom's a nice lady," Garrett mutters. "She's always been nice to me."

Sean feels something unclamp in his chest. His mother *is* nice. Even if she's misguided. Confused. She means well. Which is more than he can say for Lexi. Her betrayal. He thinks of her standing with Megan, the two of them, vicious and snide. *Ungrateful little silver-spoon-fed brat.* His mother's words have a ring to them when he repeats this phrase in his mind.

Sean's mother waves again, sweet and ordinary in the doorway, her face scrubbed free of any makeup, her lank hair in need of a wash. Harmless. That's what he wants to plead to Megan: Don't you see she's harmless? Whiling away the hours online with a bunch of lonely people, wasting their time on wild theories, searching for a greater purpose, a mission. And why not? It was as understandable as anything, wasn't it? For a moment, he wishes he were much younger so that he could run to his mother and be enveloped in her arms, her warm, soft chest. He would weep, and she would soothe him like she did when he was a little boy.

Beside him, Garrett waves back to her—a goofy, friendly swing of his arm—and Sean feels a sliver of fondness for him, this clumsy neighbor of his, ungraceful in his rough humor and his hurt. It *does* seem unfair that all the polished, lovely people of the world—the ones with good bone structure and even smiles who hardly have to study yet ace all the standardized tests, the quick-witted and the beautiful—should have everything without a thought. He sees the depth of his previous offense, the way he took all this for granted, moving throughout the world as if success were his birthright. No wonder Garrett treated him with such scorn. But Sean understands now. They're brothers, he and Garrett, Sean thinks, a warm rush of gratitude filling him at the unexpected sources of kindness in the world. Unlike Lexi, who stood like a false door, nothing at all behind her.

"Want to see something?" Sean asks, taking out his phone.

He unlocks it, pulling up one of the flirty photos Lexi sent, and handing the phone to Garrett. The image is nothing really, a PG-13 selection at most—Lexi posing in bra and panties, wearing a cowboy hat and a come-hither look—but it reveals the intimacy they'd shared. Proof.

Before Sean can stop him, Garret scrolls back through Lexi's messages. He raises an eyebrow.

"Hey, that's private," Sean says.

Garrett scrolls quietly, then shakes his head. He is smiling now, or maybe it's a smirk.

"Holy shit," Garrett says. "Oh, it's both of them! Dancing!"

"Stop. Give me my phone."

"Take it easy, dude. Just browsing."

And before Sean can take his phone back, Garrett has already typed in his own number and pressed send. Sean hears the ding of Garrett's phone in response.

"None of that's for you," Sean snaps. He's thinking of the one video in particular. Lexi would kill him. She had, in fact, snapped it so it would automatically delete. But he'd recorded it. The video was simply too good to give up. But if Garrett has seen it—his stomach has done a flip-flop at the thought.

"Like I said, take it easy," Garrett says. "I sent myself a photo. Lexi the cowgirl. For my personal enjoyment. We're pals, right?"

"No one else sees it. Please."

"Hey, listen. You see that story in the *DTH* about the series of break-ins over in some of the off-campus student apartments? My dad's been working on the case. They're about to release some security footage."

Sean shakes his head. Garrett's dad is a cop, making Garrett another of the handful of scholarship students at the school, someone whose parent isn't a CEO or hospital department head.

"No, why?"

"Ahhh, don't worry about it, man. You'll hear more about it soon enough," Garrett says, and he smiles a smile that can be described only as smug, secretive, self-satisfied.

He raises his arm for a fist bump, which Sean feels obligated to return. The moment between them is lost, though, like a door closing. Garrett's face has turned stony again, unreadable to Sean. There is a rumble, then the crack of lightning nearby. The rain pounds, a white sheet.

"I should get home."

"Thanks for the ride," Sean calls, although he wants to say something more. He pauses for a moment, wanting to restore their previous rapport, wishing to find the right words, but he cannot locate them, so he exits the car, darting through the pelting rain to his front door.

His mother opens the door and ushers him inside. He stands, dripping in the entryway, ready to unleash the tirade he's rehearsed all day long—but there is something in her face now that he cannot bear to break. She seems happy for the first time in so long. She is wild-eyed but thrilled.

"I have to tell her. I have to find the mother."

"What mother?"

He follows her, still dripping, up the stairs to her darkened office. The monitors glow like a holy relic in a vault.

"The mother of the poor man who's been falsely imprisoned. That poor man is innocent."

There, on one of her computer screens, are news articles featuring photos of a beautiful girl—the murdered girl, his mother's college roommate. Karlie. In one photo, the girl is laughing, her eyes crinkling shut, her hair lush and blonde behind her. The next photo is another from the crime scene. The girl—and it is surely the same girl—is lying, arms akimbo, shirt hiked up, on the floor. The dead girl from before. Zoomed in, and even more gruesome. The photo is a violation. It pains Sean; he turns away.

"They got it all wrong," Sean's mother says, her words freewheeling and too fast. "Toby. The one in prison. He *couldn't* have done it. Plus, there are all these other suspicious connections."

She pulls up another photo of a young man, dark-haired, not much older than Sean himself, wincing at the camera.

"This guy," Sean's mother says, tapping the retina display with her finger, "died by apparent suicide not long after Karlie's death. I knew him. I met him once, actually. But the circumstances of his death are suspicious. He was her friend. Ian. He'd recently left a cult in the western part of the state, and what I learned from talking to this documentary guy, Brian, is that he'd also taken a class with Jacob Hendrix, my old professor. There are so many threads that tie back to him."

THE VELDT

Her cheeks are flushed. There is a drop of sweat making its way slowly from her forehead down her cheek. All the photos and documents behind her on the screen swirl together like a proliferating malignancy. Sean's mother clutches herself in a kind of swaying, rocking hug. He wants to stop her, but she's so lost in her sick, sad certainty—this mystery she believes she's solved.

"Mom," Sean says, softly, because he cannot bear it. How does he explain it to her? The fact that this is all nothing but a mirage? A sick, slick valley of illusion? A metastatic phenomenon, ever expanding?

"You helped me earlier, Sean."

"Mom, please."

"It's the BMW. With the single headlight. I was stuck on that detail—there's something there I can't put my finger on—but that's not the part that matters right now." She laughs. "The car doesn't matter if you can't drive!"

"Mom."

"Don't worry, we're going to work on getting you ready for your license," she says, her eyes briefly lighting on his face, her words pouring forth in a way that makes him certain she'll remember none of this. "We'll go get your learner's permit this week."

It's happened one other time like this, a couple of years ago, shortly after Sean's maternal grandfather finally died. A former pastor, he'd been sick for years. Epilepsy, and then diabetes, heart trouble, other things Sean couldn't keep track of. He hadn't thought of his mother and her father as particularly close, but she'd gotten worked up during the months after his death, sleepless, overzealous, just like this. He'd found her internet browser open to pages featuring high-end Swedish baby strollers that cost as much as used cars, handcrafted small-batch prenatal vitamins, elaborate wraparound infant carriers made of organic hemp. It had unsettled him slightly to see his mother poring over such things—his parents were old! And done with having children! But later he took it for what it surely was—a midlife crisis of sorts, his mother's reckoning with her own mortality, the mourning of her lost youth. The way birth and death abut each other, two startling bookends; a thematic pairing he might tackle for an AP English paper. Figuring that out pleased him. He wishes he could figure out this episode. He recognizes the off-kilter way she talks again now, her absent eyes, the staleness of her breath. She will not sleep, possibly for days. A flurry of internet activity will consume her. He will have to tell his father, plead with him to intervene—he's still listed as her emergency contact after all, and the divorce is not final yet. A phone call will be made: Sean's father speaking in a hushed voice to his mother's doctor. Then, a strong sleeping pill.

The great mystery, the conspiracies, his mother's book, will all turn out to be nothing.

"I have to get in touch first," his mother continues. "I'll go from there. I'm putting the pieces together. I'm uncovering the real story."

"Sit down, Mom," he says, guiding her to her chair. She's hot to the touch, almost feverish, lit from within with conviction. He's lost the heart to chastise her. Instead, she leans her head against his shoulder, nestling into him, almost feline. It's been worse, he thinks, now that he and Ethan have started dividing time between her house and his father's new place, but he does not say this. Instead, he strokes her head, soothing her. Her hair is unwashed, and he can smell it—an animal stink of oil and fur. It occurs to him that he cannot remember the last time he's seen her clean and dressed, not wearing days-old pajamas.

"I've had a breakthrough," she whispers, tipping her head up to gaze at him again. "I'm going to put things right. I owe that to Karlie."

It is an approval-seeking look, he thinks, and she is smiling so broadly, with such hopeful expectation, that she is tearing up. Sean has the uncomfortable feeling he's bearing witness to a private moment, a kind of existential culmination of thought and feeling, and he ought not to be there.

"Sean?"

"Yes?"

"I said something. To one of your classmates. I haven't been getting good rest, you know? And with this whole investigation, I'm preoccupied—"

"I know, Mom."

"I don't mean to make things harder for you, is all . . . I'll make it right with that girl."

"She *is* kind of a silver-spoon-fed brat."

His mother laughs sadly and nods, searching his face for something else, something he cannot give. Sean can't bear to make eye contact with her. Her lips are dry, chapped to the point of cracking, painful to behold. There's a raw, tearing sensation in his gut, and he fears he might cry.

"Let me get you some water," he says abruptly, turning to head downstairs, calmly, although his heart is pounding. He will, he thinks, have a talk with her, gently, about stepping away a little bit, spending less time online, about the dangers of conjecture, the toxic alacrity with which conspiracy theories spread, the dangers of engaging in debate in the comments—although maybe it's unnecessary to say all this now. He can see the contrition in her face.

Downstairs, he stands at the sink for a long moment, longer than he needs. Through the kitchen window, streaked and fogged with rain, the world outside looks midnight-dark, almost subterranean. He watches the headlights of a passing car float down the street murkily, like a submarine moving underwater. All this will pass, he thinks, if he can outlast it. He gulps some water directly from the sink, cupping his hands, realizing for the first time how parched his throat is, how hot and dry. He shakes droplets off his cheeks. The refrigerator purrs softly behind him.

"Sean?" his mother calls from up the stairs, because she is waiting still, her voice tinny and far-off, forlorn. He turns the tap on again and fills a glass.

When he returns to her, the glass cool against his palm, she is holding his phone, holding it out to him. It dings, then dings again, and again a third time, a fourth. There's an uncertain look on his mother's face, all that unadulterated joy from her discovery replaced by something unnameable.

"I wasn't trying to read them," she says, offering his phone to him. "But you're getting lots of texts. About a video?"

The blood rushes to his ears in a torrent, a sound so loud it's a deafening roar. Sean closes his eyes, and it's all he can hear: the roar of lions. They move softly through the yellow veldt grass where once there were walls. The lions are coming, this time for him.

Garrett lied to him. That video of Lexi—he *did* see it, and now he's shared it. Does it count as revenge porn? Probably, Sean thinks. No, undoubtedly. Sean will be ruined.

There's a strange peace to it, Sean realizes—to the lions. An end to the anticipation. The worst has already happened; there will be no more waiting. He will lie down, resign himself to it: their great jaws opening, the smell of meat hot on their breath.

But when he unlocks his screen and reads the texts and Instagram notifications, he sees what Garrett has done: He's shared a different video on Instagram, a video Lexi sent weeks ago that Sean had failed previously to appreciate as anything other than pure silliness. Lexi and Megan are dancing to Megan Thee Stallion in a space Sean hadn't recognized, but had assumed was another friend's room. There's a mauve bedspread over a double bed, a poster-size Van Gogh reproduction on the wall, a Carolina pendant. Sean had taken this as the room of another high school student, but now, with a lurch, he recognizes the oatmeal-colored institutional walls and flimsy built-in shelving, the murky high-rise windows for what they signify: cheap off-campus undergraduate student housing. And the silly dance he'd taken simply as flirtation, a saucy reminder for him to appreciate his good luck in love, he sees now, is actually more of a victory dance, a taunt. Lexi and Megan pluck and parade before the camera with a variety of personal belongings that are not their own: a black satin bra with rhinestones, a Taylor Swift concert T-shirt, an antique turquoise ring, a Chanel wallet. He turns the volume up. *Ohhhh, I like it,* Lexi says. *It's mine now!* Words he hadn't even registered the first time because, he is, he's realizing, hopelessly innocent. A fool.

A new caption has been typed at the bottom of the video:

> Meet Megan Nathans and Lexi Douglas! Chapel Hill's own bling ring! Instead of Paris Hilton, they steal from college kids with student loans! Attn: @253arendaleroadaptcomplex @uncpolice @chapelhillgov @brownu @brownuadmission @yale @yaleadmissions

Alongside this, there's a freeze-frame of security footage just released by the Chapel Hill police, a grainy image of two girls, one tall and broad-shouldered, the other petite. WANTED IN SERIES OF LOCAL BREAK-INS.

Sean reconsiders the recent uptick in small nice objects in Lexi's possession. The new diamond earrings, that antique broach, and most recently a little dangling bracelet with a Taurus sign on it even though Lexi herself is not a Taurus. *Oops, my dad messed up,* she'd explained. *He doesn't know astrology!* And Sean had taken this explanation at face value because why not? Her parents could afford to get her whatever she wants. He feels almost sick with it—his own naivety, his hopeless innocence—imagining Lexi and Megan together in Megan's car, idle and intoxicated on their own youth and power and boredom.

Already there are dozens of comments. From these and from the texts he's receiving, Sean has gleaned that Lexi has posted a tearful response in which she blames Megan for persuading her, calling it Megan's idea entirely. She was ensnared, peer-pressured, blinded to her better judgment, and is now filled with regret! Megan, on the other hand, seems to be playing defensive hardball now. All her social media accounts and previous posts have been deleted, according to Trevor, who is dutifully texting Sean updates. Also according to Trevor, Bryn Howard, who functions as the school's unofficial town crier, is telling everyone that Megan has lawyered up.

The whole thing is a disaster of such delicious proportions that Sean's school will soon be delirious with it, the orderly lines of their neatly tucked lives rumpled, rich with the thrill of schadenfreude masquerading as disappointment.

A text arrives to Sean from Garrett: *you're welcome, dude.*

His mother, who has been sitting quietly, watching him study his phone, clears her throat.

"It's those girls, isn't it?" she says. She says it mildly, not an ounce of emotion in her voice. "They've gotten into some kind trouble."

Sean nods. His mouth is too dry to speak.

"You know, Sean," his mother continues. "The internet. Social media. All of this." She gestures to her computer, his phone, the whole invisible web of constant interconnectedness that surrounds them. "You get onto me about it. But see? It does things. It makes things happen."

The roar in Sean's ears is diminishing, replaced by an eerie quiet. He feels the radiant heat from their flanks, sleek muscles rippling, as the lions pass him by. There's the scent of blood in the air. Sean has a queasy feeling. Far off, he imagines screaming, the tearing of flesh, vultures gathering like undertakers in dark suits as they patiently await their turn.

Truecrimesleuth.net

@rrhawkins3: My friend knows a friend who knows this guy, Nick, who worked with Toby Braithwaite (the guy serving time). He's certain Toby's innocent. He was just an easy fall guy, a way to close the case. According to this friend, Toby was trying to check up on Karlie. She'd shown up that day at the restaurant where both Nick and Toby worked, and she seemed weird. Scared. Nick apparently told the friend that there were these bruises on Karlie, and he hadn't said anything at the time, but he'd noticed it. She seemed skittish, he said—but not around Toby. She was totally comfortable with him. Karlie was sweet with Toby—did little things for him, treated him kind of like a little brother. He worshipped her. Yet another instance of the criminal justice system scapegoating an already disenfranchised/powerless person. (He's intellectually disabled—raised by a single mom, extremely limited financial resources.)

@ljollimore: What's the status of the professor she was having an affair with? He and Karlie were seeing each other for at least a year from what I've heard . . . sometime in fall of '98 up through fall '99, not long before her murder. He was supposedly ruled out, but his only alibi was his wife, right . . . ? Not the most credible alibi IMO.

@msmolly: I remain interested in the professor. The alibi seems flimsy. He also got a doctor to testify that he wouldn't have had the necessary strength due to a medical condition, but I'm skeptical of that, too—I mean, how could you know for sure? She had another friend (boyfriend?)—guy named Ian Helmsley—who also worked in the restaurant @rrhawkins3 notes above. He disappeared not long after Karlie's murder, and then it was reported that Helmsley died by suicide. The whole thing strikes me as weird—the timing, their connection, the manner of death, all of it. Interesting connection: Ian Helmsley took a class with the professor (Hendrix, guy who was having affair with Karlie). This connection was highlighted in the recent episode of

Murder Real Estate—and I'll agree with everyone here, it turned out terribly. The reenactments, yikes! But this connection was news to me. Also, have y'all heard the rumors about someone in a car who kept showing up outside Karlie's door? Might be nothing, but . . .

@dwatts: Re: Ian Helmsley. Hard not to see his death soon thereafter and imagine this could be a sign of guilt . . . But don't forget Helmsley's two housemates, also options. Both would have spent a fair amount of time with Karlie. The leader of the campus evangelical group Clay Something and the cousin he lived with. Keith? Kevin?

@msmolly: Kent. Clay and Kent. Both questioned. Alibied each other out, which is a dicey way to alibi out if you ask me. I still like the cult for it.

@shanshan5: I think the cult's a stretch. Makes for a good conspiracy theory, sure, but you've got your obvious line of suspects in the men who were Karlie's affiliates: Jacob (professor), Kent, Clay, and Ian (the latter three were all housemates, which is interesting).

@rayray49: @msmolly Bond of Faith?

@mark5: @rayray49 Yep. I live nearby, next county over. All sorts of rumors about bribery and coercion, you name it, at BOF. Even some kind of "study abroad" they run that amounts to indentured servitude . . . People have been looking into them for years . . .

@ljollimore: @shanshan5 Agree with you. Of those, Ian is deceased. This guy Kent works in a law library out in Oregon. Clay and Jacob are still in NC. Apparently the documentary production crew for *Murder Real Estate* is trying to interview all three of them but keep getting flat-out denied. Got a buddy who was helping produce the show, and he told me.

@rayray49: I like Clay for it. Creepy youth pastor type? Young evangelist or whatever? Somebody should have looked deeper into him . . . He owns a car wash in Hickory now. My brother lives there.

Anonymous ID: RTV63XYK Sat 9 Mar 2019 No. 45376 VIEW REPORT

Mockingbird.
Why go around the 3 letter agencies?
Who has the military code?
This is not R v. D battle.
POTUS with great power. You think Soros will defeat? Fantasy.
Like a storm cloud passes, so go those who simply follow HRC, like lemmings.
Watch Bezos, Wayfair, Oprah, Obama, etc. Follow $.
Child sex slaves = un-American.
Mockingbird 7.20.19.
Dove over raven, raven over flood.
Ravens in fight, ravens in flight.
Yellow November crave. Crave raven.
<clown> insurance in big tech.
Follow Soros money.
Mockingbird. Mockingbird.
God bless fellow patriots.

level 1
wandapops
1 year ago

Repost of one I did in a different thread, but this one haunts me:

—Karlie Richards, 19 yo woman murdered in her college dorm over winter break. It was an exceptionally intimate manner of killing (strangulation. Plus, there were other marks on her body, signs of assault). See this article in *The Cut* for more (tw: sexual violence). This piece was written by an L.A.-based writer who graduated from UNC School of Journalism a few years after the murder, and the piece definitely implies there was much more to the story than the case the prosecutors brought, so many weird details they ignored.

Toby Braithwaite, the man currently in prison, was a busboy (I think?) at a restaurant downtown near where Karlie hung out. He's developmentally disabled. It was a total coerced confession (like that poor kid from *Making a Murderer*).

FWIW, this wasn't in the article, but a lot of people say Karlie inadvertently uncovered a church fraud scheme—someone in her friend group was involved. Some kind of unemployment fraud? She learned too much and was going to speak up—so she had to be done away with. It was staged to look like a crime of passion, but it was a hit job.

I believe the real killer is still at large.

Share
ReportSave

level 2
Bombastickstick
1 year ago

She was killed in off-campus apartment, not dorm. Also, the author of article in *The Cut* only refers to this obliquely, but there does seem to have been some connection to a religious organization Karlie was affiliated with. This "church" was a front for lots of financial interests. Think Jim Bakker but much more secretive, minus the televangelism . . .

Also, FYI, as mentioned in the other thread related to Karlie's murder: local urban legend about the Weeper DOES relate to this case! Toby Braithwaite, who is currently serving time for Karlie's murder, was found outside her apartment crying several nights straight after she was killed. He wouldn't talk at first. People say that's the origin of the whole thing. It's how the rumors got started—although obviously it couldn't be Toby, since he's incarcerated, but perhaps a sort of copycat? Some sick person (people?) inspired by this slightly disturbing tidbit from the case started sneaking up on people, like maybe as a sick joke or dare or something? It happened to my former roommate's aunt, years after Karlie's murder.

Share
ReportSave
Continue this thread

level 2
Comment deleted by user
1 year ago

There was also a murder plot thwarted in western NC that seems connected to Karlie's killing. Another woman, a social worker, who knew too much. Look it up. Check out the *Charlotte Observer* articles on Bond of Faith Fellowship.

level 2
tortollafree
1 year ago

I heard that same rumor but remain unconvinced. Hadn't Karlie also recently broken up with a boyfriend?

What's also interesting is that per reports, there was a gun found in Karlie's apartment that had never been fired. It's what today one might refer to as a "ghost gun," meaning it was assembled from a kit, from parts, so that there's no serial number. No background check required, no registration, etc. (Look online and you'll see how easily you can order one of these kits now.) You have to assume it was hers . . . had she gotten it recently? After the breakup? And why?

18

Share
ReportSave

level 2
roombaskyler
1 year ago

I have a friend who lives nearby—her mom's sister went to school with Karlie. Her mom's sister believes it was a serial killer—there were four other murders in college towns in the South during that time period with victims who were young women of similar age, similar profile . . . although method of killing very different, which raises questions. And just to complicate things further, I'll also underscore what someone else already mentioned: that the "friend" of Karlie's, Ian Helmsley, died by suicide not long after her death—torn apart by grief?? Or guilt??? Or murdered by someone who needed to silence him and who knew how to stage the death to look just like a suicide?

58

Share
ReportSave
Continue this thread

The Dark Forest

By the time the bus winds up the road leading to the correctional facility, most of the passengers have already gotten off. Only Sheri and two other women remain. They are heavyset, with lank hair, nicotine-stained fingers, and unreadable faces. Like Sheri herself. Although they offer no greeting, she's seen them both here on the bus before. *The Mothers' Club*, she thinks. A club no mother would want to be a part of. And yet, together they regularly trudge past the guard's station and up the walkway to the visitor's entrance and security checkpoint. They will do so again today, holding a collective silence. Sheri will pause first to leave her brown bag lunch at the base of an oak on the grounds. She has done this every visit for some time now, and not once has anyone ever taken her sad sandwich and lukewarm can of Sprite. The guards will not let her bring any food to share with Toby. She's tried. Even the kindliest guard, the old one with white tufts of hair sticking out over his ears, simply looked at her and shook his head.

The bus groans to a stop, and the women stand.

Sheri grimaces—the sciatica. She realizes how she must look now, ugly and used up. Bitten-down. Old. Toby, her baby, is, what, forty-three? Forty-four? She has to think a moment. He is and will remain childlike. That's what the doctors explained to her back when he was born, although they put it differently, furrowing their brows, holding out a box of tissues in case she became distraught. Anoxic brain injury, they'd said. A relatively mild one, it seemed, all told, and nothing she could have done to prevent it. It was an act of God. Of fate. Happenstance. Marking him with a kind of specialness, an anointing of sorts. Her baby. Forever her baby. But she'd known all along. She'd known from the moment of his conception that he'd be special. Mothers always say that sort of thing after the fact, but for Sheri, it had been true. The two daughters who came after him, pretty, sassy, smart-mouthed girls, are grown up now, with children of their own. Her girls grew up quickly, savagely. Creatures of fang and talon. Yes, they are self-sufficient women now, Jackie and Margie, but they were never like Toby. Both girls defend their brother, have always defended him. They maintain the fact of his innocence still— especially Jackie, who has argued they ought to attempt appeals, petitions, crowd-funding. After listening to that podcast *Serial*, she made more phone calls, tried to find a new attorney who would appeal Toby's conviction and reopen the case. Sheri has countered by reminding her of the expense. They cannot afford it. Nor can they afford new heartbreak—is it worth opening oneself up to slim hope again? Is it worth ripping the seams of those scars back open? When Sheri says such things, Jackie shoots her mother a pained look, a look that questions Sheri's commitment to her boy. *You still think he might've done it*, Jackie says, and Sheri can only wince, can only respond with, *I know he's a good boy*.

It is an achingly beautiful early December day, the sky a pure blue with depths that appear almost indigo. Exiting the bus, Sheri's eyes water at such saturated color. The green from the patch of lawn is thrown into high relief. If winter is coming, this day has yet to get the memo. If she did not look at the building beyond her, she might imagine she is on the grounds of a storybook boarding school. The prison itself sits squat and gray, a forbidding structure, a place where misery seems to seep out of its concrete slabs. She cannot bear to think of Toby inside; it makes the beauty of the day seem like a cruel withholding. Toby does not deserve such a hard place. He was gentle from the start, otherworldly. She'd understood this the very first time he'd looked at her as a newborn with fathomless eyes, his tiny red face crinkled with ancient concern.

Sheri ducks off the walkway, crouching to hide her lunch by the tree. The two other women plod ahead. Sheri watches as the brown door closes behind them. They will pass through metal detectors, nodding numbly at the guards. She will soon follow. Toby will greet her with a blank and sleepy smile. They have him on medications that leave him slurring and slowed. It's unnecessary, Sheri thinks, a solution to a problem that does not exist, because he was always peaceful and happy before. He would never, as she's claimed this whole time, hurt a fly—at least, she amends silently to herself, not on purpose. There is nothing inherently wrong with having the mind of a child, but there are always dark forces at work that might take advantage of that. Mistakes she could not, given such goodness, have possibly foreseen.

"Excuse me."

Sheri whips around. There is a tall young woman wearing sunglasses and a baseball cap standing behind her, far more conspicuous-looking in her attempt to be incognito. Sheri squints, trying to determine from where this woman appeared. There are staff parking lots at the far end of the complex—maybe there. She isn't wearing a uniform, though; if anything, she seems ill at ease, uncertain.

"I'm sorry, I didn't mean to startle you," the ponytailed woman says. "But are you Sheri Clark?"

Sheri takes a step back. The old wariness floods her, like it's twenty years ago again, right after it happened. Reporters followed her outside the courthouse, showed up at her door, knocking, shouting, pestering. The worst, though, was the seemingly sympathetic bystander: always a woman not immediately identifiable as a journalist, someone who offered Sheri a cup of water or a handkerchief, who spoke to her in a hushed and sympathetic tone, guiding her away from the throngs. Someone who, it seemed at first, was trying to help, but who later turned out to be press. Some help they were. Sheri saw how she appeared in the news clips: flustered and frumpy in her best floral church dress, pleading in her thick accent. (She could hear it on that newsclip, shocking next to the polished vowels of the news anchors.) What a hick, she thought before realizing that she was seeing herself. She watched herself then with the eyes of the viewers, and the sight shamed her.

"I know you?" Sheri asks. She knows that her response is rude, her tone sharp. She can see the way the young woman bows her head slightly, an apology of sorts. Again, her eyes flick to the side, like she's assessing the area for danger.

"You don't." The woman bites her lip, and for a moment Sheri feels almost sorry for her. She seems so young, so uncertain. "My name's Joy. I've got a letter for Sheri Clark."

Sheri shakes her head now. She wants to gather a great blob of phlegm and release it right in the woman's face. She's dealt with all sorts of fools and charlatans over the years, scam artists or journalists wanting access for an exclusive interview.

"Please," the woman, Joy, says. "If you *are* Sheri . . ." She presses a sealed envelope toward her, her hands shaking. "You look like him. Your son. I know he's innocent."

The whole thing makes Sheri want to laugh in the woman's face. What does this stranger know? Visiting time is dwindling. She needs to see Toby, then return here to the scratchy crabgrass and eat her sandwich in peace while she waits for the bus back home.

"I'll take the damn letter," Sheri says, plucking it from the woman, and then—showily, grandly—she lifts it before her and begins to tear it right down the middle. Trash. She will treat it as such.

"Stop!" The woman grabs her arm and takes the letter back. "He's innocent. Someone else was watching her."

It's enough to give Sheri pause, that old familiar wave of hope. Cynicism has not totally inured her yet—although over the years she's heard it all—mediums and psychics, false confessions and tips. It's left her weary, wary, but no, not without a shred of hope.

"What are you after?" Sheri growls, and the woman cowers.

"Nothing," she says. "Only trying to do what's right. I emailed you."

"I don't check my email," Sheri says, but she is softening. The woman trembles like a rabbit in a glade. Sheri is unused to being the intimidating one, although over the years she's learned. A necessary skill, it turns out.

"You ever watch that show *Murder Real Estate*? They just filmed a new episode, and I helped. Someone was lurking around Karlie's apartment. Someone driving a car."

Sheri flushes. There's a strange pride, a certainty, to the woman's voice, and yet to Sheri, the woman seems a little unhinged. She knows that the story of the girl's murder will soon be featured on one of the episodes. Her daughter Margie told her. She won't watch. More trash. She's refused to watch any of it: *Dateline, 20/20,* one-off true-crime drivel on the Oxygen network. Sheri hasn't watched a single one of them. And the funny thing is that back before all this with Toby, she'd loved that sort of thing: the foreboding voice-over narration, the hokey reenactments, all those pretty murdered girls, last seen smiling in family snapshots posing by a Christmas tree or wearing pearls in their senior yearbook photos. Afterward, the whole business made her sick.

"I don't watch that garbage."

Sheri takes the envelope back from the young woman and tucks it into the inner pocket of her jacket.

Joy nods, then turns to flee.

"Wait," Sheri says. "Why do you even care?"

"I knew her. Karlie. We were friends. I think she thought I was the one out there that night." The woman pauses, tipping her face upward as if looking for some clue in the blue expanse of sky. "I believe I might know the person who actually killed her, and, well . . . this is the least I can do."

Her face catches the light now, no longer shadowed by the brim of her hat, and Sheri can see she is older than she'd thought, although deceptively slim-hipped, long-limbed, and slight of build. There is silver frizz amid her dark hair, and the tender skin near her gray eyes is dry and lined.

"The person who did this. It wasn't your son . . ."

"That's not your problem."

"Please," the woman says, and she hands Sheri a small card with her name, Joy Brunner, and number. "There was someone else. This letter. It's from Karlie. Read it. It might help you."

"Thank you," Sheri says, although she has no idea what she's thanking her for, and by the time she's said it, the woman is gone.

Sheri trudges up to the visitor entrance and pushes through the door to the security checkpoint. She lets them pat her down and scan her bag.

Inside, she sits in a plastic chair and waits until he shuffles out to her in his jumpsuit and shackles: her son, her sweet son. Toby.

SHE'D BEEN HAPPY when Toby got the job up at Rosemary Street Grill as a dishwasher. So much better than him just hanging around downtown all day, asking for change. And he'd found the job all by himself. It was a thing she admired about her boy—his can-do attitude. He was an adult, he'd told her. It was time for him to take care of her. She knew that before Rosemary Street Grill, Toby had picked up odd jobs here and there; she knew that at times he'd panhandled. But this was his first proper employment, even if it wasn't on the books. She remembered the first time he'd been paid, all in cash, and how he'd thrust the envelope stuffed with small bills at her. How he'd beamed.

Toby didn't have a father. That's what she told him, at least. And in a way, Sheri had come to believe this fully herself: Toby, a being she alone had devised then willed into being. She'd assembled him whole cloth from nothing but the stuff of herself. The girls had a father who was, yes, an asshole, but who existed in a concrete and knowable way. Bobby Braithwaite, with his shaggy hair and fart jokes and—after the divorce—weekend breakfast excursions with the kids to Bojangles and the flea market. You had to give Bobby credit: He'd been good to Toby, had continued to include him, upholding the deal implied by the bestowal of his last name, a thing he'd done, to his credit, unquestioningly when he and Sheri had married when Toby was only six months old. Bobby was only an asshole in the routine sort of way, like all the rest in the rogue's gallery of exes among Sheri's friends at work. He might even be counted a decent guy, by some standards. There is no animus there, not any longer. Especially not after what happened to Toby. Bobby checks in on her now and then, dropping off overbaked casseroles made by his very Baptist new wife, Cindy. Bobby can afford generosity these days. He's done well as a contractor. Fancy million-dollar places in Briar Glen with granite countertops. Any rambling he needed to do he'd already got out of his system; by all accounts, he's a good husband to Cindy.

It is better now that Sheri is used to things. It's amazing what one can grow accustomed to: her son sitting across from her in chains wearing a prison-issued jumpsuit the color of sludge. Toby is smiling—of course he's still smiling, that's his nature—but there's a dullness to his gaze, a crust of dried drool always at his mouth. He has gained weight in prison, and every so often he runs his tongue across his lips, making a rabbity sniffing gesture, a kind of tic. She's brought it up with him before, but he seemed unbothered. As with everything else, she's become used to it.

"Mama," he says, and takes her hands in his, briefly, before a guard says something.

"Toby," she exhales, realizing how the encounter outside has rattled her. It has brought to mind old questions she learned long ago to avoid because they are too painful. Innocent, guilty—he is her son. He would never wish to hurt anyone. She bars the door to any other thought.

"You sleepin' okay?" she asks, because this is the pattern of their visits, their dialogue rote, the questions and answers almost catechistic in nature.

"Doin' the best I can, Mama. Doin' just fine."

"Eatin' well?"

"Not bad, not bad."

He is still there, her boy, his eyes glassy behind the thick lenses of his glasses, the soft folds of his face and neck, the sparse, shorn, graying hair.

"Jackie and the kids send their love. Margie and her boys, too. They wanna get over here to see you when work allows."

He nods at this.

"You takin' care of yourself, Mama?" he asks.

"Oh, I am."

She could let it go on like this, their ritual exchange. The words themselves do not matter. They are mere filler. She loves him. He loves her. That is what they are saying, over and over again. They are encircled, however briefly, in a kind of warm, golden bubble, the two of them—a precious, delicate enclosure she should not disrupt until visiting time ends.

Instead, she mentions the letter.

"I met this lady," Sheri says. "She says there's proof you didn't do it."

He looks at her, removes his thick glasses and rubs his eyes, then looks again. It's strange seeing his face like that—pink and bare, naked without the glasses she's so accustomed to. He's legally blind, but his eyes as a boy were always so soulful, bright. Now there is nothing—an empty look. He might as well be wearing a mask. Is this the medicine, too? Or is it a thing he's learned in prison, this impenetrable look, a gaze of such blankness it reveals nothing?

Only once at the very beginning of this nightmare did they ever discuss it—that girl's death. It was soon after she'd found out, when the police detectives had shown up looking for him, when she'd wept and howled, and she'd pulled him back into the kitchen with her, hissing into his ear: *Were you involved?* The lack of a firm, immediate denial from him had thrown her. Plus, there was something in how he had eventually responded—a twitching of his eye, the way his gaze fell away from hers, the mumbling uncertainty to the words he spoke—that made her fearful about pressing further. It reminded her of the time he'd gotten himself in trouble earlier, looking into some young girl's window—an innocent thing, really. Puppy love. He hadn't known how it would seem. He hadn't known any better—but all the same. It might be construed as a sort of pattern, she realized. All Sheri could think about then were those little moments, which stood out to her with a sudden, terrible clarity, at Rosemary Street Grill when she'd come to pick Toby up and caught him watching that girl—Karlie. She'd had a thoroughbred's sheen to her. Her hair sleek and glossy, and her big, white teeth almost always revealed in laughter. She looked expensive—that's what Sheri had thought. She looked like a girl people had spent time and money on, a girl to whom good things would come easily. Sheri saw how Toby's eyes stayed on her. She'd known he sometimes followed her after his shifts, but she took it as a harmless thing, the way a puppy follows its owner or a schoolboy moons after a crush.

It wasn't a kind thing to admit, but a tiny part of her had felt relieved when she first heard the girl was gone. Then, as more of the horrid details came out, she felt bad for thinking that, even if it was only a tiny part of her, her worst self. Later, when the police came to talk to Toby, she felt a sickness hit her, and a plausible story—the sort of story in which the police might be interested—occurred to her. It was suddenly very easy to imagine how Toby might be involved.

When her cousin Grace over in Burlington had offered Sheri a loan, suggesting she use it to hire a private investigator to help clear Toby's name, Sheri had accepted the money but used it instead to hire a better defense attorney, someone other than the court-appointed attorney who looked a day out of law school—the more practical strategy, she'd argued at the time. Although a lot of good that had done.

She hasn't trusted herself since then to ask Toby about that poor dead girl, suggesting, perhaps, some lack of steadfastness on her part, a fidelity best trusted if only tested so far—for although he is deeply good, her child, her innocent one, Toby did grow to inhabit the body of a man, and men, as she's always known, have needs. The body will have its way. It has always seemed so unfair to her—like asking a creature of starlight and mist to inhabit a rusty, muck-filled cage. To expect Toby to live, burdened, in the form of a full-grown man—it's not right. She sees that so clearly now. Had she possessed the necessary enchantments to do so, she would have frozen him as a boy of maybe nine, ten at most. A vessel to match its contents. It would have been safer that way. None of this would have happened.

He yawns very deeply then, like a dreamer surfacing from sleep. His eyelids flutter, and his lips twitch into a very sad smile, and for a moment— just a moment—she sees him again, his old self, both foolish and wise. He opens his mouth to speak. Nearby, another visitor is kicking the vending machine and cursing, but they are still encircled in that soft bubble of golden light—almost alone. The chatter of the other visitors, even the irate vending-machine kicker, melts away. She can sense that he is about to say something profound, her sweet boy.

"Didn't do what, Mama?"

Their surroundings shift suddenly, even the quality of the light returning to an ordinary bleary fluorescence. The voices of the other inmates and their guests return in a sibilant rush, puncturing the bubble. Sheri notices a roach skitter along the baseboard in the corner of the room. The sticky floors and tables, cheap particleboard, the machines full of stale peanuts and Orange Crush—it's offensive to her. It is, in fact, a thing she's been dealing with her whole life—this lack of regard. As if she won't notice. As if it's what she, and people like her, deserve. And yet where she works—at the university, down in the health sciences building and sometimes over in the law school—she actually takes pride in her work with environmental services. It's not easy with what the students leave for her—gum and moldering sandwiches, crisp excavations from nostrils, and once, even, pee in a trash can and a bloody tampon trailing its tail like a dead mouse on the carpet, because they are nothing if not filthy, those so-called brilliant minds, the students. Graduate students, at that. She has heard the horror stories from her colleagues who work in the freshman dorms, the undergraduate library—there, they say, it is even worse. And yet she moves invisibly, remedying such filth.

She offers cleanness, correction, even though no one ever seems to offer it to her.

And here, with her son, his dreamy obliviousness to such lifelong disrespect offends her. She is isolated in her outrage.

"Kill that girl, Toby," she hisses. "What do you think?"

It's harsher than she intends, but if he is perturbed, he reveals no trace of it. Maybe it's his native equanimity. Maybe it's the medicines that have made him slurred and docile. Or maybe it's a stoicism he's learned in prison, given what he's surely faced. She's heard how it works, the alliances and allegiances, the distorted replication of family life behind bars. She can imagine how someone like him might need a protector, might be made to do things, in order to survive. Jackie always tells her to shush, not to think of this whenever she brings it up, or when she used to bring it up, way back in the beginning. She doesn't anymore—it's yet another line of thought to which she simply shuts the door.

Whatever the origin, his placidity in this moment is maddening. She is the one who is ostensibly free, and yet he, in his seeming obliviousness, has left her to suffer alone in her roiling uncertainty.

"Karlie," he whispers now, and it is a name Sheri has never said, not once, because she has hated her—even in death. She has hated her—that dead woman, that dead *girl*—for her smug, untouchable beauty, for the way she has ascended to a sort of sainthood, for the vile way she has ruined their lives. It is unforgivable, what that girl, *Karlie*, has done to them. Especially when, from all that Sheri can tell, Karlie always had, in her brief charmed life, everything.

She looks at Toby now. His eyes have misted over behind the fogged lenses of his glasses, the look on his face one she cannot recall seeing, not in some time—the longing in it apparent, even now. There are many fates, she thinks, that are worse than death.

"That's the one," Sheri says, and her voice is pinched. Their time is almost up. She can see one of the other women from the bus gathering up rosettes of crumpled tissues into her arms as if they are blown roses, pale and plentiful. Another inmate has already gestured to the guards. He stands from one of the adjacent tables with the arthritic slowness of an old man, although Sheri can see that he is young, probably not even in his midthirties.

Toby is impassive. She wants to snap her fingers, pinch him to attention. Instead, she leans in close, her voice an urgent whisper.

"Some lady says she's got evidence you didn't kill that girl."

A guard calls time. The screech of chairs being pushed back under tables, as if in audible protest, follows. Sheri looks at Toby—lovely Toby, maddening Toby, turning slowly to dust behind these prison walls—and inexplicably, he starts to laugh.

"Of course I didn't, Mama," Toby says, wiping his eyes, like it's all been a big joke, a joke that Sheri is only now starting to understand. "I could have told you that. I loved her."

His words are so matter of fact, so guileless that they must be—can only be—true.

And he rises then, joining the orderly shuffle and step of the others, being led back to their concrete cells, but Sheri does not move. There is a sick taste deep in the back of her throat—metallic and strange—and a wave of nausea that she can name only after it passes. Guilt. Guilt at the thought she's long held in the deepest part of herself but never dared name, never dared address, and then a pure, fleeting relief. How could she have let doubt whittle away her faith? To convince her of his guilt? Her son is innocent. And with that, grief pummels her once more.

The door shuts, and he is gone.

LOVE IS NOT a thing Sheri ever expected her boy to understand, although perhaps it is a meaningless word. Or, it is merely a word—a crude tool, like other words, designed to achieve an end. The softest sort of cudgel, but a cudgel nonetheless. She herself has no grasp of it. There's Bobby Braithwaite—that was something, but it wasn't love. And before that, the graduate student. Which wasn't love, either—she knows that now.

Sheri avoids thinking of the graduate student, but when she does, he remains ageless, frozen in time, with his thick, wavy brown hair that curled at his ears, his big, ungainly shoulders. The way there was almost always a splotch of ink at his shirt pocket because, as he told her, he was devoted to ink pens. He was old-fashioned, even then. It was the mid-1970s. The other male students wore darted shirts and bell-bottoms; the women, ribbed sweaters tucked tightly into skirts. But no, not her graduate student. It was like he'd stepped out of another place and time—his shirts were too large in the body and tight in the arms, like they'd been handed down from someone else. He wore stiff pants that were threadbare in the knees, tatty and brown. And yet he was beautiful.

She'd gotten the job at the university through her mother—funny how she's stayed there all these years. Back then, though, it was simply called janitorial services. She and her mother were among the few white women on staff. It wasn't considered a desirable job, not among the others in the neighborhood where they lived, even though many of them were also looking for work. But Sheri's mother was practical. *It's a job*, she'd said, *and a state job too, so don't go putting on airs*. She'd handed Sheri a mop and showed her where the broom and the rags and cleaning solutions were kept. Another woman named Marlene had conducted her through the buildings she was to work in—three of them, adjacent to one another on a quad. Two looked noble and historic, and the other like it had been dropped in from the Soviet Union. What went on inside those classrooms and offices seemed, at the time, like a grand mystery to Sheri. She and the others—women and girls, since the men were relegated to work outdoors as groundskeepers, or were called in only for specific issues as part of the maintenance crew—came in during the evenings so as to be unobtrusive.

"These brainiacs don't want you underfoot," Marlene said, but there was more to it, Marlene's face said—things she didn't have to explain, but that her eyes explained for her—and Sheri understood then that as hard as things were for her, they were harder for Marlene, for all the other women who emptied the trash and scrubbed the restroom stalls. What Marlene meant, Sheri intuited, was that the work would go better for them if they stayed unnoticed by these sons and daughters of ease and fortune.

And yet she noticed him right away—one of the few people there so late into the evening—and did not want to avoid him. The first few times she'd seen him deep in the stacks of the library. Later, he started lingering, in his office on the first floor of the adjacent building. It wasn't technically *his* office, as he later explained, but a shared graduate student office. That was why he stayed late, for the peace and quiet, he told her—although it seemed to Sheri after their first encounter that he started staying for her.

"You're captivating," he'd said to her the seventh or eighth night she'd seen him there, passing by him with her mop. He'd been sitting at his desk with one foot propped up on the table, a mountain of grim-looking books piled before him.

She blushed and looked down, but he took her free arm in his hand and studied it. She held the mop, an awkward chaperone, in her other hand. She'd gone to the lake over the weekend with her cousins but had stayed hidden in the shade, well aware of how easily she burned, and now she was overcome with shame at her pallor. Absolutely ghostly, particularly against the graduate student's hand, which was large and capable-looking and tanned.

"I'm too pale," she whispered, and it was a wonder he heard anything, her voice was so timorous and small.

"Oh, no," he whispered back. "Like meringue. Or crème fraîche."

He lifted her arm to his mouth and kissed it gently on the softest part below the divot of her elbow, the flesh so translucent-pale it glowed faintly blue. Sheri was sixteen and a half. She'd had boyfriends. But no one like this.

"I'm sorry," the graduate student said, either abashed or tremendously good at making a show of it. "I'm overstepping. I ought to know better."

"It's okay," Sheri said, even though she wasn't sure if it was okay or not, but that was what you did—you put the other person at ease, you smoothed things over.

"No." The graduate student shook his head, burying his face in his hands now. He shuddered, his entire upper body quaking, like he'd shocked himself. "You see, I grew up in a cold household. There was no touch. No human warmth."

Sheri hadn't known what to say to this unprompted confession. The man tipped his head up again toward hers—hesitant, hopeful.

"But then I left," he said. Then, as if this were all part of a lecture and she were his student: "*I found myself in a dark wood.* You know that?"

When Sheri didn't respond, he shook his head slightly, seeming to chuckle at himself.

"You're like stumbling upon a bit of light in a dark forest. It took everything for me to break away and make it here. Everything. Sometimes I'm still surprised by what I discover. I'm surprised by it all."

Sheri blushed and nodded, and even though there was a strangely rehearsed quality to his gestures, there was still something about the graduate student's voice, the words he chose, that made his speech seem like poetry.

He looked hard at her. She saw that he was older—late twenties maybe? Early thirties at most. His eyes were hazel, flecked with gold. He had long lashes. He smiled sadly at her, and it was the sadness that won her over. He was handsome without being overly so—a tiny white scar above his lip. She wanted to reach out and press her finger to it but did not.

He put his hand very gently on her waist—a reassuring touch, and warm. The mop in Sheri's hand toppled to the floor.

"Would it be crazy if I told you I think I've fallen in love with you?" the graduate student said. "I keep seeing you, and . . ."

She swallowed and nodded—eagerly, fervently, because yes, it was crazy, but she felt it, too. She'd felt it from the start.

"I'm Jacob," he'd offered.

"Sheri." She could barely speak.

He pulled her closer to him, an embrace, and it was nothing like it was with her high school boyfriends, who all seemed so young, so vague and shapeless, by comparison. She was not totally inexperienced, and yet this, this was something else.

He was holding her so close she could feel every inch of him, pulsing with want, with longing, for her and her alone. Back then Sheri had been a pretty enough girl, but she knew she wasn't a beauty. She wasn't one who caused men to stop and stare. But there, in the office with the graduate student, she'd turned extraordinary. She could feel it in how he beheld her and clung to her, the way he spoke. And yet he did not, would not, kiss her, even though she held herself so poised for it, so at the ready, that she felt herself begin to shake.

"I have to finish the fifth-floor bathrooms before shift ends or I'll get in trouble," she finally whispered, and he released his grip on her.

"I'll be here," he said. "Either here, or my usual spot in the library. Tomorrow. Waiting for you."

And she picked her mop back up and smiled at him. She thought of the stacks, all those dark groves of books looming over her.

"In the dark forest," Sheri said, and his face was like moonlight breaking through the crooked arms of the trees when he smiled.

She returned the next day. And the next. And the one after that. He was always there, waiting for her, either at his preferred table in the stacks or his office, or, sometimes, smoking a cigarette outside the building. She never left any of her work undone, but somehow learned to be faster, more efficient, so that she and the graduate student had time together in that little office.

He'd brush her hair back behind her ears, painstaking with his touch, handling her with far more care than the high school boys she'd known, like she was a rare and fragile object that might shatter in his hands. There was a reluctance to his caress, although beneath it, she could feel the fierceness of his desire. He told stories to her about growing up in Richmond with his authoritarian father and delicate, sloe-eyed mother, a former debutante and DAR member sedated into a perpetual dream state; the creak of the floorboards as he crept up to his bedroom; finding solace in stacks of books, although never the right books, never the practical tomes that would make a man of him. *Fairy stories*, his father had noted scornfully, when he even bothered to notice his son. *Fluff and puff.* They'd sent him in his tie and blazer to an elite boys' prep school, a place of braying bonhomie and hideous bathroom assaults deemed "pranks" enacted by older boys upon the younger ones, overlooked by the administration in the name of brotherhood and tradition. He'd hated it there—his childhood home, that horrid school, the slow ticking of clocks, cold walls, brittle furniture he was not allowed to touch, the shrill voices of adults who reprimanded rather than spoke. His essential solitude was so all encompassing, so pervasive, he felt it surround him like a miasma, impenetrable, it seemed. A thing no force or person could ever pierce. It was a childhood so different from her own, and yet in some fundamental way, she felt she understood.

"My sweet boy," she cooed to him, ruffling his hair, soothing him, although he was more than a decade older. Yet he elicited this from her, a softness she did not seem to possess in any other aspect of her life. He touched her with an awed hesitancy that suggested inexperience at times, and a bold confidence that belied it at others.

She believed that she was educating him. He'd told her he felt undone by her, unsure, his eyes welling up as he spoke, and so she led him gently, guiding him through what she'd learned but crudely in the back seat of a borrowed Chevrolet. All the while he spoke to her with such reverence it made her feel powerful, like this was a gift she was bestowing, her corporeal self, her very being. Their time together seemed to bring him to such a vulnerable, frenzied state, a state of such intensity that she was certain she alone could coax him to it, then, mercifully, usher him through.

In those months, she did not question that they'd end up together. Even though they only spent time together in his cluttered graduate office with its mustard-yellow couch, the dust from old book pages and dead skin cells rising softly around them, the hot, metallic smell when the radiator cut on, even though no one else in the world ever saw them together, their future seemed a certainty.

"I've been lonely for so long," the graduate student whispered into her neck. "I've been so lonely. Until I met you." Even though she knew his name—Jacob. Jacob Hendrix—she often still thought of him as *the graduate student*, his role, the space he inhabited in her mind marked by the peculiar magic of that phrase.

She held his head against her breast while he cried to her. A basic need, this simple human communion she offered him. This was the equalizing force, she thought—her age held in counterweight to something that remained so deeply innocent in him, her body rich with secrets balanced against his learning.

"I love you," he'd said, and Sheri's heart buzzed on hummingbird wings in her chest.

Later, Sheri's mother would demand to know who'd done it to her, who'd inflicted himself upon her and left her in such a state. Her mild-mannered mother yelled that she'd hunt down the man who'd forced himself upon her daughter, kill whoever had done this to her baby girl. Sheri said nothing, knowing that she'd been the one who'd led the graduate student down the road to perdition. It was *her* fault—her reckless desire, her love. Or it was no one's fault at all, but rather the will of God, one of those accidents that turn out to be a blessing. She could imagine it—how the graduate student would throw back his head and laugh when she told him of her pregnancy, happy tears gathering in the corners of his eyes.

After she'd endured her mother's tirade in loyal silence, Sheri snuck off to the graduate student's office to find him. She went in the daytime, wearing her ordinary clothes—a borrowed skirt and a little striped turtleneck sweater that she thought looked appropriate for a future professor's wife. She wanted him to see her and imagine all the things she was imagining.

But outside the building she saw him. He was with a thin young woman, dressed tidily in a tight sweater and flared jeans, and a tow-haired toddler. They were standing beneath a large tree that stood near the quad, a shaded area with benches on which students might sit and read or eat their lunch. The woman stood on her tiptoes to give the graduate student a kiss, and he received this kiss with casual familiarity. Sheri stood breathless, watching. The toddler clung to the graduate student's knees, gesturing to be lifted upward, and Sheri heard him laugh and shriek as the graduate student obliged. "Daddy," the baby yelped in delight. She saw then, even at that distance, the glint of gold on the graduate student's finger, his ring catching sunlight as he lifted the little boy up. His hands had always been bare when she'd been with him. "Daddy!" the little boy cried in glee, and the graduate student nuzzled the child fondly.

Had the earth yawned open beneath her feet and swallowed Sheri, had she combusted into millions of particles of stunned indignation right then, she would have welcomed her own dissolution. It would have come as no greater betrayal, no greater shock.

SHE SLEEPS ON the bus ride back home, clutching the letter against her chest, vaguely aware of the shadows dancing against her cheek as they travel, a pattern of warmth and cool while she dozes. *The dark forest*, she thinks, although it is a dream-thought. Toby is hers and hers only, the graduate student a figment of the past. She'd never told him about Toby. Instead, she let her mother's story become the truth—and it might as well have been, given what he'd done to her, the way he'd turned her into a fool. During the entirety of her pregnancy, Sheri's mother had insisted on dragging her to the Sunday service at her church, even as Sheri's belly grew bigger and bigger, a cautionary tale for the other girls.

But she'd walked into that church stony-eyed, fierce, staring straight ahead, breathing the stale air, and indulging her own private reveries as the preacher droned on. The worst devils are devious in their attack. With their treachery, they turn you into the agent of your own demise.

She'd asked the boss to transfer buildings. And she's stayed there ever since. She was aware when the graduate student left for a position elsewhere, then returned to the university as a professor, aware when he left again, then eventually returned in his retirement as an old man.

The bus pulls to a stop in town with a heaving lurch that throws Sheri back against her seat. She can see her daughter Jackie waiting in her Nissan in the parking lot, grimacing with impatience. Visiting hours never quite align with Jackie's time off, but she is dutiful about giving her mother a ride home. Although she's a beautiful woman still, Jackie has a hardness to her: her carefully shellacked nails, the small, hard muscles in her shoulders, her auburn hair perfectly smoothed into submission. Jackie's looks are armor—Sheri knows this, and it pains her sometimes. She envies it, too.

Sheri rises from her seat, following the shuffle of the other ladies off of the bus, none of them young, none of them truly old, yet all of them walking with the hobbling gaits of the weary or the infirm. It could age you beyond your years, being in this Mothers' Club.

Sheri's tucked the letter in her jacket pocket. Once she sees Jackie, she fears she'll have to open it. She can feel it, like the need to sneeze or sob, a thing welling up inside of her and demanding release. She wants to know what the letter says. But she also can't bear to know, can't bear the disappointment if the letter turns out to be false or useless—wild ramblings, the false insights of a self-proclaimed internet sleuth or laptop psychic.

Sheri opens the passenger door to Jackie's car and lowers herself gingerly inside.

"How is he?" Jackie asks without looking at her. It could seem like coldness, but Sheri knows deep down that Jackie loves her brother, that she is tender beneath her facade and can't bear imagining Toby there.

"He's fine," Sheri says. "Good color to his cheeks." She sighs heavily, watching Jackie's face in profile as she puts the car in reverse and eases it out of its spot.

"Some lady found me outside," Sheri says. "Gave me a note. Says there's someone else. That Toby didn't do it."

"Does she have any new evidence?"

Sheri shakes her head, unable to answer. The view ahead of them turns to a blur of asphalt and scrub pine. It feels like she's swallowed something round and globular, too big to go down. She's aware of Jackie beside her, erect as ever in her bearing, shifting slightly in the driver's seat.

Jackie jerks the car over into a BP gas station with a suddenness that rattles Sheri's skull. She stops the car and turns to her mother.

"Give it to me, Mama," Jackie says, extending one perfectly manicured hand. Obediently, Sheri reaches into her jacket pocket to retrieve the letter and hands it to Jackie.

They are silent while Jackie reads. Sheri stares out the windshield, watching two men, the younger in overalls, the older one with a belly like a sack of grain hanging over his belt, step out of a rusted green truck. Beside them, a black Mazda pulls in, and Sheri sees two girls—obviously college girls based on their clothes, the way they carry themselves, like everything around them is a source of wry interest and amusement. Jackie's brow is furrowed in concentration beside her, and Sheri's leg starts to shake.

Jackie takes a deep breath and puts the letter down gently on her lap. She swallows.

"This letter seems legit, Mama," Jackie says. "Toby can't drive, and the girl mentions someone creeping around her apartment before she died. Someone with a car."

Sheri nods, remembering the trial, the things they said about her boy, the story the prosecutor had concocted—a fantasy. And yet the longer the prosecutor had spoken—a slick man with long, tapered fingers and a sweep of chestnut hair, hard, sparkling eyes—the more she herself had come to believe him. Although the story he told, the one she started to find credible, seemed to be about a different Toby entirely, a boy she'd never known.

"That proves nothing. They said he took a bus."

"But the letter says someone else was watching her, someone with a car. And that matches something one of the witnesses said, about a car driving up right before the girl died—remember?"

"They'll say he could've taken my car."

"No," Jackie says. "It wasn't your car. You never owned a BMW."

Jackie taps the letter again.

"And what about this?" she asks. "What'd the lady say about why the girl wrote it this way? See?"

She points, and Sheri sees the specific words haphazardly underlined, the odd use of quotation marks. The *"BMW."* It's a fact she might have noticed but made nothing of—a quirk of youth, maybe.

"She didn't say. I don't imagine it means anything?"

Jackie looks at her mother hard, then shakes her head firmly, pulling out the card with the woman, Joy's, name and contact information.

"No. It's weird. I'll call her and ask. I watched that codebreaker documentary the other night, and this may be nothing, but . . . it's weird."

Sheri swallows and nods. There are too many things that make it improbable now—the fact of Toby attempting to drive in the first place, a car that wasn't her old Ford Taurus. The letter, with its odd typography.

"Okay. But this letter alone. It's not enough."

Sheri starts to weep—because the letter alone *does* prove something to her. The college girl returning to her Mazda catches sight of her through the window and winces briefly as she gets back into her own car. Jackie—stoic, practical Jackie—also starts to cry.

"The letter's not nothing," Jackie says. "It's new information. Somebody with a BMW. Watching her. We could push harder. Hire a private investigator."

"I'm sorry, baby," Sheri says, but she nods, taking her daughter's hand in hers and lifting it up, pressing it hard against her cheek, like a compress. She squeezes her daughter's hand like she could wring the bones out of it, pretending she's never faltered—that she's never once doubted, her faith constant all along.

The Weeper

Maggie's favorite online instructor claimed that it was only when she'd been attacked that she learned how strong she really was. Samantha J had fought with every ounce of her being: biting until she tasted blood, clawing off ribbons of flesh, jabbing an eyeball to brutal soup, screaming like a banshee—anything not to be dragged into her assailant's car. She'd realized that her instinct to live, her spirit, was indomitable. Luck? Sure, there's luck. But there's also grit, determination, sheer will. Back then, in her former life, Samantha J had been a law student. Now, this moment of survival is part of her origin story; she's got a long scar on her neck to show for it, which she wears proudly. Not only did Samantha J access her own inner strength, but she felt it connect with an even greater vital force—external to her and yet part of her, holy and infinite. A kind of oneness with everything. That's when she'd experienced her revelation: if she survived this, she would change her life. Get honest with herself. Follow her passion. And Samantha J would share what she'd learned with others.

"Are you, too, missing something? Do you long for something more?"

Samantha J says this through the tinny speakers of Maggie's laptop as she leads the class through a loving kindness meditation. Imagine a glowing yellow orb, Samantha J says, hot to the touch, dormant until your time of need. This is your inner strength. Your love. Let your love flow forth unto the world.

Maggie, eyes closed, knees stiff, worries she will not know how. This strength—when the time comes, how can she be sure she will find it? Maggie breathes, in and out, deliberate. She wishes for such love and knowing.

This morning, the slow, watery light falling through the window, Maggie allows herself to return gently. When she opens her eyes, there is Samantha J, framed in the little window of her laptop screen, all sinewy golden limbs and tousled, honey-colored hair. Samantha J beams at Maggie; she is beaming at everyone, all the invisible others who are fellow devotees: *#samanthajsquad #bodsquad #bodyandmind #sjmindfulnesschallenge #sjmindfulmoms.* Samantha J's voice is like melted butter. Maggie is cross-legged on the hardwood floor in the near-empty bedroom of the new house. She often wishes she could curl up against Samantha J, letting all her doubts dissolve against the beautiful, sleek certainty of Samantha J's honey-butter person, her comforting proverbs.

"And remember, you woke up this morning! Let's make today count!"

The little window clicks shut and Samantha J is gone. Maggie's open email fills the screen now, the pile of unread messages amassing accusingly.

Outside the bedroom, Maggie can hear the sounds of the two boys. They're in the kitchen, fussing over something: a clatter of silverware, the sound of something liquid sloshing to the floor followed by the crack of ceramic shattering. They are adolescents, these boys, twelve and nearly sixteen. Her soon-to-be stepsons. She will forge an alliance; she must. But the boys still eye her coolly—an interloper. A rival. Maggie cannot bear to be disliked; it gnaws at her.

She rises from the ground with a groan. *The body* does *know*, she thinks. At least, she'd known from the moment she'd taken a sip of her favorite LaCroix, pamplemousse, and suddenly been able to taste, instead of the crisp, bubbling grapefruit, the intrusion of a hundred new flavors: aluminum notes from the can, traces of oil left by human fingers, the very molecules of whatever chemical blend of flavoring had been used. It was like licking a cold metal sink touched by a thousand different hands. Her nose turned canine. The aromatic world sharpened, multiplied twentyfold in its complexity. The air held crowded multitudes of odor when she sniffed. A wolf lived inside her, its teeth sharp as blades, ready to rip out her entrails with a hunger so fierce it was nausea. She must eat or die, the wolf whispered, tearing at the pink lining of her stomach with its jaws. She needed a hunk of bread so desperately, so urgently, it felt like revulsion. The wolf, with its biological imperatives, ruled. Her mouth filled with saliva and she wanted to retch.

She was pregnant.

She told John before she'd even taken a test. A terror akin to joy coursed through her and had hardly relented since. The pregnancy granted legitimacy to her position, an acceleration of status that seemed almost to rewrite where she and John had started things (as two grown adults in business attire fumbling over each other in an Olive Garden parking lot after hours, inauspicious yet undeniably titillating). Did she witness relief in his face at the news? Comfort at the thought of such an impending obligation? It may be that he loves her. It may also be that he is a man who cannot abide being alone, for whom an affair is ultimately too taxing, whose true preferences align with old-fashioned respectability.

She is *bigly pregnant* now, *big-league pregnant!*—whichever one, who could say?! Maggie adopted these terms in a spirit of bitter irony and now cannot let go. She's a connoisseur of such things: assholery on Twitter, memes, neologisms spread by memes, assholery spread by memes, memes spread by assholery, Twitter feuds, all the ludicrous excesses of social media under the current regime. John says it's because she's younger, a native of the internet; Maggie says it's because she prefers laughing sidelong at distractions over facing doom head-on. She likes to see the comic element in her villains whenever possible—a questionable strategy, according to John, but one that has allowed her to continue loving her mother and other relatives back in her hometown. *Relatable*, John says to her. *You're so polished, but you're still so relatable.* Which is, perhaps, a kind of criticism, when Maggie stops to think about it. Samantha J is not relatable, but she is enviable, admirable, a supreme act of self-creation. And John's ex-wife, Joy, is not relatable—not in the slightest.

"Boys!" she calls now. Rising heavily, she grasps the corner of the bed. It is the one piece of furniture they have so far. There are other items on order. John loves her; he wants to start fresh, he says. A new love, a new house, a new start! The truth, Maggie knows, is that John is terrified of Joy and does not want to ask her for any of their old furniture. Maggie understands. She has met Joy several times herself—tall, imperious, and gray-eyed like a goddess, with the long, lean muscles of someone with no appetite for fun and a tolerance for long stretches at a rowing machine. Someone who reads the *New Yorker* and has well-argued opinions. The impossibility of Joy's approval feels to Maggie like a shard of glass in her side, a desire indistinguishable from hatred.

"Boys?" she calls again, more hesitant, making her way down the long hall to the kitchen. John will already be at the credit union, working. She has a showing to get to.

When she enters the kitchen, Ethan and Sean look up at her in the way of raccoons caught rummaging at night. A package of cookies sits open on the counter, a carton of milk warming outside the fridge, a knife sticky with strawberry jam in the sink. The boys say nothing at first. Beady-eyed spies for their mother, Maggie thinks. They'll grow closer to her with time, John promises. And the baby. The baby!

"How's Piglet?" Ethan, the younger boy, finally says.

"Yeah, Piglet's growing," Sean adds, with a nod toward Maggie's torso, and she flushes, clutching her belly, which is almost certainly no bigger than yesterday. She feels acutely conscious of her body before them, her full breasts in the thin tank top she wears, aware that these boys, these children, are teenagers tumid with hormones—well, one's a teenager and the other almost. *Piglet* is their name for the new baby, originating not long after the time Ethan dissected a fetal pig in class. It's a fond name, John insists, because bestowing a nickname, any nickname, is an act of fondness. John is pleased by it. *Piglet*. He uses it, too—innocently—and Maggie must smile, act unaware that they are all, by logical extension, calling her a sow.

Ethan and Sean are *advanced*. Intellectually, that is, if not emotionally. Scary smart, Maggie thinks, although perhaps this is only her assessment. She grew up in a country town where the children were only ordinary smart, at best. She lives now in a university town full of professors and doctors at the academic medical center so it's to be expected that their children are often in possession of alarming intelligence. Worse though, Ethan possesses subtlety. He's learned to hide behind the fact he is only twelve. Puberty has not yet caught up with him—skinny chest, spindly, hairless arms. Maggie must play along, pretending to believe he is still naive as to the impact of what he says. By contrast, Sean, the older boy, holds himself with great seriousness, at a remove, caught up, certainly, in his own adolescent dramas. Recently, something about a leaked video, an online argument in which the boys' mother was involved (Joy! Smooth and imperturbable Joy! Although John has told her otherwise, and lately, seeing how frazzled Joy has appeared, haggard and wild-eyed, Maggie has started to believe him), and a breakup with the girl who is a grade above Sean, a girl who used to appraise Maggie coolly, devastatingly, with the knowing eyes of an adult. Sean is distraught, John has told Maggie, but around her, he is nothing but aloof, contained.

"Piglet's enormous! Must have been those enchiladas your dad made last night!" Maggie leans back, thrusting her belly out farther, cackling amiably. Like a clown. This is what she's been reduced to, in her desperation to win over these boys. A clownification of self. Embracing her role as the butt of every joke. The boys seem to delight in her humiliation, all the while liking her no better for it. John insists otherwise. *They wouldn't tease if they weren't growing close with you*, he claims. *That's why they do it—they'd only tease someone they really like.* She does not ask if they tease their own mother in such a manner. She's witnessed how they behave with Joy. She knows the answer. Joy is untouchable in her authority.

"It's gonna be pretty annoying if Piglet cries all the time," Sean observes mildly, as if commenting on a change in the weather.

"Piglet the pest. Piglet the party pooper," Ethan adds.

Maggie smiles, feeling how tight her cheeks are, willing the muscles to hold in position. She must appear unfazed, even delighted, by the wry comments of precocious children. This is the way of things now, at least when they are there, these cool-eyed emissaries of their ice-queen mother—she is rendered a buffoon, fit only for mockery, here in her own home.

There's a turbulent emptiness in her stomach. She needs to eat.

"Have you guys heard about the Weeper?" she asks, letting the question curl up deliciously but keeping her voice casual. She's reminded of being a teenaged babysitter, how she couldn't help but tell the children stories they were too young for. She knew that it was a bad idea, but it was hard to resist the power she possessed, her eyes watering as she held the children in her thrall, recounting tales of men with hooks for arms and demented callers tormenting babysitters from inside the house. Each time, she ended up scaring herself—the sounds of the quiet house magnified in menace once the children were safely tucked in bed. A dripping sink, the tick of a grandfather clock, an opossum scuttling across the back deck.

"No," Ethan says. "Who's that?"

They are staring at her, waiting for more. She notices now that they aren't properly dressed. There's a red smear of jam at the corner of Ethan's mouth, and he has an atrocious case of bedhead—but let him go to school like that! Maggie thinks. Let them both arrive late! This will reflect badly not on Maggie, but on their mother. This is the one perk of her position, the sort of guerilla warfare she could choose to wage.

"Well, it used to be just an urban legend," Maggie says. "Back when I was growing up, people who claimed to see the Weeper described this shadowy figure. He'd appear late at night, if you were alone. You'd sense him before you could make him out, and then you'd hear the sound of this horrible weeping. Like the worst sound you've ever heard. The most horrible sound in the world, people said."

"And then what?" Ethan asks.

"Something terrible would happen, I think," Maggie says. "Unless you could prevent it somehow. The Weeper was kind of a bad omen, I guess."

Sean looks up from his phone—an appraising look, deciding whether she's worthy of his time and attention, Maggie thinks.

"I heard about this at school," Sean says. "The Weeper's back. Or someone's out there pretending to be the Weeper."

Maggie nods at him.

"That's right. People in my office have been talking about the Weeper a lot because several real estate agents have been targeted. He looks for people who are alone. Say an agent goes to set up an open house, or to check up on a listing and gets a weird feeling, like another person is there, too, watching, but when she looks around, there's no one. No one else should be there yet. She tells herself it's just nerves . . . so she keeps doing whatever she's doing, tidying up, looking around"—Maggie looks at the boys, leaning forward a little so she can speak softly, creepily to them—"and then, there he is. Dressed all in black, wearing a mask."

Maggie inhales. Piglet has left her breathless. Ethan's eyes have grown big, and Sean has made himself studiously casual, seemingly more interested in the ingredients list on the box of cereal, but she can tell they are rapt. In their faces she can see not only hints of their sharp-faced mother, but also of John—kind, curious John. Fretful, serious John.

"What's he do next?" Ethan whispers.

"He makes you weep, dummy," Sean says, but his voice lacks confidence. He frowns into the box of cereal, as if one of the ingredients has offended him, putting it down. "Right, Maggie?"

Maggie shrugs.

"I'd definitely weep," she says, leaning forward again, speaking in a hush. "If someone grabbed me from behind and—" Here, she makes a menacing gesture, her hands two pincers.

Ethan flinches, and a dark look passes quickly over Sean's face before he recovers his look of perfect neutrality. She has not told them the part of the story that bothers her most: It is the Weeper who weeps. People have speculated that it must be a fetish. Maggie's colleague Robin knows another agent who knows someone else who claimed to have details. Maggie shivered when she heard how he does it: A figure approaching silently from behind, holding you, covering your eyes, his breath hot at your ear. There were things that he whispers, she's heard. Bad things. Sad and terrible things. Confessions worse than threats.

"That's all?" Ethan asks.

"Some people say they think he's followed them afterward. And he's taken cash from people's bags."

"That's the dumbest story I've ever heard," Ethan announces.

"Yeah. It's not very scary," Sean adds, but he speaks quietly. Thoughtful.

Maggie feels herself stiffen. She's been skittish lately—a result of the pregnancy maybe, or these stories of the Weeper, the way that Joy looks at her whenever she picks the boys up, her lips pressed into a hard line. She's felt haunted—by something, or someone—in the beautiful new home she's making with John. John, the house, the baby: It's all a dream she'd stopped allowing herself years ago for fear it would never arrive, yet here it is. And now some jealous entity wants to snatch it from her. She's sensed eyes watching her through the kitchen window at night. The picture windows in their living room feel far too revealing, as if every evening she's performing a dumb show for a stranger hidden somewhere in the darkness outside.

"Well," she says. "Your dad's worried. He wants me to be careful."

"Be careful."

"Don't let the Weeper get you."

"Let's get you boys to school."

Ethan looks at her with all the derision a twelve-year-old can muster.

"Don't you even check my mom's Google calendar? It's a teacher workday."

"Your mom is so organized," Maggie says, although she knows it's John who manages the family calendar. It's a trick she's learned from Samantha J: When you feel yourself brimming with irritation, focus on something you can honestly appreciate in the other person and say that instead.

THE BOYS HAVING been successfully managed (a morning of video games for Ethan, followed by a lunchtime playdate for which he'll be picked up by the other child's mom, all arranged in advance by John; Sean, left on his own to complete homework and whatever else fifteen-year-olds with phones and Wi-Fi did these days), Maggie departs for her morning. Inside the plush leather interior of her Acura (all paid off, thank you very much, long before she met John), she feels comfortable again, at ease. Sure of herself.

She is a good real estate agent. It's a competitive market, but she does well, which appeases her nagging sense of doubt, especially here, in this land of advanced degrees and biotech startups. She is a country girl by birth and upbringing. It's taken years of studied awareness to shave off traces of her drawl. A little bit Southern is okay; this connotes warmth, gentility, mint juleps. Too much Southern, though, and suddenly you're conjuring squirrel meat, Confederate flags, and hookworm. Maggie's native accent is pure squirrel meat, but she's learned to dial it closer to debutante.

Easing onto the ramp to the highway south, she wonders about Marla Cherry, a public health researcher, recently divorced but with a generous settlement from her ex-husband, along with two small children, hoping to purchase one of the new builds in Briar Glen. The house is almost finished other than a few minor things, like the wiring and lights, which are being completed today by the electrician. Briar Glen is one of the more popular neighborhoods Maggie serves, perfect for families. There's a neighborhood clubhouse and swimming pool, plentiful trails, and because it's over the county line, the taxes are better.

Maggie's phone dings and she glances down. Robin, her colleague, confirming her schedule. She and her officemates have adopted a system of extra safety measures and check-ins with one another. Daylight meetings, and only at times when there will be others on-site, along with a careful system of notifying one another where they will be and when. If any aspect of a client meeting seems odd, or if the property in question is remote or isolated, they'll team up.

Today, though, the sky's the innocuous bright blue of late autumn, and there are families eating at outdoor tables at one of the little cafés near Briar Glen. A cluster of children walk along one of the paths behind a father bicycling with his young son. The extra precaution seems unnecessary, even laughable—which is exactly the reaction Maggie's mother had when she mentioned the Weeper to her.

"Oh, baby," Maggie's mother said over the phone. She paused to exhale because she was smoking, always smoking, then laughed a hoarse laugh. "That's not much of a story, now, is it? I've heard *much* worse."

"No, Mom," Maggie explained patiently. "You don't understand. Someone is *hiding*, waiting for people to show up alone, in these isolated spots. Then he rushes you from behind and grabs you and covers your eyes—"

"Does he hurt you?" Maggie's mother finished. "Rape you? Try to kill you?"

"No. I mean, I don't think so. But that's not the *point*, Mom," Maggie answered. "He holds you and *weeps*. He weeps right into your ear, and you can't move with all his weight pressing against you. You can't see. You can't escape his grasp. Who's to say what else he might do?"

She shivered reflexively. This is, to Maggie, the most upsetting part—a strange and shaming detail, for some reason, something so weird and humiliating about it. This stranger, holding you close, with such terrible intimacy, to weep. Weeping hard, his face so close to yours, his whole body pressing against you so that you feel his every shudder, smell his scent: men's cologne and stout beer, an underlayer like wild onions, not entirely unpleasant, or so Maggie's heard. A strange sort of violation. Robin told her that her friend Kathy told her that Susanna Beam over with Fonville Morisey felt her whole face grow wet under his rough palms, saturated with those tears. When he'd finally released her and fled, she'd been too scared to move—standing there with her eyes squeezed shut, frozen. No one had actually gotten a visual ID on the guy, but Maggie could picture him in her mind's eye: faceless, masked, dressed like an old-fashioned cat burglar.

Her mother laughed.

"Honey, if that's the worst of it, I'd spend my worries elsewhere. Lord. You don't know the weirdos I've run into over the years, and I kept going. Didn't let none of them bother me. Remember that man who kept stealing our mail? Or our neighbor on Laurel Ave. who kept showing up everywhere we went, eyeing me like a shark and claiming it was always just a coincidence? And all those phone calls?"

"Those were telemarketers, Mom," Maggie said softly. "But this is true. It's happening. Right here. I know from friends of friends."

Her mother sighed over the phone, pointedly ignoring her.

"That poor soul. He sounds off, sure. Like Lenny. Remember Cousin Lenny? But I think you're gonna be okay," Maggie's mother said. "You just keep visualizing success. I'm so proud of you, honey. I keep sending prayers up."

And this was the infuriating simplicity of Maggie's mother, a woman with little formal education, a smoker's laugh, and a deep affection for *The 700 Club*. A woman who has been alternatingly too trusting and too suspicious, sending checks from her meager disability to televangelists, but changing the locks whenever she thought she was being followed around Kmart—a woman Maggie has spent her whole life loving but trying not to become. Maggie's mother, who still trusts that if you believe in the abundant life, it will manifest—and so what if it hadn't come true for Maggie's mother herself, because *Maggie* had been blessed! And Maggie's mother believes her efforts played no small part in that. It is an act of love, Maggie knows. And yet she still invests every effort into shaping herself into her mother's opposite.

Maggie pulls into the nearly finished house at the far end of Oak Street. Soon, there won't be any more space in Briar Glen. There will be more new developments farther out, more planned communities. The scope of Maggie's territory is spreading ever outward, amoeba-like, into what used to be sleepy small towns, now absorbed into the greater urban area.

Fifty-Three Oak Street sits at the end of the cul-de-sac, a lovely, spacious brick colonial. There's a battered white truck parked in the drive—not the sort of car Maggie imagines a mother of two children, someone looking to buy a house in Briar Glen, would drive. It must be the electrician's.

She maneuvers herself out of the driver's seat. Piglet turns inside her. Piglet. Now she can't help but call the baby that, too. People raised their eyes at first because yes, John is more than a decade older—a well-known and well-loved appraiser that everyone in Maggie's office uses. But Maggie herself is twenty-eight, hardly a child bride! She's a self-made woman, besides—not some hapless trophy wife.

Her pregnancy was admittedly unexpected. She wanted a baby, yes, because it seemed like a thing one did, or rather, a thing one might eventually regret not doing. But she resisted relinquishing her body to another creature. She'd seen the other women in the gym who'd had babies, and how even the fittest of them still bore the traces of pregnancy long afterward, their belly buttons no longer cute indentations but forever turned into tiny, puckered frowns. But it wasn't simply that; motherhood seemed to alter you irrevocably in other less immediately obvious ways. There was the harrowing exhaustion of it, an acknowledgment of your own diminishing role in the world, your unavoidable decline.

Even more than a baby, she'd wanted constancy. Someone who cared where she was, if she'd eaten something besides cereal for dinner, if she was sad or happy. The baby, the mere notion of the baby, brought her such a person in the form of John. The baby made her matter, her fate now truly important to someone other than herself and her mother.

At the door, Maggie presses the combination on the lockbox and enters. She can smell wood shavings and fresh paint. Her footsteps echo in the emptiness. It's a grand house, or it will be, with all the requisite trimmings: granite countertops, modern light fixtures, stainless-steel appliances. She's learned how every detail is important, how it all comes together to create a fantasy of what a life there will surely be. This is Maggie's gift—it's in painting a vision, sharing it, in believing it herself. Perhaps it's emerged from growing up with a taste for something more. As a little girl, she checked out lots of books from the library, studied television shows in which smiling middle-class families lived in clean, well-lit houses. *Champagne taste on a beer budget*, her mother said. But then her mother had also believed in Maggie, had lifted her up, calling in to those tanned, handsome television preachers, sharing the story of Maggie's poor daddy and his accident at the factory, a tragedy she spun as a tale of inspiration—her brave daughter! She would overcome; the Lord would bless her with success! And it was with the settlement from her father's employers that Maggie was able to go to school at State, where she joined a sorority and learned to cultivate a look she associated with fancy girls who grew up in Charlotte or Raleigh, learned to erase almost every trace of who she previously was.

"Hello," Maggie calls out to the electrician.

There is no answer. Maggie walks slowly through the empty foyer, to the open kitchen and living room. There are French doors at the back, leading to a large patio. The backyard is big enough for a pool. She reminds herself of the square footage, the comps, then checks her phone again. Nothing. She doesn't like to hound her clients, but maybe she'll give Marla five more minutes before she checks to see if she's lost. She walks to the French doors and gazes out to the patch of woods behind the neighborhood. There are more trails back there and a picturesque little creek.

"Hello," she calls again.

A clatter from the laundry room startles her—the sound of something hitting the floor with a thud. Maggie feels a jolt in her spine, presses herself back against the door, ready to turn the handle and bolt. She knows she is overinterpreting everything, but she cannot help it. The heavy tread of footsteps follows, someone large and male, coming toward her.

A man stands in the empty room looking at Maggie. The electrician. He is neither old nor young, neither fat nor thin. His face is nondescript, shadowed by the low-pulled brim of a baseball cap. He is dressed in black arc-flash coveralls. The way he stands there, struck by her, watchful, makes her think she has surprised him. Perhaps he forgot there was a showing. She is relieved not to be alone; rather, she *should* be relieved.

"I'm Maggie Ryland," she says a little breathlessly. "The real estate agent. You must be the electrician."

The man says nothing, but it's an amiable, awkward silence—the silence, perhaps, of someone shy who has been taken by another party unawares.

"Sorry to sneak up on you," she says. "I said hello a couple times when I came in."

"I had headphones on," the man says flatly.

There's a pounding in her head, and she can't quite convince herself to extend her hand for a handshake.

"You're pregnant," the man observes.

"I am," Maggie says, laughing slightly. "Jesus. I'm also a nervous wreck. I'm glad you're out here working today. I've got all these stories about the Weeper on my mind. I keep freaking myself out."

The man says nothing at first. Although his eyes are obscured by the brim of the hat, she can tell he is studying her.

"You scared of him?"

Maggie laughs again—nervous, fake laughter. He is odd, the electrician, but his company has to be better than being alone.

"Obviously I'm scared. It's creepy. Don't you think?"

The man appears to think for a moment, then shrugs.

"People need to do certain things, I guess."

"But it's a horrible thing to do to someone," Maggie says. Her mouth, she notices, has gone dry.

Again, the man seems to assess this, tipping his head down so that his face is fully obscured by the brim of the hat. He cracks the knuckles in each hand, one by one, very slowly.

"I don't think he'd bother a poor pregnant lady," the man says finally. "People have no decency these days. But they ought to."

"You've got that right," Maggie offers weakly.

Her phone dings. The tightness in her chest has returned and there are a swift series of recalculations occurring in her brain—which she dismisses. This poor, socially awkward man means well. She's just spooked.

"That must be my client," she says, almost apologetically. "She's here. I'll let you get back to work."

"I'll see you around," the man says, with perfect neutrality. He ambles away slowly.

At the door, Maggie finds a fortysomething woman standing there. Marla Cherry. The atmosphere in the house has shifted again. The day is sunny. Maggie feels silly. Her relief buoys her as she leads Marla Cherry through the house: the kitchen, the upstairs bedrooms, the living room and den.

"And here we have the laundry room," Maggie says, walking backward as she leads Marla along. "Which is spacious and connects to the three-car garage. I believe we've got an electrician working here today as well, so we won't get in his way."

She turns to see a young blond man in overalls. He looks up at them and smiles. His T-shirt, Maggie notices, reads G&B ELECTRICIANS.

"Oh, I must have run into your colleague earlier," Maggie says.

"Only me out here today," the young man says, still smiling. "Must've been somebody else."

MAGGIE'S OTHER APPOINTMENT that day is with the owners of one of the large apartment complexes near the university, 253 Arendale Road. Alissa, the commercial real estate agent, would normally handle this, but she is not quite ready to return from her maternity leave. Maggie has been helping cover. John has encouraged her to use this as a moment to pivot entirely.

That's where the real money's at, babe, he said the other evening, massaging her swollen feet while Piglet turned at awkward angles inside her. *Babe.* It was when he called her that she could see herself as merely one in a series of possible women—interchangeable companions, pleasant broodmares, each indistinct from the next. Her feet in John's hands looked lumpy, common—like her mother's and her mother's sisters. Mountain women, ornery and solid, built for trudging up hillsides and birthing ten-pound infants. Her peasant feet betray her. She looked away.

The Arendale Road complex is an older one, one that has existed in various iterations, under several management companies, servicing the housing needs of raucous undergrads, for decades. Maggie knows it well, but pulling into the parking lot, she is struck by how shabby and run-down it looks up close. Each unit opens directly outside to exterior corridors and stairs, like an old-style motel. There is a forlorn-looking swimming pool surrounded by a fence in the center of the complex. The pool in obvious disrepair only cheapens the place further.

At the office, there's a note on the door from the owners, explaining they've had a break-in and are filing a report. The owners suggest Maggie walk down and find them at wing C, which sits on a slope that overlooks a park below.

Maggie passes a few residents as she walks through the lot, but it's mostly quiet. It's midafternoon, so she figures many students are still on campus. Although sunny, it's cool out, and she pulls her oversize sweater close around her. The encounter with the man earlier in Briar Glen has unsettled her, but she reassures herself that he must have been another contractor. She is simply reading something sinister into everything.

As she rounds a bank of parked cars, she sees that wing C is clearly under renovation. There are commercial dumpsters and piles of pulled carpet outside. It's even quieter now, eerily so. The park that Maggie can see down the hill is unpopulated. There is a wave of something, like cold air from a cavern. Sadness. It envelops her.

Maggie makes her way around the perimeter of the building, dodging empty soda cans and balled up fast-food wrappers presumably left by the contractors. No one. There is no one here. But she feels it—a sudden awareness. Her breath catches, thinking of the strange way the man in Briar Glen looked at her earlier, of all those times at home in the evening when she'd felt something similar—eyes on her, watching from outside while she put plates into the dishwasher or wiped the counter.

Trust the body's wisdom, she tells herself, but remember that paranoia is simply another form of self-obsession. Not everything revolves around her. The world does not hold its breath, awaiting her next move with either joyful expectation or animosity. She's a minor piece in the grand scheme of things, and there's peace in accepting that. But she shouldn't be stupid—if she's cued that something's off, she ought to pay attention. It's a balance. Samantha J had offered this as an answer once in an interview Maggie read. She too must neither over- nor underreact. Maggie breathes in and out, very slowly, a meditative breath.

And then she hears the weeping.

She freezes. The weeping is low in volume but anguished. Like the sound of a wounded animal. Surely whoever it is has heard her approaching through the leaves. But no, the person keeps crying. She walks a bit closer, and there, sitting on the walkway outside one of the units is a kid, face pressed to knees, weeping. The kid is slight of build, but tall, lanky—a teenager, maybe, or a very young college student; Maggie cannot yet say whether it is a boy or girl.

She steps closer. Although she cannot see the kid's face in full, Maggie can see a profile—a sharp nose and chin that reads as feminine to her. Maggie feels certain now it is a girl. She feels a twinge of something—a memory, one she's nearly forgotten, when she herself was maybe fourteen, waiting outside the school for her mother to pick her up after all the other kids had left. It was cold out. She was crying, too. It wasn't long after the accident with her father. It was like she'd been tainted by it—his death—and her classmates seemed afraid of her. Her mother was hardly leaving her bedroom at that point. Maggie had felt so alone.

"Hey," Maggie calls out, but her voice is too tentative. The kid doesn't hear her, just sobs with such a ragged sadness that Maggie wants to offer something—a gentle touch on the shoulder perhaps, a glass of water.

"Hey," Maggie says again to the girl, stepping closer now. She puts her hand on the girl's shoulder and kneels down. "You okay?"

The girl sniffles, her small shoulders hunched forward, and Maggie prepares to bestow the small comfort for which she herself once thirsted. The girl lifts her head and turns to look at Maggie.

The girl is not a girl. Not a kid at all. Her face is withered and old, the flesh hanging loosely. Her clothes are shabby, shapeless. She looks at Maggie full-on, and the unexpectedness of it takes Maggie's breath away.

"Go away," she says. It's a ragged voice, the voice of someone who has seen many battered decades.

Maggie is already backing away. Horrified at her own horror. Desperate and ashamed. The yellow orb of her own inner strength is unsummonable; she is nothing but wind whooshing through emptiness inside.

Maggie flees. She runs faster than she thinks she's ever managed to run, even prepregnancy. She runs all the way back to her car, panting, and drives home.

Later, when the owners of the complex text and call to find out where she is, she simply doesn't respond.

BY THE TIME John gets back home, it's been dark for hours—the early, deep dark of the approaching solstice. Maggie has been in bed, meditating. Or, at least, she started off trying to meditate, letting the sound of Samantha J's smooth voice wash over her until she fell asleep. It's a harried sleep, marked by shadows leaning over her, the sound of harsh weeping at her ear.

"Maggie? You okay?"

It's John. He is sitting on the side of the bed, his hands on her shoulders.

"Hey, I got a call from your office. Your client called. They were worried."

She manages to sit up. John rises from the bed and hits the light switch. She blinks.

"I was sleeping," she says. A partial truth.

"I see that."

"I didn't feel well," Maggie says.

"I'll text Roy and let him know," John says, rubbing his temple. He looks old to her in this sudden, garish light—and tired. "That Arendale Road complex is a piece of shit anyway."

"I should get dinner going," Maggie says. There is a crust of dried saliva at her mouth. She feels strangely disoriented, almost hungover. The day, the afternoon, feel like a strange dream.

"Relax," John says. "Sean ordered pizza."

She rises to follow him out to the kitchen. There, the boys sit at the table, chattering happily. Compared to the darkness outside, the kitchen is aglow with warmth and light. It is the kind of family scene that Maggie might have only dreamed of as a girl in the cramped apartment she shared with her mother, the blackout curtains drawn, air stale with smoke, the television always on. Ethan looks up midbite and smiles at her—a rare and bright thing, like a winter bird appearing. Sean has already finished his meal, and when he takes his plate over to the sink, he returns with a new plate and a fresh slice of pizza, offering it to Maggie before he retreats to his adolescent burrow, his books, his laptop, his text threads with his friends. Maggie accepts the plate of pizza from him with undue pleasure—such a simple gesture. She could weep herself at this small act, from gratitude.

It's all filled with promise. She can see that now.

I am so lucky, Maggie thinks, and then it occurs to her that this is exactly the sort of reflective moment of appreciation that Samantha J would want her to have, and she thinks it again. Her place is not so uncertain as it often feels. She is a legitimate presence here, with her loved ones, in her home. She must savor this.

"You have a good day, Ethan?" Maggie asks, and the boy nods politely. It's moments like these that make it all seem possible—a future in which the boys like her and they all get along, in which they are a family.

They sit with her, John and Ethan, while she finishes her pizza, and Ethan recounts the small dramas of his day. John smiles at her across the table—the smile of teammates, a smile of solidarity.

When she's finished, Maggie carries her plate to the sink. She rinses the dirty bowls left over from breakfast to put everything into the dishwasher. It's when she straightens that the sight outside the kitchen window catches her eye.

It's Joy standing there.

This is hard to believe, especially after what happened mere weeks before. Joy had appeared outside their window just like this, and then, what? She'd had a fit of some sort? A seizure? John had taken Joy to the emergency room at Maggie's insistence. No matter how strained their relationship, Maggie wasn't about to let John's ex, the mother of his children, die in their front yard. Although a part of her wondered if it was all for show. Joy seemed sheepish, reluctant to go to the ER—so much so that Maggie felt certain that episode would be the end of it. But no, here she is again. Joy, the money-grubber. Vindictive Joy, who cannot let John go; Joy, who wants to drag them all down with her into her sorrow. She steps into the radius of light from one of the streetlamps and the contours of her face show more clearly, as if she's been spotlighted to begin some performance.

Maggie feels a wave of understanding pass through her—all the nights that she's felt herself being watched by someone—along with pity. It has been Joy all along. Every single time Maggie's had that unsettled feeling, the feeling of being watched. Gray-eyed, imperious Joy, poised Joy, with her intellect and her advanced degrees, all her noble talk about the women's health nonprofit where she works. All this time Maggie has feared her, has wanted her approval—and now she sees that Joy is no different from any of the rest of them. Sadder, maybe. More alone. Even in her well-tailored clothes, her stylish boots.

"Ethan, buddy, if you've finished up with your pizza, I want you to go ahead and put the trash out at the curb. Okay, kid?" John says.

Maggie turns toward Ethan and feels another twinge. She could let this happen, let Ethan find his mother there—cold and lonely. Pathetic. No longer the brisk, capable woman he's accustomed to. Maybe this is even the natural moment for such a rupture. He will pull away soon anyway, enter puberty, turn surly toward Joy. Perhaps this will be how she steps in—the natural entry point for a younger, cooler adult in his life, quasi-maternal, yet not.

Ethan groans, rising and tucking his chair back at the table. Maggie looks back out the window; there is something about Joy's face. Is she crying? Maggie can't be certain from this distance, but she knows now: She can't let Ethan see her. He is too young. She must allow him a bit longer before he faces such inevitable disappointment.

"I'll go," she says eagerly.

John scoffs. "You're pregnant," he says. "Besides, this is Ethan's chore. Don't let him wriggle out so easily."

"I can still push a trash can," she counters. "Plus, I'm really stiff from the nap. Honestly, it'd do me good."

Ethan glances at her gratefully, and she walks out the side door to where their trash can sits. She allows herself to be noisy, hefting it to an angle, letting it clunk. She wants to give Joy plenty of warning, to allow her to avoid being confronted—but as Maggie pushes the trash can down the long drive, it seems like Joy has been immobilized. She stands in the circle of light as if she's frozen.

Maggie says nothing as she approaches, but she continues to let the trash can rumble along, making as much noise as she can, like she's warding off a bear.

Joy still doesn't move. She's as erect as a soldier at attention, as if waiting to receive Maggie. She's holding something—a full canvas bag, bulky and soft.

It's then that Maggie sees the outline of another figure, standing farther behind Joy, watching her from a cluster of trees at the edge of the property.

He stands there, cloaked in darkness, scythe-less, but otherwise like an old-fashioned image of the grim reaper. She knows it is the man she encountered earlier at Briar Glen. She knows it with such surety it's like her bones have been irradiated. She is lit from within, buzzing with energy. She blinks, and he's obscured again by shadow. There is a weeping sound, only Maggie cannot say whether it's him, or Joy, or a guttural sound rising from her own throat.

"I've been going through some old stuff," Joy says without any greeting or preamble. She seems unaware of the shadows that swirl behind her. "Clearing things out. I found some things. In case you could use them."

Her words are practiced, matter of fact, as if this is a speech she has prepared and rehearsed. She must register some wariness on Maggie's part because Joy's tone shifts.

"Although maybe I shouldn't have come up like this . . . Not after last time. I should have called first. I wasn't thinking," she adds, her hand moving up to her mouth, covering it. An automatic gesture. She's prattling in a way that reveals that she is nervous. Behind her, the darkness seems to contort and deepen.

"Joy," Maggie whispers, stepping closer. "Shhhh. Behind you."

She puts her hand onto Joy's shoulder, gently, and feels her flinch. Maggie pauses, listening for it: that nocturnal figure in the foliage, his horrible sound. The Weeper. A sound of old grievances, a warning. A lonely moan. A vague shape flickering in the bright and tender dark.

"Maggie?" Joy says softly. "I don't think there's anyone there."

Maggie blinks. She feels a little light-headed. The shadows have shifted again. She's wondered for a while if Joy is okay. But now she realizes Joy must be wondering the same about her. Joy looks different, too, particularly compared to their encounter a few weeks prior. Better. Of the two of them—Maggie, trembling, staring into the shadows, and Joy, standing tall and calm—Joy appears to be the one maintaining her equanimity. She's neatly dressed. Her hair is smooth, and she's wearing cuffed tweed trousers and a button-down shirt. This version of Joy is the more familiar one. Maggie exhales, then takes a long breath back in, and for the first time since seeing Joy, her lungs seem to fully expand.

"Listen," Joy says. "I really didn't want to upset you. Not after . . . last time. But like I said, I've been going through a bunch of old stuff, and I found some nice baby clothes I'd saved." She thrusts the canvas bag toward Maggie. "I thought the boys might like it if their new baby sibling wore something of theirs . . . I mean, probably they won't be sentimental enough to care, but I thought maybe you could get some use out of them. If you want." She tilts her head toward Maggie. "They're clean. I washed them."

Maggie accepts the bag from her, but she is crying now, silently. This is a gesture she'd never dreamed Joy might make—brusque, proud, wounded Joy. This small, unexpected act of generosity, its poignancy, guts Maggie.

Joy steps back, clearing her throat. "You all right?"

"It's been a long day," Maggie says, eyes burning, the taste of salt in her mouth. "But I'm all right. Thank you. Really. You didn't have to do this."

Joy shrugs. "I know," she says. "But I'm going through a lot of old stuff. It's been weirdly cathartic. Getting rid of stuff I've been hanging on to. It's freeing."

Maggie nods. Something strange is happening to her—a sensation, a warm tingling in the back of her head.

"John might have mentioned my college roommate who was murdered? I've been looking into it. I got a phone call from the sister of the guy who's in prison, and she asked me something that reminded me of an old joke . . . Anyway, I don't need to bore you with all this, but I feel like I might have had a breakthrough."

Joy sounds proud, and Maggie nods again, with too much enthusiasm.

"Maggie?"

It's John calling from the house.

He seems miles away. Maggie's body is alive with new knowledge. She could laugh—the threat is not Joy, has never been Joy! Strangely, they are allies—whether Joy is aware of this or not. She will have to explain it to her at some point. It would be a mercy, Maggie thinks, to take Joy's hand right now. To hug her, to let her cry. They are sisters. The threat is elsewhere. It has always been elsewhere. The threat is all around them, but here, together, they are briefly safe.

"Just a minute! I'm fine!" Maggie shouts back.

The darkness rustles. The gaping nothing yawns blackly. An abyss. The weeping. The horrible weeping; it is so close her ears are full with it. Like ringing in one's head. Like the loud white sluice of total silence.

Who is weeping? Joy. The Weeper. Maggie herself.

She closes her eyes. She breathes. The yellow orb is hot to the touch, like Samantha J promised, and shoots through her with a power that can hardly be contained, a surge of energy that will be either her triumph or her undoing. Maggie is stronger than she's ever realized. She will not fear the electric strength that surges through her.

The night is almost soundless now. There is no more weeping. Joy stands receptive beside her, breathing, as if she already understands and is waiting. The shape in the darkness is, for the time being, gone, and Maggie is filling herself with warm, golden light—light that shoots from her fingertips and toes and onto everyone, onto the whole, lost world.

1999

Karlie Richards
Eng 46
Prof. Lang
January 1999
Introduction

    Hello. My name is Karlie Richards. I'm eighteen years old and grew up in Sycamore Grove, NC. This is my second semester. It's hard to know what else there is to say. When you asked, Professor Lang, for us to write about ourselves, I was stumped. I'm nobody—and I signed up for this course to learn about the modern novel.

    "Don't overthink it," you said to us that day in class, dusting a bit of chalk dust from your hands before tucking them into your pockets. (I like how your very gestures are professorial. Also your tweed jackets and wireless glasses. I know you're reading this, Professor Lang, but I like when the little details of college match what I imagined.) "Let's start with someone close at hand," you said. "A real person. You. How might *you* read on the page? As a character?"

    You went on then about wanting a sense of who we are, the forces that have shaped us, our experiences, our temperaments, the events we've encountered. The problems we've faced. Just as we'd be considering characters in the novels we'd read, we would consider ourselves. What we *want*. What *drives* us. As you were talking, I thought it was a weird assignment, but I also thought you might be onto something.

    When Colin, the guy in our class who went to Durham Academy and took creative writing already in high school and wants to tell everyone all about it, said, "Piece of cake. Our generation's *really* good at navel-gazing," some of the class laughed, and Colin looked at you in this overeager way, like he hoped you'd recognize him as some kind of intellectual peer who was already in on the joke. But you didn't smile or even look at him, which I appreciated.

    "Perhaps," you said. "Although what I'm asking for is a little self-examination rather than navel-gazing. Who *are* you?"

Who am I?

I'm stalling, avoiding the question.

Sycamore Grove is a small town in the western part of the state you pass through on the way to the mountains. There's not much to do there. My friends and I used to drive in the evenings and sit on the hood of the car by the movie theater or the old railroad tracks, letting the mosquitoes bite our legs while we talked. There were these outrageous sunsets you could watch spill tropical fruit colors on the freight cars. We talked about nothing, but it felt significant somehow, like we were on the brink of something.

I was a smart kid. People praised me for the things I did well, and I liked that feeling. I sought it out. I had a boyfriend, too—clever, with curly brown hair and books by Sartre on his shelf, which was a way of making a point where we grew up. My boyfriend had a fraternal twin brother, and it was like something out of a fairy tale, the way they were both complementary and opposite. One twin was a science whiz, the other twin a genius at the humanities; one twin taciturn, the other garrulous; one twin devoutly religious (my boyfriend), and the other twin (my boyfriend's brother) only nominally so—but the trappings of Christian youth worship-culture suited them both. It was a big thing in Sycamore Grove.

My boyfriend was the handsome one. He and his brother were in a Christian ska band (please don't laugh, Prof. Lang: Circa 1995, where I'm from, this was—perhaps still is?—incredibly cool), and my boyfriend—Tyler was his name—and his twin, Mark, and I would travel around to other little western NC towns to play shows on the weekends along with the two other guys who formed the band. I'd watch girls in skater pants and baby-doll tees and cross necklaces try to talk to my boyfriend. He was the local teen idol, the singer. Mark hung back, aloof or shy or both, absorbed only in his drumming, in the quiet labor of hauling equipment from battered gymnasiums back to the car. I'd watch Tyler interact with these girls after the show, listening to what they said, clasping their hands in this brothers-and-sisters-in-Christ type of way, sometimes praying with them. But then he'd hold my hand. The real way. We were a perfect couple, and, I'll admit, it was a little intoxicating. Sometimes I'd catch a glimpse of us together in a window or something, and it was hard not to gaze at our reflection.

We listened to a lot of music on Tyler's back patio. Not Christian ska—secretly Tyler didn't even like ska, but he liked being in a band. He liked the adoration he received when he performed. But we listened to other music. Patti Smith, Joy Division, Sonic Youth, Neutral Milk Hotel—CDs you had to drive to Charlotte or Asheville to get, an effort that indicated your uncommonly good taste. We loved sitting out there, listening. And then we'd go inside and kiss. There were strict parameters to that kissing—Godly parameters that now strike me as sort of arbitrary—but Tyler had a way of making the slightest contact pulse with longing. He loved God and God made all things, and you could feel that abundance, its intensity—if that makes any sense. Not that you want to know this, Prof. Lang, but you've never kissed until you've kissed an adolescent boy who has committed himself to Christ and thus may go no further . . . But anyway, we'd nestle under one of his mom's old quilts watching Kieślowski's *Trois Couleurs* trilogy (because they were some of the few foreign movies we could find at the video store to rent, and they suited our sense of ourselves). Occasionally Tyler's brother would walk in, and we'd straighten up and fold our hands in our lap and make room for him to sit with us. In addition to being Godly, we wanted to be artists. Part of something bigger and more meaningful than what we saw around us.

We felt we couldn't relate to the rest of Sycamore Grove. Tyler and I didn't see any similarities between ourselves and the golfing Baptist bankers in their Duck Head shorts, the ladies in the Junior Charity League. Maybe we were snobs. I don't know. But we felt different.

As for my family, my dad's an accountant. My mother was a middle school English teacher who quit to stay home and raise my sister and me. She's prone to episodes of depression. When I think of my childhood, I think of the quietness of our house: the red-and-gold plush rug my mother kept in the living room, the grandfather clock ticking in the hallway, the steady whirr of the air conditioner because my mother likes to keep the house very cold. A mausoleum, my sister called it. There is a polished wood hutch filled with china my mother collected. We never use it. It's to look at, I guess—which is kind of the theme of our whole house. It's a very nice house filled with rarely used things too fragile to touch. I hate it.

My parents didn't grow up in Sycamore Grove. I think people perceived them as strange—outsiders—even though my dad has a respectable job. We are awkward together at home, my silent parents, my sister, and me. A lot of the time my parents were preoccupied with my sister, who started getting into trouble early. I guess that's why I leaned hard in the other direction. A good girl, a high achiever, and popular to top it off. I made myself into her opposite. That's how I got so involved in youth group at church.

But by the end of high school, I couldn't wait to leave. I couldn't wait for college. I was genuinely excited, but there was also an event I wanted to distance myself from: a bad accident that happened midway through my senior year. With my boyfriend after a late-night Christian ska show up in Boone. When I say "accident" people always assume I mean a car accident. Usually I don't bother to correct their assumption.

It wasn't a car accident. We were outside, at the back of this old farm where the show had been held. I remember the sky was flecked with so many stars and it was dark enough to really see them. Tyler was being silly and expansive, talking about how God had worked in his life, saying all the silver-tongued stuff he used to say, about the universe and God's plan and Kierkegaard or whatever. He'd recently gotten a big scholarship to Vanderbilt and even though he downplayed it, I knew it meant a lot to him. There was a cluster of teenage girls, younger than both of us, just freshmen, watching him, admiring him, hanging on his every word. I could tell he was eating it up. And he hopped up onto this wall—like a retaining wall type thing—at the back of the property. Like it was a dais or something and he was preaching a sermon to those girls and they were rapt. What he didn't realize was that while it was a low wall on the side where we stood, the ground sloped sharply on the other side. There was a big drop-off. We were in the mountains. Everything there is built on this steep grade. But anyway, he was up there gesticulating, arms thrown wide, and he was saying something—that's the worst part now, I can't remember what he was saying, but I do remember his face, lit by the glow of a single flashlight one girl carried, moon-pale in the night, ebullient. He was wearing a white T-shirt, which, along with his face, seemed to glow up there. Tyler was radiant, but I was tired at that point. Irritated. I wanted to go home.

"Hey!" I said loudly. "Look behind you! What *is* that?" I wanted to shift everyone's attention. I widened my eyes. To be funny, I guess. Someone had been talking about mountain lions earlier.

Tyler turned with a start. Mark had walked up to join us, and I saw something—a shadow—pass over his face, as if he knew already what was going to happen. Tyler seemed to wobble and lose balance above us. I watched his arms start to flap, and he was suspended there for this long, drawn-out moment, like he was preparing to fly.

He survived but he wasn't my boyfriend anymore, not after that. It was a bad fall. Unlucky. Everything about it—how he happened to land, where. It's not a topic I mention now that I'm at college. It's a memory I'm always trying to forget. I'm surprised I'm even writing about it. I tried to lean hard into my faith after Tyler's accident. I wanted to be good. I wanted to *excel* at being good. I wanted discipline. Order. Like maybe there *is* a divine plan at work, a reason for everything, if I could only figure it out.

But lately, I've started to doubt all that. More and more I worry that Tyler's accident was meaningless. Simply an accident. That's all. I see other students having fun, doing things I've never allowed myself to do, and I wonder. Maybe I've been approaching everything from the wrong angle. Sometimes I wish I had the type of parents or older sister I could call and confide in. I wonder about this particular role I've been playing so well: *Karlie*. Karlie. KARLIE. You repeat your name enough times, you don't even recognize it as your own anymore. It becomes meaningless. Gibberish. A random string of letters I've carried around all this time, mere noise, a certain alignment of sound and syllable. **Karlie**.

I wonder if it's time to reinvent her.

Universal Love

Spring 1999. UNC Chapel Hill. The sky a brilliant Carolina blue, temperature mild. The parents arrive, for home games, for weekend visits. They come in minivans and station wagons, weather-beaten sedans and hatchbacks, occasionally a shiny Audi or Lexus, creeping uncertainly down Cameron Avenue, jamming the intersection by Carolina Inn and Columbia Street. On foot, they meander across the quads, fanning their damp, splotched faces with folded campus maps, pausing to beseech their offspring to pose for photos by a columned building or beneath overhanging blossoms in the arboretum. *Were you able to get tickets to the last game?* one father asks, because here the Dean Dome is the space for collective awe, for either the gnashing of teeth or rapture, for chanting TAR! Heels! TAR! Heels! They are full of questions and curiosity, these parents, ambling like eager sightseers in a new city.

Mostly, Joy believes, these visits are an excuse for the parents to spy upon the lives of their newly independent children—for the anxious and overinvolved ones to bustle through campus, the mothers in Ann Taylor capri pants and visors, the fathers all looking like middle managers in polo shirts and khakis, their paternal paunches settled at their waists like fanny packs. A parade of sturdy middle-class Americana. They want to walk the same routes their children walk to class. Some of them, the alumni, want to relive something. Others, the parents of first-generation students, want to taste a bit of an experience they've never had.

Parents will take their children out to lunch at local institutions, like Mama Dip's, serving plates of buttermilk fried chicken and sweating glasses of sweet tea; they'll ask loud, enthusiastic questions during campus tours. Fraternities host afternoon barbecues for the families of new pledges; the sororities, mother-daughter teas. This kind of tourism is good for business in town, for the selling of Carolina Basketball T-shirts and baseball caps from Johnny T-Shirt or Shrunken Head, burritos from Cosmic Cantina, cups of iced coffee from Carolina Coffee Shop. Football games in the fall, basketball in winter, class reunions on the weekends in between. Soccer games, lacrosse, baseball. Visits just because. The parents come. There will be predeparture Wal-Mart runs for bags full of supplies. Dorm room minifridges stuffed full of provisions: bottled Frappuccinos and bags of string cheese, Yoplait and Diet Coke. Shelves packed with boxes of Cheez-Its and Clif Bars, Bic pens, and family-size bottles of Pantene, because it's what the parents can do—a love offering for their darlings, their hope of hopes, their precious offspring.

Neither Karlie's family nor Joy's visited during the fall semester, not even for the official Family Weekend held in October. This surprised Joy—not her own parents' absence, but that of Karlie's. Although Karlie does not discuss her family, or any aspect of her life before college for that matter, Joy still expected her to have the kind of pleasant, preening parents who would show up at any opportunity, eager to promenade along with their sparkling daughter, witnessing the shimmering facets of her life, meeting all her friends.

It seems instead that Karlie has emerged wondrously de novo—parentless, like Aphrodite from sea foam. Joy might have dared ask about this, but a wedge already divides them: Karlie is spending more and more time away from their dorm. The professor. Joy's professor. She has seen him one evening, with Karlie, escorting her back across the quad like an old-fashioned suitor. This is the real question Joy dares not ask: What's happening between Professor Hendrix and Karlie? Research, supernatural mystery, or mortification of flesh? Spiritual communion or bodily consummation? Every prospect is horrible to consider. Joy is, as always, left alone.

And yet, now it's Joy's parents who have insisted on coming for the weekend—despite their interest in Joy as an autonomous human historically having been minimal, despite the fact Joy has no fascinating new life to display for them, no mother-daughter sorority teas, no good lunch plans.

"But Daddy's so sick," Joy says on the phone to her mother the weekend before. They hardly ever speak, none of them are talkers by nature. Joy's parents evince a partnership so close it's atomic. Discussion hardly seems necessary; they orbit each other in an impenetrable silence. "Are you sure?"

Her father has taken short-term leave from the pulpit while the doctor adjusts the levels of his medications.

"We'd really like to come," Joy's mother offers plainly.

"I don't have anything to take you to," Joy confesses, regretting briefly that she's not a sorority pledge, that she hasn't yet glommed onto the Christian fellowship Karlie attends, that she doesn't have the singing voice to join the women's a cappella group.

"No need for a fuss," her mother says. "We'd just like to see your life. Where you live. How you spend your days."

Her parents had not been able to help Joy move to campus, her father having been recently discharged from the hospital at the time. Instead, a member of the local congregation with a son Joy's age had volunteered to help. Her parents have not set foot in Chapel Hill so far. Joy imagines them in a Burke County that's so distant it might as well be another world.

"But Daddy's not well. It's too much trouble."

Her mother clears her throat. Joy knows by that sound that her father is there, listening in the background. "We'll decide what's too much trouble, Joy," she says. "And besides, your daddy's doing better. They've fixed his meds. He wants to see you."

Joy hears her father cough. This, she knows, is the closest she will get to an outright declaration of her parents' love.

NOW THAT HER parents have arrived, Joy's embarrassed. That's the truth of it. There is the hesitant way they walk, like their very presence demands apology, and the outdated nature of their clothes. Thrift and modesty are virtues—Joy knows this—and yet she wishes that someone might take her mother to Talbots, or wherever it is other mothers shop, and buy her some cheerful red cropped pants and a boatneck top. Instead, Mr. and Mrs. Brunner appear as if they've emerged from an old photo—not a really old photo, which might hold the allure of something antique, but a photo five to ten years out of date. Joy has hoped that Karlie might absent herself. It's not a request she'd ever make, but one she hopes Karlie might intuit and offer. They've been talking less and less at this point, Karlie being so often gone, and although Joy has tried to create a semblance of their previous ease, increasingly they move past each other in their shared space with the stiff, scrupulous politeness of strangers. The other day Karlie's shirt smelled of woods and spices, a cologne or aftershave faint but distinctive, a smell Joy recognized as Professor Hendrix's. There was another smell beneath that, a murky, bodily smell, like the sea and pollenating pear trees, moss and underarm sweat. A private, almost acrid odor, unfamiliar to Joy, yet instantly recognizable.

But Karlie does not make herself scarce. Instead, she greets Joy's parents herself, patient and polite, the quintessence of a lovely college freshman. Her desk is neat and orderly; Joy's, by contrast, is a ruckus of papers and gum wrappers and empty soda cans. Joy's mother sits in her desk chair uncomfortably. Joy's father, lanky and long-jawed, looks unnaturally thin. His face is sallow. It's obvious he's ailing. He moves through the girls' dorm room, studying its features, running a hand along Joy's lavender comforter, as if inspecting the place, determining its sufficiency. He comes to a stop at the window overlooking the quad. The grass is a lush green. Two shirtless boys throw a Frisbee back and forth. Her father frowns, watching them.

"Well," Karlie says brightly, "Pastor Brunner, Mrs. Brunner, we could take you to lunch at the dining hall. It's actually pretty good."

Joy, who initially doubted everything about this scenario, feels a rush of gratitude so overwhelming it subsumes any irritation she initially felt, gratitude so intense that she could hug Karlie, who is missing a picnic hosted by the Gathering, her Christian group, to be here with Joy's parents. She sees now the generosity and wisdom in Karlie's thinking: She is excellent with parents. It occurs to Joy that maybe this is her way of making amends over the situation with the professor, her way of wordlessly indicating she's perhaps even done with all that, and that they might now return to the friendship they had before.

Joy has mentioned in the past to Karlie her father's health status—not the specifics, only that he's been unwell. Karlie seemed to absorb this information and understand implicitly that she ought not ask follow-up questions. Now, Joy watches Karlie taking in Joy's father's appearance—the temporal wasting, his sallow complexion, the sparse hair that remains like downy feathers on the crown of his head—with a cheerful lack of recognition, a convincing pretense that there's nothing remarkable to observe.

"Please," Joy's father says in response, "call me Frank. And that sounds like an excellent idea."

They maneuver down the hall of the dormitory to the elevators, exiting into the blue-bright day. Joy blinks, noticing how Karlie has slowed her pace to match her father's, how Joy's mother hovers anxiously at his elbow, available to steady him if necessary.

The dining hall is large and newly redesigned, featuring numerous food stations, a salad bar, sleek, silver soft-serve machines, cereal dispensers and waffle makers that are available all day. It's less crowded than it usually is at this time on a Saturday, but they aren't the only ones who've brought visiting parents to dine. This reassures Joy—like she's doing something right, showcasing the quotidian sights and sounds of university life.

"Here," Karlie offers, guiding them to a table set back near one of the windows that overlooks the Pit. It's a thoughtful gesture, the way she's found both a view but also chosen a table that's accessible—easy for Joy's father to return to the food stations for seconds. As always, Karlie has a way of noticing things and making minor, unspoken adjustments in consideration of others' needs. These are exactly the kinds of details Joy always manages to overlook, despite her efforts.

They sit at the table with their trays, and Karlie instinctively pauses. Joy's father offers a blessing. They bow their heads, letting the hum and clatter of the rest of the diners wash over them. When they raise their forks to eat, Joy feels a little wave of something unfamiliar: contentment. This is how it ought to be, her parents here, witnessing her life, meeting her dearest friend. And for a split second, that's how Joy thinks of Karlie again, as her dearest friend. She has the strange, dreamy sensation that nothing of those past several months with Jacob Hendrix has happened. Karlie is the charismatic leader of Bible studies, the bubbly best friend to all—even to prickly, alienated Joy, whom she met those very first days of the school year.

Joy takes a bite of roasted potato, fragrant with rosemary, noting the food is particularly good today, as if the cooks themselves have put in an extra effort to impress the out-of-towners.

"So, Karlie," Joy's mother begins only minutes into their meal, "tell us about your family."

Joy's father makes a funny sound before Karlie can answer. Joy looks and sees that far-off look in his eyes, like someone is speaking to him from a great distance, someone only he can hear, that great Father-God voice imparting a message for Pastor Brunner to convey to his flock. Oh, no—but she is immobilized, a hunk of roasted potato poised near her mouth. She watches her mother's hand dart toward her father's arm, a helpless, clutching gesture. It's going to happen. It's going to happen here, in front of everyone. Here, for the whole dining hall to see.

"Help me get him to the floor," Joy's mother says to her, but it's Karlie who responds. She jumps from her chair to assist while Joy sits helpless, frozen in place. Joy watches blankly as her mother and Karlie help her father to the ground, watches as they push back the chairs, clearing a space for him to seize.

It starts. Joy's father's body moves unnaturally, hideously contorted. A current moves through him, an unseen bolt of lightning. Joy cannot watch; she cannot stand to watch this yet again. Still seated, she turns from her father, her face growing wet. Joy's mother and Karlie kneel on the floor on either side of him. A crowd has gathered around them.

"Stand back!" someone yells. "Give them space!"

The entire dining hall has grown quiet, the focus narrowed onto Joy's father as under the beam of a spotlight. Karlie looks up into the crowd.

"Someone call nine-one-one," she orders.

And although she feels removed from herself, Joy can admire the calm of Karlie's voice, the authority of her tone.

Time has turned elastic and illogical, slippery. When the paramedics make their way up the escalator and into the dining hall, it could be mere minutes that have passed or millennia. Joy cannot say.

What she does notice is that all the savory lunch smells have been supplanted by the rising smell of shit, a watery brown puddle beneath Joy's father.

Joy cannot look. She also cannot look away. The crowd has parted for the paramedics, who work with solemn efficiency, moving Joy's father onto a stretcher, and Joy has the light-headed sensation that they are all on a stage, she, her mother, her father, and Karlie, performing for a live studio audience. She has failed to step up to her role. Failed utterly. But the show must go on. Joy rises from her seat, finally able to move, and hastens to her mother, her father, with arms outstretched. Her mother's focus is elsewhere. She nudges Joy out of the way. Joy, who is useless. The studio audience heaves a sigh of collective relief when the paramedics exit with Joy's father. He offers a weak thumbs-up from the stretcher to a smattering of cheers and applause. The smell of hot human dung has permeated Joy's nostrils so deeply her eyes burn.

Her father disappears from the dining hall.

The day is ruined. Joy weeps.

LATER, WHEN JOY'S parents are gone, their visit abruptly concluded, Joy returns to her dorm room from a long study session at the library. She feels both grateful to and chastened by Karlie—so much so that Joy's been avoiding her, unsure she will ever be able to speak to her again, her gratefulness leaving her abject, tongue-tied. So humiliatingly in Karlie's debt is Joy that she cannot speak of it. Karlie, with her cool head and obvious competence, must be appalled at Joy's uselessness. Karlie must also understand her better now, her circumstances, and there's relief in the thought that these facts will require no further explanation.

Joy buys a cookie—one of the giant ones they sell at a stand beside the library, a cookie she knows Karlie loves. It will serve as a small thank-you, a token. The reason will go unsaid. Joy trusts Karlie will understand.

But while she's crossing campus back toward their dorm, she spots them. Karlie and Professor Hendrix. They sit on the stone bench beneath the majestic Davie poplar. If one didn't know any better, it might be a brochure-worthy scene, a demonstration of the deep academic commitment of educator toward student, the two surely engaged in some sort of Socratic dialogue, partaking in an outdoor office hours of sorts. They could be discussing revisions on a paper or an article they've both just read. But Joy sees the way Professor Hendrix's body curves toward Karlie's, protective, proprietary, and she sees the sheen of Karlie's bright hair, the way she tips her head back in laughter at some quip he's offered her. She leans close, too close toward him, and then there is the moment that almost undoes Joy. He touches Karlie. Her professor brushes something away from her cheek. It's an almost innocent touch, a gesture with plausible deniability, and yet Joy sees how his thumb lingers there. Like a lover. Or like a father with his child.

Like a *father*. Joy could vomit. The entire visit with her parents changes tone yet again, the color draining from it. The whole thing reads differently on a second look. Karlie's kindness, Joy sees, instead as a kind of greed, a constant usurping, a need to be needed, and wanted, and loved. Joy never asked for her help. What she thankfully accepted before reads now as yet another betrayal. Karlie takes everyone from her with her relentless charm, the great, gaping imperative that she be liked, preferred. There's an undeniable avarice to her seeming generosity—Joy sees it now.

Karlie looks up and sees Joy standing there. Her gaze seeks to capture Joy's, but Joy resists. She turns to leave, hurrying in the other direction, across the quiet upper campus quad toward Franklin Street, where she finds an empty bus stop. She sits, pulling her knees to her chest, embracing herself. The cookie Joy bought as a gift has broken within its wrapping inside her bag. She pulls it out and opens it. She chews great hunks of it, hot tears gathering in her eyes. The cookie tastes like sand, the crumbs of it dry in her throat.

When she finishes eating, Joy goes into the nearest coffee shop and dries her face with a paper towel in the bathroom. She continues wiping until her cheeks are nearly raw.

Then she goes to the housing office and rescinds her roommate request for next year. It's finally clear to Joy, who does not read the subtle signs, not like Karlie. Karlie, who sees God's Truth in how the light falls, finds answers in the clouds or the sudden affirmation of a four-leaf clover or a cooing dove. No, that is not how Joy sees things. Poor, obstinate Joy needs Truth to smack her in the face, to repeat itself over and over, to be writ small and large and larger again until she can see. Until she can *understand* what ought to have been obvious all along: She cannot keep living with Karlie.

The More Loving One

There are worse things than falling in love with a girl. Jacob Hendrix appreciates this, even if others—his wife, for one—do not. His wife, Lila, indulgent though she is, takes these frequent crushes a little personally, Jacob knows, although she has never said a thing. Her imperviousness is part of her charm, and for her to admit annoyance would be to relinquish some part of her power. She's sleeping now, his wife; he is the early bird in their household. He'll prepare her toast the way she likes, along with a cup of chai, because he always does. This is how they live, under the tyranny of ritual niceties.

Jacob considers this as he pours half-and-half into his coffee, a lovely white bloom, softening and mingling beneath the surface. He likes to watch the way the colors blend. The changing hue always makes him think of skin tones, the great variety—but he knows better than to make such comparisons aloud, having once, as a younger man, written a poem in which he likened a girl's complexion (favorably, of course!) to café au lait and was told by his professor—a woman herself, it should be noted—that he ought not describe women's appearances in terms of caffeinated beverages or any consumables, really, especially if he hasn't deigned to depict these women as also having personalities. She was a real snot, this professor—the very reason he'd dropped his English major, if he's being honest—and despite the appealing rigor of her pencil skirts, the hose she wore with precise little seams running up the backs of her calves, her sleek and perfect bob that practically demanded ruffling, Jacob never fell in love with her, not one iota. Her skin, he'd noticed that day, had been like potter's clay, clammy and unappealing, and her intelligence, a bitter thing, taste-ruining, like the loose grounds at the bottom of a cup of coffee.

The toast pops up. Its shade is off, so he presses the lever again. Toast should be the color of wet sand, like the color of the inner arm of a girl he'd taught last semester, the one with large, chestnut eyes. *What do you compare me to?* Lila once asked him, and he'd been stunned. A lifetime of delectable similes, rhapsodizing over such great buffets of flesh and longing, and truly, with regard to her, his own wife, the thought of her as something else had never occurred to him. *Incomparable*, he'd said to Lila, who is pinched and sallow, though striking in her way. *That's you. Incomparable*, and she'd laughed, pleased, although Jacob knew that to him it was not entirely a compliment.

There is the muted howl of dogs outside. His hand shakes as he lifts the mug. The coffee trembles forebodingly. He is a god, creator of earthquakes. With his left hand, he clasps his right wrist, trying to quell the tremor, but the quaking does not stop. He puts the coffee down, then tries again, lifting it with his left hand instead. He takes a sip. Through the kitchen window, he can see his neighbor Diana outside, wearing specialized workout gear that does not suit her. She appears to be stretching, preparing for some vigorous exertion. The dogs howl again, obligingly. Diana is responsible for these dogs—rescue animals, anxious and snapping, dogs no one else will touch but that Diana loves with abandon. He hates dogs. A childhood neighbor of his had raised German shepherds on her property, and she raised them mean. Diana's exercise clothing looks new and preposterous. It is cold out, mid-November, and her breath comes out in white puffs. He has never seen her out there like this. Ordinarily, she rushes back and forth from her Volvo station wagon in saggy slacks and button-downs and loafers. Jacob is aware that Diana's husband has recently left, and he pities her, red-faced in the cold. The defiant jut of her chin, her bleak determination—it's a little appalling, really.

Shall he get the paper now and be forced to wave to her? Speak?

He and his wife have been passingly friendly with Diana and her husband, Doug. A younger couple, stuffy and ungraceful, with a whiff of 1980s-era striving to them—even though it's 1999, practically the new millennium! When he'd first heard they were moving in, a couple in their midthirties without children, the wife a new, hotshot hire at the law school, poached from a Big Ten university, he'd allowed himself to imagine something different—a woman who was polished and gaze-able, a man of understated intelligence with whom perhaps he might share a nip of bourbon on the weekends. But Doug had been unbearable. Honking laugh, a tendency to deliver nasal disquisitions on tax code, backslapping bonhomie with an edge to it. And private equity—what is it, really? A place former Northeastern lacrosse goons end up, Jacob supposes. Poor Diana. Maybe she is better off without Doug. She has her esteemed faculty position, her hard-luck dogs.

He opens the door and steps out in his robe, one foot, two feet, careful over the threshold. The cold air startles him, burning his throat. He's learned of late to grasp at handholds, to steady himself. If he moves slowly enough, he is fine. The trick is avoiding overconfidence—something the doctor accused him of when he'd refused his recommendation of physical therapy recently. *It will help,* the doctor had promised, his eyes beseeching, *at least until we see how you respond to treatment.* The setup of the clinic had been such that he'd been able to see the physical therapists and their patients in a kind of open gymnasium across the hall. Cheerful young women assisted doddering old men and shrunken old ladies, calling brightly to one another across the room. Not one of them moved quickly or fluidly, those enfeebled gym goers. It had made Jacob want to die. He is only fifty-six.

"Jacob Hendrix!"

He is halfway down, in a kind of crouch, the newspaper at his fingertips. Diana. Her voice, more cheerful than it ought to be, unsteadies him. He pauses, gripping the doorframe. A wave of dizziness passes over him. There's that numbness in his foot. One of the dogs in Diana's backyard issues a desolate moan.

"*Bonne journée!*"

Her words are white plumes. And her blithe obliviousness is an astonishment. He is able to push himself back to standing with an effort he hopes is not noticeable. His and Lila's Volvo sedans, silver and gold, sit in the drive like two sentries. Only make of car he's ever trusted. God bless that Swedish engineering—superior, Jacob thinks, to the engineering of the human body.

"Diana Cathcart," he says. "Off to France soon, aren't you?"

She nods, approaching him as if he's invited her, as if his presence has provided her a much-needed excuse to pause her exertions. There's a bit of hair plastered against her forehead. Her cheeks are pink, like those of an overgrown child. Her proximity is novel, unappetizing.

"I should be using the time to write," she says, shrugging. "But I'm trying something new. Starting fresh."

"That's the spirit."

"Language school in Nice has always been a dream of mine. Just never felt practical."

"Good for you, then."

He can smell it now, coming from the kitchen—the toast has burned. He will have to start again. Otherwise the day will go all wrong. He tips forward a bit more, and there is that sharp pain again in his back, an electrical hand seizing him, traveling up and down his spine. He recalls the doctor's face as he described the MRI, a few white smudges scattered here and there, it seemed to Jacob, at least until the doctor pointed them all out—and then he could see they were everywhere, like pale mushrooms sprung up after a rain. It looked bad. *It's bad, isn't it?* he'd asked the doctor, a neurologist, himself a pale, mushroomy thing, chinless with a sparse blond goatee and a habit of frowning meaningfully. *We can't predict the disease course yet*, he'd said. Jacob realized the frown was meant to convey empathy. *Primary progressive, secondary progressive, relapsing-remitting, clinically isolated syndrome*—he'd read the patient handout dutifully, but it had felt like reading about life on another planet.

He rises again, the newspaper clutched under his arm.

"How are you feeling?" Diana asks, and he can see it, the terrible knowledge of his situation, rippling across her face. Her voice has gone soft, solicitous, like she is sad—oh, so sad for him—and here she is, a woman abandoned by her husband! Doug, run off with another man! Such public betrayal. Jacob's mouth has gone sour. Lila had promised she would tell no one. But maybe it came up, the way women are wont to gossip, trading personal disasters, commiserating their way to closeness.

"Sorry to hear about Doug," Jacob says.

She steps back as if struck. He's said it too gruffly, he realizes. Defense turned offense. But now he cannot stop himself.

"I saw them once," he continues. "Doug and that man. At Mulligan's. The way they were sitting. So close. They kept looking at one another . . . I should have known. I'm sorry. I should have said something. Saved you the trouble."

It is unnecessary, he realizes, the level of detail he is offering, this unasked-for apology—it is, in fact, a further humiliation to her. But being sick has done this to him, left him desperate and greedy for whatever shreds of agency remain. Only last night, he'd been felled by sudden weakness getting out of the shower and had to call, naked and shivering, for Lila to help him.

Diana has gone rigid now. Her lower lip is white from where her teeth press into it. No, she is not dumb, he realizes. She sees what he's doing.

"Lila brought me zucchini bread," she says, studying him.

He nods, and the strange, electric zap travels down his spine. *What was the first symptom you noticed?* the neurologist asked, and he described this, although no, it had not truly been the first symptom.

"She's a wonderful woman. You're so lucky. To have a happy marriage."

Her face is still and flat as a coin, her words double-edged.

"Oh, yes."

He lowers his eyes, clicks his lower jaw forward into a underbite, a nervous habit from youth. *You're trying to provoke me*, his father always said. Jacob had grown up in Richmond, in the Fan, his family one of the old, good families, the ones who traced their history back to the founders. His father was a member of the Commonwealth Club, an attorney who was well known in town, a man who carried a twenty-four-karat-gold pocket watch and got professional shaves and enjoyed martini lunches with clients. He made partner before he hit thirty, a fact he was constantly mentioning to Jacob. Jacob's mother was beautiful and prim and nervous, a member of the Woman's Club that met at Bolling Haxall House. She was easily prone to tears, an anorexic back before anorexia was even fashionable—there was hardly a name for it then, her insistence on cottage cheese and celery, her dainty birdlike bones. She had a taste for barbiturates and a doctor who delivered. What Jacob can remember now are the long silences, his mother in bed. The return of his father each evening was like the threat of bad weather, a looming storm. They were practical people, his parents, who showed up in fine clothing to the Episcopal church on Christmas Eve and Easter only, social visits, the obligatory showing of face for any proper Virginian. Jacob had been expected to go to law school, to join his father's firm, not to marry young and study, of all things, the sociology of religion. *Your childhood warped you*, Lila has said to him in the past, on many occasions, but she's said it gently, in a way that he's always taken as permission. For leniency with himself, for a kind of psychic recompense.

"She's gorgeous," Diana says, her voice almost a whisper, turned intimate with the information being conveyed.

Jacob looks up, startled.

"Just stunning."

He knows she is not talking about Lila.

"I've seen her here," Diana continues. "With you. She drives that old gray Honda, always parks it two blocks away." She flushes, as if on his behalf, but her eyes are hard. She thinks she could destroy him if she wished. He can see now how she would be in a courtroom or in front of her law students: stark, impressive, ferocious with knowledge.

She's talking about Karlie, obviously. He misses Karlie fiercely, but the loss is becoming secondary to his own physical suffering, his ailment having intensified an already present self-obsession. At least, this is what his father would point out—what he *did* point out, through the duration of Jacob's childhood and adolescence. Although what he meant, Jacob thinks, is that Jacob did not worship his father fully enough, did not cower and bathe him in the glow of paternal adulation. He was, Jacob will admit, slavishly devoted instead to the urges of the flesh. And good at it, too. From an early age he'd been a charmer. What a thrill, to recognize one's own power, to see what one could do, to be so full of amorous energy—well, it wasn't necessarily a bad thing, but it was a thing you had to share. *And can you believe it, right after losing the girl I love—my soulmate!—after she dumps me, I learn my body's falling apart?* He imagines himself explaining it all to a nodding bartender, someone discreet and nonjudgmental, as befits the profession. He remembers when Lila was studying for her nurse practitioner exam, recalls the grotesque mnemonics. *S2-3-4 keeps the penis off the floor.* Bodies in all their complexity broken down to a child's nursery rhyme. The deepest humiliations turned singsong. But maybe the loss is not final. Maybe there is hope—a dangerous, marvelous thing.

"She's a student," he says. "A very talented one I hope to encourage."

His choice of articles is a precise one: *a* student, which is the truth, although the elision suggests she was Jacob's student, which she was not. He met her through one of his actual students: a girl whose searching loneliness was so raw, so palpable, so mollusk-soft, that he'd wanted to protect her, to offer her a shell, a carapace. As so often happened, his initial impulses became muddled with other things, but through her, he eventually found Karlie. Karlie inspired something else in him. A cruder person would have called it lust, but Jacob knows better.

"Hey," Diana says. She throws up her hands as if to say *not guilty*, although she understands what she is doing. "None of my business."

"It's nothing anyway."

She puts a finger to her chin as if struck by an idea. "Oh, hey, you know who Lila would love? My friend Selene. Do you know her? Robert Parker's wife?"

Robert Parker is the chair of his department. Diana smiles a tight smile, and he mirrors it. It's a threat, this baring of teeth. Little does she know, he thinks, of Lila's steadfastness. They are together, he and Lila, like left arm and right, a fact that remains true whether you like your left arm or not. But Selene is another matter. He wants to laugh harshly in Diana's face, to say something quick and cutting that will dismantle her.

But before he can do anything, she steps closer, her warm breath clouding his face, and touches him. Her fingers against his cheek are soft. A suggestion. A challenge. He cannot move. And then, she turns and begins huffing down the block—a jog!—in that ridiculous outfit. He steadies himself against the doorframe and makes his way back inside.

Lila is awake now, and he sees her in the kitchen, wearing one of her black velour tracksuits. She is a tiny woman, pocket-size, with a startling efficiency to everything she does. She is still quite appealing, actually, if one doesn't mind severity—sharp cheekbones, thin shoulders, the bright and powerful eyes of a bird of prey.

She looks up at him, the burnt toast pinched between her thumb and index finger—such a lapse is unlike him.

"Diana," he announces, as if this explains everything. "From across the street. She's going to France on her sabbatical. It also seems she's taken up jogging."

Lila sniffs. "She's been chatty lately," she says.

"Lonely, I guess. She means well."

This latter part is clearly a lie, but Jacob says it anyway, as if saying it will make it so. Lila raises an eyebrow, silently placing fresh bread into the toaster. Already this morning, though barely started, has leveled him.

The girl. She was everything Lila was not. Karlie. Her soft cheeks, her earnestness, the fervor of her faith—it had awakened something inside of him. He understood how she'd seen him at first: a stodgy sociology professor, a fixture of the university, part of the establishmentarian intellectual atheist elite. But then he'd proven himself to her. Although he hadn't grown up religious, he knew his Biblical history from grad school. And he, too, had a taste for wonder. He'd felt some glee in that—this appetite they shared. There was something about Karlie that he simply couldn't get enough of—not a physical thing, no, although he found his whole body wound itself tighter, practically vibrating in anticipation, when she was near. Finally, he'd figured out what it was: her purity. Her kindness. Her vast joy in small pleasures. She believed in signs from God, and she saw them everywhere, not in an egomaniacal way but in one that resulted in an abundance of kindnesses—the homeless man humming gospel songs downtown, the crying boy in the grocery store—little nudges everywhere, nudges he, like most people, chose to ignore. Which was not to say she was a saint—oh, no. He's also seen her acts of petty selfishness, how she could sulk when not given enough attention, the laughing, reckless way she'd treated his affection. He was almost certain she was also seeing someone else—some fresh-faced boy her own age. There'd been hints of it, vague mentions of a friend she needed to meet, the way her eyes darted when she spoke of this friend, a careful avoidance of pronouns—and who could blame her, although he felt a terrible needful aching at the thought. But even in those moments, there was something guileless to her. In Jacob's world—one of faculty cocktail parties and witty repartee, of cynical jokes and layers of self-conscious irony—he'd not known such a thing could exist. It was like discovering a hidden glade of such loveliness, such untouched beauty, that you could not help but enter into it, even if it meant trampling all the most delicate flowers.

"You missed a phone call," Lila says, taking care not to look up. "From Robert."

It is unusual for Robert to be calling him on a Saturday. Again, there is that strange tingle up his spine, although this time he thinks it's old-fashioned anxiety.

"What did he say?"

Lila takes a sip of her chai, careful to remain untroubled. She is demonstrating to him, he understands, the demeanor she wants him to maintain. "Just for you to call him back."

Jacob feels the pricking of pins and needles in his feet. He sighs, lowering himself to a chair at the kitchen table. Karlie, of course, is not the first of his loves. He has operated like this, making pets of his chosen ones, always young women, right in plain sight, because how better to hide a secret than in the open, behind excellent guidance and charm and numerous teaching awards? He *is* a good mentor. No one can deny it. He thinks often of Plato's *Phaedrus*. Anyone who denies the erotic tensions inherent in mentorship, well . . .

Lila studies him, her mug below her nose, hiding her mouth. "The computer upstairs," she says quietly. "It automatically logs onto Instant Messenger under the name Karliegirl80."

He blanches. It is Karlie who showed him AOL Instant Messenger, something she said all the students used. He'd chosen a screenname, ProfPlum71, then quickly developed an eager, Pavlovian response to the creaky-door-opening sound that played when someone entered and the yellow humanoid shape. Karlie had been the only one he ever added to his friend list.

"Do I need to be worried about anything?" Lila asks, still exceedingly calm, patient. But her eye twitches. She's been working longer hours at the clinic, not getting enough sleep, worrying about him.

"No," he says, shaking his head, although Lila knows. She's known about all of them, but it is a thing about which they never speak directly, by unspoken agreement. "She needed help with a paper but couldn't make office hours. Must have signed on."

He feels a sliver of irritation at Karlie because how could she be so stupid? It must have been that last weekend they spent together, the last time he spoke to her or saw her, when Lila was at a conference. While he was preparing the salmon steaks, pouring wine into two nice glasses, Karlie was in the living room reading on his couch, her sock feet tucked sweetly beneath her bottom like a schoolgirl. But she must have slipped upstairs, unable to bear missing high-import messages from her silly nineteen-year-old friends, the inflated dramas of their late-adolescent lives.

"Good," Lila says. "Now's not the time for further complications."

Karlie is the only one he's ever dared invite into his home. She was different by the end. He hoped he'd be renewed by her, restored to some kind of prelapsarian state, ferried back into the soft golden light in which she seemed to reside. Instead, he'd ruined her and humiliated himself. That last night together, after he'd touched her neck, her waist, her hips with such gentleness, such obvious adoration, she laughed sourly at his eventual failure. *I'm sorry*, he'd whispered. *I love you so.* And that's when she'd laughed again, pulling her clothes back on roughly—the sweatpants with the lettering down the leg, standard-issue college girl stuff, like she was nothing but ordinary—and said, *It's okay. You're old.* He'd recoiled as if scalded. His failure that night had broken some spell, causing Karlie to revert back to the mundane form of a callow youth.

They have not spoken since, but he's longed for her to do something—send a message? Apologize to him?

In a way, he feels vindicated by his diagnosis. He wants to call her up and tell her so: *It's not old age, you see! It's demyelination!*

But now there is the prospect that she's filed some sort of complaint against him. No, it wasn't possible. She wouldn't. Someone else, then? He thinks again of the student who'd introduced them, Karlie's roommate—a churning, serious girl, intelligent in her own right. A memory surfaces, of the roommate waiting outside his office building, watching him leave with Karlie. Is it his own revisionism at work, or does he distinctly recall the look of jealousy on her face? A woman spurned, he thinks. A girl.

Lila moves neatly to the sink to rinse her mug, then pauses at the window. "Diana has one of her rescues out," she says.

He rises and joins her at the window. The dog, muscled and broad shouldered, leaps at Diana boisterously. She bats at him, stepping back. The dog lunges this time, and Diana falls, the dog atop her now like a human lover, its face nuzzling hers. Jacob feels sick and turns away.

"I don't think they're playing," Lila says uncertainly, right as Jacob sees it. There, on the floor, beneath the refrigerator, winking up at him. Karlie's lost earring. One of the gold stars she'd been wearing their last night together. He remembers now, her hand pressing one bare earlobe, the way they'd both searched under the coffee table on hands and knees but found nothing. Gratitude surges through him. He'll reach out to her and return it.

He's brought back by a shriek. The scene outside the window continues to unfold. Diana's twisting under the dog. Jacob remains motionless, watching, but there must be something—a tensing of his hand into a fist, a new tightening of his jaw—that Lila observes.

"We'll call for help," she says. "Don't." She clutches his arm, grabbing the nearby cordless phone from its cradle.

But he's realized what Karlie would say the earring is: a sign. From God, presumably, although Karlie is the conduit. The message is clearly intended for some better soul than he, but he's right there; it's unavoidable. He shakes Lila off, making his way decisively toward the door. A strength he hasn't felt in months courses through his limbs.

Outside, coatless in the chill, he walks directly toward Diana and the dog. He sees its muzzle flecked with blood, the steam coming from its nostrils. Its jaw is clenched on Diana's forearm.

"Jacob!" Lila cries, as if from a great distance. He's past heeding her at this point, so absorbed in the moment, the way it's slowed down to allow for perfect focus, the kind one might only ordinarily achieve through sustained meditation or prayer.

The dog side-eyes him warily without releasing its grip. Diana, panting softly, says nothing. There is a fallen branch on the ground nearby because yes, Jacob thinks, sometimes it's true that the Lord will provide. As he picks it up and swings with all the newfound potency flooding his body, the dog snarls, releasing Diana and charging at him instead. Jacob feels a searing pain in the soft meat of his calf, but it's a pain like elation—proof of all that's mighty even when the flesh is weak. He holds the branch aloft, triumphant, preparing to swing at the dog again, knowing already, even as the pain blooms into a red radiance, that no matter what—all the girls he's loved and lost, the frailties of the flesh—he will remember this moment, when he was strong and good.

Nov 12, 1999

To Whom It May Concern:

Please excuse Karlie Richards from classes through the remainder of the semester. She is dealing with an urgent family issue at this time. She will make up the work and complete the final as soon as possible. Thank you for your patience and understanding in this matter.

Most sincerely,

Nancy Lane Richards (her mother)

Dear Sir or Madam:

My daughter Karlie has been unwell. She is unable to attend class for the remainder of this semester, but will make every attempt to complete her outstanding assignments in a timely fashion. Thank you for your support as she recovers.

Truly,

Nancy Lane Richards (mother of Karlie Richards)

To Whom It May Concern:

Please excuse Karlie Richards from classes through the remainder of the semester. She has embarrassed herself before a member of your faculty. (Although let us be clear: He was behaving badly himself, which has become painfully clear to her on considering details of the situation. One might call him, in fact, a charming predator. Predatorily charming. And what was she even seeking from him in the first place? Paternal approval? Something closer at hand than God the Father, aloof and enthroned in His clouds? Sad. Desperate. Embarrassing. She's a smart girl; she should have known better.) As such, Karlie must now avoid campus at all costs. She will make up the work accordingly and complete the final. Thank you for your patience in this matter.

Most sincerely,
Nancy Lane Richards (her mother)

To Whom It May Concern:

My daughter Karlie Richards has been ill of late. Lovesick? Sick in the head? She has ruined many things: a friendship, the potential for mentorship with an interesting professor (who did in fairness turn out to be a lust-crazed creep, a situation she indulged and even encouraged for a while because it flattered her, apparently. She found him very wise. Ha!), and possibly two real possibilities for an actual relationship. She has also very likely ruined her good standing with a campus Christian group and her reputation. She is a bad, bad girl. I have always found her worthy of reproach myself. She wearied me—this is probably why I spent so much of her youth in a state of existential malaise, locked away in my darkened bedroom. Whoever has been following her is likely mad at her, too. Please consider her absences from class for the remainder of the semester to be excused absences; she needs time to consider her errors and woes, repent her sins, etc.—if she even still half believes. (In God?? Was that ever real? Or was that all for show, Karlie? Please share with us.) She will make up her missing academic work, at my stalwart maternal insistence. I myself am a former teacher; thus I do understand. She is the reason I was always deeply mired in sorrow, although I did not admit this to her because, poor girl, she would not have been strong enough to bear it. It was not a pleasure to be her mother, nor, do I imagine, is it a pleasure to be her college professor or graduate teaching assistant. Thank you for your service.

Truly,
Nancy Lane Richards

To Whom It May Concern:

My daughter Karlie Richards is really quite unhinged. Perhaps she is turning out like me? (I'm well aware this has always been one of her worst fears.) All those years clapping her hands and singing glory-glory songs, praising Jesus, doing winter coat drives for the homeless—oh, she was not fooling anyone! I know a flimsy facade when I see one. I know a fraud. God, if He's up there, knows a striver. He knows when someone's full of false show, overeager to please, and surely it annoys Him. As for earthly troubles, someone has been following her. She's not thinking straight. I myself can't say she doesn't deserve it. A harsh reprimand is almost certainly in order. Have her ways been sluttish and vile? Yes. I was never religious myself, but I've always carried myself with dignity, whereas Karlie, slavering, panting Karlie, cannot help but lap up even the most paltry morsels of affection. By what measure was that ever love—or faith? When was it ever anything other than selfishness disguised as virtue? Please forgive her when she skips class. Father, forgive her, for she has sinned. She will likely not show up for the next several weeks, but she will try to complete any final exams/assignments.

Sincerely,
Nancy Lane Richards

To Whom It May Concern,

Please excuse Karlie Richards from class for the remainder of the semester. As the great poet Robert Lowell once said, "My mind's not right," and "I myself am hell" and "I watched for love-cars." The thought of cars is bothering her, of one car in particular, how it creeps up to her door, that single headlight running up the wall. She can see it from her bedroom. Karlie is dealing with several Intractable Problems. I am her mother, so I would know. I cannot give details. Possibly, she is simply Overwrought. Hysterical. Please excuse.

Yours,
Nancy Lane Richards

Dear Professor Hindelmann,

The truth is that I almost gave you a note supposedly written by my mother asking to be excused from class for the next several weeks. But I couldn't even write a fake note properly. I couldn't write one without hating myself. Plus, I respect you too much for that, and I'm trying to be a more honest person. (And the notes I attempted to forge all turned out very badly, so maybe as a creative writer I'm not actually that good . . .) If you might find it within your heart to forgive any of my upcoming absences, I promise to turn in all of the poems for my portfolio soon. I will try to make it to class. I really will. You're a great professor. But I'm having some problems. I've upset a few people, and it will probably be fine, but . . . I can't make any promises about my attendance. I anticipate having to miss class. Sorry to be vague. I hope you will understand, and that you might still recommend me to continue on to Advanced Poetry Writing.

 Sincerely,
 Karlie

The Gathering

If the world ends when the clock strikes midnight, Joy figures she'll be here, alone, in her near-empty high-rise dorm when it happens. For reasons she cannot fully explain, it feels like a punishment she probably deserves. The campus is a ghost town. Joy's sophomore roommate, Eliza—nice enough, but hardly a close friend—has gone home to Wilmington.

And yet someone is knocking at her door.

Joy shifts in her twin bed, neither fully awake nor asleep now, listening. The person knocks again, less hesitant, louder. In her dream, Joy was sitting on a grassy embankment near a community soccer field talking to her former best friend, Rachel. Sun-dappled Rachel, fair and freckled, throwing her head back in hiccupping laughter. Smiling Rachel, bathed in all that leafy, green-gold light. Rachel has vanished. The relentless knocking comes again.

One must seek special dispensation from the university to stay in the dorms over the holidays, an option mostly reserved for international students. Joy is not an international student, although people often assume she is because of her stilted mannerisms (so unforgivably out of sync with all the effortless Jesses and Jens and Amandas) and her clothes, which appear off-brand and strange on her, even when she's had the chance to shop at chain stores (the Limited! Abercrombie & Fitch!) frequented by her more fashionable peers. Joy is from everywhere and nowhere, the product of a peripatetic childhood—at least up until her father became sick and put his missionary work on hold, returning to western North Carolina—which makes her socially useless. A weirdo.

"Jooiiiiiieeee," a voice calls. "Joooooooeeeeee."

It is Tatiana, the Ukrainian girl. Her suitemate. Tatiana is an information science major with a tight little crew of friends from her program, but she's also rabidly inclusive of Joy at any opportunity, a facet of her personality that Joy finds alternately admirable and off-putting. She imagines Tatiana standing there, waiting, peeling at the lavender-sparkle polish on her bitten-down nails, one hip jutting out in annoyance. It's almost eleven A.M. Joy is still fully horizontal, gummy-eyed, wearing the oversize knockoff *Simpsons* T-shirt—*Burt* Simpson, flipping a bird from his skateboard, purchased from a street vendor in Cape Town—that she sleeps in. Even now that she knows better, she's more of a Burt than a Bart Simpson girl anyway. Her nomadic upbringing has left her unmarked by proper American youth culture. Her shirt is musty with sleep-sweat and she isn't wearing pants, only the saggy cotton underwear her mother purchases for her in bulk.

"JOOIIIIEEEE," Tatiana says again from the hallway. "It's New Year's Eve!" She overenunciates, speaking an old-fashioned English that is entirely out of place here, a habit born of ESL classes taught by British expats. "Two thousand zero, party over, oops out of time."

The mysteries of data and computer science confound her, but Joy imagines a cartoon sequence of events: digital clocks exploding, computer screens reverting to the year 1900, the bright ticker tape of the stock exchange flickering, then going dark, a melt of overwrought motherboards, like butter left out in the sun. She has heard Jerry Falwell raging from the television screen—*A worldwide revival is coming. Get your canned food and guns. Prepare ye for the rapture!*—as the silent boy from downstairs sat watching in the common area, mesmerized. Even the nonreligious carry an expectant weight, ready for something—the future!—to swoop down and alter things inexorably.

"I'm not dressed," Joy says, but her door is not locked, and Tatiana has already pushed it open. Tatiana's body is absurdly, almost parodically beautiful—ripe to bursting in the feminine ideal. But her lovely face is riddled with cystic acne, the kind of curse only some vindictive goddess could inflict on a mortal given a rare gift, a cruel set of checks and balances. She enters the room and throws herself over Joy's roommate's bed with exaggerated languor, oblivious to, or tactfully ignoring, Joy's bare thighs, the ragged elastic of her ugly panties.

"It's New Year's Eeeeeve," Tatiana says again, like it's an important announcement, a concept to ponder.

It's also the eve of Joy's birthday. She will turn twenty on January 1, 2000. Tomorrow, should tomorrow come. It's a special date for a big birthday, her mother says on their most recent phone call. And as for the whole Y2K panic, well, that's nothing more than a bit of sensationalism to jazz up the news cycle. There may be a few technical glitches, better to withdraw some cash ahead of time, just in case, but otherwise, nothing to worry about. Her mother—distant, preoccupied, and oblivious—is focused only on Joy's father's illness and subsequent retreat from the world, the pastorship from which he will most likely have to step down.

She is, to her parents, a third party to be benignly tolerated. A pleasant inconvenience, like an elderly dog—a pet, an obligation they must check in on now and then, but ultimately not part of their essential dyad. Every cliché that's ever been said is true of Joy's parents: They are battle mates, comrades, life companions. Lovers? This is hard for Joy to fathom, but in all practical matters great and small, they face the world together, their bond impenetrable to outsiders, including their own daughter. Her parents have lived at almost as many addresses as Joy has lived years on earth, relying on their unassuming faith, the goodwill of various parishioners in new zip codes, eking by haphazardly yet graciously, despite abysmal credit scores and a semi-forgotten daughter. Her parents' home address is in Burke County, the childhood home of Joy's mother—though Joy feels no connection to it. She was narrowly parachuted in for junior year at a North Carolina high school. She has in-state tuition at the university but might as well be from Mars.

"You are coming with me to the Gathering, yes?"

Tatiana is involved in the same large, all-campus evangelical group that Karlie once attended, which leaves a certain taste in Joy's mouth. But now that Karlie has stopped going, Joy has acquiesced, accompanying

Tatiana, on occasion, allowing herself to be courted by the group's relentlessly smiling members, who seem to have an uncanny ability to sniff out the awkward, the stilted, the friendless. Joy has the self-awareness to find these overtures insulting, and yet she has started going from time to time out of pure desperation. As an antidote for loneliness, it is better than nothing. She and Tatiana are not friends exactly, but they are both equally excluded by the larger social fabric of the university and thus often find themselves thrown together. Friends of convenience. There are always Gathering-sponsored events. Free pizza and a speaker sharing slides of missions work in the slums of Johannesburg. Movie night (PG-13 only) at the house of one of the senior girls. Candlelight and acoustic guitar and sing-alongs. Purity pledges. Cheerful girls wearing Bonne Bell Lip Smackers and guys in pastel Izod shirts. By senior year, there are always at least twenty Gathering couples announcing their wholesome engagements. Everyone has the flush of American health to them. By contrast, Joy feels worm-ridden, anemic, the pallor of her days in a moldering international school apparent. Perhaps there were not enough hormones in the milk she drank. Or she did not get enough of the rectangular lunchroom pizza and tater tots doled out to American schoolchildren.

Joy keeps a silent record of her wry observations regarding the differences between members of the Gathering and herself, all for the benefit of an imagined version of her former professor, Professor Hendrix, even though she and the real Professor Hendrix are no longer talking. She can envision the corners of the imagined Professor Hendrix's mouth turning up in amusement, and that is something. Or, rather, it is not nothing. It is a thing to think about when one is all alone.

"What else do you have to do?" Tatiana asks, lolling all over Joy's roommate's throw pillows. Eliza would have a fit. "I'm basically the only other person here." She arches her back, driving herself into the mound of bedding.

It's an almost sexual gesture, Joy thinks, Tatiana's elaborate wallowing on the bed. Her pustular cheeks nestled in pillows, her head thrown back in the approximation of some ecstatic pose, her pinup breasts straining against her shirt. Tatiana is completely unaware, like a toddler or a puppy; her body a toy she wields recklessly.

Joy must look away—there is something wrong with her. It descended on her suddenly, like a fever. Joy sees sex everywhere, written into the crude geometry of buildings, the blushing cleft in a stone fruit, the way a stranger licks his mustard-smeared lips outside the dining hall. Every protrusion in the natural world, every crevice. She herself has the skinny body of a child but the mind of a monster. She knows nothing other than her own damp imaginings, snippets from a friend's parent's Cinemax, the shrieks and whispers of the other girls at a high school sleepover.

The gods have cursed Joy, too—she is a stick figure with a wild and heaving brain. People not infrequently take her for a girl of twelve. All rigidity and right angles, yes, but her thoughts are darkly luscious with want. It is terrible, a pain exquisite in its indefiniteness, to be trapped in the sexless body of a child when her mind is fully formed, womanly. Her longings land indiscriminately, like those of an adolescent boy, everywhere, on everyone—guy or girl, fish or foul, even inanimate objects. The pleasing swoop of an abstract statue left her in a fit of lust for days. Although her parents, studiously avoidant, allowed her to listen to the careful talk led by a stammering high school health teacher, a talk that emphasized how normal such preoccupations were, it is clear to Joy that there is something wrong with her, at least with regard to degree and intensity. She is a freak. There is no ready outlet for such burning.

Perhaps this is why virgins turn to God, Joy thinks.

". . . and I talked to Ji-Yoo and Maria and they're going, but they might go out for burgers beforehand. But some of the juniors are meeting up at Lila's before they go to Clay's place, so we could start there. Or we could go straight to Clay's," Tatiana continues, and Joy realizes once more that she's let her attention lapse.

"Sure," she says, and Tatiana sits up on the bed.

"Sure, what?"

"Whatever works."

"You driving us?" Joy asks because Tatiana is one of the few undergraduates on campus with access to a car. It's an ancient gray Cadillac—inherited from an elderly aunt with U.S. citizenship who lives up in Virginia—an overtly old-lady car that still smells of White Diamonds perfume and cigarettes that she allows, to her credit, friends from the Gathering, including Joy, to borrow frequently.

"Oh, yeah," Tatiana says. "In my sweet, sweet Caddy. We're gonna take the Big Mama Wagon out for a spin. But no, I told Kelly and Rae they could take it to Raleigh tonight. It's not far. We can walk!"

Joy laughs, despite herself. The car's nickname is a joke that's stuck. It was Karlie who christened Tatiana's car the first time she saw it, in all its rickety, precarious splendor, during their freshman year. The Big Mama Wagon. *But hey*, Tatiana had pointed out with her typical good humor, *wheels are wheels*.

Tatiana smiles. She might have crusted cheeks, a raw and angry chin—but her smile is bright and inviting. She claps her hands together, making a gesture like she's praying, or rather, giving thanks for a small prayer answered. Joy can see the glint of the tiny gold cross necklace Tatiana always wears, a winking temptation nestled against the cleavage revealed by her scoop-neck shirt.

"Tonight we're going to party like it's 1999."

Joy forces a grin. Even she knows the reference, a song people have been playing repeatedly throughout the month. Since having been introduced to his music, she loves Prince—the humor, the funk, the gyrations—but like all her passions, it is perhaps a little unseemly in its degree, so instinctively she keeps it hidden.

Somewhere above them in the firmament, the heavenly clock clicks forward on its gold hands, either toward oblivion, or toward a new millennium.

CHRISTIANITY IS AN inherently apocalyptic religion. Mainstream Christianity, with its gleaming edifices fitted with big-screen TVs and coffee bars, is simply in denial. Joy knows this. She took an honors seminar last semester on apocalypticism, and before that she'd taken Professor Hendrix's class on the Second Great Awakening and Modern Evangelicalism—although it was best not to think of that course, or of

Professor Hendrix, now. Joy realizes the doomsday cults, the fringe Christians bracing for the end times, are in many ways more accurately hearing Jesus's message. There's an honesty there, a real commitment, an acknowledgment of the message most others—members of the Gathering included—seem to ignore. With them, it's all about the blessings of God's bounty: new cars and job promotions, gifts doled out by a benevolent cosmic Santa Claus. In a way, it makes her respect her own father, the plainness of his vision, his practicality and asceticism—even if now it's a lapsed vision, a failure—all the more.

It is cold, dark enough to be midnight even though it's not quite eight P.M., and Joy is following Tatiana up the steep paved slope that separates South Campus from the rest of campus as well as Franklin Street and downtown. Across the way, they can see lights over near Kenan Stadium.

"Come on," Tatiana says. She is wearing a midriff-baring spaghetti-strap sequined top despite the chill, a grandpa sweater layered over top, wide-leg skater jeans that may or may not still be in style but have clearly been thoughtfully chosen. Her eyelids are a carefully applied iridescent gold. Her efforts are touching to Joy, who has made no effort at all—other than to finally put on pants and brush her teeth. No, that is a lie—Joy is wearing the most beautiful pair of panties she owns, soft and buttery, trimmed with lace. Lingerie, really. A foolish indulgence no one will likely ever see, but something that feels like a good secret, the fabric cool and promising as she pulls it up her skinny thighs. Otherwise, she is dressed like an ordinary tomboy, harmless and unassuming.

"A few people are going to Waffle House afterward," Tatiana says, her words white puffs in the cold. "We're invited. If we want." There is satisfaction in her voice. Landing an invitation to a Gathering-derived subgroup is a social coup.

Joy nods, knowing that she herself was not specifically invited, but that Tatiana is including her as a kindness. They're huffing their way up the hill, which is brightly lit by all the stadium lights, but turns into a shadowy pathway behind a series of midcampus dorms. She wants no part in this, really. Is it sadder to wait out the rapture alone? Or to meet up with a bunch of people who cannot, as per the dictates of godliness, *not* feign being your friend? She has been to such Gathering-sponsored events before, which all tend to have the feeling of the church lock-ins she went to with a friend back in Morganton—innocent, titillating, sparkling-grape-juice-drenched affairs.

"Tomorrow's my birthday," Joy announces, surprising herself. They are nearing the main quad in the upper campus now, trees like noble old men glowering above the manicured grounds, classical buildings that look like halls of great learning, architecture meant to inspire the mind to its highest potential. Wilson Library, Old Well—symbols of an institution, the whole arrangement coalescing into postcard images of what a university ought to be. Joy can see several other clusters of students, laughing, expectant. A beautiful girl, bare-legged in a skimpy dress, wearing Y2K-shaped party glasses passes by. A boy in slouchy jeans holding a party horn hurries past, leaving behind a cloud of cologne.

"Happy birthday!" Tatiana says, clapping her hands delightedly. "I'll get everyone to sing to you at midnight."

"Oh, no," Joy says, instantly sick at the thought. All those eyes, turned toward her. Everyone assuming the attention is something she sought, was hungry for. "No, please don't. Really."

"Come on," Tatiana says, and she pushes Joy gently in the shoulder. Joy's arm warms at even this fleeting contact, her nerves all lit up, receptive. It's so rare that someone touches her.

When they finally arrive at the address, Clay's place, Joy sees an ordinary apartment complex—low-slung, putty-colored buildings surrounding a silver banquette of mailboxes. There's a peeling sign that reads CRESTVIEW MANOR. Clay is one of the adult leaders hired by the Gathering to help lead the various campus branches. Like all such leaders, he's still young himself, a recent graduate, and ruggedly handsome. Charming in an effortless sort of way. The kind of person who has been on many hikes and backpacking excursions and who carries a whiff of an outdoor educator about him. His faith journey is one big Outward Bound mission. But his apartment seems discordant to Joy in its bleakness. There are two rusted bicycles lying in a heap by one stoop, a busted lawn chair, a child's teddy bear, rain-sodden and blinded in one buttonless eye. She has filed Clay in her mind as a responsible adult, and this does not seem like a place where responsible adults live. Crushed beer cans litter a porch. Across the parking lot, Joy can make out an immense-seeming figure sitting in the shadows on a front stoop—man or woman, who knows—but the person catches Joy staring and waves, calling out, "Y'all at the wrong spot, baby girl?"

Joy doesn't answer but follows Tatiana through a door in the center of the horseshoe-shaped complex. Inside, the room is warm and buzzing with chatter. Tatiana squeals in delight, rushing over to hug two of the other girls. It's crowded, the air thick with the smell of pizza. Across the room, Joy sees Clay tilt his head toward them in greeting, mouthing hello.

Tatiana tugs Joy through the press of bodies. Jen B. and Brad and Curtis, Leah and Claire and Jessie, Jenn F. and Beth and Danny, Melissa and Tai-Li. More faces she recognizes but cannot match to a name. She should know most of them by now, but something in her brain seems to be shutting down. She is thirsty, suddenly far too hot in her jacket. It's silly, but she has an end-of-the-world cramp in her chest, like a stitch from running too fast and too far. If all of this—ephemeral, beautiful, ridiculous—were to fade away when the clock strikes twelve, would she even miss it?

"Whoa, Joy. Hi."

A male voice.

They have made their way over to the table laden with Domino's boxes and two-liter sodas, plastic cups and paper plates. Clay presides over a cluster of freshman girls, leaning back casually against the wall, propped on one foot like a stork. This person who has spoken stands nearby, beside him. It takes her a second, but Joy places him: her high school friend Rachel's older brother, Will.

"Hi," she says uncertainly. Sweat is beading under her armpits, a creeping redness overtaking her face. She has not seen Will since she left Burke County. Rachel is away now, at a small Presbyterian college in South Carolina. Joy has not spoken to her, not since the matter of the letters.

"Clay and Kent and I graduated together from State," Will says, offering an explanation she hasn't asked for. "I didn't expect to run into you here tonight."

Tatiana is paying attention, hovering near Joy, awaiting an introduction. Will is clean-cut, tall, and handsome. "How do you two know each other?" she asks.

"She went to high school with my sister," Will says. "I'm Will, by the way." He extends a hand toward Tatiana, and she accepts it, smiling up at him.

"We were best friends, his sister and I," Joy says, but her throat is cracked and dry and the words come out softly, almost inaudibly, and neither Will nor Tatiana are paying attention. A moment, she realizes. She is interrupting their moment—always someone else's moment, never her own.

What she wants is to ask after Rachel. Maybe to pass along a brief message, a hello. Or try to explain herself. There was the matter of the letters—letters never meant to be seen by anyone else, but letters that Rachel's parents found. Joy's face burns to think of it now, the nakedness of her words, all that pure, untarnished feeling. The purest thing, really. She and Rachel. They trusted each other. A friendship so intense it kept Joy up at night sometimes, yes—but that was all. She wouldn't have dared sully that. It was special, the inexplicable connection they had. She didn't fully understand it herself. And yet what had Rachel's parents said when they called Joy's parents? They were disturbed by the content of those letters. *Disturbed.*

What's this hullabaloo? Joy's father had asked her, and Joy hung her head, a throbbing in her chest. *I quoted John Donne*, she'd said, which was true, or part of the truth at least.

I wonder, by my troth, what thou and I / Did, till we loved? Were we not weaned till then? / But sucked on country pleasures childishly?

They were both smart, bookish girls, and the words were so beautiful, this poetry from their AP English anthology. Such a surfeit of beauty one could hide behind it. *Sucked on country pleasures childishly.* Yes, it also sounded kind of dirty, but in a good way. Like a Prince song.

Will and Tatiana continue talking, laughing with each other. Someone has turned up the music too loud, Shania Twain, of all things. Joy feels queasy. It's all too much, and she can no longer pretend that any of this feels natural to her.

Will touches Tatiana on the arm like they are old friends. He is glancing at Joy, watching her watching him—and she sees his face, the way he looks at her: wary, sad.

She can't tolerate it any longer.

Joy turns, pushing her way through the tiny kitchen, crowded with people, pressing her way through the bodies, a sea that reluctantly parts for her. A group of guys clustered around the small kitchen table playing spades look up at her, mildly curious. She is no one. Just another unfortunate, swept into the fold of the Gathering. There is a sliding glass door, and Joy heaves it open, making her way to the tiny back patio and yard. She slams the door closed and then stands in the cold night breathing, each breath a pain in her lungs.

It is searing air, cold and clean though tinged with woodsmoke drifting from somewhere. She can feel the low thump of bass from a car idling beyond the little fence that encloses the back patio. The chatter and music from inside Clay's place is muffled. Somewhere else—in Morganton, probably, at a warm dinner party gathering with soft, tasteful music playing—Rachel is sitting down to celebrate with their old friends. Joy has not heard from her now for almost two years. It is a loss she ordinarily avoids considering.

"Hey," someone says. A shape rises from the shadowy corner of the yard.

She had not seen him there. A man. His face is obscured, but she can see the red tip of his cigarette.

"Sorry," she says. "I didn't know anyone else was out here."

The man steps closer, dropping the butt of the cigarette and crushing it under his heel. He shrugs.

"Not bothering me. It's too crowded in there, but I don't mind a little company."

As he moves closer, his face catches the light from inside, and she can see him: a youngish man who is still clearly older than the typical undergraduate. Late twenties, early thirties, she estimates. He is dark-haired, two-day stubble on his face, raffishly handsome. He lifts one hand toward his forehead, offering her a sort of salute, and she can see the black script of a tattoo on his wrist but cannot make out the words. The entire effect of him, his look, is decidedly non-Gathering-esque.

"Ian," he says, and now he's close enough that she can smell liquor on his breath. She can read the cursive script of his tattoo: *seven trumpets*. "I'm Clay and Kent's housemate."

"Joy," she offers.

"You into all that?" He tips his head toward the glowing kitchen window, the partygoers inside.

She shrugs. "I take it you're not one of the Gathering leaders yourself?"

His laugh is wonderfully husky and warm, like deeply whorled wood.

"I don't think they'd have me," he says. "But Clay's a decent guy. We got linked up by chance when my previous sublet ended, but it works." He gestures again to the apartment. "I don't mind these little things."

"That's nice of you. I mind them a good bit."

He laughs again, appreciative, and she flushes. There's a dark magic happening, and she can feel the pull of it, an inescapable gravity that Ian emanates. His voice has a mesmerizing, gravelly quality. She wants to keep listening to him talk. "What do you do, then?"

"I work in a restaurant. Here," he says, patting a plastic bench set against the fence. There is a patch of dirt nearby that Joy recognizes as a failed attempt at a small garden. Though it is cold, she can smell soil and rot. He sits and pats again. He means for her to sit beside him.

When she does, she is overwhelmed by his warmth, the closeness of his body, its enveloping maleness. A convergence of odors—cigarette smoke, his deodorant, and something beneath that, pungent and animal.

"You want some?"

He has extracted a flask, and something about this so satisfies her notion of him that she laughs, letting herself bend forward, cackling unselfconsciously.

"What? Is that a yes or a no?"

She clutches her belly and sits, trying to catch her breath. A fit of giggles has overtaken her, and she can't quite quell them. "Yes," she breathes, and he hands her the flask. She takes a burning swig. It is a sensation she has not experienced since the last time she visited Professor Hendrix during his office hours. "Why not? Y2K. The world's ending, right?"

He leans away from her, as if appraising her anew.

"So you think so, too," he says. "A fellow apocalypticist."

She takes one more swig and hands the flask back to him, their hands touching.

"I don't know, maybe."

She thinks of her parents, distant and tiny as posed dollhouse figures. Of Rachel, lovely and self-possessed as ever, taciturn and brilliant, wearing a party dress and a foil New Year's crown somewhere else, kissing someone under the soft fall of tossed confetti. She imagines Daliesque clockfaces dripping into gelatinous blobs, the firecracker pop and fizz of desktop monitors exploding.

"Yea or nay? Place your bet."

"Sure," Joy says. "This could be the end."

There is a loosening in her joints, and she allows herself to relax against him, a hundred different warm points of contact between their hips and shoulders.

"Heaven's Gate," Ian says. He has lit another cigarette, and as he takes a drag he squints as if concentrating on something. "Remember? They had a certain panache. A boldness. No waiting around. Hitch a ride on Hale-Bopp."

Joy can remember the newsclips, the uniformly dressed men and women in their Nikes, the plastic bags over their heads. She gives a reflexive shudder.

"Not into mass suicide, huh?"

He passes her the flask again. Her hands are reckless against his as she accepts. If the world ended tonight, it would certainly simplify things. She drinks. His hand is on her cheek, fingers brushing her face light as butterfly wings, yet rough.

"Oh," she says, leaning the tiniest bit toward him.

"Eyelash," he says, showing her: a black comma stuck to his forefinger. He looks at his watch, then looks at her. "Well, I hope you didn't drink anything inside—did you?"

She starts to laugh, but then there is the way he's looking at her. Serious. Actually a little scared. Her words catch in her throat. "Umm, no, I mean—" She gestures to his flask as he takes another drink. She watches the cords of his throat, the snakelike motion of his esophagus.

"I'm kidding. Lighten up, kid."

He puts an arm over her shoulder, offers her another swig.

"I used to hang out with people like that . . ."

He shakes his head, looking at his watch again, continuing.

"Religious types. You know, Clay means well, but . . ."

He scoots closer, blowing a warm, ticklish breath down her neck as he speaks. "Shit gets real weird real fast with them. Recruit, recruit, recruit. They've got a mission."

"Yeah. It's kind of insulting how badly they think I need to be saved," she says.

"Fuck 'em."

"Fuck 'em," she echoes, and it feels good. Freeing.

He laughs again, appreciatively, and she can feel how it pleases her, a warming fire in her belly.

"That's what I like: Someone else who's hell bound. Company. For when the world ends."

Joy shudders a little, suddenly aware of how cold she is despite how close Ian is sitting. She can feel a persistent pounding, like a distant train approaching, and it takes her a moment to realize it is Ian's heart.

"You have a dark sense of humor," she whispers.

"Do I?"

He smiles then, his teeth sulfuric in the light cast from the kitchen. A devilish smile. Beguiling. He leans toward her, cupping one hand at the nape of her neck the way male leads in movies do before they kiss the female lead. Or the way debonair killers do before they—

"You look like a little girl."

Her stomach, sour with his liquor, drops. Relief and disappointment simultaneously. He is still holding her though they're about to kiss.

"Oh," she says, and she turns away. A stupid thing to say—nothing at all. A syllable, a small, pathetic sound. As if she has failed to say the right thing, to *be* the right thing, yet again.

"No, I mean . . . I like it," he says, and his face is close to hers, leering and wolfish. "Shit. That sounded bad. I didn't mean it like that. You look young. It's the way your face seems so earnest. Or open, or something. It's nice to look young and earnest, but I don't mean it in a creepy way."

"Oh," Joy says again, and a part of her is horrified while a part of her rejoices. Her heartbeats thud inside her groin, a steady thrumming in the pith of her. Finally, she thinks. Someone sees. A tiny frond of wanting unfurls inside of her.

"We could get out of here if you want," he says. He offers it mildly, like it's merely a suggestion, like choosing ranch dressing over Italian.

She pulls back, studying him. "Get out of here?"

"We could go somewhere. Really celebrate. Before the world ends. Before they all drink the Kool-Aid or whatever."

She makes her eyes bug out and does a throat-slitting gesture in response to this, then grins at him. Who is this intrepid new person she's playing suddenly? A confident girl, capable of sass and humor.

"Seriously though," he continues. "We could do whatever. Hang out."

He's brushing the hair back from her face now, and Joy's startled not by the boldness of his hands, but by the way she knows intuitively how to respond. She moves one hand gently, tentatively, to the nape of his neck and caresses him there, this small, soft part of him untouched by the sun. He needs a haircut. It's the sort of suggestion a mother or girlfriend might make. She lets her hands move downward slowly to the small hard muscles of his upper back, his maleness new and strange to her.

"Oh, wow. I mean . . ." What does she mean? She lets her sentence taper into nothingness and waits for him to supply the rest of it for her. His right hand traces the helix of her left ear. It's hard for her to take a full breath. She is bewildered by his wild proximity, almost overcome by it. The contents of her stomach—pizza, whatever was in Ian's flask—slosh uncomfortably. She's tipsy. No, she's well past that point.

The door slides open, a yellow spill of light and sound falling onto the back patio. It closes again. Even in her present state Joy notices the way he has maneuvered himself slightly away from her, increasing the distance between them almost imperceptibly. His hands have fallen away from her in the process.

A girl stands there holding a red Solo cup. She is beautiful in an old-time way. Her blonde hair falls in loose waves over her shoulders. She is someone Joy has not seen in such a long while now that the sight of her, like a once-familiar song, causes a catch in her throat. Joy can hardly speak.

"Karlie," Ian says, retracting farther from Joy. There's a guilty quality to his movements.

"Karlie," Joy whispers.

Ian has straightened beside her, alert to Karlie's presence and at attention. The space between his body and Joy's opens even more—invisibly, but Joy can feel it. "You two know each other?" he asks.

Karlie smiles, perhaps a little sadly.

"Freshman roommates," she says.

"Oh," Ian says. "Small world."

"A happy accident," she says. "We don't run into each other much these days."

Ian stands. "Karlie, Karlie, Karlie," he says, murmuring the name like it's a refrain. He moves toward her in a way that, to Joy, feels choreographed. She can see it in how they stand, how they look at each other—there's a familiarity there. A history. History repeating itself. A game, and Joy is always the loser. Everything before with Ian, she'd misread. An idle joke played by the universe at Joy's expense. But this—what she is witnessing between Ian and Karlie—this is real.

How can one person take so much so easily with so little effort? Joy feels a wordless thought, more of a feeling, and the feeling is one of deep cramping in the recesses of her gut, in her churning, liquor-soaked stomach.

"Let's get out of here," Karlie says, and there's something—the faintest wobble, barely detectable—to her voice. "It's good to see you, Joy. We should catch up sometime."

"Definitely," Joy says, but the word comes out strained, barely audible. She can feel herself receding into the background. Once again, it's like she's no longer truly present but rather a part of the scenery, a tree or a rock or a bit of shrubbery, which is how she lives her life. The previous moment, rich and tantalizing with risk, with potential, is gone.

Ian brushes his hands against his thighs as if he's removing dust. He turns to Joy, shivering by herself on the plastic bench, nearly forgotten.

"You're welcome to join us if you like," Ian says offhandedly. "You know, two's company, three's a party."

Joy glances at Karlie before answering. Karlie's face is a mask, unreadable in the dimness. "I think the saying goes two's company, three's a crowd," Joy says.

"Suit yourself," Ian says, and Joy imagines there's relief in his voice, his invitation nothing more than an offer born of politeness. "But you get this as a consolation prize. I don't need it."

He hands her an airplane bottle of vodka and smiles at her apologetically, his face hollowed by the yellow light cast from the kitchen window, turned waxy and skull-like. Karlie scoffs. There is a lurching in Joy's stomach, a spasm like she's going to be sick. Karlie raises the red cup to her lips to drink, and for one panicky moment, it occurs to Joy that it might not be in jest, what Ian said earlier, that maybe, just maybe, something very bad is about to happen.

"Don't!" Joy yelps. "Don't drink that!"

Karlie pauses, a strange expression on her face, studying Joy as if for the first time. A look passes quickly between them, and Joy appreciates what it is: sudden mutual understanding. The kind of divine transmission of knowledge she's only previously read about. Joy is missing out on nothing, Karlie's eyes tell her. Not tonight. They are actors in a play that's already been written, the scenes already blocked. It's not too late for her, Joy, to bow out, to go home. Ian lets out a bellow of laughter.

"Relax, kid," he says. "I told you earlier. I was messing with you."

"I know," Joy says, and the firmness of her voice surprises her. "I was joking, too. Good to see you, Karlie."

Almost imperceptibly, Karlie nods.

"Well, little lady," Ian says amiably, like he's a server in a restaurant at which she's been dining with her parents, like he's relieved to be escaping her, slightly pained by the awkwardness of their previous encounter. "It's been real. See ya around." He winks at her, then adds, still using his jokey, cowboy-waiter voice. "If the world don't end."

Karlie's nose crinkles slightly as if at a minor but unavoidable unpleasantness. She drinks from her plastic cup finally, a long, slow gulp. Ian throws his arm over her shoulder, and they open the latch on the gate, leaving without having to go back through the apartment.

"Happy New Year," Ian says, but already he and Karlie have dissolved into shadow, nothing more than a figment of Joy's imagination.

LATER, AFTER THE clock has struck midnight and everyone has cheered and fireworks have gone off and the world has not ended, Tatiana will find Joy still sitting outside in the cold. Joy has finished the airplane bottle. She is unaccustomed to alcohol. Slowly and then all at once, Joy knows she is drunker than she thought possible. Her stomach roils, acidic, when she tries to stand. Tatiana wavers before her, like a mirage.

"There you are," she says. She draws Joy close to her and whispers, "I heard you were hanging out back here with that drug dealer. Clay's housemate? I heard you were all over each other."

"Not really," Joy says, but there's a pulsing heat inside of her again, and she's pleased by this misunderstanding, this smallest of scandals. She is dizzy. She might tip over. She thinks of Ian, leaning toward her, his rasping voice.

"And that girl, Karlie, too?" Tatiana says. "I forgot she was your roommate. She's trouble now. That's what I heard."

Joy lifts her empty palms, a gesture of surrender, but says nothing. Seeing Karlie has jostled something loose in her—an old thirst for a feeling of mystery Joy's never quite been able to summon, never quite been able to taste.

She retches.

There is red in her vomit, from the pizza. A hunk of crust. A foul and sudden sobriety descends upon her as she realizes her shirt is covered in the recent contents of her stomach. She smells like whiskey, half-digested pepperoni, humiliation.

Another young man appears outside then. He's slender of build but broad-shouldered, lean with muscle, sandy-haired, with a wry smile that catches the ambient light from inside. Shimmering, Joy thinks. A shimmering, handsome man. Maybe she's still drunk.

"Oh, shit," he says, moving toward them. There's laughter in his voice. "More Christians out back! Y'all are everywhere."

"We have a bit of a situation here," Tatiana says.

The guy steps forward. It's dark, but there's enough light for him to make out Joy's stained shirt. Plus, there's the smell.

"Seems like you got into something harder than the Hi-C," the guy says.

"Please," Joy says. "Don't mention this to anyone. Please don't mention it to Clay."

"Secret's safe with me," he says. "I'm an unrepentant heathen myself. Kent. I'm Clay's cousin. And housemate. Merely a bystander. Part of the background. Ignore me."

The ease with which he offers this acknowledgment of himself allows something to unclench inside of Joy. A small knot of humiliation loosens. Then she recognizes him—the boy from the library steps! The one she and Karlie used to pine after! Here, now, talking to her while she's covered in her own vomit. She is always meeting the right person at the wrong time, or so Joy tells herself, since it's better than the thought that there are no right people, no right times. When Kent smiles—shyly, with a winning note of shared self-deprecation—his teeth catch the ambient light and shine. A beacon, Joy thinks. Although perhaps at this point she's being melodramatic. She's exhausted.

"Oh, Kent," Tatiana says. "It's you."

"Oh, hey, Tatiana," he says. "Happy New Year. Good to see you."

"He was the TA for one of my information science classes," she explains to Joy. "We know each other."

Kent extends his hand to Joy, and she shakes feebly.

"Why don't I get you a clean shirt and a grocery bag for that one?" Kent says. "No one will be the wiser."

When he returns, he's holding a UNC SILS T-shirt, which he hands to Joy, leaning in closer than necessary. His breath, she notices for the first time, smells like beer. There's a hint of mischief, amusement, in his voice.

"Keep it," he says. "I'd never intentionally undermine my cousin's Godly work, but I support a little wandering off the path here and there. Y'all take care. Happy New Year." Kent winks at her, then disappears inside.

"We're friends," Tatiana says, one hand on her hip, appraising Joy. "I used to have a crush on him, but I'm over it. I could put you in touch."

Joy shakes her head. Her mouth is still sour—regurgitated pizza and gastric acid.

"Oh, no," she says, horrified at the first impression she's made. "Not after meeting like this."

"Suit yourself. It's cold. Let's go." Tatiana helps Joy change shirts quickly, then tugs her back into the apartment, where the crowd is sparser and there are trampled napkins and pizza crusts littering the floor. Joy blows on her numbed, whitened fingertips, rubbing them, trying to warm circulation back into them. Her soiled shirt is tied tightly in a plastic grocery bag. Kent's SILS T-shirt is oversize and smells of men's deodorant in a way that is not unpleasant to Joy at all.

"Welcome to the Year 2000, astronauts," a heavyset kid with curly hair says to them.

"Happy birthday," Tatiana whispers, pinching Joy softly on the upper arm.

It's too late, the atmosphere inside the house deflated like the already wilting mylar balloons.

"You don't want to go to Waffle House?" Joy asks, but she can tell by Tatiana's face that the breakfasting party left without them, having forgotten their invitation.

"Nah. I'm tired," Tatiana says with a convincing heavy sigh.

As they walk back home to the dorms, Joy can feel the shift that's happened—an ineffable thing, subtle but definite. She is exhausted, and they are quiet as they shuffle through the last of autumn's dead leaves. The dorm, a great tower, looms silently above them as they approach, their keycards clattering as they make their way inside. Somewhere far-off, a sound rings out, a long note held trembling in the throat, a sound that heralds great change. Tatiana hasn't noticed, but Joy's ears are keen enough to hear.

Poetry 36 Honors
Professor Hindelmann   Karlie Richards
12/01/1999

The Arsonists in Love   *"lusted/luster"—nice!*

We lusted after luster, lit our fill
of itchy matches, loosed a quickening blaze   *"loosed a quickening blaze/to pop*
to pop and flicker, lapping up the spill   *and flicker..."*
of iridescent fuel. We'd trace the craze   *Maybe a touch overwritten? Simplify?*
of glass, testing the give of beam and joist
as lintels warped to wishbones. When they cracked,   *"lintels warped to wishbones"*
we made a wish for radiance, rejoiced   *Nice image, but is this technically*
while walls collapsed. It was a flagrant act   *accurate?*
to burn the place we lived as if we'd spare
some light for later, as if we could make love   *Nice use of enjambment!!!*
destroy itself then make its own repair—
as if the blotting shape that loomed above   *Phoenix reference?? good!!*
us molting blackened feathers were a bird   *Also, I love the rhyme pairing of*
and not the darkness we had now incurred.   *"bird/incurred"*

A+
Wonderful work, Karlie!! Excellent handling of the form—my sense is that for the most part, you are in control of it rather than vice versa. Some lovely sonic textures here, and a strong (albeit disturbing???) central conceit. Please do stop by my office hours before winter break if you're able—we missed you in several of our last workshops, although I know you've been dealing with some family issues. I'd love to talk with you about continuing your writing—but of course, I'm available to offer my support with anything!! You're a very talented writer, and it's been a pleasure having you in class. I look forward to reading your final portfolio!
                                                —Maria Hindelmann

Bonedigger

Love God long and hard enough and, likely as not, He'd do you dirty. Just to show He could. At least, that's how Ian saw it. Casual torments, little tests, ways of insisting you prove your fealty to Him. A bully God. Take your beloved son out into the wilderness and kill him, for example. Who said that? Someone petty, mean-spirited and insecure, that's who. And the congregation sitting there, hearing the story for the umpteenth time and nodding their heads, murmuring that *this* was real faith. Faith?! Ian called bullshit. And don't even get him started on the story of Job, his long-suffering mother's favorite. Also bullshit. He'd lived through enough himself to know that these were stories only people in captivity would find consoling.

"Chop the fuckin' onions, son."

It's Bill, the manager, son of the owner. Always hassling the rest of them. The kitchen is hot, no matter what season, even now, in early January, with two industrial-size fans blasting from opposite corners. Sweat rolls down Ian's face. Sweat, or tears—it's hard to tell when you're chopping onions.

"Going as fast as I can," he says, holding up his hand so that Bill can see the bandage on his finger, thick and off-white, a spackle of dried blood showing through. He'd almost lost his goddamn fingertip and all Nick, the head cook, had done was laugh—kept flipping those burgers while he laughed, too. Like it was an initiation or something. A rite of passage, which it probably was.

"Boo-hoo," Bill says. He has a pink face, two plump cheeks that bring to mind uncooked chicken breasts, and a neck like a fat, purplish sausage. "I forgot. You're crippled now."

Ian grunts in response. Bill continues cutting the moldy bits off a hunk of cheese.

Nick is plating one of their finer dishes: chicken salad on two lettuce leaves that are pale and crinkled as tissue paper. A bleak, unseasonal dish for the day after New Year's, but no matter. Rosemary Street Grill stays busy throughout the holidays, a favorite of locals and university types alike. He looks up and nods at Bill.

"He's making progress," Nick says, but he makes a chopping motion with his own hand, his eyes going big in cartoonish pantomime.

"Shit knives." Ian holds one up, pressing the pad of his finger against it as proof.

"The university better get ready for you, son," Bill says. "A genius in the rough. Real unspoiled talent headed their way."

He and Nick chuckle again. This is their running joke. The university sits only a block away, but it might as well be across an ocean. Neither Bill nor Nick finished high school. Scholarly ambition is a hilarious farce to them, a luxurious indulgence. They've all seen the antics of those undergrads! What they don't know is that Ian *is* smart. If the world operated with any sort of fairness, if the Almighty Father were a patient and loving God, meritocratic in his dispensation of gifts and just rewards, Ian would be a block over, at UNC, enrolled as a full-time student. Instead, he's here, earning minimum wage, auditing courses when he's able. He gives them a sour smile and gets back to his chopping. He is not ungrateful for small mercies. He appreciates how they've welcomed him.

He grew up in the western part of the state, part of an enclave of fringe evangelicals. Their head pastor was a woman. Loud, with big *Dynasty* hair and expensive clothes and strong beliefs when it came to child-rearing. Tie the children into chairs. Scream the demons out of them. *Blasting*, it was called. A purification of sorts, and he can still remember sitting there in the middle of the circle of adults, trembling.

It's better here, in the Triangle, working in the restaurant. Away from the church in which he grew up. Even with all the macho bravado and ragging on one another, he feels part of the Rosemary Street Grill crew now. Which is something, considering that he's an outsider. A no one.

Nick, in particular, has been good to him. They have an arrangement. Nick looks the other way when slouch-shouldered college students turn up at the back door, asking for Ian. Ian greets them with a gruff nod, grabbing something from the black duffel he tucks by the door, slipping little baggies into their hot palms. The college kids look nervous waiting for him there by the restaurant dumpsters, eyes clicking sideways. Novices, Ian thinks. Although in fairness, he's a novice himself, just better at playing his part, necessity being the mother of invention. He's careful to invite his customers only when Bill is away. Every now and then, Ian slips Nick a twenty for his troubles. Nick's got an eighteen-month-old son and diapers to buy. He understands those times when it's best not to ask questions, better to look away.

One of the college girls who helps wait tables pops in to pick up an order. She's a brunette with dark eyes and slim legs, and Ian watches her. Probably a local, he thinks, since it's winter break and most of the college-age staff are still away, visiting family. He watches all of them, these girls. Women. Drinks them up with his eyes. Where he's from, you don't get to do that. Plus, there is the stain inside of him, an evil he was infected with. It's made him wolfish, hungry-eyed. There's something sick and indiscriminate and ravenous inside of him—although deep down, he thinks, there's also a part of him still desperate to be good. A little God-fearing worm that twists about uncomfortably in his innards, a thing he can't entirely dislodge.

The kitchen goes silent while she waits, awkwardly, twisting a gold necklace at her throat. The overhead speakers play the thin melody from an old Billy Joel song.

"Thanks, Nick," she says, flushing when he hands her the plate. The door swings shut behind her, and they all release a spill of pent-up nervous laughter. They're all tongue-tied when a female is present—*females*, that's what Bill calls them.

"*Thanks, Nick,*" Bill says, his voice a mocking falsetto.

"You're jealous, man," Ian says. The truth is that *he*, Ian, is jealous. Nick, with his muscular, tattooed arms and swarthy good looks, is the heartthrob of the place, but he is married, a family man. Look but don't touch, he says with a wink.

"You and the females," Bill mutters, massaging the last bit of green off the cheese. From Bill and Nick, Ian has learned that expiration dates are merely suggestions, if you slather enough cheese on something customers will like it regardless, and a good deep-fry will pardon any number of sins. In other words, there's no such thing as waste if you have enough grease or cheese or butter.

The door swings open again, and it's Toby, the kid Bill took on as a busser and dishwasher. He is what Ian's mother would call slow. A holy innocent, that's what Pastor Janet would have said. She was big on innocents, invited a whole choir of Down syndrome children to sing one Sunday at the church, everyone sobbing at the sight they were so moved. Later, Pastor Janet organized a special weeklong equestrian-therapy camp down at the gleaming new center owned and operated by a few of the deacons. There were photos all throughout the church offices of those godsent, special children beaming atop beautiful chestnut mares. Precious innocents, Pastor Janet said, who were all too often cruelly murdered before their birth. With Bond of Faith, they had vigils, protests, prayer meetings for the unborn. He remembers following his mother to one of the clinics in Charlotte where they stood outside all day in the beating sun, holding gruesome images of human fetuses. They sang hymns together, pleading at passersby.

Back then, it pricked at Ian in a way he couldn't quite articulate, the way Pastor Janet fawned over those children in the visiting choir, how they gazed back at her with adoration. It's only now that he is certain what she so loved: her absolute power over them. The way they dared not question her.

"What's up, big man?" Nick says to Toby, who blushes. They are all fond of him, and pick on him gently, like a little brother.

"Someone wants to see you," Toby says. He is looking directly at Ian—potato face and milky eyes. There is something wrong with one of his feet, and he walks with a limp.

"Uh-oh. You better not have been out there chatting up the ladies," Nick adds, and Toby blushes more fiercely, his entire face turning scarlet.

Ian has placed his knife down carefully, more carefully than he needs to. The container is filled with chopped onions now, and rivulets of sweat and tears flow over his face. His damp T-shirt clings to him. There's an uncertain feeling, a tightening in his chest, his heart a fist, clenching and unclenching.

"Me?" Ian says. He knows so few people here: the guys from work, a few of the regulars at Rosemary Street Grill, including the girl Toby loves. Karlie. On this point, Ian and Toby are in agreement. Maybe it's her, Ian thinks. Karlie often comes toward the end of the lunch rush, sitting alone with a milkshake and her book, reading.

Toby nods. He's got a stack of dirty plates that he unloads into the sink.

No one from his old life knows where he is, not even his mother. He had to slip away in the middle of the night, leaving most of his meager possessions behind. He got a name of a friend of a friend of a friend, someone he could stay with until he got his feet under him—Clay, a Christian of the slightly less overzealous variety who was living with his cousin Kent. They needed a third roommate. Clay seemed sympathetic to exiles, a wholesome, scruffy fellow who loved soymilk and hiking and who led an on-campus ministry group. The plan had been to stay awhile with them, get established, save up money. Work and take classes at the community college eventually, then transfer to the university. Head back when he had a degree to his name, money, a paid-off car. He'd try to convince his mother then that she was better off leaving, and maybe she'd turn her back on her so-called God and join him.

"Go on," Bill says. His voice is mild, but his eyes are curious.

Ian wipes his hands on a cloth, then finds another rag and swipes at his face. It's no use; he won't be looking proper for whomever it is. Only one other time has he been summoned by a customer, a middle-aged gentleman in tweed, who looked decidedly of the academy. It was during the after-breakfast lull, and Ian was arriving to help start lunch. The man was sitting at the bar, a cup of black coffee in his hand, a stack of papers before him.

"Excuse me," he'd called.

Ian flinched but didn't turn.

"Excuse me." The man tapped Ian's arm lightly, gesturing for him to move his wrist closer so that he could inspect Ian's tattoo. Ian recognized him then, only he wasn't used to seeing him so close. He was accustomed to seeing him from a distance in a large auditorium-style lecture hall.

"Seven trumpets," the man read, adding thoughtfully, "I remember you. Your tattoo. You audited my class on cults and new religious movements."

Ian nodded cautiously.

"You're not from around here, are you?"

"Grew up in the western part of the state, Professor Hendrix," Ian offered noncommittally, his eyes on the floor. The professor's name had come back to him, and he couldn't help but add this formal address. A quirk of his upbringing, the way he was raised. A habit that, like so many, was hard to shake. "But I don't go back there. I don't talk to my family anymore."

The man seemed to consider this for a moment.

"Same here," he said. "Remind me of your last name, son?"

"Helmsley," Ian said, then instantly regretted it. Having been trained since childhood to offer quick and dutiful responses, he was terrible at concealment. Further recognition flashed in the man's eyes.

"I remember your work. You turned in a paper even though you were auditing the class. On Bond of Faith. You wrote like you knew it firsthand."

Ian remained silent. There was a creeping heat moving up his neck, the tips of his ears.

"I researched," Ian said finally, and the professor nodded.

"Please come back anytime," he said. "I'd love to have you sit in on another class, or drop by my office—"

But at that point, Ian was already walking away.

They were few and far between, the excommunicates who got away and made something of themselves. Usually, the best you could do was to make it to UNC Charlotte or Chapel Hill for a limited and heavily monitored stint, during which time you might pursue law or medicine in order to come back and serve Bond of Faith, further insulating everyone else from the outside world. That's how they did things. If you got educated, it was for a specific purpose. Young men were sent in pairs so they could monitor each other. There was no participating in campus life outside of academics.

Ian remembers his friend's older brother, how he came back from school every weekend to work for one of the businesses run by a church elder. Ian found him one morning after service, eager to ask what college life was like, and he'd simply ducked his head. There were violet half-moons under his eyes, and his face was thinner than it had been before. *I wouldn't know*, the older boy had muttered.

Exiting the kitchen, Ian wipes his hands again on the apron he wears. He's aware of how he smells, damp and alive: animal musk, wild leeks. There is no antiperspirant strong enough to withstand that kitchen. The dining area is blissfully cool by contrast, with ceiling fans placed strategically overhead turning year-round. There are booths and an old-fashioned counter, at which a few customers finish late lunches. Even though it's a diner, unfussy and casual, he feels unkempt and stinking, out of place.

As promised, a lone man sits in the back booth, the one by the bathrooms. All he can see is the man's back: sandy-colored hair, skinny shoulders. There's a plate with an untouched grilled cheese and a mug of coffee on the table.

He heads toward the guy, chest tightening as he approaches.

"You need something?" Ian says by way of greeting. He tries to make his voice gruff, no-nonsense. The man turns and looks up slowly.

The man is actually a boy, a late adolescent. He is slender, almost pretty, with sandy hair brushed in a swoop across his brow. His cheeks and forehead are still sprayed with acne, but this does not detract from his handsomeness. The worm twists inside Ian, new wariness flooding him. The boy had been fidgeting, drumming the table, but at Ian's approach, he stops, letting his palm fall open. He smiles.

"And a happy New Year to you," the boy says, pausing a moment, before adding, "Ian." He spits it out so scornfully, so definitively, that Ian finds himself wanting to wriggle out of his own name. "Remember me?"

There is something familiar but unplaceable about him. Ian recalls the big, newly built church of his youth, the halls lined with Sunday School classrooms, the smell of aftershave and wax polish, people wearing stiff new dress clothes. Worship service was an event. Respect was required in the form of attire that proved you'd trekked one county over to find something nice off the sale rack at Belk.

"Trey Wheeler," Ian says slowly but with certainty.

The boy nods. Trey Wheeler is nothing but a child in Ian's memory. The person standing before him is long of limb and wears a nasty smile.

"Your mom can't stop crying since you left," he says, so plainly that Ian knows this is true. Ian can picture his mother in her long, modest skirt, sitting in her designated pew, eyes swollen and red. The image pains him. She loves music, his mother—mostly hymns and songs of worship, but there was also the tape she'd gotten when he was a boy. Paul Simon. She loved that tape, playing it over and over on a secondhand boom box in the kitchen. There are words he remembers even now, as if from a dream—*a cartoon in a cartoon graveyard* and *diamonds on the soles of her shoes* and *losing love is like a window in your heart*. Eventually, one of the neighbors must have heard and told Pastor Janet, who did not smile upon secular influences. Then the tape was gone. *Everybody sees you're blown apart. Everybody feels the wind blow.*

"And my mom wants the disk back," Trey announces, threading his fingers together as if he is a businessman discussing the finer points of a deal. The last time Ian saw Trey, he was what—eleven, twelve? Had he been so self-possessed?

Ian swallows. He knows the disk—a three-and-a-half-inch floppy he took from the Bond of Faith administrative office. He'd swiped the key, seen the disk, and grabbed it. Collateral, Ian figured. Protection. It seemed like an act of foresight at the time. Now, as beads of cold sweat spring up along his back and armpits, he wonders if this was unwise—merely an act of provocation.

"I'm never going back," Ian says, stubborn, like a child protesting his bedtime. He feels ashamed of himself, to be so easily found, so easily rattled.

"You're unimportant. But my mother needs her disk back. I'm here asking nicely. You give it to me, my mother leaves you alone." He looks up at him, his eyes cold and pale blue—the same eyes that belong to his mother, Pastor Janet.

Bile seeps up into Ian's throat.

"I'm asking for my mother," Trey continues calmly. "But she only asks once."

And for whatever fool reason—stubbornness, defiance, the same spirit of frustration that might have led Ian to talk back to God Himself if threatened with one of his vicious tests of faith—Ian shakes his head again. His mother is still there, and his younger sisters. He needs a safeguard. Just in case.

"Tell Pastor Janet she can go to hell."

And with that—the steady click of the fans above them, a Motown song playing tinnily over the speakers—he turns back toward the kitchen before Trey can get out another word.

When Ian is back in the kitchen, sweating and chopping and wiping, something about the set of his lips must tell Nick and Bill to mind their own business. When Toby buses the booth, Ian sees that Trey's grilled cheese is untouched but the plate is broken into three pieces: a jagged Father, Son, and Holy Ghost.

IAN GREW UP on the brink of beauty, a former mill town set in the foothills, the mountains a breath away. God's country, his mother called it. And it was pretty enough, especially if one never went farther west to compare it to any of the real Blue Ridge views—God's actual country, as far as Ian was concerned. It probably helped that his mother had grown up near Tulsa, gone for a year to Bible college, soaking up all that singing and fervor, all those visions of God's abundant blessings. And that's where she'd met Pastor Janet, who had grand visions herself. Pastor Janet wanted her own church, and when she and her husband had set off to western North Carolina to start one, called by God, Ian's mother had followed.

Hard to argue with. Convincing. That's what Pastor Janet was. Even now, Ian can acknowledge it.

She's a little like Karlie. Although with her, it's different. Karlie, convincing though she is, seems to toggle between doubt and devotion, her God is one of mystery and ambivalence—at times, even disinterest. Like a willful child seeking the attention of a distracted parent, Karlie challenges her own very conception of God, then alternately attempts to please or defy Him. Pastor Janet's God, on the other hand, is one of certainties, and in this sense, they are well matched. God is a presence with whom she has immediate and unimpeded access, a God who seems to endorse her decisions completely.

Ian is meeting Karlie this afternoon, his day off. He's aware of what he is to her, a pretty college girl and former high school valedictorian, disgruntled now with the campus evangelical group: a distraction. A phase, a passing fancy, an act of rebellion. She is slumming it with him, the shady housemate of her Christian youth group leader, a guy pushing thirty, with a couple recent tattoos and a burgeoning cigarette habit, whose only education so far is a questionable high school degree from the Bond of Faith onsite school and whatever else he's gleaned through contraband secular reading material he obtained during adolescence.

He wonders if she knows what she is for him. They are not dating. They are not sleeping together. He tries flirting with other girls—striking up conversations, attempting to redirect his interest. Like with that girl the other night at the New Year's Eve party . . . but then Karlie showed up, and . . . he just couldn't. Besides, it turned out the girl was her former roommate. All roads lead back to Karlie. Always Karlie. He does not know what they are doing—*hanging out*, she calls it, as if that actually means something. As if it does not leave him in a place of perpetual ambiguity.

The day is mild for January. He walks along the main street, the one that runs right by campus, lined with coffee shops and restaurants and bars. There are golden leaves littering the brick sidewalk still, an autumnal taste of smoke lingering in the air even though the new year has recently been rung in. The Year 2000: an anticlimax if ever there was one. From what Ian can tell, there were no discernable glitches with the transition; nothing changed. There's no real heft to this new millennium. Everything is as before, the same postholiday doldrums. There are still Christmas wreaths hung on the streetlights, a few straggling college students underdressed for the weather, who shuffle by him in cargo shorts and Birkenstocks.

He approaches a chain sub sandwich shop at the opposite end of the street from Rosemary Street Grill and sees her sitting there on a low brick wall, waiting for him. Her hair sparks gold from the late-day sun. She's backlit, but even so, he can see her smile break open, releasing a radiance that surpasses everything else.

"Hey, dude," she says, and he lifts a hand to wave, chuckling ruefully. The use of *dude* seems to be a recent tactic, a way of effectively holding him at arm's length, precluding any suggestion of romance in case he's started to consider it.

"What's up?" he says. He can play along. Being around her is enough, but there's also a canine readiness to him when he's with her, his ears pricked, sniffing the air, twitchy muscles at his throat working overtime. Sure, he has almost thirty years of repression to make up for, but he cannot risk losing this thing, this friendship or whatever it is, with her.

"You hungry?"

He sees that she's already ordered. He takes a seat beside her, and she hands him a wrapped sandwich—turkey on wheat with spicy mustard, his favorite.

"Always trying to feed me," he says, although he is grateful.

Karlie has taken to doing this—not grandly, not ostentatiously, but automatically—paying for his meal before he arrives, always seeming to remember his favorite order at the local spots or chain restaurants they frequent. She says nothing about it, and he has hardly questioned it, but he can see in her face—the clean, bright, straightened teeth, the unblemished skin, her caramel-and-honey-colored hair—that she is a well-cared-for creature, loved and nourished, someone's long-term emotional investment.

He and Karlie unwrap their sandwiches and eat. It's already getting dark. Little knots of people—students who've stayed over break, townies, visiting families—pass by them, carrying a residual holiday air. Across the street, a man with an acoustic guitar is busking. He drifts from Bob Dylan to belated Christmas songs, like someone riffling through the discount bin at a CD store.

Ian and Karlie finish their sandwiches in silence. It's a thing he appreciates about her—the way eating is a business best done communally, but during which no conversation is required. Karlie eats with an intensity that reminds him of himself, his siblings, the way they ate around the dinner table, silent, serious, uncertain.

When she is done, she wipes each of her fingers daintily. "You wanna walk?"

He nods, taking her trash from her and balling it up with his own, tossing it in the nearby trash can.

"Someone stopped by the diner the other day looking for me," he says eventually. "From my old church."

She pauses, looking at him, but says nothing.

"I took something before I left."

"You stole," she says, slowly exhaling her words, "from Bond of Faith."

"I thought it might help," he says, nodding. "To have something of theirs. If my mother ever tries to leave."

The man across the street has drawn a small crowd now, a clutch of girls who have joined in the singing, their arms slung over one another in a calculated portrayal of sisterhood and happiness. Ian watches Karlie watching them, cool-eyed. There's a thing he's noticed among the college students so often—the way they appear to be engaged in a constant performance, a portrayal of some vision of themselves, of college life, that they've been fed from an early age. It's maddening to him—although admittedly, the first thing he did when he left Bond of Faith was get tattooed and take up smoking, let his near-military buzz grow scraggly and long. Somehow that seemed different to him, a way of shaking off the clean-cut rigor of his upbringing, a way of rebuking Pastor Janet and her mandate for Sears catalog uniformity.

He watches one of the girls across the street. She looks like a sorority girl, but many students are still away for the winter break, so maybe she's a local, even a high school student. He can no longer gauge ages. The girl smiles uncertainly, revealing crooked teeth. She is taller than the others, hunching uncomfortably to their level, and he can feel it radiating off her—her discomfort, her need for approval. She throws her head back in laughter, an attempt to mimic a spontaneous eruption of joy. Seeing this makes him appreciate Karlie, her authenticity, all the more.

He and Karlie begin walking away from campus, past a used bookstore and a real estate office.

"What'd you take?" Karlie asks. Her voice is disinterested—although perhaps she simply doesn't want to spook him. She appears to be watching another little clump of sorority girls across the street in their matching pink Tri Delta Fun Run long-sleeve shirts. More students seem to be back already than he'd have thought. Karlie is one of the few undergraduates—one of the few people—he's met so far who appears never to be impersonating some notion of someone. He mentioned this to her once and she'd laughed. *You've only known me a few months*, she said. *You've only met New Karlie.* And it's true, he thinks, that he first met her through Clay, through the evangelical organization Clay leads. In this sense, he and Karlie are both sheep lost from the fold. The similarity comforts him.

"It's a disk," Ian says. "With employment records. Payroll. Bookkeeping stuff. At least, I think so."

"Boring," Karlie says.

"No, see, Pastor's got a scam going," Ian says. "All these church businesses, they'd lay their employees off. Have them file for unemployment, get checks from the state. But everyone would go in to work every day anyway. Clock in and everything."

Karlie nods. They are heading down a gentle slope now. The streetlights overhead turn on with a ceremonial pop, one by one, and she lifts a finger toward each as if doing magic. *Ta-da!* She smiles at him. The one at the corner does not turn on, and she shakes her fist at it in mock anger. Ian pats the disk, secreted in his hip pocket, and feels reassured that it's still there. A nervous habit. Ever since his encounter with Trey at the restaurant, he's been afraid to leave it at home, keeping it on his person at all times.

It's a blue-black winter dinner hour that could pass for midnight, although it's not yet six. Having turned off Franklin Street, the sidewalks are empty. Ordinarily, these side streets also hum with pedestrian traffic and bicyclists, students entering and exiting a line of off-campus apartment complexes and rental houses, but not now. Between the semesters they are sparsely populated. The overall effect is like being on a forgotten stage set, is one of being left behind after a great exodus. Uncanny, Ian thinks. Although ordinary for any university town at this time of year.

"And then there are the exchange students," he continues. "They come up from one of our sister churches in Brazil, thinking they're going to stay with host families and take classes at the community college and improve their English. But she just puts them to work. That's all they do."

"You think all that's on the disk?" Karlie asks.

Ian shrugs. "I don't know. I haven't been able to look yet," he says. The truth is he's been too afraid to open the disk at a public computer in the library. She appears to intuit this, since she doesn't press for more of an explanation. "But something's on there. She wants it back, right?"

They've made their way down to a small park, the empty baseball field turned ghostly in the darkness, the swing set sinister. Ian follows Karlie to the merry-go-round, where she sits. He plops himself down beside her.

Something rustles in the brush at the edge of the playground. Ian tenses.

An opossum scuttles out briefly, then tunnels back into the brush.

"Shit," Ian says.

Karlie lets out a nervous laugh.

"Give it to me," she says. "I'm curious."

He looks at her.

"I'd keep it safe. Hide it for you. Just say it's lost. Or that you destroyed it."

He squints, watching the smooth planes of her face arrange themselves into a placid expression again. There's a twitch in her left eye, though, a flicker of dread.

A flash of memory: He thinks of his stepfather, one of the church elders, taking him down to a freestanding building they called the Lower Hall, a place where the church doled out their punishments. It was a punishment, but also a sort of terrible game. Ian gritted his teeth, squeezed his eyes shut, until it was almost like he wasn't there at all. But he knows, now, that this is how the sickness seeped into his mind, a black bile one person could infect another with. Like vampires. One must feed. One must feed on the blood of innocents.

"I could figure out what's actually on it," she continues. "While safeguarding it for you."

"You've been telling me for weeks how you're worried. How you're being followed."

"Not by your church. And half the time I'm convinced I'm making the whole thing up."

"Still. You should tell someone. Report it."

"Maybe that's what we ought to do with the disk," she counters. "Turn it in to the authorities."

"You know I can't involve the police. Not yet. Not while my mom's still there. You could file a report, though. To be safe. On the chance you're *not* making the whole thing up."

"It's nothing. I had a dumb thing with one of my professors. A falling out . . . I don't want to make anything more of it."

She explains herself no further. He looks at Karlie, so young, her neck long and white under the newly risen moon.

"I'd keep the disk safe," she continues. "Until we figure out the right people to show it to. Get the media involved. Expose whatever's going on. Take the whole place down."

"Jesus, Karlie," Ian says. "Promise me you won't. Not until my mom's out, at least. These are bad people. They do scary shit. You think because it's a *church* . . . "

She throws up her hands. "Fine. But I've got the safest place to hide it. Swear on my life—they won't find it."

She clasps her hands and will not look at him, letting the merry-go-round turn slightly to the left. He throws down a foot to stop its motion. She smiles at him sadly—a heartbreaking smile, he thinks, the way you smile when you're about to do a thing to someone else that will inevitably hurt.

He hands the disk to her. It feels like the night is watching with a thousand appraising eyes, the whisper of leaves surrounding them like a congregation of invisible voices murmuring worries and soft prayers. His mother's voice—always a prayer under her breath, worried about displeasing Pastor Janet, his stepfather, the church elders.

There were dogs in the night where he grew up. They howled every evening, issuing sharp barks of warning, then high, mournful sounds, like Pastor Janet had trained them to do it. Watchdogs trained to meanness with their keening and the way they moved like a warning, nothing but muscle rippling under sleek skin, lean and hungry, stalking the length of their chains. Thou shalt not. Thou shalt not.

Thou shalt not touch her. Karlie. But he wants to touch her, there in the darkness, her girl's face turned serious by shadow, her girl's cheek and brow still unmarked by time. He wants to touch her—her cheek, her chin, tilt her mouth gently toward his. This is the noblest of his wants. If they could run away right now, he thinks she might save him, erase the stain that seeps into his brain. He might love her and be made pure—a true love, righteous and clean, like a linen sheet flapping on its clothesline in the sunlit breeze. Get a little house and go to school, stop the backdoor peddling, all those sad baggies of weed and pills. No more trekking over to his supplier, a pathetic creature, a former veterinarian with too many cats and an opioid problem, heavy-lidded in his filthy undershirt, his whole place smelling of trash and tobacco and excrement, a man who didn't speak much but who was more sad than scary—the ghost of Christmas future, sitting there, lazily adjusting his balls. Proof you could have it all and still plummet.

She pulls away, some sixth sense alerting her to a moment pulled too taut, the danger of excessive sentiment.

"Dude," she says, and it lands like a blow. "I've got to go. But, hey, you're still going to help me get what I asked for, right?"

He groans, leaning back onto the merry-go-round so that he can see the sky, the stars blurred and blotted by the city lights, the clouds. They've smoked weed together, and he's allowed it. They've gotten drunk together, fine. He's enjoyed it, yes, and—is it bad?—hoped for more, the liquor loosening her, perhaps, pulling them together with its slow tide of inevitability. But this, this thing she's asking for—a gun? It's too much. Not that he doubts that someone might be following her, as she claims—

a thwarted admirer, probably, an unrequited crush—but a gun seems excessive. Dangerous. It's a not a thing for Nice Girls. And at the end of the day, she is still a Nice Girl. The sort of girl who might save him.

"Karlie, come on," he says. "Did we not just have that entire exchange? About how you're just fine? How you're only imagining that someone's following you?"

"Please," she says, tapping the place where the disk sits in her bag. "I'm a woman living alone. I like to be prepared, that's all."

He sighs the exaggerated sigh of his mother. "You just said that half the time you thought you were making the whole thing up."

She shrugs. "I'll pay. Two, three times whatever it costs you. Tell me the amount."

"I'll think about it."

She shoves the merry-go-round with her foot so that he's spinning, staring up into the dizzying whirl of the night.

"I'm going," she says, and he maneuvers himself upright, stills the spinning merry-go-round, and watches her go, candle-pale, into a place where the trees part. There's a short path from there to her apartment complex. She disappears, leaving only an ache in his chest.

LATER THAT NIGHT, when Karlie calls him from the bar, he can tell from the singsong slur of her voice that she's wasted. It's after one A.M. He should be sleeping. Tomorrow he's working breakfast.

"You're a mess," Ian says when he pulls up in Clay's old Jetta and she stumbles, laughing, into the passenger seat. It's a raucous undergraduate bar. There are three other girls in short, peacock-bright skirts, legs goose-fleshed in the cold, standing outside, hugging themselves for warmth.

"Take me to your place," she says, and he looks at her. She appears to understand his look and laughs, tapping his knee with her index finger as if he's a harmless old man with a quaintly dirty mind. She smiles up at him, a honey-cayenne dare of a smile. "I don't want to be alone."

And then she nestles sweetly against him while he drives, her cheek on his shoulder like a child's. Like an overtired child being driven home from the late service on Christmas Eve. He can hear her breathing softly, can smell the rum and Coke on her breath, the fine, floral-shampoo scent of her hair. He holds perfectly still, hardly trusting himself to shift in his seat.

When he leads her inside and back to his bedroom, he sees Kent, a night owl, watching an old movie in the living room. Kent looks up from the TV and nods in acknowledgment but says nothing—a placid guy, a good housemate, never one to judge or intrude. Clay's away at another one of his conferences meant to nurture and develop new Gathering leaders. And as Ian helps Karlie to his bed and takes off her shoes, he realizes this is the closest they've ever been to each other, her chest rising and falling close to his. And it's then that she pulls him toward her, to the warm, sticky sweetness of her mouth. She kisses him long and hard, like someone very thirsty finally taking a long, clumsy drink. It is a messy, enthusiastic kiss. She tastes like rum and Coke, pink two-for-one rail drinks, onion rings and ketchup, a bummed clove cigarette.

"Oh, Ian," she whispers, and his heart starts to split in his chest like an overripe plum, the rest of his body suddenly alert, rising to meet her. Her eyes catch the light and glitter in the dimness.

He is on top of her now, and she kisses him again, with the dreaminess of a drunken person on the verge of sleep. Her hands are at his belt buckle, fumbling but purposeful. He stills her hands with his own, stopping her.

"Not like this," he says to her.

"Like this," she responds, laughing quietly, teasing, although she can hardly keep her eyes open.

"Not like this," he says again, and it is only a tremendous protective feeling that allows him to gently guide her hands away. The dark part of his mind churns, then quiets—conquerable, at least this time. A test. A temptation. Her breath is slowing, and she does not resist. By the time he pulls the covers up to her chin, she is breathing softly and evenly.

He lies on his back, silent, on the floor beside her, not sleeping, unable to sleep, until it's almost five A.M. and time for him to go to work.

When he leaves Karlie dreaming whatever she dreams in his bed and walks out into the cold pitch-black of that early hour, the air is sharp in his lungs, but it feels like promise, like possibility. Ian is sleep-deprived but buoyant.

He doesn't notice the truck crawling along behind him until it's too late.

The men have been waiting for him, idling in an adjacent alleyway until he passes. They are prepared.

Ian has considered before the possibility that he might be mugged by someone going after his stash, but these men have been sent for a different purpose. They are masked and gloved, yet he knows their voices—those slanting western North Carolina vowels, the way they growl at him like it's the chorus to an old song. One of the men sounds like his stepfather, but his stepfather is long dead.

The men shove Ian into the truck bed where they bind and gag him like a trussed pig, then drive him out to a dirt road in the middle of nowhere. There, they untie him, remove the cloth from his mouth, and throw him to the ground, encircling him like ghouls. They go at him like it's sport. *Where's the disk, you fuckin' fag? You devilspawn. You shiteatin' bastard, where's the disk?* they say as they pummel him, and he can feel their unadulterated rage and joy, all the forbidden filth words snarling and alive on their tongues. Such pure release, the pleasure they take in slamming his head to the ground, rattling his brain in his skull, kicking him in the groin so hard he vomits. There's blood or tears running down his cheek, and he swallows helplessly, lapping up the salt, like a dog.

We saw you with the fuckin' girl. We saw you, shithead. You can make this easy, or you can make this hard. Tell us now and maybe we don't pay her a visit also. Maybe we don't need to touch a hair on her pretty head. Go on and tell us and you make this easier.

Kicking. Fists on him. A crunching sound. Cartilage, or maybe bone.

Squeal, you fuckin' piggie. Squeal.

They do not stop, and he feels himself tunnel inward, as if he were a child receiving punishment at the Lower Hall. Maybe this is yet another test issued by God, upping the ante, offering one more ferocious *Do you love me?* And maybe the correct answer this time is to say nothing, hold a martyr's silence. Or maybe the answer is to relent and confess, crawl weeping back to Pastor Janet, begging to make amends.

He does not know anymore.

His mouth is a gushing wound. He has swallowed a tooth. He sputters like a rat drowning in a gutter. He can feel that deep-seated instinct for survival, the urge to relent, to tell them, to beg. He curls himself into a ball, shivering, aching, broken-boned and bleeding. Maybe a ruptured spleen, God only knows. Thou shalt not squeal. Judas Iscariot.

Judas Iscariot got a crap deal. There was something sympathetic about the guy. A well-meaning fellow with a fatal flaw. Hard coming up second fiddle. Wanting things. Having ambition. The pieces of silver—they'd serve a practical end, who could deny that? And Jesus all the while showing off, running around like the lead singer in a boy band, easy and entitled.

But then again, Ian's always been a contrarian. His mother often said this of him, laughingly, when he was a little boy, and then later, when he was older, she said it, too—urgently—with a nervous jerk of her head, warning him to shut up.

They leave him there in the mud. The truck skids off into the night, its headlights slicing the darkness over the empty fields. Ian lies curled into a ball, his insides mashed to pulp. His head clangs like a beaten gong. Love God with all your heart, He'll do you dirty. Try and defy God, He'll do you dirty all the same. It's a losing bet either way.

There is a beetle beside him, its antennae twitching as it probes a splatter spot of his blood. They are at eye level, Ian and the beetle. He is no better than that. He wails into the great, black maw of sky, begging someone, something, to be merciful and to let his end, if it's coming, be quick. Thou shalt not weep and moan. Thou shalt not. Let ferocious seraphim appear, blinding with light, so righteous in their anger that he will cower. It's a sickness that grows inside of him, planted there by someone else. Already ruined. Damaged goods. Left broken and beaten, thrumming with regret.

And then it occurs to him: Even once they've figured out her address, Karlie's still at his place. He can stop her from going back home, go back with her, stay with her, protect her. If he warns her, she can be prepared. He'll help her get what she's asked for. He can save her if he can only get back to her in time.

There is no one else for miles, only the cold rush of wind through the empty stalks in the field. When Ian tries to rise from the ground, his legs judder and will not hold him. He is seasick, the ground moving in waves beneath him like a great, black ocean. There's a hammering behind his eyes, but he knows what he must do. This thought steadies him. He must find a way back—and soon—to warn her.

The Walk-In

She's woken before her alarm again. Bit by bit, Lila is losing sleep, twenty minutes here, fifteen minutes there, a steady accrual of lost time, those last, sweet diaphanous moments of slumber. It is a thing that happens with age, the broken wee hours. She was a luxurious sleeper once, a gourmand. Now she startles easily, like frightened prey, tearing right through the seams of her vivid dreamscapes. Jacob shifts slightly beside her, then settles, the comforter humped over the sleeping mound of him. He is unperturbed.

He's a good husband in many ways. She is a good wife, decidedly. The morning sun is not yet up, and their bedroom, their marital bed, is stagnant. Ordinarily, Jacob is the early riser of the two of them, but lately, he has been tired, tremulous. Like an old man. Ever since the dog bite, stitches in his leg, the infection, a certain confidence of his has been depleted. The old fizz and sparkle have flattened now like champagne the day after a party. She and Jacob watched when animal control came to take the dog away. Diana, their neighbor, wept horribly. All over an ugly, aggressive dog—and Diana needed stitches and antibiotics herself! A pitiful sight. No accounting for who you loved, or what, man or monster, beauty or beast. In this instance, as in all manner of things, Lila prides herself on being practical. It took the dog attack, but at least now Jacob has submitted to the advice of his neurologist, showing up dutifully to physical therapy wearing a pair of eggplant-colored sweatpants Lila purchased for him for exactly that purpose. A troubling sight, yes, to see him there with all those elderly people, spines curled like candy canes, their shriveled, meatless limbs, but the correct choice.

Lila shoves the covers off, pivoting her legs, letting her bare feet hit the cold hardwood floor. It's still winter break at the university, which means Jacob will stay home, and she will go to work. She works in the university's student health clinic. The life of the mind deserves a rest; the life of the body, however, is afforded no such luxury—other than sleep, the briefest respite. And even then, the body is always under assault, subject to urinary tract infections or mononucleosis, conjunctivitis and otitis media. Even these college students, their bodies wonderful in their resiliency, in the punishments they can withstand—sun and sugar and hard drinking, sleep deprivation, sex with strangers—they will test their bodies and, most of the time, come out unscathed. Lila has seen it. She's doled out penicillin or Valtrex to tearful, quaking girls who cup their neat little vulvas as if clutching a treasured pet—perhaps a hamster, or hedgehog—that has betrayed them. (Children! They are children! With acne on their cheeks and thin shoulders, the boys barely knowing how to shave, barely needing to!) During the break, there are hardly any students on campus, no classes, and yet she will still help staff the clinic. She and one other nurse, a gently gregarious woman in her sixties, will run the place while an attending covers from home. It will be a slow, windowless January day, one of those days when she travels to and from home in darkness. When she returns in the evening, she'll find Jacob still in his pajamas, sitting on the couch, covered in crumbs, brimming with delight over some delicious tidbit from one of his books. The life of the mind! When she says it to herself, the phrase drips with irony.

What is the brain but a gelatinous bundle of nerve and fat? What is the mind but an act of mythology? What is the body but a fractious empire, ever ready to revolt? These are not her words, but Jacob's. She agrees. As in most things. Not because she isn't smart; because she is. He has a way with something—words, is it? Ideas? Cajoling people? Lila's gift is quickly ascertaining the gifts of others, then making herself amenable. And what else is a wife but a tireless helpmeet?

Lila dresses quickly. She is a compact, neat person—attributes that read as competence. She cultivates this to her advantage—at the clinic, and at home. Her house with Jacob is not large, but it is tidy, despite the piles of books he builds—wild, tottering constructions that crop up like the precarious block towers of a child throughout their house. She permits this. Neatness must allow its streak of chaos or else risk seeming precious, too tightly controlled. This flourish gives them, their house, a certain desired flavor when visitors arrive. *Oh,* they all say, running their thumbs down the spines. *Oh, I've wanted to read this.* And Jacob will leap excitedly into the conversational fray while Lila, demurely, almost as if by magic, will appear bearing a tray of appetizers or drinks. This is one of her tricks, much appreciated by Jacob—her gift of anticipating other people's little needs and then—poof!—appearing at an elbow with a napkin, a canapé, a Scotch refill. It's a trick of invisibility and quiet attention. She is capable of disappearing between the warm, lissome bodies of their guests—beautiful graduate students, precocious undergrads, newly hired assistant professors. They fill the room with subtle, woodsy perfume and soft-voiced enthusiasm, smart girls, all of them, classic beauties, wearing clever glasses frames of interesting geometries. Lila absorbs it all, every detail, imperceptibly, at the edges of the conversation.

Her stomach sloshes, a sourness rising in her throat, but Lila puts the bread in the toaster anyway, and prepares her cup of chai. Ordinarily, Jacob does this for her, but not lately. He is weary. The neurologist says it's normal. She knows that when the body says sleep, one ought to listen. It is healing. It is a physiological requirement. Outside, it's not yet light, but she can see the bare trees in her neighbor Diana's yard delineated even more darkly. Melancholic trees. Through the glass, she can see the cold—an invisible tightening, something about the way the contours of darkness seem to grip the maple branches, the haggard forsythia in her front yard, and not release. A choking cold. She splutters her chai, a spot landing on her sleeve. It is too hot, too sweet—nothing like the way Jacob makes it for her. The toast goes down dryly: meager, tasteless sustenance. From the refrigerator, her stepson, Michael, beams at her from a photo wearing his graduation cap and gown. Jacob's son, from his first marriage, although who can call it a marriage, truly? They lasted barely three years, Jacob and his first wife. He was a graduate student then, his wife a little stick figure of a girl from back home with haunted eyes, their elopement an act of rebellion. They'd both been raised never knowing any material want, in icily pristine households, playing at adulthood, romanticizing their new poverty. Who could blame them? The two of them barely out of adolescence, affection-starved, bucking against the expectations of the society in which they grew up, like they were the first to ever think of such a thing? But Jacob's first wife grew weary of playing house and making ends meet. New motherhood was too much for her; she fled back home. Too young. We told you so, her parents said, happy to pay for the divorce. They sent money to Jacob for the child, and that was that. Lila met Jacob soon thereafter. A single father. She stepped in, raised Michael like he was her own. Mom and Dad, he calls them. She *is* a mother, in that sense. She certainly is. And that is enough, Jacob has always said. Because she loves him, she's always agreed.

In the bathroom, she brushes and flosses her teeth, dabs moisturizer under her eyes, pats her chicly cropped hair. She's not one of those done-up women. But she is trim, well maintained, like a high-quality vehicle with many miles on it—not flashy or new, but soundly constructed.

There are worse things than falling in love with a girl. Yet another girl, that is. Lila appreciates this, but it's still an insult. A persistent one. Even so, she says nothing. Her husband does not give her enough credit for such vast patience and understanding. Falling in love with a girl. By *love*, Lila means hopeless infatuation, and by *girl*, she figures she ought to clarify—for herself, for the meddlesome critic who lives inside her brain, for the permanent record maintained, possibly, by some remote, cosmic judge—that these have all been young women of unequivocally legal age, however absurd the flush of their youth. So no, they have not been *girls*, not technically (and thank God for that!). And yes, there *are* worse things.

Lila's breath is visible in the car as she drives to work. The heater will not warm up, she knows from experience, until the moment she pulls into the parking garage at the clinic. The sun is a harrowing orange that keeps threatening to rise as she traverses a series of little bends and dips in the road. The day has lightened to a mournful, winter white by the time she arrives.

She takes the skywalk from the parking deck toward the main hospital entrance, then continues on the pathway past the emergency room to the student health clinic. There are already people standing outside the emergency room, some of them in hospital gowns, shivering, smoking cigarettes, hunched in the cold. Although it shouldn't be, somehow it is a heartening sight to her, the way these beleaguered smokers cluster together, their impromptu solidarity of a sort. She can see the stork-like limbs of one older man, pale and purplish below his gown in the cold.

She used to smoke when she was young. When she wished to be a broody girl with big, daring eyes, one who could wield a cigarette, her mouth puckering suggestively, her dainty fingers letting it flash through the air when she gesticulated, as if to punctuate her witty remarks. And she almost was a witty girl like that. A Vassar graduate, a painter—good Lord, she wished to be an actual *artist*! But something stopped her. A nervous hesitation, a desire not to be seen as too obtrusive, a stiffness, even a formality to the way she spoke that left people puzzled and a little chilled.

"Hello," the girl says to Lila.

She's standing at the door because the clinic is not yet open. Her breath is fragrant smoke. She's holding a cup of coffee that Lila smells with envy—a thing she gave up years ago because it was too acidic.

"Hello," Lila says warily. The girl stands there trembling in her thin sweater and pajama pants, her flip-flops. Why is it that the students insist on traipsing across the campus in flip-flops year-round? The girl's hair is abundant and wavy, the kind of honey-blonde overflow you might expect to find on a mermaid: impractical, a little ridiculous, suitable only if your days were spent singing siren songs from the ocean deep. There is a turquoise scrunchie on the girl's wrist, a pink wristwatch depicting Minnie Mouse—a calculated girliness, Lila thinks, for someone with such a shrewd face. The girl is pretty but her eyes are hard, a strange mix of knowing and naive.

Lila fumbles her keys while the girl watches.

"You have an appointment?" she asks.

The girl runs a hand through her hair, flipping its golden bounty to the opposite side of her face the way a swimsuit model would. In the dead of winter. Outrageous. Lila herself was outrageous once, albeit in a different way. Cunning. Subtlety used to be a kind of art.

THE WALK-IN

"Y'all still do walk-ins, right?" the girl asks.

"Only on Thursdays and Fridays."

It's Tuesday. The girl makes a quick face—a goblin-like flash of annoyance or disappointment, the ugly, angry look of a child. Somehow, it's this face, the way it betrays her, that makes Lila soften slightly.

"We can probably get you in today, though," Lila adds. "Things slow down over the winter break."

The girl nods, shifting her weight and pulling the sweater tighter around her chest. Lila unlocks the doors, and the girl follows her silently. The lights click on, and the faint smell of sizzling dust fills the air. The HVAC system is old here, housed as they are in one of the unrenovated buildings on campus.

Her colleagues, the admin staff, are not yet there.

"Take a seat," Lila says. "I've got a blanket for you if you want."

The girl eyes her but doesn't answer, flopping onto one of the plastic chairs with all the flustered beauty and awkwardness of a young woman who cannot be marred by even the most unforgiving light, the baggiest and least flattering outfits, the most uncouth movements or expressions.

"How may I help you?" Lila asks.

"You're the nurse?"

"And the doctor and the check-in lady and the medical assistant. For the time being at least."

The girl sighs and lets her head fall into her hand. Now Lila can see it—the purplish marks on her neck, a dusky spot on one cheek, the dull bluish color beneath an eye. She's worked here long enough to know these signs—unmistakable.

"A checkup," the girl says but her voice is faraway, her eyes glassy. "Tests, maybe. Bloodwork."

"Tests?" Lila echoes.

"Whatever it is you can test for," the girl says, and she throws a hand in the air, making a vague figure-eight gesture that means everything and nothing.

Lila frowns. "I have a kit," she says carefully. "I'm trained to use it. You know. In cases of coercion."

It's quaint how she cannot say the words *rape* or *rape kit*—not here, not now, with this girl, so uncannily familiar, sitting before her.

The girl shakes her head.

"It's fairly quick," Lila adds, kneeling beside her. The front door opens and Angelique, the other nurse, enters in her puffer jacket. "We could send it over with everything else." Lila whispers this, but the girl has gone rigid, stony.

"Maybe," the girl says. "I'll think about it."

Lila sighs, rising to her feet. Her left knee pops. She does yoga regularly, but one cannot stop time, decay, the slow decline of the body, its inevitable turn to mush and rust, from woman to artifact.

Angelique pauses, eyeing the two of them as if she's sensed the interruption.

"Don't mind me," she says loudly, her voice bright and chipper. "It's cold out there, y'all. I'm gonna go turn the coffeemaker on in back." She gives a curt little nod to Lila.

During these slow January days between sessions, they don't get many appointments. She and Angelique drink herbal tea together in the breakroom with its bland walls and drawers full of plastic cutlery and tiny ketchup packets. Some days, Lila brings a novel. They each allow the other a long lunch. It's nothing like during the regular semester, when they are crawling with students—overgrown boys with acne down their necks, glossy girls in Kappa sweatshirts, anxious former valedictorians from some godforsaken county in the far corner of the state. Angelique is maternal, bosomy, with a deep, rich laugh, a graying braid that falls down her back, and a pale, freckled face. Lila is more reserved, but she can tell they appreciate it, the students—her knowledge and authority.

"Come on, then," Lila says to the girl, feeling, as she often does, motherly. "I'll take you back to a room."

LILA ONCE BELIEVED that she would be a mother—not a stepmother as she has been to Michael, whom she does love very much. (Stepmothers!

The much maligned villain of every fairy tale! The wicked women who swooped in when the goodly maidens with their milky breasts and lily-pale cheeks succumbed to puerperal fevers. The true mothers, vanished or lost, disappeared, or too good for this earth and called home to their Lord and Savior early, leaving only these ruthless women with their mirrors, their vanity, their feminine wiles—the practical ones, who survived. It used to be a thing she and Jacob joked about, back when it still seemed funny because everything, anything, was possible.) Motherhood. A tiny being would gestate within then rip her apart, tear her open into someone new. She yearned for it—the small, hot gums on her breast, that sweet weight in her arms—a physical sort of need that became a sharp pain. And then, like most acute pain, it dissipated to a vague, persistent ache.

Lila met Jacob when she was twenty-five, a new nurse in the emergency room—a concession to practicality after her Vassar liberal arts education failed to land her requisite social or artistic status. He'd been her patient. It was a story that made older people sigh and younger people squirm. *What was it?* the younger person might ask, being bold and not knowing better. *A cut, a deep cut, and you could see down to the fat, all the way to the bone,* Lila would answer, unabashed, although Jacob still blushed to hear her speak of the body and its grotesqueries. The official line had been he'd tried to slice a melon and his hand had slipped.

It was only after the doctor was gone, Lila alone with Jacob, putting a bandage over the stitches, that he confessed to her.

"I did it on purpose," he whispered. "I don't know what came over me, but . . . I have a son at home," Jacob said to her. "A baby. He's with a friend, so I need to get back."

"Oh," she said, looking at him in a way he must have read as shock or dismay. Befuddlement, really, because here he was, entirely beautiful with his long lashes, his hazel-flecked eyes, the tiny scar above his mouth that she would later learn was from a fall during toddlerhood. His hair was chestnut and gold, practically ringlets. She'd heard him tell the doctor that he was a graduate student at the university. The prospect of his fundamental sadness—when he had everything—seemed unthinkable. Crushing.

"Oh, don't look at me like that," Jacob said, turning his head from her, covering his face. "I can't bear it. I'm an idiot. You're far too pretty to be subjected to something so awful."

"How can I help?" she asked, and it was a genuine question, the true essence of her being, the one domain in which she felt complete confidence.

"Let me take you out to dinner," he said. "Please. And then it'll never happen again."

The way he looked at her in that moment: eager, pleading, earnest. It was a way no one had looked at her before. She fell in love with him, right there, on the spot.

THE GIRL IS lying dutifully on her back in the exam room, eyes flickering across the ceiling. She shifts, the thin paper crackling beneath her, and pulls the gown tighter around her chest. Her pale forearms look almost greenish in the light. Lila notices the small, heart-shaped locket the girl wears—a youthful trinket, the sort of object that might be given as a sweet sixteen birthday gift—and the multiple piercings in her ears, including one in the helix that still looks fresh.

"I like your necklace," Lila says quietly. The girl doesn't answer. Lila decides to start somewhere ordinary and specific: the cardiac exam. She warms the stethoscope on the heel of her hand.

"I'm going to listen now," Lila says, and the girl nods. She holds the bell of the stethoscope, pressing against the girl's chest: fast, but regular. She listens longer than she needs, letting her eyes fall onto the girl's neck, where there are bruises, lilac splotches, the clear imprint of fingers.

She knows she should ask Angelique to chaperone the pelvic exam, but something warns her against this. It's recommended as part of best practices, but sometimes they are too swamped. Angelique is probably busy, and anyway, she'll be quick. She helps the girl scoot forward and begins the exam, noting the labial tears. She has seen worse. Lila says nothing, other than to announce each action before she takes it, waiting to see the small acknowledgment on the girl's face before she moves her gloved hand. She swabs quickly, but with extra gentleness and care, as if she's not using a test but ministering to the girl, her touch offering a kind of healing.

"I'll need a urine sample, too, before you go."

"When will I hear about the pregnancy test?" Her face blanches as she speaks. She looks like an illustration of a child martyr.

"We should get everything back in forty-eight hours," Lila says. "Maybe seventy-two. But you should know. If you just had intercourse, it's too soon. If your period hasn't come, you'll need to take a pregnancy test again in a couple weeks."

"Oh," the girl says, and Lila can see that not only has she not considered this, but that she also probably didn't have enough knowledge of human reproduction to have known it in the first place. The dreaded Two-Week Wait—it was a term the women used the time Lila went to a support group. They met in the empty fellowship hall of a church, pulling metal folding chairs into a semicircle and gathering Danish butter cookies onto paper napkins in their laps. They welcomed Lila, warmly, without pity, but there was something rabid and terrible in the way they dissected all the details: ovulation kits and reproductive specialists, acupuncturists and thyroid supplementation. It was a horrible camaraderie they shared, a reminder of one's failing. Lila left that evening with a sense of sadness dropping into her gut like an anchor.

She and Jacob continued to try over the years, but nothing came of it. A false hope once, yes, but by ten weeks in, she bled, and that was that.

The girl begins to cry, silently. Her lovely, pale face is made ugly with red splotches, her features twisting into a ghastly mask. Her shoulders heave up and down.

Lila hesitates. It's the only way in which she is hesitant: the hows and whys and whens of human contact. Will the girl welcome it, a consoling touch on the shoulder? Will she flinch and pull away? What Lila would like is some helpful task she might complete with her hands, a busying motion, the retrieving of a cup of ice water, the drawing up of an injection perhaps, or the expert wrapping of a twisted ankle.

"I'm so sorry," Lila says finally. "If you want me to submit a rape kit, I'll need to swab a few more times. Should I go ahead?"

"That's not necessary," the girl says.

"Still," Lila says. "If it were relevant. Might as well while we're doing everything else."

"I guess," the girl says, allowing this as if it's a kind of relief to relent.

The girl is already positioned, so Lila opens the kit and works efficiently, smoothly, taking the final samples that she needs and placing them in the envelope. When she finishes, she watches the girl, and the girl holds her gaze.

But that is when she sees it (or rather, the absence of it, the asymmetry): There, in the third hole on the girl's right earlobe is one earring in the shape of a star, gold with a tiny pink stone in the center. In the corresponding hole in the girl's left earlobe is a tiny silver stud—an obvious replacement, Lila thinks. Lila knows the star earring, its missing mate. She's certain. She found it the evening after Jacob was attacked by the neighbor's dog. She had scooped it up from the kitchen floor, felt the slight weight of it in her hand. A star. Tiny, a pink fleck of stone in its center.

She could tell immediately that it was a young person's earring, the sort of object a teenager might pick up at Claire's, its post blackening over time, the cheap metal irritating the earlobe.

Jacob had been lying on the couch in the living room, an ice pack on his leg. She could hear the tinny sound of laughter, the jaunty musical theme from a *Seinfeld* rerun.

"Lila," he called to her, and she stilled like a rabbit in an open field, sniffing the air, assessing things. "Lila, my darling, come sit with me."

And she threw the earring away in the kitchen trash can, making sure to bury it deep beneath carrot shavings and the carcass of a rotisserie chicken. She went to him, let him wrap his arm around her, pull her close to him, his scent of library book pages and Old Spice. On the television, Elaine Benes was dancing, and Jacob shook with laughter. A familiar plot, characters like old friends, the cleverness of it, all comforting. She let herself soften against him. She let herself laugh.

Now, she thinks of that earring in her house and studies the girl, who is sniffling, wiping her nose on the sleeve of her gown.

"I know who you are," Lila says to the girl, whose given name on the chart is listed as Margaret. Margaret Karla—of course. Karliegirl80. The AOL Instant Messenger name on their home computer. "You're Karlie."

The girl frowns, but she is quick, this girl, and Lila sees that she is already putting the pieces together. The girl exhales shakily.

Lila feels as if a clamp has been brought down across her torso, like a band is tightening across her midsection so that she cannot take a full breath. The air escapes her parted lips in quick, shallow bursts. Her fingers have started to tingle. She cannot feel her mouth.

"Did he hurt you? Did my husband do this?"

The girl does not respond. Her eyes dart across the room to the doorway, then to the chair, where her clothing rests in a neat pile. She is calculating her escape, and Lila understands then how she herself must appear: pinched and breathless with anger, a vengeful wronged wife.

Then it occurs to her how much trouble he's had lately—since the diagnosis. The doctor had mentioned that difficulties with sexual functioning were quite common, particularly with a sacral lesion like Jacob had. So it was less likely, but was it *impossible*? To her chagrin, she realizes she cannot speak to this from any recent personal experience—it's been a while since they have tried. But no, no, that's not the point. The point is that above all else Jacob was not cruel. He had no need to get his way by force; his charms were plenty sufficient. They likely had a misunderstanding, Lila thinks, and the word sounds so much better in her mind. At worst, *a misunderstanding*. The girl, coquettish, provocative, reveling in the attention of a brilliant older man, had surely been receptive at first. Lila can imagine her coaxing Jacob, giggling and goading him on—and then, when they were in the midst of things, the girl changes her mind in a fit of pique. Lila can envision it all so clearly: the girl suddenly yanking herself away, turning spiteful. Jacob would have been thrown off. Confused at the unexpectedness of this. It was easy to understand how someone might have accidentally gotten hurt.

"I'm not angry," Lila says, stepping closer, pressing one hand against the girl's cool forearm. A risk. Her hand pulses there, hot on the girl's arm. "Truly. I'm not. But please. He's sick, you know. I'll make it right if we can just keep things private. And if there *is* a baby . . ."

Lila cannot explain how it leaps to her mind, this sudden mad vision of herself: a grandmother of sorts! The baby gnawing his fat fist, cheek against her chest as he drifts off to sleep. The sweet down of his ponderous head, his sticky, prehensile grip on her thumb. Caring for her husband's lover's child. It makes no sense. Illogical! But why not? They have the money. She'd always thought there'd be another child after Michael, but there never was. If she'd known, at the time, that he'd be it . . . But now, here, fate seems to be offering another baby! An unconventional arrangement, yes, but there, laid out as a picture in her mind, it makes all the sense in the world.

Lila's dream is a lapse, a moment of slowed time, the pause between each heartbeat lengthening to a fermata between her ribs. In those seconds, the girl is up from the examination table like a sprinter, sweeping her clothes up in one arm, fleeing the room with the gown flapping around her bare thighs. She is gone, the door flung open like a dumbstruck jaw behind her.

Before she goes home that day, Lila tucks the rape kit in a cabinet, behind gauze and betadine and bandages. It would be wrong to throw the kit out. But sometimes samples are lost, any residual DNA lost with them. It happens all the time. An innocent mistake. She'll decide what to do later, when her head is clear.

THAT EVENING WHEN Lila is back home, when Jacob has heated them both bowls of tomato soup, which he carries to the table carefully, not a drop spilled despite the shaking in his hands, she studies his face for a sign of such brutality. Is it there, in the thinness of his lips, the slightly arrogant arch of his brow? Or the fierce, almost greenish light of his eyes? No, she cannot see it.

"You love me best, my darling?" she asks him.

His spoon hovers over the bowl, his face blank, unreadable. Then his eyes crinkle, and his face softens to a smile, as if he's humoring her, amused by her peccadilloes. He lets the spoon drop back to the bowl.

"Yes," he says. "Above all else, my love. Most decidedly."

She reaches across the table to pat his hand, which feels thinner now. She almost tells him about her encounter, about how she didn't recognize the girl at first. Not when she saw her shivering like a stray outside the clinic's entrance, nor later, when the girl was undressed except for the rough gown she clutched tight to her thin shoulders in the exam room. How it was only in the end, right before the girl fled, that Lila figured it out—after that strange, buzzing intimacy had passed between them. What was it? Not love—Lila is not susceptible to it, having been previously inoculated. More like a dream, a relentlessly repetitive dream in which you must avert some disaster, close a door quickly, find someone lost—a dream you keep waking up from, wishing always you could return. Jacob would understand. They have always shared their own peculiar intimacy, a tenacious closeness that persists whether the world can fathom it or not.

"Good," she says, squeezing the bones of his fingers. "I understand you. Like no one else."

And he nods at her, like an obedient child.

He is a man of vast and varied appetites, a damaged man, Lila thinks, but what no one else could quite appreciate is his core loyalty. He is hers, and she is his. Look at how his cheeks have hollowed, the vulnerable divot beneath his collar bones. He is sick and brilliant, her beloved. Marred by his difficulties, yes, but valiant, even, in his broken way. She cannot see brutality. Or rather, no greater brutality than she can summon in herself, when the need arises. So let them be bound by it, whatever it is—call it monstrosity, or call it devotion.

Karlie

All she's ever wanted is to redeem herself somehow—to perform an act of bravery or right a wrong, to make one thing beautiful and true, pull off a bit of heroism—and yet here she is, in the middle of nowhere, trying to buy a gun. Guided or misguided, she can no longer gauge. There's a bouquet of polyester flowers abandoned on the curb, an array of cheerful lavender, yellow, and pink, petals heavy now with last night's rain, a stack of wet newspaper turned into a pile of sludge—fitting metaphors. Signs? Perhaps she was naive. Perhaps there are no wrongs to right—at least not within the limited scope of her powers. Perhaps this, here, is reality in all its entropic meaninglessness like garbage in the face, and she is only now acknowledging it.

The shopping center is empty but for a green Ford truck and a van with tinted windows parked near the dumpster at the far end of the lot. The Sally Beauty, Dollar General, Dress Barn, Rosita's Cantina, and Carter's Guns & Ammo stand sullenly in a row, like a lineup of suspects. There are no customers around, but then again, it's not quite ten A.M. on a frigid January morning. The parking lot is littered with the detritus of sad lives: limp plastic bags, an empty bottle of Colt 45, a child's soiled pink mitten. Maybe everyone's life is sad and it's only a matter of realizing it. Karlie sits in the driver's seat of her ticking car, hesitating. Her breath comes out in clouds. The car's heater is broken, so she drove the whole way with numb feet, shivering.

She blows on her raw hands and steps out.

She's meeting a guy named Rick—one of Ian's connections, a friend of a friend. Although is *friend* quite the right word?

Walking toward Carter's Guns & Ammo she pauses, aware of herself, too conscious of a potential audience. Maybe she ought to go to Sally Beauty first, amble by the window, gaze inside. Consider the press-on nails and mustache bleach, the jet-black hair dye, lipstick. A wig. Transform herself into a stranger. Return incognito, play it casual, nonchalant, someone stumbling into gun ownership by chance. But who is she even performing for? The men who are after Ian? The person following her?

The shop windows are smudged, fogged over from the inside. It's hard to see, but Karlie gazes in. Her teeth clack. She should have worn a heavier coat. She rubs her arms with icy fingers.

A gray Buick pulls up, and she feels an electric jolt, but it's not Rick. It's a woman—with elaborately curled hair and a teal windbreaker. Karlie watches the woman get out of her car wearily, heavy-limbed, as if she's just finished a long shift. She extracts a canvas bag from her back seat and slings it over a shoulder while Karlie pretends to examine a display of dusty nail polishes in the Sally Beauty window. The woman disappears inside Rosita's Cantina.

A beat-up-looking brown Oldsmobile pulls in next, and Karlie's throat grows so tight she can't swallow. But this time it's a frail old man in pleated trousers smoking a cigarette—surely not Rick. Ian said Rick was supposed to be reliable, discreet, with a clean record and excellent knowledge of firearms.

When Karlie first brought up getting a gun, Ian had told her it was a bad idea regardless of whether anyone, man or phantom, was following her. But that was before he showed up the other night, a crust of blood down the side of his face, both eyes nearly swollen shut, a tooth missing. She almost didn't recognize him. He looked half dead, his head swollen and discolored like a smashed gourd.

The church he'd grown up in, the cult, had come for him. Beaten him almost to unconsciousness, kicking him in the head and groin with their steel-toed boots, demanding he give back what he'd stolen. What's worse, they seemed to know about her—*a girl*. They'd seen the two of them together, had made vague but menacing threats. They're looking for her now, too, he told her. And the disk.

"I should give it back," Ian had said. "They're not messing around. It's not worth it."

"But this just proves how valuable the information is," Karlie argued. "We need to get the disk to the police. Or a reporter. After you get your mom out, of course . . . And after we take you to the emergency room."

"No. No emergency room. They'll find me." He shook his head. "Goddammit. I should never have taken the disk, and I shouldn't have involved you."

"It's well hidden," Karlie said. "No one's going to find it unless I want them to."

"We need to get well hidden ourselves. 'Til we can figure something out."

So instead of the ER, she guided him to the ratty motel room they found near the airport, easing him onto the bed. She paid in cash. He gave a fake name, wore sunglasses and a hat to conceal the extent of his injuries.

"Whew," she exhaled, helping him arrange himself gingerly against the propped pillows. She gave him a glass of tap water, which he gulped greedily. "You sure you're okay?"

He hadn't even noticed her own bruises, the scratches near her elbow. It wasn't the moment to tell him what had happened to her, so she was grateful.

"I'll be fine," he said, and she watched his eyes close and his breaths even, waiting until he'd fallen asleep.

Now she's here because the gun shop owner doesn't ask questions. Rick has an agreement with them. Rick's a regular, a purchaser not of guns but of gun kits, which allow for a fully operational weapon without a serial number to be constructed.

"We're getting it for self-defense," Karlie argued originally. "Why not just get a license and do everything aboveboard?"

But Ian was adamant.

"You don't know Bond of Faith," he insisted. "I don't want any record of you, me, anyone I associate with, getting a gun. Trust me. They have ways of finding these things out. I don't want anyone seeing either of us in a gun shop."

This level of caution seemed a touch excessive to Karlie at the time, but then again, who was she to argue, given how she's been behaving? Karlie presses her face against the store window, peering like a child. There aren't any customers inside, but she can see the long barrels of rifles arranged with military precision against the walls. The store is laid out like a jewelry store, with racks and glass cases, the rifles and handguns laid out on rich purple velvet, like treasures on display, worthy of lust and admiration. And they are, Karlie can see, mean and clever objects, tantalizing in their appeal.

"You want some?"

Karlie jumps. It's the woman in the teal windbreaker, suddenly right next to her, extending an opened can of Pringles. The woman lifts a stack of chips to her mouth and crunches, letting a slow, sly smile move across her mouth.

"I'm good," Karlie says.

The woman swallows and smiles even more broadly. There are bits of whitish chip caught between her teeth, and her pink lipstick is smeared. Karlie steps back; the woman looks friendly but a little insane.

"You're cold," the woman says to Karlie, glancing to the side of the building, which faces an open lot filled with nothing but dirt and scraggly weeds. "Come on. We can sit in my car and get some heat. You sure you don't want some chips?"

"I'm waiting for someone."

"I'm Rick," she says. "I think you're waiting for me."

"Oh. You're a woman. Ian didn't tell me that."

The woman laughs.

"He's smarter than I figured."

The egg-shaped man inside Carter's is watching. Glaring, or so it seems, his arms crossed over his midsection. An evil Humpty-Dumpty. Then he smiles and waves. The woman, Rick, touches Karlie's shoulder. She's misjudging everything. A shadow passes over her, a coldness, like clouds moving over the sun. But it's an overcast day, sky the color of snow, though it does not snow here, no, hardly ever. It's the thing, the shape, whoever has been following her. She whips around quickly, but no one's there.

"Jumpy, aren't you?" Rick says. "Come on."

Karlie follows dumbly and slides into the passenger seat of Rick's car. Rick turns the key in the ignition and cranks the heat up to full blast. Karlie thinks of Ian, of blood dried black along his scalp, of his crushed face and broken ribs. They're searching for him right now, those men from Bond of Faith. She could already be too late.

". . . Easy to carry, right?"

She's missed what Rick is saying. Karlie's mind is chittering like a squirrel with a box of Cracker Jack.

"Sorry?"

"I said you probably want something small. That'll fit in a purse or a small backpack?"

"Yes," she says. "Nothing fancy. With a—" She fumbles for the word—is it handle? The part that you hold on to? She makes a motion with her hand, and Rick nods.

"I chose one with a smaller grip for you. So, what I'm selling you here is not a gun, but gun *parts*. Because if I were to sell you a gun, that would be illegal, see? But nothing's stopping you from buying parts from me and then assembling them yourself. Don't need a permit or ID or anything to buy yourself some parts, you see? And all I'm doing is selling you parts . . . though I took the liberty of getting the process started. Let me do a couple other things to help you out, and then you'll take over . . ."

Rick assembles the remaining pieces quickly. She has a small drill for exactly this purpose. It's apparent she's done this many times.

"And then you're going to finish it," Rick says, taking Karlie's hands and guiding her to click the grip into place.

"And now," Rick says, pressing Karlie's hand so that her fingers curl around the grip, poised against the trigger. "You've built yourself a gun. Untraceable, but should work like a charm."

"Oh, wow," Karlie says.

KARLIE

Holding it is a kind of power. She could alter the course of things, command respect. In high school, Karlie once wrote a long, scolding essay excoriating the NRA and thoughtless gun enthusiasts. She still abhors guns, in theory. But now she also gets it on some level, the sick appeal. She likes the gun's weight in her hand, despite the implications. She is a dutiful student of literature and knows what this should mean: The gun must go off.

"I like it," she whispers, her voice trembling.

Rick chuckles like someone who witnesses this sort of seduction all the time.

"She'll do the job. For a build-yourself option, she's not bad."

"Thank you," Karlie whispers. The Buick's heater is blasting warm air on them. For the first time in a long while, Karlie feels almost calm.

"What's a sweet thing like you need with a gun, anyway?" Rick asks, plucking a stack of chips and crunching.

Karlie squints at her, letting the gun droop.

"I'm being followed. Ian got beaten up."

Rick's watching her with interest now, hands folded across the expanse of her dingy lap. There are rhinestones on her windbreaker, a dog-eared paperback copy of *The Brothers Karamazov* lying on the dash, a cracked CD jewel case promising *Ten Calming Buddhist Meditations* on the floorboard. She pops open the can of Pringles and places one delicately into her mouth, chewing thoughtfully.

"Looks like he caught up with you too," she observes after she finishes the chip. She touches her own neck lightly. "The bastard. Whoever he is."

"That was something else. A mistake." Karlie's shoulders tense. The thought of the other night, his hands on her—it elicits a deep ache in her groin. His fingers were hard. It still burns when she pees. She can feel her muscles growing taut, her grasp on the gun tightening.

"Don't point that thing at me," Rick says. "Jesus, kid. It's not loaded, but."

"Sorry."

Karlie's shoulders slump and she lets her arms fall, handing the gun back to Rick gingerly. Her eyes are welling up. Embarrassing. She looks away, out the window, where the old man is picking his way back across the lot holding a paper bag.

Rick sighs. "Hey, listen, you know the first rule of having a gun?"

Karlie shakes her head.

"Do everything you can to avoid using it. Nothing good ever comes of pretty young girls playing with guns. And keep your hands on her. Don't let her out of your sight."

"And the second rule?" Karlie asks.

Rick sighs again, hesitating. "You know you could still change your mind. Keep your money and use it to get out of town for a while, lie low."

"The second rule?" Karlie asks again, pulling the wad of cash from her bag and handing it to Rick, mashing it into her left hand. Rick shrugs. With her right index and middle finger, she presses gently against Karlie's forehead, right in the spot where there would be a third eye. The touch feels like a blessing. Karlie's ragged breathing slows. Rick looks very old, like she has seen too much of this life and it's disheartened her. She hands Karlie back the gun—Karlie's gun now—a little reluctantly.

"If you shoot, don't miss."

ON THE DRIVE back, the sky starts to clear, deepening to a blue that belies the January date. It could be spring, or early fall instead of the dead of winter. A sign, Karlie thinks. An approving sign. Perhaps God has not left her. She *is* doing the right thing by getting a gun. She will protect herself, and Ian. She will set things right.

Once she gets back to Ian at the motel, she'll take him out to eat—somewhere anonymous on the highway where they'll hardly mind his wrecked face, a breakfast-all-day sort of place with sticky plastic menus and hearty, filling food for people who are on their feet all day doing hard labor. Scrambled eggs, toast, sausage. Restorative food. Pancakes in perfect circles with the cold little foil-wrapped butters and sweet syrup. She'll pummel him with healing calories, touch his hand softly, wipe the crust of dried blood near his temple the way a girlfriend would. A *girlfriend*? The possibility has recently occurred to her. A surprisingly wholesome thought, wholesomeness being a quality she's stubbornly rejected for at least this past year or so.

But her memory of that night at Ian's house nags at her like a toothache. Her recollection of the details is foggy, but she knows she pulled him toward her recklessly. Oh, God, it was embarrassing. She recalls tugging at him, playing the role of a dumb, drunk, horny girl. He turned her down so gently she winces to think of it. What was it really that goaded her to do such things? Loneliness. When you wanted to be near someone, to feel his bodily warmth and know he adored you but resisted any actual closeness. Because that was the thing: Ian was yet another person who adored her that she'd toyed with, strung along. She was stupid and thoughtless that night, yanking him toward her, hands at his crotch. Graceless, crude, cruel. It would make sense if he hated her, if she'd blown whatever chance they could have had at something real.

Or maybe they had no chance, because of what happened with Ian's roommate. She can't tell him; it'd probably seem like her fault, given how he'd seen her behave. He'd never say such a thing, but . . . how could he not blame her, when she already blamed herself?

Still, she'll take care of him, convince him to get checked out at an urgent care at least, buy him a new shirt. Maybe they'll drive out somewhere and find a movie theater, sneak into the humming, anonymous daytime dark of a matinee. Something innocent about it, old-fashioned. A boy and a girl watching a moving picture, colors splashing their rapt faces, lost in all that beautiful artifice. No one will know them there. It'd be as safe as anywhere. She'd lean against his shoulder while the previews play. The prospect of hiding out for a while might be necessary, romantic, salvific, even. She will prove herself to him. She will do things right.

The problem is she can't find her bank card—probably buried under papers on her desk back at her apartment. Now that she's used up almost all her cash on the gun, she has nothing. Not even for the motel tonight, not for new clothes for Ian or breakfast or a movie or anything. She's promised Ian she'll come straight back to the motel. The men from Bond of Faith could be surveilling her place, keeping an eye on downtown. But it's still bright out, the day holding such a sunny innocence that any act of violence seems unfathomable. It'll only take a second to swing by the apartment. And a hot cup of coffee wouldn't hurt. She's got a headache.

The roads are clear as she drives back toward town. She checks her rearview mirror, but there is no one.

Karlie pulls in a parking spot downtown beneath one of the huge tinsel wreaths still hanging from a streetlamp. Rosemary Street Grill is open, doing a sluggish but steady business. She can see the regulars at the counter through the window—old guys, townies who come in year-round and nurse the bottomless cups of coffee, shoot the shit over college basketball or the weather.

The cook, a guy named Nick, is manning the bar when she walks in, and Toby, the sweet kid who seems much younger than his years, is wiping down one of the booths.

"We're going out again tonight," Nick offers in lieu of a greeting. "Belated New Year's celebration."

She shrugs. Maybe it'd be safer than the motel—to be out in public the whole night, partying, always with a group of people. Drinking and laughing. She'll run it by Ian, see what he thinks. But then there's Ian's swollen face, his obvious injuries—how would they explain that?

"You ought to come," Nick says, looking at her pointedly. "Seems like a strong drink might do you good. I'll call later. Apply a little friendly pressure." He nods once, like this decides things, and moves off to the other end of the bar toward a tray of clean cutlery. He lifts this and moves back toward the kitchen.

Toby, childlike in his plastic-framed glasses, smiles hesitantly and sidles up to her. He's fond of her, more than fond of her—always finding excuses to be near her, to bring her slices of pie on the house. In turn she gives him little knickknacks—usually items she finds for cheap in discount bins or from fast-food restaurants. He used to panhandle, but now he's managed to get a job here in the diner, and she feels an almost maternal pride in his upward mobility.

"I couldn't get a coffee, could I?"

Toby studies her, still smiling, and she wonders if he's noticing the bruises on her cheek and neck. Without a word he moves to the other side of the counter, pouring her a to-go cup.

"Here," he says, and she sips, feeling her headache start to lift already. But she's still tired, oh so tired.

She pulls out her last couple dollars, but Toby waves her off.

"Thank you. You're always so sweet to me."

He follows her out the front door. There's something about his face, how he's looking at her, his small bright eyes blurred behind his thick lenses. She must be throwing out a distress beacon, something only discernable to infants and animals and people who are slightly touched.

He stands there, still wearing the dank apron he wears at work, studying her.

"What's wrong?" Toby says, and he gestures to his own face, the mirror location to where there's a dull bluish splotch on her own.

"Nothing—oh, I have something for you, too."

His eyes widen.

"It's one of those little *Pokémon* toys Burger King's giving out."

"Karlie!" He beams at her, clapping his hands once in a way that almost breaks her heart. Ever since she learned of his dedication to all things *Pokémon*, she's been on the lookout. She wishes such a small gesture could make her own face split open with such joy. Ian has pointed out the intensity of Toby's gaze, his murky eyes watery behind his fishbowl lenses, how his infatuation with her borders on creepy, but she knows that's not right. She can still recognize adulation that's pure.

"I'll go grab it and bring it right back for you," she says. "I have to swing by my place anyway. Give me ten minutes?"

He nods at her.

"You're beautiful and good. Like a princess."

"Oh, no, not really," she says too briskly, her voice husky, threatening to break. She turns from him, almost rudely, and slips into her car while he stands there, watching her go, waving.

EVEN THOUGH THEY aren't close, Karlie's sister, Becca, is wont to offer occasional well-earned wisdom. That's what five stints in rehab will do for you. *Life lessons*, Becca says. *It works if you work it.* She told Karlie a story once, from when she'd stayed at a recovery center down in Georgia. She'd made a friend named Dave who'd had a bad football injury as a freshman walk-on. Started with pills, moved on to shooting up. But he was finally clean. Hopeful. At night, he and Becca talked about what they wanted to do in their sobriety. When he got out, he told her, he would try to get his job back, file for joint custody of his baby daughter.

But then one night he looked off. Rattled, pale. Becca couldn't figure out what was wrong with him until he broke down and told her. He'd seen someone—or something. Following him. He'd seen it the other night, and now he was seeing it everywhere. A shadowy shape, racked with sobs.

"The Weeper," Becca said, and then she told Karlie about a story some of the old-timers told. There was a rumor about an apparition that foretold a death. An urban legend.

"The last night he was alive, Dave saw the Weeper again. This time he got up close. And it had his own face. Dave's. Dave couldn't move a muscle, and the Weeper just got closer and closer to him, wearing his face, crying."

The very next day, Dave was found only three miles away in a parked car, dead, with the needle still in his arm.

Karlie must have looked credulous because Becca had laughed bitterly.

"Nothing but druggie ghost stories," she said. "It's not the Weeper that gets you. It's the smack."

Later, Karlie read in one of her literature classes about seeing one's double. A doppelganger. Another harbinger of death. Or rebirth, maybe—phoenix-like rebirth, if you were an optimist. A myth, nothing more.

Karlie does not want to believe in such things. She prefers a notion of the world governed by benevolent guiding forces, ablaze with signs and signals should one care to look. If she can still believe in such a world. But something has been following her. Like a recurring nightmare.

There are things she tries not to think of, but the avoidance of them cobwebs the corners of her mind. If she could do things over, she thinks.

Again. Set things right. Maybe that's all the Weeper ever was—the clang of one's own bad memories.

"Why'd you leave?" Ian asked her not long after they first met. He was talking, she knew, about the Gathering. It had been late, the wee hours, and they'd been drinking.

"I needed a change," Karlie said. "I wanted to stop playing a role. Looking for approval, you know?"

Ian said nothing, waiting for her to continue. They were sitting on an old picnic bench at the park below her apartment complex. The sun was coming up in long, pastel strands beyond the trees. They had not slept at all, but Karlie wasn't tired.

"But then I felt like I was just playing a different role, still looking for approval, not from God but from . . . all these other people."

"And now?"

She shrugged. She'd been thinking of the professor, Professor Hendrix, how pleased she'd been at first by his attention, how she'd known from the start that his interest in her went far beyond that of a teacher toward his student, far beyond benign paternalism. She saw how he looked at her, how he listened when she spoke, and it gratified her. It warmed a small, lonely part of her that had been shaken by the absurd arbitrariness of things. If God Himself could not be bothered to supply order, then she could supply it through the power of her own intelligence, with Jacob, quick-witted and sought-after, his classes always overenrolled, there to nod approvingly. Until their last night together when she'd seen the flimsiness of it all—and what had she done? Laughed. Like a wicked child. That ended things pretty effectively. She was like a pampered brat breaking toys.

She pictures Ian now, and the way he decorously declined her advances that night. Her face burns at the thought. She tries to conjure an image of her high school boyfriend, Tyler, his face gone waxy after the injury, the sour smell he'd emanated when she visited him once at the long-term rehabilitation center—yet another person she'd ruined. Even dear Joy—who is smart and lovely and good, but filled with doubt, so she carries herself hunched and uncertain. Karlie had tried to make amends with her, like the time Joy's parents visited—she intuited how hard that visit would be for Joy, so she tried, tried to be a true friend—but it was too late.

She sees them: all her mistakes lined up in a row, like haunted dolls on a shelf. They merge into a single black shape in the periphery of her vision, inescapable as a bad smell, a cloud that follows. Following like the sound of that gray Cadillac with a busted headlight pulling up outside her apartment and idling there. The "BMW," they all called it. The Big Mama Wagon. A bad joke. She's borrowed the car herself. Tatiana lent it out to everyone. So it could be almost anyone . . . only now she's starting to feel more certainty as to who's been driving it, watching her. And maybe it's her own fault. Maybe, despite appearances, she brings blight wherever she goes. Maybe that's what's been happening all along. There's freedom in finally acknowledging it.

"Maybe I'm me at last," she'd finally said to Ian that day. "Maybe I don't need approval from anyone."

AT HER APARTMENT, all is quiet. The late-afternoon sun is dropping lower in the sky. The place still smells of the Indian takeout she got two nights ago. The dirty cereal bowl in her sink, the pile of books on her living room floor, and the T-shirt she shucked onto a kitchen chair all lie unperturbed. There's a light flashing on her answering machine—a message from the woman at the clinic. The nurse. Lila. Jacob's wife. An added humiliation. So far the tests that have come back are all negative, she says. Her voice on the recording is studiously neutral. Professional.

Karlie has been having flashbacks to what happened. There's no word that feels quite accurate for what he did. Well, there *is*, but she can hardly name it in her thoughts, no more than she can name him. Even with it unnamed, she shudders.

She knew from little things he said that he'd grown up with an alcoholic father. He was terrified of turning out like that, he'd told her. He'd seemed so solicitous and gentle at first. She'd turned to him, after she stopped seeing Professor Hendrix. After she'd laughed, after her laughter had revealed the situation for what it was: human, ugly, inappropriate.

What a little fool she'd been to acquiesce for so long, although it had felt like an antidote to something else. To Tyler, maybe. Tyler, so vulnerable and wide-eyed, so easily moved by beautiful music, by the majesty of the world. So painfully sincere in his Christian belief. It was hard to think of him without wincing. The countervailing weight of Jacob's cool intelligence, the way everything—including religious fervor, *especially* religious fervor—seemed to present itself as an object for study. But then his professorial confidence, once so reassuring, seemed more and more like mere cynicism. And he was sick, which reminded her, in an awful way, that he was old. That last time, when he couldn't . . . She'd felt awkward—scared, really, because it was a reminder of sorts, wasn't it? It shook her. Like those memento mori they'd discussed in her art history class. She hadn't liked seeing his frailty.

So she turned to *him*, instead, the unnamed one, who was certainly more age appropriate. That wasn't the issue. He was easy to turn to. He'd been waiting there patiently, in the wings. She'd noticed his interest in her from the start. She'd suspected he had a crush on her, a way of showing up places where she happened to be. But he was careful not to push it, flattering and attentive in a cautious way. The car, the "BMW"—she'd even developed a hunch at some point, a gut-level inkling, that it might be him. But she hadn't had proof, not at first.

Sleeping with him that night, right on the heels of calling things off with Jacob, was nothing like what a good Christian girl would do. Unlike Jacob, he'd been rough with her. It was surprising given the quiet, hesitating way he always spoke, the way he stooped under the weight of his heavy textbooks walking across campus. He was so rough it felt like welcome punishment—something she deserved. She wanted to be emptied out, shattered into pieces, un-Karlied into someone blank and new. But there'd also been something broken in him—or so it seemed. A deep hurt, a loneliness she'd recognized and to which she'd been drawn, vain enough to think that, in offering herself, her body, she might fix it. But sleeping with him only unleashed it further. Afterward, he seemed to take the whole thing too seriously, following her like a stray dog she'd made the mistake of feeding, mooning after her with his wounded puppy eyes. She wasn't ready for that. Neither for the gaping hole that seemed to open up when he drank too much, nor for the neediness he mistook for love.

One night, that's all it was. But he'd been smitten. Had begged her to meet with him again over the ensuing weeks, to hear him out, let him plead his case. He'd started showing up outside her classes. Waiting. And finally, she'd relented. That very night at Ian's, after he'd gently rejected her then left. *He* showed up, right in Ian's bedroom where she slept, almost too intoxicated to stand upright, reeking of bourbon, his eyes turned to voids. He'd moved toward her, lumbering, like a bear. Talking about true love. Begging her to save him. She told him no. He'd become unrecognizable. A monster. She kicked him, scratched at his face. He didn't listen. It only seemed to make him press harder, use greater force.

Since then, he's called twice and left messages. She could tell he wanted to smooth things over. He probably hardly remembered the details. He wanted to meet up, to talk. *To make sure there were no misunderstandings.* He spoke like a politician, in the passive voice. A blackout drunk who had an inkling that there were things he'd done that were not good. Even so, she guessed, the story he told himself was almost certainly different. A story of star-crossed love.

Karlie glances at her watch—it's only been five minutes since she arrived. She might as well grab a clean set of clothes for herself. She puts on a fresh pair of jeans, a new shirt, runs her fingers through her hair. Wakes up her sleeping Microsoft laptop, but there are no good new emails there—no more clever or gently chiding messages from ProfPlum71. For weeks she thought it might be Professor Hendrix driving up to her place, idling in the car outside, working up the courage to knock, maybe, to issue her a professorial dressing down for her bad behavior. But then she actually saw the car: the Cadillac. Then she thought it might be Joy, even wrote Joy a letter. An overdue apology, in part. But deep down she knew all along, or at least suspected. The messages, the missed calls. He'd also have access to that Cadillac.

She shivers. She misses Jacob, actually, in spite of herself. If nothing else, he possessed a comforting self-certainty, a way of looking at the world's complexity with detached amusement. It had settled her to be near him, as if she too were a clever spectator watching petty dramas unfold from on high.

There's a noise in her kitchen, something soft and heavy shifting. She flinches. The air in her apartment, still redolent of curry, is not right. The gun is in her waistband, but she doesn't trust herself to use it. If anything, its presence undoes her further, makes her aware of how far she's in over her head.

"Ian?"

No answer.

It's a foolish, desperate question on her part. Ian is miles away, probably sleeping. Her spine prickles. She tiptoes around the corner, and there they are.

Three large men stand in her tiny kitchen—powerful-looking, with broad shoulders and guts, big functional muscles built by doing manual labor—looking at her like they've been waiting. There's something starched about them, the way their shirts are buttoned all the way up to the top. Clean-shaven. No tattoos. White, southern men with wedding rings. Potluck men, church supper men. Fathers. God-fearing husbands.

Outside her kitchen window, she can see the sun dropping quickly, the fast-approaching winter night.

"Well, there she is," one of the men says softly. "Lady of the hour."

Karlie is frozen. She looks into the faces of these strange men and knows they are the ones who came after Ian. This time they haven't even bothered with ski masks or disguises. They are emboldened, on a righteous mission, blessed by the Lord.

"'Though hand join in hand, the wicked shall not be unpunished,'" one of the other men says, and his eyes seem to twinkle with punitive delight.

"'But the seed of the righteous shall be delivered,'" Karlie finishes.

The man whistles his approval.

Karlie straightens her shoulders.

"Your friend said he gave you something that belongs to us," the man says.

"I destroyed it," Karlie says. "You can leave Ian alone now."

The man chortles.

"You know the parable of the lost sheep," he says, stroking his own pitted cheek with mock tenderness. "Gotta return him to the fold."

"Where's the fuckin' disk, Karlie?"

She stiffens.

"I told you. It's gone. Search the place."

Her hand goes to her hip, to the shape of the gun resting coldly there, but she's clumsy and obvious. The youngest of the men dives at her. He plucks the gun from her easily, tucking it into his own pocket with a smirk.

Her gun, Karlie thinks. A sad joke, an anticlimax, a dud. If her gun goes off in a forest but there's no one there to hear it . . . She thinks of Ian, bruised and vulnerable in the desolate motel room. The man strokes the butt of Karlie's gun gently with his large, chapped hands.

"Poor little girl," says the biggest man, the one who seems to be in charge. "You don't know what you've gotten into." She notices the butt of another pistol poking out of his pocket. They're armed; of course they are. The big man nods to a red-haired man, who heads to Karlie's bedroom. She turns to follow him.

"You stay here," the big man says, gesturing for her to sit. From her bedroom, she can hear the sound of drawers being emptied, clothes flung from the closet onto the floor, light fixtures removed, carpet ripped up. A floaty, disconnected feeling, almost like tranquility, overwhelms her.

She can hear that the man has moved to the bathroom now—clatter of pill bottles, the sound of his hand sweeping the contents of her medicine cabinet onto the floor.

Something flickers in the corner of her eye—a shape. Someone else, some other entity, watching.

It's nothing, though. A trick of the eye. Night has fallen fully, deeply, sullenly. A January darkness. Most of the other residents of the apartment complex are still home with their families for winter break.

"I got zilch," the man says upon his return to the living room.

"Will you please leave now?"

The redheaded man looks at Karlie like she's a fool, but she stands, following him to the door.

KARLIE

"Sit your ass back down," one of them says, but she cannot listen. She can only follow, a cataract of words tumbling out of her in desperation.

"The disk is gone. I swear. I destroyed it. It's not Ian's fault. Leave him alone."

She can hear how her voice is rising to a near-hysterical pitch. Hot tears are springing to her eyes. Her gun in that man's pocket—the gun she got to protect herself, protect Ian. There is, she can see, a dead bird on the walkway outside her apartment, and it is wrong for so many reasons—its beady, vacant eyes, the fact of a robin being out and about in the depths of winter. It's wrong. It is a sign. But from whom? Meaning what?

"Please!" she shrieks, and one of the men turns and walks back to where she stands, illuminated in the doorway. He slaps her in the face so hard she recoils. Her nose is bleeding: bright red splotches that splat into a picture of a dozen roses on her floor.

"Go on out there and tell Pastor we're ready for her," the man says, and he pulls Karlie back inside her apartment.

HOW LONG KARLIE sits on the floor of the apartment clutching her knees to her chest is uncertain. Her bones ache even though—strangely, it seems to her—the woman did not hurt her. *Pastor*, the men called her, and she wore the long, old-fashioned-looking skirts of a pioneer woman, her graying hair pulled back in an elaborate twist. She was tiny, fierce, with small, sharp hands. This woman, Pastor, had not hurt Karlie, but she humiliated her, handling her roughly, like livestock, and this has made all Karlie's old injuries from the other night flare into acuity. Something in her head feels knocked loose; there's a clicking in her jaw, a spinning sensation when she tries to stand. One of her ankles that seemed wobbly the other night now aches with the bite of the rope cutting into it. The pastor had bound Karlie's ankles and hands together with rope before she left, but it is only haphazardly done, the hands far too loose and the ankles far too tight.

Before she left, the woman had looked at Karlie long and hard, and then she spoke, her words like a curse. "I don't need to lay another finger on you. The Good Lord's spoken. 'For wide is the gate, and broad is the way, that leadeth to destruction.'"

She moved gracefully then, swishing in her long skirts, shutting the door softly behind her and leaving Karlie bound on the floor. Karlie's cordless phone rings once, twice, but it's beyond her grasp, tucked in its base, and whoever it is calling leaves no message on her answering machine. She could yell for help? Would someone even hear her? But her tongue's a dead lump in her mouth; she cannot think. In the long minutes that follow, Karlie manages to free her hands bit by bit. Her feet have gone numb by the time she manages to unbind them. It feels like she's gone into a state of shock.

Once she's free, she grabs her phone to call Ian's motel room. No answer. Police, she thinks, but then remembers the flash of fear and anger on Ian's face whenever she'd brought this up. *You don't understand*, he'd said to her. *You don't understand what they might do to my mom if I involve the authorities.* Karlie tries the motel room again and again, pleading under her breath for Ian to pick up, but he still doesn't answer. She finally gives up.

Her car keys are gone. She'd watched the big man scoop them up into his rough palm before he left. She imagines he's tossed them somewhere onto the shoulder of the highway by now.

Her chest is too taut to breathe. Ian will come to her, she thinks. He was probably already worried when she failed to turn up. He's almost certainly looking for her. She counts her breath over and over, losing the numbers, starting over. A pair of headlights moves across the wall of her apartment, and she holds her breath—but they pass. It's no one. There is no one here but her and the long, shadowy fingers of her own thoughts. Her pulse fills her ears with a kind of whooshing sound. The night is endless.

She prays.

It has been a long time since she's prayed. The words come to her mind only slowly, a ball of tangled yarn. She speaks to God falteringly, with anger and apology. It used to be that even beginning such a private conversation would fill her with an upwelling of peace, peace that passes understanding. But now there is a deep knot in her stomach. The blood

KARLIE

rises and falls between her ears, oceanic. It's difficult to think, impossible to formulate a thought. But surely, He, a loving God, will understand—her failures, her doubt.

A headlight arcs across the wall again. An engine cutting off. A car door opening, then shutting. *Ian*, she thinks hopefully, wishing to make it so. *Joy*. But she knows who it is. It's him, driving the Cadillac. She recognizes that single headlight, the sound.

There's a knocking at her door. It is very, very late. Or very, very early. It is tomorrow. Tomorrow will never come.

Karlie exhales and rises gingerly to her feet again. Her twisted ankle hurts but does not betray her. She hobbles, as quickly as she can, to the peephole. "What do you want?"

He does not answer. He knocks again, louder this time. More insistent.

Her hope is desperate, clutching at possibilities. She's afraid of him, yes, but tonight she's met people she fears more, and he is, after all, Ian's friend, his roommate. A deep exhaustion is setting in, the aftermath of panic and terror, and all she wants is help, for someone to help her. It's hard to take a full breath. It's hard to think. She draws the chain and opens her door.

Kent stands there with a weird sort of half smile on his face. The bruise on her neck throbs at the sight of him.

"You won't answer me," he says, his voice like a hurt little boy's. "I keep calling. Why won't you answer?"

Her arms shake, the adrenaline subsiding. For a moment, she's simply relieved it's not the men from the cult.

"Shh," she says. "You've got to get out of here."

"Not until we talk," he says, pushing his way inside her apartment and closing the door. She can smell his breath. Whiskey. His eyes are red.

"I can't right now," she says. "I'm in the middle of something. I'm . . ."

He seats himself on her futon, makes a scoffing sound. "What? You expecting guests?"

"No," Karlie says, swallowing the lump in her throat. "Ian's in trouble. His old church. They sent guys after him. To hurt him."

Kent laughs softly, regretfully. "Dude's involved in so much shit. Trust me. I've heard about that church. You don't want to get involved."

An obvious thought occurs to her—*Kent drove*. She could use the car to get to Ian.

"Maybe I could take your car. Borrow it and look for him. You could rest here. Sober up."

He laughs sourly. "I don't own a car. You know that."

"Tatiana's car. You know what I mean."

"Too dangerous. I told you. Ian's involved in some real messed up shit."

He reaches from the futon and grabs one of her hands, pulling her toward his lap. "Please," he says. "Just sit with me a minute. Let's talk."

She pulls back hard, managing to jerk her hand free from his grasp. "No, Kent. It's late. I'm hurt. I'm tired."

He throws his hands up in protest. "I only want to talk," he says. "Karlie. Please."

"If you aren't interested in helping me, please go."

"You're mad about the other night. I wasn't myself."

"Go, Kent."

"Karlie," he says.

She can hear the pleading in his voice, desperation muddled with the overemotionality of a deeply intoxicated person. "We have a connection. You know that. Remember the bird you saw? The bluebird that flew right over us and you said it was a good-luck sign?"

He reaches for her again, clumsily, with his bearlike paws. This time, he pulls her to the futon with him. He draws her toward him, too close. She tries to resist. She knows this about him—he's a bad drunk. That was the problem the other night. He transforms into someone else—black-eyed and soulless, blundering and cruel—once he starts drinking. So different from the version of him that she and Joy had imagined when they first spotted him on the library steps, so different from the shy, thoughtful person he seemed when she'd only known him from afar as Clay's earnest roommate, his cousin. Kent grabs her shoulder too hard. It hurts. He's hurting her. She pulls back, but he's got his other hand on her back now, his liquored breath in her face.

"Kent, you're drunk," she says. "Go home. We can talk another time."

"You love me," he says, and he's pressing himself against her. There are tears on his face, his voice a sound so raw and wild she almost pities him, but he's hurting her, drawing her into the bulk of him. "And I love you. You're the only good thing that's ever happened to me."

She knows that she cannot let it happen again. She twists hard. It startles him, and she breaks free, steps back from him, away from the futon. His mouth pops open, and he rises, bellowing like a wounded beast. The sound reverberates. He is terrifying and pitiful. Her whole body quakes.

And that's when she grabs the antique brass lamp her sister gave her and swings at him. It lands squarely. She can hear the sound of bone crumpling on bone in his face. It's a good feeling, satisfying. Better, even, than what she thinks the gun would have given her. The base of the lamp is heavy. He looks stunned for a moment, clutching the side of his jaw, and then he's lunging at her—Kent, gentle Kent with his hardscrabble childhood and wavy brown hair, the one with the dreamy look and tortoise-shell glasses she and Joy first spotted on the library steps—is scrambling toward her, grabbing her. She panics and steps away.

There's blood dripping from somewhere, a splotch of red on Kent's cheek. She touches her own nose testingly, but then he's on top of her, shoving her to the ground, the lamp tumbling from her grasp.

"Dammit, Karlie," he says, although the sound is like a moan.

She writhes and twists beneath him, thinking of advice she shared with Joy once, back in those early days of freshman year: If you're being attacked, you have to shock your attacker. Throw a fit. Go crazy. Let him think you've been seized by some other power, holy or unholy. Hiss and shake like you've been possessed. She tries. She flails. His fingers are tight on her throat. She can't breathe.

"You love me," he whispers, but he is weeping. His grip tightens. He tries to fix her with his stare. She won't relent. With her eyes, the one free part of her, she looks away.

On the ceiling, there's a watermark shaped like an angel blowing a trumpet. She's noticed it there before. Some days it's looked more avian, but today it is decidedly seraphic. *A sign*, Karlie thinks, with a shifting meaning. A sign, now, that she will triumph. Even though she cannot at present take a breath. She cannot breathe, but there's a strange clarity descending. It's a feeling like exultation, like the best possible high. She feels herself summoned to some nearly celestial plane. It's better than any drug, she's absolutely certain—*What a trip*, she'll tell her sister, *you wouldn't believe*—and she almost wants to laugh, to explain all this to Kent, who is better than this, deep down, in his true self, like so many people—*They know not what they do*—but she can't tell him, even if she could form the words, so far off does she feel. Hovering. Preparing to takeoff, to fly. She wants to tell him about the experience that he's missing, how much bigger things are. The universe! He doesn't even know. Her eye is trained on that angel on the ceiling. The angel will keep quiet until the time is right. Karlie will not lose sight of her no matter how hard he grasps. A calm overwhelms her. The peace that passes understanding. Karlie will not break gaze. What holiness. Her limbs still. Her face slackens.

The angel blows its horn.

Dark

She's limp when he leaves. Nonresponsive. Not dead, surely, but sleeping. Oh God, surely. Simply passed out. Gonna wake up sore and miffed. More bruises. Pissed off. He'll deserve it—her wrath, her vengeance. Mad as hell. An unfortunate misunderstanding. He'll get flowers, make it up to her.

The whiskey's wearing off, beads of cold sweat are breaking out on his forehead, but steady hands, steady hands. Shit. He's shaking. His hands are really shaking. Claw marks on his cheeks from where she tore at his face. Jaw busted from where she swung the goddam lamp at him. Broken bone? Is his jaw sitting crooked now? Can't close his mouth quite right, blood seeping from his nose, from somewhere.

He pulls the hood of his sweatshirt up over his head, touching his cheek lightly. Doubt's seeping in. She's fine. She'll *be* fine. Fury's subsiding, leaving fumes, regret. He tastes copper and salt, like biting your own tongue. He's depleted, an empty windsock. Yep. He fucked up. Got to stop drinking. The trouble is she won't *listen*. Wouldn't listen. He loves her, too. Legit *loves* her. He knows she loves him, too—good God, he's felt it and was made new! What his daddy always said the love of a good woman would do. What he always swore to himself he'd find: something different from what his own mama and daddy had, the way they spoke to each other. How they acted. The drinking. Good God. He swore he'd never be like that, say all those things.

One thing his daddy loved to say about his mama: *Got a mouth on her, the fat bitch,* laughing and laughing even though Kent's mama would be standing right there, seething, that pulse going in her neck like a warning. Truth was she could give as good as she took, Kent's mama, the old harpy. Slapped him across the face when he was just eight years old and left his cheek with such a big, red welt that he had to tell the teacher it was a fall, that he'd tripped and landed funny—hell, how was he supposed to turn out? Hot temper ran in the family. Good Lord, considering everything, he really turned things around. By the time he'd made it over to their aunt's place, with Clay, things were a little better. They took care of each other, he and Clay. *Praise Jesus!* Overall. Most days. He turned out pretty good. Not as good as Clay, maybe, but he's in school, getting an advanced degree.

Hands fishing in his pocket for his keys, and he can't steady them, but it's not the drink. Nerves. The afterglow of burnt rage. There's a star blinking overhead like it's a worried eye. Bluish, maybe? A satellite?

Oh, shit. She didn't look good, did she? Doubt seeps in. She looked bad.

Or God looking down on him, and He's fucking DISPLEASED.

KENT, I SHALL SMITE THEE, SON. I'M FUCKING DISPLEASED. That old cinematic God-voice in his head. Sonorous, like Charlton Heston in one of those movies his mom watched. *SINNER.* God, buffered by clouds, spoiled and out of touch, sitting at a blissful remove from everything. Guy's kind of an asshole sometimes.

Passed out is all. He saw a twitch, right? A little flicker at the eyelid. She'll be mad as hell when she wakes up and he'll deserve it. Oh, good God he's fucked up again. It's the drink. It's his goddam genes. All those times, borrowing the car, driving up to her place, palms damp, trying to work up his courage to knock. Should have brought flowers.

Keys fumble to the ground. Is it the cold? Why are his hands so numb? Fingers like chunks of clay. Maybe he should go back in, just to check on her, you know? Put a pillow under her head. Set out a glass of water for when she wakes, head throbbing. Make an anonymous 9-1-1 call. As a precaution! She's fine. She'll be fine. But she didn't look so good, did she? When he left? The way he felt something giving, giving, gone until he let go. How she went limp beneath his grasp. That stillness when he left her. Oh Jesus, he hadn't meant to. Maybe he should call somebody, to check in on her, so they could help . . .

There. Face. Shape. Looking at him. A jolt through the spine.

Someone in the darkness. Watching him. That moonfaced kid. Doughy face, beady eyes. Slow kid from the diner—that's who. Reminds him of his little cousin back home. He loved that cousin of his, babied her. Little girl with the eyes like—you know, the eyes like that—and the sweetest smile. She was special. *You got a real nice way with her, Kent,* his aunt would say, because he's a good guy, at the core. The sort of guy who'll go out of his way to be nice to a kid with problems of the brain. He and Clay, they were both good guys, despite what they'd gone through. Considering. And if the religion had stuck with him like it had with Clay, well! It's funny where religion takes and where it doesn't. It took with Clay. His cousin was downright corny with it, all hokey and fervent, but he was for real. Clay meant it. He felt something Kent could only pretend to feel.

Kent saw too many flaws, all the discrepancies, like watching a pageant put on by children. You wanted to indulge them, clap real loud, sure, but everybody knew it wasn't *real*. Meanwhile Clay saw magic, holiness. But Kent had still gotten out, not by faith but by his smarts. Quick in school—*brainy*, his aunt called him. *Brainy boy getting hisself a big ol' scholarship.*

His head is starting to pound a little bit, like somebody's knocking on it. Brain's melted to sauce now. His one asset, and he's intent on ruining it. And yeah, he knows this kid standing out here in the cold. Ogling him from the shadows. God knows how long he's been here, this kid. Toby. Coke-bottle glasses. From Rosemary Street Grill. That's where Kent's seen him.

"Hey! You know Karlie?" Toby asks.

But Kent's hustling to the Big Mama Wagon. A piece of shit in need of a new headlight, but it does the job when Clay's car is in the shop. He fumbles at the car door without answering, his meat-hands cold and useless. His thoughts are clearing. A sudden, hideous sobriety is settling in along with a headache. Door of the old beater won't open. Needs to get his own car and stop having to borrow this piece of shit. He's got to go.

"Karlie? You know her? 7C?" The boy won't give up, looking at Kent with that big, pale face, white as the moon.

Kent pulls the hood of his sweatshirt around his face, tucking his head to obscure it further. A little practical voice inside his head is piping up. Best not be seen. Best not have a witness who can attest to seeing him here.

"Nah, man," Kent says. "Never heard of her. You know Jen and Katie? 18C. I was over there."

The lie comes fluidly. His voice is hoarse—had he been screaming at her earlier? At Karlie? A glob of mucus gathers in the back of his throat and he swallows it down. Thank God for the dark. String of snot running down to his mouth, a salt taste. Jesus, is he crying? Hustling away from this big ol' slow boy like he's a scaredy cat 'bout to piss his pants and weeping like a goddam infant. Oh, mortal sin. Oh, sinner, lost to God. Weeping and gnashing of teeth.

"Oh," the boy says solemnly. "Karlie's real nice. Told me she got a present for me but then she never came back so I came down to check. I couldn't find her so I got worried and came back."

He can't respond to that. He won't, scurrying away like a goddam rat. This kid's killing him, all mournful and serious, looking for his treat. For his Karlie. Jesus Christ. Kent's nose is running and he can't breathe. Slams himself into the driver's seat of the car, and guns it. Peels off toward his apartment. Got to get it together. Toughen up. No more going soft at the sides. Like his dad used to say. Too tender-hearted. Fuck it. Fuck that kid. Sayonara, moonface. Hasta la vista, bad dream.

Once he's home, he can barely remember the drive back. A ghost-blur of what was illuminated by the single working headlight, his face throbbing, lids slipping down so he could only half see, so he had to yank them back up by hand. Couldn't see the road, really. Only Karlie. The image of Karlie, her eyes going dull and far-off, stuck in his mind.

Inside the apartment, he locks the door. Dead-bolts it so even Ian can't get in. Staving off what? Who? He's lost now. Chains of darkness. Gnashing of teeth. You done fucked up, son. (Sonorous God-voice, gone softer now, nothing but a sad and distant whisper. Not angry, but disappointed, ashamed. Mortal error, Kent. Things aren't looking good. God, she was still, wasn't she? Karlie. He's fucked up. Real bad. *I'M FUCKING DISPLEASED, SON. CAST YE THE UNPROFITABLE SERVANT INTO OUTER DARKNESS.* Can't even think of Clay, his gentle, freckled cousin, his best friend, the way he'd look at him if he knew.) He's shaking still, unsteady, backs himself right into the end table and knocks over one of the lamps. It crashes to the floor. Fit to wake the dead—shit, shit, shit. *I SHALL SMITE THEE, SINNER.* Shattered glass. Him and lamps tonight. Jesus. Oh, sweet Jesus.

"Hey, man, that you?" Clay calls groggily from the back bedroom. "You okay? Just getting in?" Clay's voice is murky, still middream, half asleep. He sleeps the deep, innocent sleep of a child.

Speak of the devil. "Yeah, it's me," Kent says, steadying his voice. Calm, real calm. Natural. "Nahh, I've been here. Musta got back right after you went to bed. Finishing up that movie I was watching. Startled me, you know? I just knocked the lamp over. Ha. Total klutz. Sorry to wake you, man. Sorry."

His heart catches in his chest. He's overexplaining himself to Clay—dear Clay, good Clay—but best establish his presence in the apartment the entirety of the evening with his trusting cousin. Best make it emphatically clear. He, Kent, has been here the whole time.

"No problem. Night, man."

Kent's throat is parchment paper, rasping when he tries to breathe. He fills himself a cup of tap water in the kitchen. It tastes of greenish pipes, moss on a stone, but he swallows it anyway, then pours a finger of whiskey to clear the murk of it, to light the back of his throat and quell the juddering of his immortal soul.

Kent sits in the darkened living room, finally turning on an old movie: Audrey Hepburn plays a blind woman, fending off con men and murderers who are searching for a lost doll filled with drugs. The men will do anything to poor sightless Audrey to get it. The lights go off, the lights go on, the lights go off. Hidden in the dark.

There's a knock at the door. It's not quite five A.M. He knows who it will be: gruff men, so-called men of the word, searching. And with their arrival, there's a kind of solace. A helplessness. He was never in control. Things are falling neatly into his lap as if according to some master plan, although he cannot take credit for the stratagem. God's plan. Karlie was done for anyway. A goner. He's merely a bit player who stepped in, accelerated things. An accident set against a larger web of villainy. He is hardly at fault.

The knock comes again. He rises, stiff-kneed as an old man, and moves slowly to the door. Fated. He is an actor in a shadow play, every motion already choreographed, bound by destiny.

He opens the door. The men standing there, heavy-faced and somber in their work clothes, ask for Ian, where is he, how to find him.

"I don't know," Kent says. The honest truth. The breath has all been knocked out of him. A hollow shell. A dead man. No, he thinks, Ian is the dead man. This thought occurs to him with almost complete neutrality despite his love for Ian, for Clay. His friends! There's no feeling left. He could try to warn Ian but there's no way to reach him. Kent has already started to absent himself from the situation, like he used to do, back when he was young.

The men at the door make their way inside, and Kent offers no protest. They search the small apartment quickly. There's nowhere to hide. They shove Clay awake, demand to know where Ian is. Something in his bewildered face must read as truthful. Clay doesn't know. Satisfied, they leave. Kent can see the outline of their weapons—a suggestion, an implicit promise.

"We'll find him," the biggest man says as they exit the door. "Always do."

The door closes and Kent sinks back to the couch, head in his hands—the ache building.

"Dear God," Clay says. He's turned pale. Always the delicate one. Gentle and good. Kent feels the urge at least to protect him for all this ugliness.

"Ian's deep in some shit, man. Nothing you can do but pray."

Clay stands there, vulnerable-looking, bare-legged in his boxers. Frightened.

"Go on back to bed, buddy," Kent adds softly. "I'll wait up."

Clay nods mutely, complies, disappearing to the back bedroom. Kent sits motionless on the couch. Audrey's frozen on the screen—for how long, God only knows, but the night is endless now. Nothing but endless night. His right temple beats with a steady pain against his fingertips.

The phone rings. At this hour. His heart skips, but his hand falls to the phone, an automatic gesture. Karlie, he thinks, although this makes no sense. She won't wake up for a while now. Won't wake up—

"Kent? That you?"

Ian.

Something breaks inside of him. A torrential awfulness bursting forth.

"Oh, God. She's dead. Karlie's dead."

He's weeping into the line, breathless, blubbering. Another part of him, hovering high above, watches his broken animal self with cool neutrality. His diaphragm spasms. He can hardly breathe.

There is silence on the other end of the line for a while before Ian speaks.

"Kent," he says slowly, carefully. "What the hell are you talking about?"

Kent's crying like a lost child, sick with guilt and regret and sorrow. Oh, God. Lord, have mercy. He can hardly form words.

"I went over there," he manages to say. "To talk with her . . . Oh, Jesus. I'm crazy about her. You should know that. She's something special. There's no use hiding it anymore—" His voice breaks. He hears Ian swallow on the other end of the line. Kent's mouth is dry. Takes another swig of the tap water—like iron and lukewarm algae, but wet on his tongue.

"Oh, God. I loved her. I swear to God, I loved her. I didn't want anything to happen . . ."

"Kent, you've got to get it together, man. Is Karlie okay? Tell me what happened."

Kent attempts a deep breath. Long skeins of mucus and tears clot his throat. He tries to clear them out, to breathe again, to explain.

"She was on the floor when I left," he says carefully. "She wasn't moving. Oh God. She didn't look good . . ."

He's going to tell Ian, Kent thinks. He's going to confess—it was an accident. He just wanted to talk to her, to get her to hold still. To listen.

But he was caught up in it all. He was holding her too hard, and yes, he was angry, too, goddammit he was mad—she was making him so angry, not listening like that, making a fool of him, after he'd waited for her so long—but he didn't intend to . . . The urge to explain all this to Ian builds up in him like the need to sneeze. Kent takes another swig of whiskey, which burns through the core of him. Devil-water. He can think again. Strategize. Problem-solve. The world reconfigures into sharpness, clear lines and contours. He can see with newfound clarity. The fact of Karlie's unnatural stillness when he left. A searing image in his mind, reappearing. She is dead. Karlie. Acknowledging this plain truth confers the thinnest horror—he feels it, a slickness to his palms—but already it's a sensation he's distancing himself from, like a balloon cut loose. A trick he learned in childhood, this way of detaching, floating up, up and away. A survival tactic. Ian would never understand. An accident! Kent sees all this now—the obviousness of it. Ian loved her, too. Karlie. They both loved the same girl, and he, Kent, has hurt her. Oh, dear Lord, it was an accident, it was . . . But he's practical, adept at managing misfortune. Already a plan is forming, tantalizing in its obviousness. A small relief. A gift.

"Bond of Faith," Kent says. Another lie based on a kernel of truth. It emerges so easily, the absurd elegance of its offering: new villains. Worthy villains, villains who make sense, slotting into the role perfectly, and thereby absolving him. He meant no harm. He loved Karlie. There's a moral logic to his substitution.

"It was those guys from Bond of Faith, man. They came here, too, looking for you. I went to go check on her, but it was too late. They'd gotten to her first . . . I haven't called anyone yet. I didn't want you to get dragged into it, you know? I was hoping to tell you first. To warn you."

"Oh, no," Ian says. "Oh, God, no."

Kent can feel his heart rate slowing, the calm, distanced way he's observing himself in this scene. All the panic has fled his body. He's passed it along to Ian instead. He can sense it, even through the phone line, the way Ian's voice recoils from the words he speaks, a visceral dread he's transmitted like a horrible disease.

"Oh my God. Karlie's dead?"

"Those bastards," Kent says, soothing, soothing now. In control of the situation. Director of the tragedy. "It's awful."

"Oh, God. It's my fault," Ian says. His voice breaks. "I'll never forgive myself."

For a moment, something twists inside Kent—a little niggling thread of doubt, of guilt, hearing Ian—but he takes another sip of whiskey. It settles. It's like being in an airplane, far above everything. He can see for miles, the patchwork ground, the miniature houses like toys, human figures so small they are almost ants. He can see and understand how it will all play out, so when he speaks to Ian again, he is serene, nearly godlike in his omniscience, his capacious understanding.

"What's done is done. You're gonna have to learn to forgive yourself, man."

2019

When We Were Gone Astray

The lady shows up while KC's working the desk in the crappy little office of the apartment complex. The semester having drawn to a close, most of KC's fellow tenants are home for winter break. Silver tinsel droops around the office door, and a little stereo system plays a rotation of holiday songs at the owner's insistence, although KC tends to skip the merry ones. He prefers eerie Christmas songs in a minor key, the ones that hint at the creepiness of the story: an innocent girl impregnated by the Holy Ghost, yet another mortal woman undone by man or god. Endless iterations of such stories since the times of ancient Greeks—strip away the yuletide cheer, and you're left with an unsettling sequence of events in which a peasant girl emerges as a folk hero while God does as God does. But no one in KC's hometown ever talked about it like that.

"Hello," the woman says shyly, the doorbell still jingling as she enters.

KC's tapping a pencil to "God Rest Ye Merry Gentlemen," sipping enough cold brew coffee to ruin his sleep that night and skimming the *New York Times* home page on his laptop. The office is overheated, permeated with the dank odor of a gym locker room. And yet KC likes it. There's a perverse freedom in remaining here, all the other students having left for their childhood homes, joining picturesque families by mantels hung with stockings. He is abandoned, mercifully and terribly alone.

"Can I help you?" he asks.

She is tall and gray-eyed, this woman, dressed in professional-looking cuffed trousers. Her eyes dart around the office like she's scanning it for something. Maybe she's a parent, he thinks, trying to secure last-minute housing for her kid next semester.

"What's your name?" she asks.

Startled by the authority in her voice, he tells her on reflex.

"KC," she repeats, rolling the two syllables over her tongue. She seems to consider him in a way that makes him feel vulnerable, beholden to her somehow. Drawing closer, she lowers herself so that her eyes meet his. He remains seated, holding her gaze, although he lets the pencil fall still against his palm. If the woman moves in any closer, their noses will touch. He watches her breathing.

"I need you to take me down to unit 7C. It's important."

He looks at her, unblinking.

"No, ma'am," he says. "I'm sorry. Hard no. It's off-limits. I've gotten in trouble for that before."

"Please."

"There's nothing to see. I promise you. Despite what those murder-freaks think."

He watches her face to see if he's offended her, but she regards him stoically.

"Please," she says. "I'll pay you. Five minutes, tops. You can stay with me the whole time. I won't touch anything."

Outside, the late afternoon is already turning a pre-solstice dark. A sliver of moon sits above the trees, framed in the grimy rectangle of the office window. The string of twinkling holiday lights on an automatic timer cuts on, outlining the doorway as if it's a portal to somewhere magical, and the darkness, the lights and music, the intensity of the woman's gray eyes create an atmosphere of possibility—annunciations and heavenly messengers. *For unto us*, KC thinks, *a child* . . . the words pressed into his mind for so long they've never really left him. The lady is perfectly still—a statue. Only her eyes plead with him.

He sighs, rising. "Listen. I would, but I can't. I almost lost my job last time." He lifts his hands in a helpless gesture.

The woman stands, turning from him. She walks to a small corkboard, inspecting the various takeout menus pinned to it. He can feel her intake of breath, readying herself for one final volley of words.

"Please," she says, only this time she's not making eye contact with him. She touches an old flier from Pepper's Pizza, a local favorite, now defunct. Her fingers trace the words next to a pen-and-ink drawing of an everything slice: *A sunny place for shady people.*

She explains.

There was a letter. A letter mailed twenty years ago, lost, and yet—miraculously—it recently turned up in an old book. A letter from Karlie Richards, the girl who was killed here, in this complex. This lady's friend, her freshman roommate. The letter led to certain questions. It prompted her to action. She began to dig back into Karlie's murder, to research it. And she discovered things—things that made it seem like the case was handled incorrectly. Incongruities. She realized that she had to show the letter to the woman whose son is currently in prison for the crime. There was no other choice. Maybe she was moved to do it, maybe it was pressed upon her heart—you could put it that way, if you were a believer. Or maybe her conscience finally kicked in. Either way, now the letter is being used in an appeal—the mention of someone stalking Karlie, in a BMW, only it wasn't an actual BMW. It was an inside joke, one this lady had forgotten. And the man currently in prison would have never had access to that car, plus he's legally blind!

"We're so close," she says. "You know the backlog of rape kits? There's a rumor online that there's one for Karlie, done shortly before she died, but it went missing. If we could find that, if we can appeal the case . . . But I need something else. I need your help."

The woman watches him, to make sure he's absorbing what she says. Her face shines like a prophet. Or a lunatic. KC nods patiently.

"I need you to let me into her apartment," the lady says. "Karlie believed in signs. Signs from God," She pauses, glancing at him again. "She was the type of person who saw things—angels, faces, birds. She'd point out patterns anybody else would miss, notice all the smallest details. She used to lie on the floor and, you know, pray. I think she was trying to tell me something. I know they'll search her apartment again, but I just need to look. I feel like it needs to be me, you know? There might be things they wouldn't notice. But I might. There's some other message from her, I know—I'm ready to receive it."

The woman stops short. Up to this point, there's been a level of excitement to her voice that could indicate either crackpot or savant. It's like she hasn't talked to anyone in ages, words have been overflowing faster than she can grasp. But now she's caught up with herself. She lets the flier fall back against the bulletin board and turns squarely toward KC again, flushing, as if for the first time hearing how she must sound.

"I know what you must be thinking . . ."

"It's not that . . . I just can't let you in there."

"I mean, maybe it's nothing. But I have to check."

"I'm sorry," KC says, and he is. In the background, the Merry Gentlemen have moved along to "Jingle Bell Rock," which feels mawkish, offensive even, given the moment. "Listen. You could come back another time. When the owners are here. And explain to them."

He knows what the owners will say, but he can't simply offer her nothing. She seems to understand this, looking down at her hands, which are large and square-nailed with long, tapered fingers. Strangely elegant, KC thinks. And inexplicably, he reaches toward the lady, taking one of her hands into his own. He holds it. She blinks but accepts this gesture.

"Thanks anyway. I'm sorry to have bothered you."

"There's nothing there. I promise you."

"I know. But maybe it's something tiny, something only I'd appreciate?"

"I'll put in a good word for you," KC says, because it's the least he can do.

She sighs. "I'll leave my card."

He squeezes her hand. She's a stranger. She is no one to him. For a reason he can't explain, old words again surface in his mind, a rote offering of kindness.

"Peace be with you," KC says.

She tips her head toward him, and he releases his grasp. "And also with you."

The lady is gone, the door jingling shut behind her.

It's too dark to see her slip away to wherever she's come from. The music continues tinnily. KC shivers. All that late-day caffeine is giving him palpitations, but there was something in what the woman said that's snagged him. He waits five more minutes to make sure she is really gone, then he grabs the large ring of keys. He exits the office, locking the door behind him, and walks to unit 7C.

Down at the vacant wing, all is hushed but for his breathing. He glances over his shoulder. Scaring himself, he thinks. He's let this woman's appearance, her jangly energy, get to him. He works here; he has the authority to check up on things. This is ordinary surveillance of the premises, he tells himself, a routine check.

The key to the apartment sticks, but he shimmies it back and forth until the lock gives. He pushes the door open and clicks the lights on. The apartment is as vacant and anonymous as it was the last time KC saw it some weeks ago, the floor still bare and splotched. There's a new scattering of dead insect husks, but otherwise, it's completely unchanged.

There's nothing to see. As expected. The woman was crazed by grief, or guilt. The trauma of losing her friend. He should leave, go grab a bite for dinner.

But KC walks to the center of the living room, near the spot where he'd sat with Lydia. There's nothing—no special marking or irregularity. He circles a moment, the way a dog might before it finds a spot to lie down, and then lowers himself to the floor. Although it's bare and dirty, he lies on his back, the cold seeping in through the thin fabric of his shirt. Closing his eyes, he crosses his arms across his chest like he's atop a funeral bier. Across the state, his family is gathering at the dinner table, the Christmas tree aglow behind them. The caffeine has created an insistent ache in his chest. His ribs tighten when he tries to breathe.

He opens his eyes, letting them absorb the expanse of the ceiling, which is a dingy eggshell color.

There's no sign, no clue, no cryptic message—only blank, white space. Emptiness. An absence onto which anything might be superimposed or imagined. He stares into the nothing of it. *Swan*, he thinks. The long neck and feathers. The only break in the monotony is an oblong watermark there—not quite a swan, he thinks, but he can see now how Lydia might have interpreted it that way. To him, it's almost person-shaped, if the person were wearing a long gown or dress. Maybe someone in a choir robe, extending an arm toward someone else out of view. The more KC studies the watermark, the more person-like it becomes. He thinks of somewhere else, somewhere warm and far from there lit with glowing candles, where a group of people, people he has not yet met, a chorus, their voices rising in unison, sing tidings of comfort and joy, comfort and joy.

The image blurs. KC wipes his watering eyes with a fist. The person-shaped watermark reassembles itself—not reaching, he realizes, but pointing, toward a vent in the corner. Now that he's seen it, he cannot unsee its obviousness: a figure, pointing adamantly toward the vent. It's a crazy thought, an absurdity, but the lady has shaken something loose in KC, all the dormant credulity of his childhood uncoiling, stretching, rising on animal-legs within him. A primal capacity for meaning-making. He ought to check. He ought at least to look.

The contractors have left one of their stepladders outside of 13C. KC scrambles up, brushing himself off, and goes to grab it. Returning, he positions the ladder beneath the vent and climbs.

He pries the metal grille off gingerly. It's dusty, but almost entirely loose, KC realizes, only two of the screws securing it in place. For a moment he hesitates, feeling foolish, but then he reaches his hand, blindly patting the space inside. Nothing. Nothing but dust and grime—until his hand lights on something. He slides it out.

A floppy disk. An old three-and-a-half-inch, obsolete. A typed and folded sheet of paper. He slips both into his shirt pocket, slides the grille back in place over the vent, and descends the ladder.

He glances toward the ceiling once more, a shiver moving down his back. A lucky guess. An instinct. Could be junk abandoned by anyone, but still; he'll call the woman and tell her.

KC walks back to the doorway and turns off the light. The figure on the ceiling disappears, merely a stain, the room awash in dark.

During KC's senior year, deep in the throes of the pandemic, he'll be invited for a meeting with the dean and given the news that an anonymous donor has given him a retroactive scholarship, a sum sufficient to pay off the entirety of his loans. "The Karlie Richards Fund," the dean will tell him over Zoom. "One of our alumni has started it. A classmate of Karlie's. One of her old roommates. Instrumental, I'm told, in the reopening of the case." And at that point, KC will have heard: about the new person of interest, a librarian, and about how the floppy disk he found instigated an investigation into a cultlike church in the western part of the state.

For now, though, KC knows none of this. There's only the empty, darkened apartment, its long-kept secrets, the floppy disk, the folded paper he's found.

He exits and locks the door.

December 2021
Carolina Alumni Review
In Memoriam Margaret Karla "Karlie" Richards (1980–2000)

River Song
by Karlie Richards

It's a given
to rove rivers
but never, no,
twice to rise
from the same river
riven via
its own traverse,
shivering over
stones grinning
white as teeth grit,
ever singing.
Vie to trace egress
to source, verging
tributaries riving
the very groin
of earth, siring
grove after virgin grove,
giving vigor.
We are goners,
everyone,
roses riveling,
resigned.
Let the river rinse
us clean, reverse
our course, one sign
we sing and serve,
engrossed,
until we cross
into sweet verse
spilling at the mouth.